I0600240

The Lightness of Rain

a novel

TERRI HANAUER

the three
tomatoes
The Three Tomatoes Book Publishing

Copyright© 2025 Terri Hanauer

All rights reserved. No part of this book may be reproduced in any form or by any electronic or mechanical means, including information storage and retrieval systems, without permission in writing from the publisher. The only exception is by a reviewer, who may quote short excerpts in a review. For permission requests, please address The Three Tomatoes Publishing.

Published: August 2025
ISBN: 979-8-9926661-8-2
Library of Congress Number: 2025911355

For information address:
The Three Tomatoes Book Publishing
6 Soundview Rd.
Glen Cove, NY 11542

Cover and author photos: Mark Hanauer
Cover design: Nancy Nimoy
Interior design: Susan Herbst

This novel is a work of fiction. Names, characters, places, and incidents either are products of the author's imagination or are used fictitiously. Any resemblance to actual persons, living or dead, businesses, events, or locales is entirely coincidental.

PRAISE FOR THE LIGHTNESS OF RAIN

"Hanauer takes you inside her extraordinary characters in ways I've never encountered in a work of fiction. Her stream of consciousness, poetic and imaginative prose dances and twists from one revelatory line to the next. *The Lightness of Rain* is innovative, exploring the complexity and depth of the characters in ways that take the art form to a whole new level."

~ **Tom Schulman** – Academy Award Winner for *Dead Poets Society;* screenwriter of *Honey, I Shrunk The Kids* and *What About Bob?*

"Hard to believe this is Hanauer's debut novel! Her gifts are on full display in this fast-paced, genre bending novel – which is imbued with a literary lyricism and the punch and pop of a page turner you grab at the airport and can't put down. A seamless mashup."

~ **Cathleen Young** – HUMANITAS Prize winner for television; The Christopher Award for *The Pumpkin Wars*

"A debut novel of great scope and passion. A deeply insightful, evocatively written and inspiring journey."

~ **Gary Goldstein** – IBPA Award for Excellence in Fiction for *The Last Birthday Party*; author of *The Mother I Never Had* and *Please Come to Boston*

"A riveting story of three complex female characters who turn their lives around in order to fulfil their destinies. A captivating novel that kept me turning pages even though I didn't want it to end. A must-read!"

~ **Thaao Penghlis** – Emmy-nominated actor; author of *Places* and *Seducing Celebrities, One Meal at a Time.*

In every generation, there are thirty-six humble,
righteous people who hold up the world.
If it weren't for them—all of them—if even one of them were
missing,
the world would come to an end.

-The Talmud

Nobody, not even the rain, has such small hands.

-e.e. cummings

GRACE

SEARCHING

ALISON

January 4, 2018

Aʟɪꜱᴏɴ ɴᴇᴇᴅᴇᴅ ꜱᴏʏ ꜱᴀᴜᴄᴇ. The only thing still safe to eat in the fridge was the veggie rice roll, stuffed with carrots and cucumber, and wrapped in seaweed. The bottle was so far back in the cupboard she had to get on her toes to reach it. She was just about to twist the cap open when she looked at the "best used by" date: 4 January 2015. That was her forty-seventh birthday. Exactly three years ago. Today was her fiftieth.

She poured the soy sauce down the drain and walked to the side of the house, trying not to spiral as she threw the bottle into the blue recycling bin. There was her car, a light green Ford Mustang convertible. She couldn't remember the last time she drove with the top down. It made her feel too vulnerable, exposed like that. She opened the trunk. A small suitcase lay there, packed and waiting for a spur-of-the-moment trip, along with a pile of old calendar books she was going to shred. 2015 was easy to find. She looked at the January pages. The fourth was a Sunday. And then that thing happened to her—that rush like hot cement melting into her gut.

There was a red star on the date of her forty-seventh birthday in the 2015 calendar. That was the day she left Vincent. It was the day she decided to go incognito, become one of those middle-aged women who wear clogs and no makeup, someone no one notices anymore. She was tired of all the lies, especially the ones she told herself. It was a self-imposed exile. She disappeared into the landscape, and that was fine with her. She still had her teaching, of course. But she was done trying to find love. She would look inward instead, and she would write.

Alison was curious. She went to the blue bin to retrieve the bottle of soy sauce. She gripped its neck and smashed it against the garage wall, dragged a piece along her arm—just a small scrape, just enough to break the skin. It had been years. It hurt a little, like she expected it would. It wasn't the same as when she was twenty-one and reeling from heartbreak.

She licked the scarlet beads off her skin so the wound would heal faster. That's what her best friend Suzy told her when they were in high school. Suzy's arms and thighs looked like stained glass windows without the stain or the glass—just the lead seams that held the irregular pieces in place.

They'd been in an all-girl band, Juicy Kisses. Suzy was the singer. Alison was the drummer. She felt her heart brighten whenever they played. That feeling happened again with Jesse. But with him, there was more, so much more. It had been true, their love. Truer than anything she felt, ever again. She didn't want to think about him now because that always led to—

Alison looked down. A pigeon feather lay on the dark, oil-stained garage floor. The late-day sun was hurling golden spots onto her car. It looked like it had freckles. Or maybe little scars. She had a few of those from her early twenties, her Juicy Kisses days. She told her lovers and husbands make-believe stories about the art on her body. *I was a painter's model and fell out of his studio window. I survived a small plane crash. I was locked in a building, and the only way to escape was to jump through the glass doors.*

But they knew, her lovers. They toasted each other's suffering with vodka and cocaine, continuing their passionless pretense of romance when their true love was the alcohol, the powder, the pain.

Alison went back inside. She had to pack some of her clothes and books and call the Salvation Army to arrange a pickup. That's a good one, she thought. Will I really get salvation from an army? Then came a sound she hadn't heard in a long time—her own laughter.

Her African grey parrot, Jagger, sang, "Can't get no! Can't get no!" It had been two days since he'd chirped anything, probably because it had been two days since Alison had said anything. Her laugh set the bird free. Jagger squawked again. "Can't get no! Can't get no!"

Golds and reds splashed through the iridescent pearl sky. John Turner would've signed this canvas. She unlatched the kitchen window and watched Jagger fly into the Santa Monica sunset. Two years ago, the bird flew into her open window like a tourist in need of an Airbnb. He'd be back in a day or three—they had an understanding.

Suzy and Tumaini were taking her out later to celebrate her birthday. Alison went to the bathroom, turned on the cold water, and splashed her face. She looked at the birthday presents she bought for herself—lipsticks in the tin box that once held loose-leaf Darjeeling tea from her trip to India. They were falling all over themselves like the Pick-Up Sticks of her youth. A pale shade of burgundy called Very Berry Berry caught her eye—she twirled it on her lips like she was putting icing on a wedding cake, each delicate stroke a loving wish for the happy couple. Her tongue moved across her mouth. It tasted like blueberries. Alison unbraided her long red hair. She looked at her reflection and smiled. She was remembering herself. She was still pretty in that tired sort of way. She was still... what?

With her free hand, she wiped the mirror clean, then kissed it, again and again, until the surface was Very Berry Berry. Her face was fractured in the purple gloss. Her gray eyes were filled with bitter sweetness—or was it sweet bitterness? Funny, she thought, and laughed again, a roadwork of tiny lines appearing on her soft cheeks.

A ladybug flew in the bathroom window and landed on the edge of the sink. It let Alison nudge it onto her left thumb. It walked across her fingers and stopped on the fourth one, the ring finger.

"I want to begin again." Alison brought the ladybug up to her lips. "It's my fiftieth birthday," she whispered, "and I want to begin again!"

It opened its tiny wings and stopped in mid-air for a millisecond. There was a moment between them, an eye-to-eye, a heart-to-heart, a secret shared—before it flew out and disappeared into the brilliant horizon.

There was a faded Post-it Note taped to the bottom right-hand corner of the mirror. It read:

"Be of service to others. There is no greater love."

With the tube of Very Berry Berry, she wrote on the mirror just above the note, "Best Used By."

Alison wasn't ready to put in a date.

~ 3 ~

WANDA

March 15, 2019

Y OU COME HOME DRUNK.

Wake me with your mouth on mine. Your tongue ticklin' my tongue with the promise of other places you'll tickle.

You pull my head back, jagged blade scratches against my throat.

"You know what, Wanda?" you laugh. "I'm gonna carve my name on your neck."

And then you kick me in the stomach.

My head turns and sees the crinoline skirt hangin' in the closet. You twirled me faster than anyone ever twirled me—goin' round and round like a merry-go-round where the horses go up and down, up and down in circles—in circles, like that 45 of Elvis singin' "love me tender, love me sweet."

First kiss in the bar. First burst in the bed. First punch in the head. The pain, the thrill and then the pills—hard and round like your fist.

My hair tears off into your foul, ink-stained Jesus Loves grip.

"Bitch!" you yell.

"I'm your wife!" I cry.

You wear the drippin' crown of holy thorns as you sink into me.

fallin'

               flyin'

       trippin'

                     dyin'

I drop to the floor.

Another kick. But not yours this time. Hers.

And then the flood between my torn-up thighs, your acid whiteness slitherin' outta me, the rush of Satan swimmin' for his life.

So handsome you were at the weddin'. Real nice tux. Blue suede shoes.

Your knife drops to the floor, wet floatin' on the River Nile. The Pharaoh's daughter doesn't pick it up. I do.

I push it into you. Hard and deep. Bloody waters streamin' out.

You fly fallin' down.

My breath is shallow, sharp. I hurt all over—inside and out.

She kicks again. Just like her father, I think, and I almost smile.

I lie down in the shadow of 'til-death-do-us-part' 'cuz I'm the mother of your child. It was rainstormin' the night we made her.

Remember?

Diamond slivers of rain. Thunder like cymbals crashin'. Our lovin' so holy, so fine. She arrived in a flash of lightnin' like God himself placed her in me. So her life is mine to protect.

I touch my belly—round and hard.

"Don't fuck with a pregnant woman," I say.

I grab the cash in the can under the kitchen counter. I grab my yellow bag. No time to pack it. I grab the cross hung on the wall next to the pictures of us from the photo booth that time on St. Anthony Street. I was sittin' on your lap. You tickled me and made me laugh so hard, I was fallin' off you and onto the floor.

Remember?

You're not sayin' anythin'. You're just lookin' up at me. Scared. Kinda like I've been feelin' these past three years.

So I light a match and I burn you down.

The night ignites—and I start runnin'.

I hear her singin', "Love me tender. Love me sweet..." I touch the best part of me and say, "I will, my darlin'. I will."

I stop 'cuz I see the words "Thou Shalt Not Kill" big and red behind my eyes. I'll do anythin' to defend myself, but a killer I'm not.

So I go back and drag you out by your boots.

And I start runnin' with all the sacred saints singin' at my feet, Mother Mary flyin' by my side, and Father Abraham leadin' the way to the blessed Greyhound bus.

~ 4 ~

TRISHA

July 4, 2017

Trisha plied low, jumped high, grabbed the top of the shredded curtain hanging from the window rod, and tore it off. She was scrubbing the grimy stucco walls of her new place, hastily vacated by an old pot dealer, who had moved back east to be with his mentally challenged adult son who'd just won $650,000 in the New Jersey Lottery.

She landed soft on the balls of her blistered feet. The hardwood floor was shellacked with a dark green wash. She decided it made the living room feel like water. She could never afford Malibu, so she created her own private ocean in West Hollywood.

It had taken eight days to drive cross-country from Toronto. Now the boxes were stacked near the destinations of their contents—plates in the kitchen, clothes in the bedroom, linens in the hall. Trisha labeled everything with huge capital letters and red hearts. This was her new home. This was where she'd start a future.

Somehow.

Trisha threw the curtain into a green plastic bag. Apparently, the dealer was a creative dude. There were stashes of weed frozen in ice cubes in the beat-up tray in the freezer, in a violin case in the garage, in a ziploc baggie taped behind the fake fireplace grate. Tightly rolled joints were stuffed into the hollow handle of a hairbrush threaded with strands of long white hair, abandoned in the rusty medicine cabinet.

She lit one up and decided to hide these treasures in the bottom of one of her ice skates. Skating was one of the skills Trisha brought with her from Ontario where she grew up. Hiding things was another.

She exhaled the misty potpourri. It was getting late. The sun was almost behind the slim view of two-dimensional buildings to the west. Even though she was a fresh transplant, Trisha already had the trendy schizophrenic attitude toward her new home. She loved L.A. She hated L.A. Pirouetting across the room, she flushed the roach down the toilet and continued to dance through the empty spaces of the fourth floor, 750-square-foot apartment on N. Palm Avenue.

Her phone rang. It was her mother. Trisha declined.

When she was seven years old, her mother told her, "There was something beautiful about being pregnant. It was the time I loved you the most because you were inside of me. After you were born, it was never the same."

Brigid O'Connor was a sullen woman who spent her days at the sewing machine, tailoring other people's special garments, repairing other people's torn treasures. Trisha remembered only one dress her mother made for her. They bought the rest at Honest Ed's. It was white with little yellow flowers and had a little yellow cardigan to go with it. She wore it during the summer she turned ten. The weather was so hot and sticky. Thunderstorms poured down every other afternoon. She'd run to her father's bar, O'Connor's Pub, on Carlton Street after school, soaking wet and shivering, the dress clinging to her skin. Geoffrey O'Connor had wanted a son. When Trisha was born, he tried his best to hide his disappointment, but he couldn't quite love his daughter the way he knew he should.

"Here, show us a step," her father would say when she arrived. "Come on now, Trish, let the folks see how good you are."

He took down his fiddle and she danced a jig.

"Good job, Trish." Uncle Barney patted her on the head.

"You've got some talent," Old Aunt Fiona applauded. "Too bad *The Ed Sullivan Show* is off the air, or you could've been on that for sure."

Trisha curtseyed and glowed, nourished from the tips of her toes to the top of her head by the audience's praise.

"Better be off home now, Trish," her father tapped her shoulder. "Help your mother."

Then she'd walk home shivering, clothes still damp, still clinging. She'd unlock the front door of their small house on Salisbury Avenue, make sure her mother was in the back room sewing, then turn on the TV and wait for a commercial. It didn't matter which one. She knew them all by heart. The only time her parents looked at her with pride was when she performed.

"Better beans make better coffee," she'd recite the phrase back to the pretty people on the screen, holding up an imaginary jar. "Maxwell House. It's good to the last drop."

She'd hug a sofa cushion and dance to the percolating beat, pouring out the pot into the cup. "Better beans make better coffee," she'd belt like Mariah Carey.

Trisha was most comfortable when she was pretending to be someone else.

"You're a performer, you are," her mother said one evening at dinner.

"That's what I want to be." Trisha placed a bowl of beef stew in front of her father.

"You're not pretty enough," he said.

The kitchen table was set like it always was with no tablecloth, cutlery piled in the center for each person to take their own, and paper napkins. The clock on the wall was old, brought over from Dublin in 1985. It had been her mother's father's clock, with a red-painted cuckoo bird that popped out every hour.

"Now, Geoffrey, don't say things like that." Brigid reached for a spoon.

"Why not? Truth is truth." He sipped a glass of Guinness. "Lots of professions out there. Let her be one of them." He reached over and tousled his daughter's yellow curls. "Right, Trish?"

"I love acting," she said, looking down at the floor.

"You're only a little girl," he said, wiping the foam off his mouth. "What do you know?"

It was seven o'clock. The cuckoo bird popped out, chirped seven times, and disappeared back behind the tiny door.

"Your father's right," her mother said. "There are lots of other professions."

If no one chooses me, Trisha thought, I'll choose myself.

She worked harder than anyone she knew. Her high jumps were famous due to her sturdy thighs from childhood gymnastics. She studied Irish folk dancing as a young girl and continued into her teens. She rode streetcars and buses in subzero temperatures to get to her classes. She worked unpacking and refrigerating bottles at her father's bar to trade for lessons.

In her early twenties, Trisha appeared in the touring productions of *Riverdance* in regional theatres across Canada. She was in the chorus, one of forty young women and men who formed the undulating lines of kicks and hops that imitated the movement of the river. Her pleated skirt covered the bulky muscles that held her back from ever becoming a soloist. They said she looked too much like a Clydesdale, and not enough like a Thoroughbred. She knew exactly where to focus when she did the pivot turn. Her balance was clean. Her positions were correct. She never stumbled, not once. The front row girls could trip or fall, and it didn't matter. They had that illusory loveliness that pulled the eyes of the audience. Trisha was always the character dancer, the barmaid, the farmer's wife, the whore. She ended up in the back, far from the amber glow that worshipped center stage.

Trisha wanted more than this. She wanted to be seen, needed to be seen. She took ballet classes in every city she toured, but her short legs and broad toes made it impossible to get lead roles. She didn't like the idea of anything being impossible.

If she couldn't dance as a soloist, she'd find another way on stage. Acting was her first love before her father poisoned the well. She would finally follow her dream, even if she had to leave Canada to do it.

She enrolled in university so she'd "have something to fall back on," like her father always said. Then she worked in bars and restaurants to save money for her future. Getting work papers for the U.S. was not going to happen—not unless she fell into a priority group of candidates. Nursing was one of those professions that could transport her across the border. She was already in her fourth year at the University of Toronto studying for a degree in Communications, but she hated it. With the right marks, she could transfer to the Lawrence S. Bloomberg Faculty of Nursing 2-year accelerated program.

Trisha was excited to share her plan with her parents. She'd have a career to fall back on and at the same time, follow her dream. She brought red roses to the Sunday night dinner.

"Let me get this straight—" Her father's forehead creased. "You want to become a nurse...so you can become an actress?" He put down his fork. "In the States?" He glanced at his wife, who rolled her eyes as she passed him the bread rolls.

"That doesn't make any sense at all," her mother said.

"I'm close to thirty." Trisha pushed her unfinished colcannon to the side. "If I don't do it now, I never will."

"Well, it's a bad idea." He sat back in his chair like it was a throne. "I won't help you financially, if that's what you're asking."

"I'm not." Trisha straightened her blouse.

"What's the matter with you?" He hunched his shoulders. "I thought you were smarter than this."

"It's my passion." She wanted to escape the house just like she'd wanted to all her teenage years. Instead, she clenched her hands into fists and placed them in her lap.

Her mother got up and stood like a queen behind her husband.

"You should understand, Dad. Didn't you do the same thing?" Trisha's voice came out louder than she intended. She sensed a seed of confidence growing in her body. "You're always telling me how you came here with a dream, right? How you worked fifteen years on the assembly line at General Motors in Dublin. How you scrimped and saved so you could move here and open your own bar.

So what about your own daughter, huh? Can't I have a dream?"

Dad slammed the table with his hands. "What about you? What about you? We did it all for you! And now you want to abandon us?"

"Look how you're upsetting your father, Trish. Shame on you!"

"I just want to be happy—"

"Be an actress at your age?" her father shouted.

"Yes!"

"So what, you're going to leave Kenneth? Your mother and I actually like him."

Trisha stared at the cuckoo clock. It wasn't even close to eight, which was when she would usually get up and leave with a Tupperware full of leftovers.

"I broke up with him."

"You've lost your mind, Trish," her father sighed. "He makes a good living. He's a decent man—"

"He's a boring man!"

She'd been dating Kenneth for nine months. He was the son of one of the longtime patrons of her father's bar. He was thirty, a real estate lawyer, nice-looking, played hockey on weekends, and adored his large, Irish family. He was "a catch" by any standards, except when it came to Trisha's. There was no chemistry between them, sexual or otherwise. He never wanted to see a play or attend a dance concert. All he wanted to do was watch sports and hang out at the pub. He was more her parents' type than hers.

"I've got to go," Trisha pushed her chair away from the table.

"But we haven't had dessert yet, Trish." Her mother stepped in close. "I made bread and butter pudding."

Trisha retrieved her heavy wool cardigan from the closet. She loved the cool autumn breeze that fluttered up from Lake Ontario. I'll miss that, she thought.

"Sorry, Mom. Got lots to do tonight."

"What could you possibly have to do that's more important than spending time with us?" her father asked.

"Spending time with me." She slammed the door behind her.

So Trisha put in the work. She did everything she had to do herself—secured a loan, switched majors, graduated with an RN degree, and applied for jobs at hospitals across Los Angeles. After months of searching, she secured a position in a hospital in East Hollywood, which got her a work visa—and six months later, there she was in her new apartment in West Hollywood, just in time for the Fourth of July.

She popped open a half bottle of La Marca Prosecco, poured a glass and watched the fireworks sparkle over the Hollywood Bowl.

"To passion," she toasted herself.

It was her Independence Day too.

~ 5 ~

ALISON

February 1, 2018

Aʟɪsoɴ ᴡoᴋᴇ ᴜᴘ ɪɴ ᴀ fierce sweat. Was it from a disturbing dream or the ongoing persistence of menopause? Her pajamas were drenched. She peeled them off, shivering in the space between dark and light, and crawled back into bed for another hour of sleep. But her mind wouldn't drift off. Instead, it was racing through images of Jesse from when they first met. For some reason, he was coming out of hibernation—where he'd been for years.

∞

It was 1988. She was twenty years old...

Alison was out on her own for the very first time. She liked her studio apartment on Vista del Mar in Hollywood, just off of Franklin Avenue. It was on the second floor of a large colonial revival complex with curved red clay tiles and white stucco walls. When she moved in, the building manager informed her that Marilyn Monroe had lived in the building.

"Who knows," Mr. Kuznetsov reddened, "maybe even in your apartment."

He was a huge blotchy-skinned man from Azerbaijan with a brown walrus mustache and wild black eyes. He ran around in a Rolling Stones Tattoo You T-shirt and a bewildered grin on his face. He still couldn't believe that a boy from Baku was living in the same place a movie star had lived, a movie star he fantasized about throughout his teenage years.

The apartment was the perfect location, walking distance to the Hollywood Hills Coffee Shop she worked at on Franklin near the entrance to the Hollywood Freeway. Every night she'd get offers to party with some drummer or guitar player. She always said no because she promised herself she didn't want to get involved with anyone until she knew what she wanted to do in life. Then Jesse walked in.

It was 10 p.m. and he ordered the all-day breakfast special— three eggs, three pieces of bacon, hash browns, toast, strawberry jam, and a pot of coffee.

"You just get up or something?" Alison asked.

"Kind of." He drew his shoulder-length brown hair into a ponytail. "I'm going to shoot Hollywood by night. No glamour. Just gritty, real stuff, you know?"

She watched his green eyes sparkle. "Sounds exciting."

"My name's Jesse." He held out his hand.

"I'm Alison." She placed hers in his.

"Nice to meet you!" they said, overlapping each other, and laughed—two twenty-somethings at the beginning of their adult lives.

Jesse put his Nikon on the table and pulled a roll of Tri-X film from his bag. Alison stood there fascinated by his fingers dropping the canister in, threading the film like a magician rolling a coin across his knuckles.

"You shoot?" Jesse asked.

"No."

"My uncle got me a Kodak Brownie when I was ten. I've been taking pictures ever since and I'm never going to stop."

"You're lucky," Alison said. "You know what you want to do, what you want to be."

"Yeah." He clicked and advanced a few frames. "You an actress? Most waitresses in Hollywood are."

"No," she laughed. "But I was a drummer in an all-girl rock band in high school. Does that count?"

Juicy Kisses had broken up because the keyboard player and the rhythm guitarist went off to college. Suzy, the lead singer, signed with a big time manager and was trying to make it as a soloist. She stopped returning Alison's calls. They hadn't spoken in over a year. Alison was starting to miss her.

"Did you love it?' Jesse smiled up into her gray eyes.

"Drumming?" Her cheeks flushed. "Yes."

"Then it counts."

Alison's pen slipped out of her hand, but Jesse caught it before it hit the floor. Something happened in that instant when his hand shot out and rescued the pen—they talked about it later—an intimacy, a connection, an opening of the heart.

"Nice catch!" she said over her shoulder as she headed towards the kitchen.

The next night, Jesse walked in at the same time. Alison was at the register, counting her tips.

"Good evening," he said.

"Breakfast?" she mused.

He shrugged and pulled out a handful of pens from his jacket pocket. "Here," he presented them to her. "Just in case..."

There was something about two people laughing together that felt more intimate than kissing—looking into each other's eyes, allowing themselves to be seen.

"Want to come to a party with me?" he smiled, exposing two dimples.

She was about to shake her head "no" when he pulled a small camera out of his shirt pocket and started taking pictures of her. She laughed and drummed on the counter with her fingers, and for a minute, they were dancing to the harmony of his clicks and her hands.

"When?" she said, freeing her hair from its braid.

"Now."

They sat in her kitchen the next morning, still happily hungover from booze and sex. She handed him rye toast with peanut butter and strawberry jam.

"I'm going on tour to shoot Bon Jovi. A few cities on the West Coast, then Europe. Want to come with me?"

She held up the coffee pot. "More?"

"Yes, please," he nodded.

Alison wanted to go to college, but she wasn't sure what to study—maybe music, maybe education. That night at dinner, she told her parents she was thinking of traveling with Jesse.

"Are you sure, Ali?" her mother asked as her fingers grazed the delicate cross on her necklace. "You hardly know him."

"I'm sure. I mean," Alison jumped up from the table, "what an experience I'll have! Europe and Bon Jovi! I'll learn so much about music. How could I not go?"

"Easily," her father dug into the salad. "You could not go."

"Do you feel safe with him?" her mother asked.

"Yes. I do. And don't worry, we'll be traveling with about twenty people—the tour organizers, roadies, publicity people..." Alison grabbed a dinner roll and sat down. "And he knows what he wants in life. I find that inspiring. And he's kind and funny—"

"Okay, okay, I guess you're going." He touched his daughter's hand. "Just remember, you can come home anytime. We'll wire you money if you need it."

"Thank you!" Alison kissed him on the cheek.

"I hope you know what you're doing," her father said.

"I do," she assured him. "I really do."

"And be careful, Ali," her mother reminded. "Don't get yourself in trouble."

∞

Alison blinked open her eyes. The alarm was ringing. She had to get up, go to a Thursday morning meeting with the English department, and then teach a full day of Shakespeare. Whenever they got to *Romeo and Juliet*, she thought of her romance with Jesse—at least the beginning, before the poison and the dagger.

∞

Alison and Jesse's time together lasted three beautiful months on tour—San Francisco, Seattle, Portland—then Dublin, Rome, and Paris.

Alison left the tour early because she wanted to spend time with her parents before they departed on their first cruise—a two-month voyage to Australia and New Zealand. She stayed over at her childhood home, on Vesper Avenue in Van Nuys, a cotton night-gown waiting in the middle drawer of her old oak dresser. They watched *Jeopardy!* while her father did the crossword in the *L.A. Times* and her mother crocheted. Their latest project was drying on the balcony of her apartment on Vista Del Mar. It was a multi-col-ored afghan of patchwork squares, the yarn collected from unrav-eling their old sweaters. Alison was proud of it. She couldn't wait to show it to Jesse.

"He's amazing, Dad, really," Alison said.

Her father folded the newspaper. "We look forward to meet-ing him when we get back from our cruise," he said.

The nausea began three weeks after Alison returned from Par-is. She ran to the bathroom and threw up in the toilet. She inspected her breasts in the mirror. They were tender, and a tiny bit bigger.

Jesse had sent two postcards, one from Berlin and the other from Warsaw. There was nothing romantic in either one, or even intimate. Maybe his emotions were in code. "This place is weird. Full of Nazi ghosts," he wrote from Berlin. From Poland, "Warsaw is sad. I'm shooting clouds here. Sometimes I wonder if my work has any meaning." She couldn't decipher the love.

She wanted to tell her parents the news, but that would mean a choppy transatlantic call to a cruise ship eight thousand miles away. But really, she wanted Jesse to be the first to know. He was coming home in a couple of weeks. In the meantime, she'd start tak-ing good care of herself. She gave up red meat and sugar. She quit her job at the coffee shop before they left for Europe, but that meant she didn't have a place to go to every day, or a source of income. She owed her parents a lot of money for helping with the rent, so she found another waitressing gig at a Greek restaurant on Cahuenga, still within walking distance from her apartment. She worked five nights a week from 5 p.m. to 11 p.m., and one of the chefs would drive her home. His name was Niko, charming and ambitious. He always wanted to come in for coffee, but he stopped asking when he turned out to be the first person she told.

"I'm pregnant," she said.

She did it so he would stop pestering her, and it worked. He stopped driving her home. It felt weird that Nico knew while Jesse didn't. She walked home by herself now, staying as far from the street as possible, blending into the shadows of trees and houses. She was a mother, a huntress, looking out for trouble before it found her.

The day Jesse returned, he was jet-lagged and hungry. She cooked him steak and roasted potatoes, poured him a tall glass of burgundy. He talked about the guys in the band, the schizophrenic city of Berlin, the sunsets at Tempelhofer Feld, Checkpoint Charlie, and the modernization of Warsaw. He wanted to go back and take pictures of places that really mattered, like Auschwitz and displaced person settlements throughout Germany. He talked about going to India to photograph the slums, then maybe he'd take a ship to Australia to document the Maori. He wanted to grow as an artist. He wanted his photographs to stand for something.

He fell asleep on the couch. She wished the crochet blanket was dry so she could cover him with it.

In the morning, he joined her in bed. He unbraided her hair and spread it out around her head—a flaming crown to her pastel body. She opened herself to him, and he took her like the waves take the beach, rolling in from the horizon, then back out and then back in again.

She cooked him scrambled eggs with warm, fluffy croissants. The butter was soft. The espresso was strong.

"Perfect," he said.

Their love was so easy—like two halves of the same circle, fitting together without seams. She wanted to tell him that she didn't get her period. She wanted to tell him she was going to have their baby. She wanted to tell him that it was all meant to be. But Jesse had a faraway look in his eyes as he gazed out the window.

"I'm really starting to feel it all happening for me, Ali," he glowed.

"All what happening?" Her inner pulse quickened.

"My career!" he turned to her. "I can't believe I didn't tell you last night. I'm going to New York to shoot an album cover for Bruce Springsteen, and two agencies want to represent me. Two! And they have contacts all over the world. One said they could get me gigs in Japan. I mean, fantastic, right? They do a lot of movies and want to hire me to shoot posters. I could really start to make it happen, you know? I can feel it."

She wiped some jam off her fingers. "But what about taking photographs of things that really make a difference, like you said last night?"

"Oh yeah, I wanna do all that. And I will. I'll go to Japan and shoot a movie poster, and then I'll fly to China and take pictures of villages along the Silk Road, and then maybe take a train to Tibet and visit monasteries and photograph Zen masters and who knows what else. And you can meet up with me."

The butter was melting in its dish. She picked it up. She welcomed the cold rush on her body when she opened the refrigerator door. She stood there, staring at a carton of milk like it was the Oracle of Delphi. Her back faced Jesse's back.

She wanted to tell him she was pregnant. She wanted him to take her in his arms and tell her it was the best news he could imagine. She wanted a miracle.

He swallowed what was left of the coffee. "More, please."

She closed the fridge door. It was just the sounds in the room that carried her now—the hum of the refrigerator motor, the drip of the faucet in the sink, the ticking of the clock on the wall, the clinking of the spoon against the plate. She poured him more coffee.

He stood up. "This is my time!"

She sat down, shifting her feet under the chair. Her ankles felt dry. "That's amazing, Jesse!" She was happy for him. She really was. But why was her stomach doing a somersault all of a sudden? She calmed herself by touching his arm. "You're so talented, I'm not surprised. This is just the beginning for you."

Jesse took her hand and kissed it. Then his eyes opened wide as if the greatest idea had just popped into his head. "I hope you feel this one day, Ali."

"Feel what?"

"Passion for your art," he beamed.

"Me too," Alison gazed at the floor. "I guess I'm still searching."

"Hey, play drums!" His fingers danced on the tabletop. "You said Juicy Kisses was a happy time for you, right? Join a band!"

"Yeah, maybe," pulling her legs into a cross-legged yoga position. "I'll think about it."

Jesse slipped his jacket on. "Oh, I almost forgot!" He took out two photographs. "I have something for you."

In one picture, the two of them stood on the Pont de la Tournelle, his arms around her, Notre Dame behind them. They looked like they were one person.

"It's beautiful," she said. "That old Frenchman was a good photographer."

The second picture was just her, alone in front of the gum tree at Jim Morrison's grave in Père Lachaise Cemetery.

"I love this," she murmured. She wanted him to say he loved her, that they should be together, that a baby would be perfect—

"The rest of the photographs will be ready when I get back from New York." He studied her face. "What's the matter? Are you okay?"

She rose from the chair. Her eyes met his. She didn't look away. Instead, she moved into him. Kiss me, she thought. We are two halves of the same circle. Just kiss me and we'll figure it out.

He kissed her, longer and deeper than she'd ever been kissed. She was going to tell him. She really was—

"Man, this is what I've dreamed of Ali! A beautiful woman, shooting all over the world, making art! No hassles, just good vibes. Right?" He moved to the front door.

She couldn't bear to drag him down. She and a baby would be a "hassle." He was too young to have a family. He deserved to live the life he dreamt of. So did she...

"Right." She rubbed her eye.

"Anyway, gotta go," he looked at his watch, "but I'll call when I get back from New York and we'll do something. There's this country western club—I shot Blue Öyster Cult there. The Palomino. You heard of it?"

Jesse ran back and kissed her again before she could answer. Then he walked out down the stairs to the pink stone pathway that led to his van. Alison closed the door and locked it. She rocked back and forth and couldn't stop the truth from streaming down her cheeks. She wanted to wrap herself in the afghan and roll away. But it was still damp with that odor of wet wool that made her even sicker.

After she vomited the scrambled eggs into the toilet, she went to find the Yellow Pages.

The next day, Alison arrived in the waiting room of the free clinic, signed the permission forms, and skimmed through the magazines. Nothing held her attention. All she could think about was how empty she felt. Jesse was at the beginning of his career. He was only twenty-five years old. They hardly knew each other. Yes, there was chemistry—more than chemistry—there was the possibility of true love. But a baby? They used condoms—but not always. It was a mistake. It wasn't planned. It wasn't fair to tell him. It wasn't fair to ask him to change his life. None of it was fair. And now she would never tell her parents, ever. They were against abortion.

A doctor's assistant brought her to a room, more like a ten-by-ten cubicle with a navy curtain that separated it from its other half. Alison placed her palm against the shiny topcoat of the bare white walls. Her hand slid down the surface, leaving a faint trail of sweat. She'd never even thought about having a child. She was too young. What about her life? Maybe joining a band was a good idea. She loved playing music and wanted to travel. Alison put on the gown and waited on the examining table until sleep took over.

"You alright?" The assistant shook her awake half an hour later.

"Just tired," she said.

"If you're not sure..."

"I am." Alison pushed herself up. She was only twenty. She couldn't raise a child alone, and she didn't want to burden her parents. They were heading into retirement.

"It'll be uncomfortable, and there'll be bleeding afterwards. Wear pads, no Tampax for the next month. No sex. No baths. No swimming. You don't want to get an infection. Do you understand?" The assistant waited for her to respond.

Alison gripped the hem of her hospital gown. She could never tell Jesse about the pregnancy or the abortion. It would only cloud their relationship.

"Do you understand?" the assistant repeated.

"Yes," said Alison.

"Then come with me," she said softly. The assistant had seen so many women like her—Alison knew that. At least she didn't feel judged.

The next room was big, metal, cold. If she didn't tell him, was that a lie between them? And if that was so, then could there ever be true love? Was their relationship already doomed? Alison lay on her back and positioned her feet in the stirrups. A high-up window held back the day with its shades pulled down. A shred of sunlight stole its way along the edges of the pane.

The assistant came back with a tall woman behind her.

"I'm Dr. Humphries," the woman said. "I'll be performing the procedure. Do you have any questions?"

"No," Alison answered. The odor of bleach and Ivory soap burned her nostrils.

"Then let's begin."

The doctor spread Alison's knees apart. The speculum sent an ice-cold spasm throughout her body. There was a pressure in her abdomen, the sound of a vacuum cleaner, the smell of burnt flesh.

"Almost done," Dr. Humphries stated. "How're you doing?"

Tears slid down Alison's temples. The assistant wiped them away.

∞

Alison stepped into the shower. She wanted to wash away her memories of Jesse, but the spray of hot water only brought them crashing back. The morning's pre-dawn sweat wasn't menopause. No, it was caused by the fractured nightmare she had just dreamt of Jesse coming back to her abandoned apartment those thirty years ago. In the dream, Alison was watching through Jesse's eyes.

"She moved out," said the building manager. "Didn't even ask for her security deposit back."

"What? She—she moved out? Did she leave a forwarding address—or anything?" Jesse paced.

"No, nothing." Mr. Kuznetsov ran a comb through his hair. "You try calling her?"

"Of course! Her phone's disconnected."

Mr. Kuznetsov nodded like he understood, like he'd had lots of girlfriends disappear out of the blue. "Sorry, man. Women, ya know?"

Jesse's hand shook as he handed the manager a sealed manila envelope. "Could you give this to her when she comes back to get her mail?"

"They never come back," Mr. Kuznetsov slid the comb into his pants pocket, "when they leave fast like that."

Jesse's chest tightened. The manager leaned in.

"Hey, you know," Mr. Kusnetzov lowered his voice, "Shelly Winters used to visit Marilyn Monroe here. I'm told they had pretty wild parties. Plenty of drugs. Lots of group sex. You hear that too?"

Jesse walked back to his van. He sat with his head in his hands for several minutes before he tore open the manila envelope. He came to tell Alison that while he was in New York, he realized he'd been too focused on his career the last time they were together. He wanted to tell her that he really missed her, that he loved her and that he wanted to be her man.

Jesse let the Paris photographs from Père Lachaise Cemetery slide out—Alison dancing with the spirit of Jim Morrison, the radiance of fifteen flashlights shining on her nakedness—their last pictures together...

∞

Alison stepped out of the shower. She toweled off, promising herself she'd get through *Romeo and Juliet* as quickly as possible. All these Jesse-related thoughts were getting in the way.

~ 6 ~

WANDA

March 17, 2019

I BEEN TRAVELIN' 47 HOURS from Mobile when I get off the bus.

I took a pink blanket from the Greyhound lost and found when we stopped in Houston. It seemed kinda lonely and waitin' for someone to pick it up. It smelled like baby powder when I breathed it in, and maybe it was a whisper from God I'd done the right thing. So I held it to my belly and prayed all night long. I prayed you're alive, Travis. I prayed I won't go to prison. I prayed my baby will be safe. I thought of your knife on my neck and then in you, and I prayed to God for all the forgiveness He's got.

The bus lets me off on Hollywood Boulevard. It's not a real station, just a place where you see the Hollywood sign— 'cuz there it is, stuck right into the mountains. There's a red brick church to the left of the parkin' lot, its big white cross stretchin' up to the sky. Across the street's a car dealership. More cars than I ever seen in one place. Nobody buyin' 'em.

I start walkin' to where the sun's settin'. I guess that's west. I don't wanna spend another minute in today. I come up on a buildin' called The Museum of Death. It's got pretty red flowers hangin' over a door of white bars. I freeze when I see the big skull painted on the front window, taller than me, maybe five feet wide. It grins like it wants to chew me up and spit me out as its eyes go round and round, like they're hypnotizin' themselves. Did you send death here to watch over my every move? Are you everywhere, no matter where I hide?

"No! You're not gettin' me, Mr. Death," I whisper even though I know it hears my thoughts. Like you do. "You're not gonna take me down!" I yell and kick its glass chin.

I cross the boulevard and head into the neighborhood. Dirt is the color of everythin' here. A man sits outside the Motel El Centro, watchin' crows on the trees above his head. They ain't palm trees— they look like someone dipped a feather duster in a barrel of violets and sprinkled 'em all over the branches. I walk closer. I want to feel the little flowers fallin' on me like how I imagine snow falls. I've never seen it for real, just in movies. But now it's snowin' violets. I walk behind the man, but he don't notice. He's too busy cryin'.

There's a tiny flower on his hair. I reach out for it and lift it off. He jumps real fast and puts his hand up to protect himself—but when he sees what I did, he steps closer. His cheeks are wet. His eyes are full.

"My grandmother died this morning. In Mexico."

"I'm sorry," I say.

"She'd do something like that," he says.

"Like what?"

"Like you taking the flower out of my hair."

The crows lift off all together and fly away.

"You want it back?" I hold it out to him.

"Sure." He takes it and puts it in his shirt pocket. "It's just something she would do, that's what I'm saying. Something thoughtful like that. My grandmother's sending me a sign she's alright. Everything's going to be alright."

I figured some angel's busy sendin' a whole bunch of signs. But how come I only see 'em sometimes? I think they're always there. I mean, how else is God gonna reach us?

He points to his seat 'cuz that's when he notices I'm pretty big.

"Please sit down," he says. "My name's Ricardo."

"I need a room," I say.

He wipes his cheeks with the cuff of his jean shirt. "Well, I'll tell you what, there's a small room next to the office. Come on, I'll show you."

There's a cot shoved up against a light blue wall. It has a nice white pillowcase and a nice white sheet.

"How much?" I ask.

"For a couple of nights?" He looks 'round the room. "No charge."

"How come?"

"I'm the manager. You brought me a message from my grandmother, so if you want it, you can have it."

I need a place to hide in 'til I figure out what to do. The baby's comin' in a month. "Thanks," I say.

I fall into bed. The next day, he knocks on the door and I open it. He's medium height and strong lookin'. He's like a Rembrandt paintin' with the light hittin' the side of his face. His skin is rough. He's got a scar on his left temple. It's almost faded. But I see it 'cuz that's what I do.

"Are you okay?"

He sees I've been cryin' so he comes back with juice, eggs scrambled with red peppers and onions, white toast and coffee and leaves me alone. He does the same thing for two days. On the third, he asks a question.

"Can I stay and eat with you?"

We eat beef enchiladas that are covered all over with purple onions and green tomatoes, just like a tablecloth I remember in a Mexican restaurant my father took Betty Ann, Janine and me to that had so many colorful vegetables painted on it we got even more hungry just lookin' at it. I tell him 'bout that while he watches me eat like he's a mama bird makin' sure her baby's gettin' big and strong.

"So, where you from?" he asks.

I wanna tell him but I don't, I can't—'cuz he could be like that Mr. Death I saw when I got off the bus. He could be your secret agent, workin' undercover, tryin' to trick me and bring me and the baby back to you. A bounty hunter.

"Florida," I lie.

"Your neck okay?"

My hand flies up to cover my wound—what you tried to do to me.

"I see you got scratches on it," Ricardo says. "You need a first aid kit?"

"It's fine," I say. "Don't worry 'bout it."

He's embarrassed now, sorry he asked.

"What about you?" I say changin' the subject back to before. "Where you from?"

"I come from a place called Tequila."

"Well, I won't forget that name."

He cracks a smile.

"It's where they make Tequila," he says.

"I sure hope so," I say, "or what a silly name for a town!"

He looks at me like he don't know if I'm bein' funny or makin' fun of him.

"You want some?" he asks.

"Can't," I say, lookin' down at my baby bump.

"You pregnant?" he asks.

"You blind?" I say, and we both laugh.

"You should go one day," he tells me. "My family's there. Just ask for the Lopez Cafe in the town square. Everybody knows it. There's a fountain in the middle of the zócalo. When I was a kid, I used to throw pesos in it. I made wishes."

"What'd you wish for?"

"I can't tell you or it won't come true," he says.

"You know what I'd wish for? Some more of 'em beef enchiladas."

"You like 'em? I made 'em. I work in a restaurant and go to chef school. That's why I'm here. When I learn everything I need to learn, I'm going back to Tequila and start my own place."

He brings me a couple more. While I'm eatin', he pulls out an old guitar from the closet and sings me some Mexican songs. His voice isn't as deep as yours. You know I love your voice, Travis. It's beautiful. When you sing to me late at night, it helps me fall asleep. You're like healin' tea. I've been missin' it. Ricardo's voice is pretty. Like a girl's, but still a man's sound. All I can think of is him bein' on *The Voice* and how Blake Shelton and Kelly Clarkson would both want to coach him. They'd fight for him and get up outta their chairs and beg him to be on their team. I tell him that. It makes his cheeks go pink. I don't tell him all four chairs would turn 'round for you.

"Hey, you know what? I don't know your name," Ricardo says.

He senses I don't wanna tell him, so he answers for me.

"I'm gonna call you Angel 'cuz my grandmother sent you. That fine with you?" He gets up.

"Wait," I say, and hug him real close. I don't know why I do. I just want to.

"Hey, no problem, honest," he says. "If you want a nicer place, you can stay in my room."

I look at him like he's crazy.

"No weird stuff, I promise. There's two beds. There's a kitchen and I'll cook for you because that's what I really love to do, and I need to practice, and you could tell me if its good and stuff like that."

So I do. He doesn't come near me, though I know he can't sleep. On the third night I go over and put my hand on his back kinda gentle.

I never done this before. That's always you. You don't like it if you ain't the one to start things. This time it's me. My fingers touch Ricardo's shoulder and move in close. He turns to me. His stubble is soft, not coarse like yours. His breath smells sweet like peaches. I lay my head on his chest.

I know we speak in different languages all over the world, but I think we hold each other in the same way. It doesn't matter that he's somebody Momma would hate just 'cuz she could, just for the honey-color of his skin. It doesn't matter what anyone thinks 'cuz in my heart I know he'll never hurt me. All we do is hug each other. It's enough.

"*Dulces sueños,*" he says, and a peace comes over me for the first time since I lit my life on fire.

~ 7 ~

TRISHA

August 12, 2017

Erika was a would-be screenwriter who could only work with Daft Punk or k.d. lang playing in the background. That's what brought them together at a neighbor's garden party one Saturday afternoon. Trisha was going through some CDs she'd brought when Erika came over to see why it was so quiet all of a sudden.

"Where's the music?" she asked.

"You like k.d. lang?"

"Are you joking?" Erika twirled around. "I saw her at the Universal Amphitheatre, and the women in the audience were screaming so loud, she practically begged them to stop so she could do her set."

A bee buzzed near Trisha's head. She stepped back. Erika stepped forward.

"Then I threw a pair of sexy red panties on the stage, and the audience went wild again," Erika smirked.

Trisha gazed at Erika, five-foot-ten, lean and muscular with sun-kissed skin and shiny black hair. A dancer's body, she thought, the kind I should've been born with. Trisha's hair was just above her shoulders, dirty blond and curly. She wore it up in a rubber band to make it seem like she didn't care what she looked like, even though it took her ten minutes to get her curls to look as nonchalant as they did. Her eyes were honey brown, framed by round tortoise shell glasses. She wore a pair of white capris and a matching white shirt with the collar turned up. Her lipstick was brick red, her eye shadow a metallic blue, the eyeliner a dark brown painted with a slight wing at the end. She looked like a pretty 1950s secretary.

Erika's exposed sculpted muscles, her metallic-coated black jeans and red crop top with accentuated shoulder pads placed her in the near future.

Trisha couldn't help herself. She reached out her fingers.

"May I?"

Erika grinned. "Knock yourself out."

Trisha skimmed Erika's taut stomach with the back of her knuckles.

"Oh my gosh," Trisha retreated, the tiny hairs on the back of her neck jumping. "I've never done that before."

"Asked? Or touched?"

Trisha blushed. "Both."

k.d. lang's "Consequences of Falling" started playing.

"I haven't seen you around," Erika said.

"I'm new."

"You sound British."

"Nope. Canadian."

"Like k.d. lang. Nice."

"Yes."

"No, I mean Canadians are nice, right?" Erika flirted.

"I guess. But nice never made it to the finish line. And that's why I'm here."

"Darling, that's why everyone's here."

They went to The Abbey and shared an order of pumpkin pancakes.

"You realize I'm gay, right?" asked Erika.

"Yes."

"I'd like to take you home."

"I've never..."

"That's no reason not to."

Trisha pulled on one of her curls. Sex with Kenneth and the other men had been unfulfilling. She'd never felt like she was the true object of their passion. She wanted that badly—to be desired, to be longed for, to be needed. Maybe this would be different.

Erika was Trisha's first woman. Trisha was—well—Erika couldn't remember how many women she'd bedded.

"What difference does it make?" Erika asked two weeks later. They were sitting wrapped in a fleece blanket on the red leather sofa in her studio on Courtney Avenue. A bottle of Prosecco and a plate of freshly baked chocolate chip cookies sat next to the laptop on the secondhand coffee table.

"I want to know," Trisha said. "I just do."

"Okay," Erika sighed, shrugging her shoulders. "I'll figure it out."

Erika had to call up a couple of her longtime friends to help her run the numbers. The final count was twenty-five.

"Twenty-five women?" said Trisha. "I've only been with one—

you!"

"But you've slept with guys," Erika teased. "I haven't. That should count for something, shouldn't it?"

"Four," Trisha said. "I've had sex with four, and they weren't anything to write home about."

Erika took a bite of a cookie. She offered the rest to Trisha, who shook her head.

"Do you want to sleep with a couple of people to catch up?" Erika asked. "That'll be okay with me if you do, as long as it's just sex." She smiled, pouring Trisha some more to drink.

"You won't be jealous? I mean, what if I fall in love?"

Erika unzipped her jeans. She tugged them off, throwing them on the floor, then unbuttoned her shirt and tossed it to the jeans. She kissed Trisha's mouth as her hand traveled under her skirt.

"If you do, you do. But I think we have something special, and I want you to feel free, so I'm willing to take the chance."

Trisha put her hand on Erika's back and pulled her closer.

"And, if we do have something special, and it turns out I'm your one and only woman," added Erika, "I don't want you deciding years from now that you want to do some extramarital exploring. So it's a preemptive strategy, so to speak."

Trisha lay back, her golden curls splayed out on the red-and-black brocade cushion. She liked these Spanish apartments with their high, curved ceilings.

"And what about you?" she murmured. "Do you get to sleep with other people too?"

"Me?" Erika said. "I don't do anything with anybody. I'm too busy writing, trying to get to the finish line." She gently massaged her new girlfriend's inner thighs.

"Feels nice," Trisha said.

"And whatever you do," said Erika, "don't tell me about it. Okay?"

"Okay," Trisha whispered, her voice caught in her throat, her body aching to expand.

"Nothing. The woman. The man. The sex. Nothing. Understood?" Erika said. Then she stopped.

"No! Wait, what are you doing?"

Erika opened a small drawer under the coffee table. She pulled out a pink vibrator.

"Do you have them everywhere?" laughed Trisha.

"Yep," Erika turned it on. "And this "catch-up arrangement" stops when we move in together if we move in together. Agreed?"

It buzzed. It trembled. It sang. "Agreed," Trisha moaned, as it traded places between them until their bodies rumbled in unison like an aftershock.

They drifted off to that special after-climax place that is sleep but not, dreams but not, peace but not. Twenty minutes later, Trisha was ravenous. She reached for a cookie. Erika was already back at her computer, writing. There was a look of determination on her face that Trisha had never seen before. That, and complete contentment. How could these contradictory emotions live in the same person?

Later, driving home, Trisha wondered about the "catch-up arrangement." Were a couple of sexual encounters really enough to even out the score? If they stayed together, she'd always be lacking in experience. She'd be at a disadvantage. So, no, Trisha thought, a couple of encounters is not enough. She wanted more. Much more.

Erika knew about Trisha's longing to shine in the spotlight, her need to win at something and her fierce competitive streak. You couldn't cross the Canadian—U.S. border to become an actress without one. But she didn't know how deep the need bled.

Before she and Trisha got really serious, Erika made it clear that a baby had to be in the cards. Otherwise, no deal.

"Do you want to have a child?" Erika asked.

Trisha was getting dressed for an audition. She was up for a one day part of a hooker on *Days of Our Lives*. They'd been dating for three months. They were falling in love. Looking at Erika, you wouldn't assume she wanted to settle down and start a family. But she did.

"Look, I don't want to get too invested and then really disappointed. That's happened before. So I swore to myself that exactly ninety days into a relationship, no matter if that day fell on a birthday or Christmas or Valentine's, I'd ask the question. Today is November 12, 2017, three months to the day we met."

"I'm listening," Trisha said.

"I was going to have one on my own, but my periods are too irregular. Like almost non-existent sometimes." Erika cleared her throat. "So, do you? Because if you don't, then we can't go any further. But if you do, then it doesn't matter when, but it's got to be you."

Erika stood there, leaning against her bedroom wall, still in her white T-shirt and panties, coffee cup at her lips, waiting for the answer before she dared take a sip.

Trisha pulled up her black net stockings, clipped them onto the garter belt and looked at Erika. "That's a pretty big ask, don't you think? I mean, we've just been together—what—three months, right? And I'm the one who has to have the baby?"

"I wish it could be me," said Erika. "I think pregnancy is so beautiful. It's a symbol of all that's possible in life." The morning haze flowed in through the blinds, covering her in a shimmering veil of paleness. "So, yes, unless we adopt. Which is fine with me—but I'd like to try first. I mean—have you try if you want to," Erika pushed away from the wall.

Trisha put on her fuck-me pumps and crossed to the bed. When she was working on her nursing degree, she spent time in the maternity ward at Mount Sinai Hospital in Toronto. She'd watch the newborns on her lunch break. They looked like tiny aliens, otherworldly caterpillars bound in their cotton cocoons. The first time she held one, she was surprised by how light and perfect it felt. She'd been oblivious to the part of her that had a lot of love to give—not the romantic kind of love she'd read about, but the parental kind of love she'd never received. She overheard a new mother say, "I'm thirty-two years old. He's three days old. I feel I've known him my whole life." Trisha wanted to feel that way about someone.

"Let me get this part first," she joked. "Then I've got to go to work. I have an eight-hour ER shift. We can talk about it tomorrow."

She picked up her French demi-bra, slipped it on, and turned for her lover to clasp—but instead of clasping it, Erika tossed it aside and cupped Trisha's breasts in her coffee-warmed hands. She kissed the nape of her neck and then turned her around and sat her on the edge of the bed.

"I'm going to be late for my audition," Trisha murmured.

"It'll be worth it."

Erika's tongue traced the edge of the stockings and then the garters that held them up. It traveled to the lace panties. Erika slipped them down but only as far as the tops of the stockings. With the same power of their first night together, she brought her partner to an early morning climax.

"Your turn," said Trisha.

"No," said Erika, standing up. "Think about my being wet all day, waiting for you to come over."

When Trisha walked into the audition room, she was greeted by a female casting director and her gay male assistant, who ran the camera. Trisha remembered her morning on the edge of the bed. She let herself blush as she slated her name to the camera. She had one line.

"Do you want to?" she gazed into the lens.

Trisha felt herself get aroused at the naughty thoughts she was having. She was definitely, as her acting teacher said, "in the moment." She lifted her skirt, exposing the garter. She felt a rhythm in her body come out of nowhere.

"Do you want to?" she asked again, dancing, tossing her head back and laughing.

On the way to the hospital, Trisha's agent called and told her she got the part. Trisha cried with happiness. It was her first acting job. She left a message for Erika. She knew there would be champagne for a late dinner that night.

But she kept asking herself: Do you want to? Do you want to? It had only been three months. How could she say yes to Erika? Three months was nothing when it came to relationships. Erika was ensconced in the gay world, with plenty of friends and ex-lovers. She'd never been with a man, and never wanted to, because she always knew who she was. She always knew what she wanted. Trisha was barely in any world. She was a baby immigrant, a baby actor, a baby bisexual. And now Erika wanted to know if a baby was in their future together. A baby having a baby? The thought was too scary for Trisha. It was too much, too soon. What about her career? It was just beginning. Would she be a good mother? She didn't have good role models with either parent. It was unfair to ask the question so soon after meeting. It was too soon for an ultimatum.

Do you want to?

I don't know yet, Trisha thought. I don't know.

~ 8 ~

ALISON

March 12, 2018

Aｌｉｓｏｎ ｗａｌｋｅｄ ｉｎｔｏ ｈｅｒ ｈｏｍｅｒｏｏｍ. It had the familiar odor of sweat and perfume–teenagers dangling in limbo. The kids in her classes said she was their favorite teacher. They liked how real she was, how open and encouraging. They felt safe in her class. She'd be teaching a short story by Hemingway and connect a sentence to a personal memory, shake her head and laugh out loud, or get emotional and talk about it. She'd ask deep questions. She'd listen without judgment. She told them about her drumming days on the Hollywood Strip and touring with Juicy Kisses. Some of her students' mothers remembered Alison from the band. They thought she was kind of famous and kind of cool. She'd reference old rock songs, and even the occasional contemporary hit. She'd share how embarrassed she was in the red-and-white wool go-go pants her mother knit for her fifteenth birthday party, or how she burst into tears when she heard John Lennon was assassinated, or how she saw her geography teacher scratch his butt when he thought no one was looking. She even shared that she was contemplating a change.

Alison moved to the window and gazed out across the football field onto Pico Boulevard. She'd lived in Santa Monica for twenty years, in a rent-controlled complex with a communal courtyard. The coastal city had a beautiful beach and an eclectic assortment of takeout places to fit her mostly healthy, mostly single lifestyle. She was a fixture at the Tuesday night Santa Monica City Hall meetings, ready to fight the landlords on any attempt to hike the rent. She lived below her means, so she had plenty in the bank between her savings and investments from the proceeds of her parents' house and their life insurance.

As a pale mist tumbled in from the ocean, Alison wondered how much longer her life would last. Her parents died in an accident in their early fifties. Who knows how long they would have lived? Maybe to seventy or eighty, at least. That could mean twenty or thirty more years for her, plenty of time—to do—what? Something was changing. Her body was hovering above itself, a hummingbird just before it chooses its next blossom.

Alison waited until 4:30 p.m. to walk into Principal Tumaini Otieno's office, once most of the kids had gone home. It was a medium-sized room paneled with dark wood. A worn green sofa rested against the wall under a large, sepia-toned photograph of Santa Monica beach in the 1930s. He was sitting at his massive desk that was covered with paperwork.

"What's up, Ali?" When she didn't respond immediately, he added, "What's wrong?"

Alison closed the door. "You know, I started teaching here at SAMO over twenty years ago. I was almost thirty then, and I was really excited to share my love of literature—"

Principal Otieno rose from his chair and walked to the window. His blue shirt had sweat stains on the back and underarms. His mauve tie with laughing frogs hung loose around his neck. He was born in Kenya and had the kind of face you didn't notice until you were forced to—face to face in a crowded elevator, standing near under an awning in a thunderstorm, sitting beside in a darkened theatre—his nose flattened out above his top lip, his black hair short and thick, his smile wide and contagious. He resembled a young Sidney Poitier.

"You're a great teacher, Alison."

"Tumaini, please let me finish." She sat on the arm of the sofa. "This isn't easy."

"Okay," he shook his head. "Go ahead and ruin my day."

She relaxed a little. "Now that I'm fifty—"

"You're fifty?" he feigned shock. "Really?"

"Very funny," she smiled. He joined her, and for a few seconds, they were Ali and T—good friends. Then they resumed their professional roles. "Let me finish, sir, please—"

"But you're such a great teacher, Ms. Bishop—" Principal Otieno added.

"Now that I'm fifty," she continued, "I want to be the student, the one discovering new worlds, the one curious about her future—"

The sound of laughing students running down the hall interrupted her thoughts. That freedom, that carefree feeling of youth. That's what she was missing. That's what she wanted back.

"What did you plan to do with your one wild and precious life?" Tumaini quoted Mary Oliver. "Is that what's going on here?"

"I think so. You know these last three years have been hard—good, but hard. I've been on my own, trying to find myself..."

It was already getting dark outside. March was a dreary and cold month in Santa Monica.

"I'm almost the same age as my parents were when they died..." She pulled her sweater close to her body and crossed to his side of the desk. "I can't stop thinking about that."

"I understand, dear one," he put a hand on her shoulder. "I understand."

She was hungry. She'd been too nervous to finish her sandwich at lunch, knowing this was the day she would give notice.

"And all the financial stuff is worked out so—I'm going to retire in January of next year. I wanted to give you plenty of notice."

"Thank you," he nodded. "So what are you going to do?"

"Travel. Write. It's going to be my next chapter." Alison let out a deep sigh. "Thank you for not making this harder than it already is..."

"I'll need a letter of resignation so it's official." He slipped on his jacket.

"It has nothing to do with the school or my students." Her voice broke a little. "I will miss them."

"I know, Ali. To be perfectly honest, I'm happy for you." He reached out his long arms and pulled her into his chest. "You're finally celebrating yourself." Then he stepped back and perused her face. "Fifty, really?"

"Yes, really!" she laughed and headed for the door.

On her way to the parking lot, panic raced up her body. She got into her car and sat for a moment, clutching the steering wheel, breathing deeply. She had changed her career before, from musician to teacher, but why was she so scared now?

∞

Her relationship with Jesse ended when she was twenty. She needed to discover a passion then, an enthusiasm for something, just like he had with photography. After the abortion, she gave Suzy another call. She needed a friend. When they were in high school, they used to come home past midnight after performing at a party and sit on the porch, smoking weed and drinking Coors. Suzy would sing "Total Eclipse of the Heart," and Alison would accompany her with drumsticks on the metal banister, at least until the neighbors started complaining.

But Suzy still wasn't calling her back. So she went to Suzy's parents' house on Hatteras Street, not too far from her own parents' house, and knocked on the door.

"Alison, honey!" The front door swung open, and Mrs. VanDusen's strong arms reached out, pulling her into her mighty bosom. "It's so good to see you!"

"Is Suzy here by any chance?" Alison pushed away gently.

"Ah, honey, she's in Arizona," she said, wiping her hands on her blue-checked apron. "Been there for a while doing rehab."

"Oh! That's..." Alison crossed her arms. "What happened?"

"Drugs and alcohol, honey. Bad ones." She tugged at her twisted bra strap. "No visitors, no contact with the outside world, nothing." Mrs. VanDusen exhaled like a tea kettle the moment before it starts to whistle. She untied the apron and folded it over a chair. Alison noticed that the hem of Mrs. V's blouse was crooked. She'd missed a button.

"I'm—I'm so sorry, Mrs. V.," Alison said. "Suzy and I lost touch after Juicy Kisses broke up, and I still feel bad about it." They'd been good friends. They'd sung in the choir at school before spinning off into their own band. That's how they'd met. Suzy sang like she was touched by God—that's what everyone said. Alison reached into her purse and pulled out a pack of cigarettes.

"Still smoking those Lucky Strikes, huh?"

Alison nodded. "I promised my mom I'm going to quit."

Mrs. VanDusen took one. Alison joined her.

"They back from that Australia cruise?"

"No. Another couple of weeks. They're having a great time, but my father gets seasick sometimes."

They smoked in silence until Mrs. VanDusen sighed again. This time louder and deeper.

"Suzy started playing clubs, singing, traveling the country, having a real good time." Mrs. VanDusen flicked her ashes onto the cement porch. "Then that evil Mr. Fred Parker—her so-called famous manager—started taking her to parties, got her hooked on cocaine and vodka 'til she was stealing cash from my purse, forging checks, taking money from the family savings," nodding her head up and down like a bobble-head toy on a dashboard. "So I called the police."

"You—you had your own daughter arrested?" Alison inched back. She couldn't believe a mother would do that.

"It was for her own good." Mrs. VanDusen took out a tube of chapstick and ran it back and forth over her lips like a windshield wiper. "They said they wouldn't press charges if she got help. And that's what she's doin' now." She smacked her lips together and puffed at her cigarette, but it'd gone out. Alison held out her light, but Mrs. VanDusen shook her head and tucked the cigarette into her blouse pocket, and the chapstick too.

"That's..." Alison trailed off, searching for the right words. "Good." It wasn't what she wanted to say.

"Yeah, it's good. What's left of her college money's going to rehab now—but it's good."

Alison stubbed out her Lucky Strike on the old banister she used to drum on, then slipped the half-smoked cigarette back into the box.

"Suzy's got another month to go and then they evaluate." Mrs. VanDusen sat down on the front steps. "What are you up to? Heard you live in Hollywood now. Better be careful. Lotta drugs in Hollywood."

Alison sat down beside her. She still had cramps occasionally. She was having some now. Dr. Humphries said it was to be expected the first four weeks or so after the procedure.

"I'm back home on Vesper Avenue. My folks don't know yet. I'm going to surprise them when they get back. It didn't make sense me working at a restaurant just to pay rent, you know?"

Alison wanted to talk about the abortion and why she never told Jesse and then disappeared from his life. She wanted to talk with a therapist but couldn't afford it. She wanted to tell her parents but couldn't do that, either. So she buried it all as best a young woman could. She thought maybe she'd confide in Suzy if she'd been home.

"Please tell her to call," Alison said. "I'd really like to see her."

"Will do." Mrs. VanDusen patted Alison's hand. "You still play the drums?"

"Haven't for a while."

"You were good," Mrs. VanDusen smiled. "Real good!"

"Thanks!"

Mrs. VanDusen was lonely for her daughter. Alison was lonely for her mother. The two women hugged each other tightly.

"Take care of yourself, honey."

"You too, Mrs. V." And she ran down the steps.

When Alison got home from Mrs. VanDusen's, she unpacked the drum set in the garage. The feel of the sticks against her fingers was like touching the hand of an old friend. She played for hours, embracing the power of the sounds. It was like therapy, this pounding out of pain, this exorcizing of loss.

Two weeks later, Alison picked her parents up at LAX.

"Jesse and I split up," she said on the 405. She'd never lied to them before, but she couldn't tell them what she'd done. They'd be so disappointed in her.

"I'm sorry," her mother said. "Can I ask why?"

"He's focused on his career." Alison changed lanes. "And I need to do the same, so it's a good thing."

"Are you alright?" her father asked. He looked at his daughter's reflection in the rearview mirror.

"Yes." Alison stared straight ahead. "And I decided I'm going to be a drummer! And I moved out of my apartment, so you have your daughter back."

"Well alright, then," her mother said. "Welcome home to all of us!"

Alison was ready. She curled and teased her hair to look like Sheila E's, the drummer for Prince, and went searching in Hollywood for gigs—The Roxy, Whiskey A-Go-Go, Gazzarri's. She wore red sparkly lipstick, royal blue eye shadow, push-up bras, high black boots, and played drums like it was her calling.

Suzy got back from rehab a month later and called Alison to come over. They sat on the front porch like old times, except there was no more weed and no more Coors.

"I really learnt a lot getting clean and sober." Suzy sipped from a bottle of Seven-Up. She'd gained back the weight she lost to her coke habit. Her shiny brown hair was cut in a bob, framing her beautiful, heart-shaped face.

"Like what?"

"I'm sorry for not returning your calls. I was into dark stuff." Suzy hugged her knees to her chest. "But that's over now."

"Good."

"I realize my voice is a gift." Suzy looked up into the star-filled sky, "And I'm not gonna waste it anymore."

They both sat beaming like little girls who'd just been granted a wish.

"That's the best news I've heard in a long time." Alison squeezed her friend's hand. "How're you gonna do that?"

"Oh, I'll show you how!" Suzy leapt to her feet. "Girls just want to have fun..."

Alison accompanied her by using her own body and the banister while Suzy danced into the house and led Mrs. VanDusen outside.

"Now what's all this about?" laughed Mrs. VanDusen as her daughter swayed her to the music. The three women jumped around like Cindy Lauper had infiltrated their bodies.

"I'm gonna dedicate all my songs," sang Suzy, "to love and happiness, Mom!"

"Oh hon, you make my heart sing!" said Mrs. VanDusen.

"Let's get Juicy Kisses back up!" shouted Alison. "What do you say, Suzy? You're clean and sober. And I'm free as a bird."

∞

Alison started up the car and drove out of the teacher's parking lot. She liked thinking about Suzy. It calmed her down.

Alison and Suzy had tried to put the original members together, but two of them were still in college, so they replaced the keyboard player and rhythm guitar. The new Juicy Kisses rehearsed and played parties and clubs all over the Southland. They even got good enough to open for The Pandoras, an all-female garage punk band on their second American tour.

Alison had fallen in love with one of the roadies—a tattooed, curly-haired, thirty-five-year-old named Arlen. He was her first after Jesse. Arlen built motorcycles and lived in New Mexico. He was well-read and funny. She admired his intellect and how he analyzed literature. Alison had always loved reading, so finding a partner who could discuss books was thrilling for her. They were a two-person book club.

They'd traveled to India together and she stayed with him on and off for a couple of years when she wasn't on the road. They grew vegetables, made wine, and did a variety of drugs. But then he wanted to get married and have a family, and she didn't. The thought paralyzed her. Images of Jesse flooded her dreams. Her stomach ached. She packed her bags and flew back to stay with her parents.

In 1993, when Alison turned twenty-five, Juicy Kisses broke up for the second time. The era of the female-band was ending. The teenage fans were getting older and changing their taste in music. And the band members were changing their taste in lifestyles. Living on the road had lost its charm. Most of the women wanted stable relationships and families to come home to.

Alison was unhappy and unemployed. She quit doing drugs cold turkey because she needed a clear head to figure out why her two relationships hadn't worked, and why she didn't know what she wanted to do with her life. She'd abandoned Jesse because of her secret and left Arlen because he wanted kids. Did one have to do with the other? Yes, she realized. She didn't want to re-live any kind of possible loss. It would be too painful. So she closed off her heart.

But there was one thing she was still open to. Books. The women in the band traded them back and forth like tubes of lipstick—mysteries, romance novels, biographies—anything and everything. If anyone was looking for Alison, they'd find her reading. "Just like 'Rush,'" Suzy joked. They were the band that was famous for being avid readers.

Alison inhaled Toni Morrison, Saul Bellow, Tony Kushner, Donna Tartt, Jane Smiley, and Tim O'Brien. She wanted to jump into their worlds and live there for a while. Hers was still crowded with Jesse, and all the things she had and hadn't done five years earlier. She could escape into literature and forget about herself. Books gave her peace.

"Why don't you study English?" her mother suggested. "Then you can share all the knowledge in that beautiful, brilliant mind of yours."

That's when she found her second calling. She'd become an English teacher.

Alison drove home along Ocean Park. She passed Merrihew's Sunset Gardens and Bob's Market. Their familiarity comforted her. The anxiety subsided. Now that this would be her final year as a teacher, she could look into the future. She could look up Jesse if she really wanted to. And she did want to.

After all the men in her life—her two ex-husbands, the married professor, and more than a handful of casual encounters—there was always Jesse. He'd been her first sexual experience, her first love. She remembered the song playing at the Hollywood party that first night they were together. It was Bon Jovi's "Runaway." She remembered how their mouths met, and their tongues tasted each other for the first time. She hadn't even known what an orgasm was until they spun each other with such force and grace that their insides surged and liquefied into each other.

Perhaps the first love is the truest, and all the loves after are an attempt to get back to the innocence, "back to the garden" as Joni Mitchell sang, back to Juliet on the balcony and Romeo climbing up the vine. "Come, gentle night; come, loving, black-browed night; Give me my Romeo." Back to the beginning, before it all crashed and burned.

There was always Jesse because I ran away from him.

Sometimes she wished she'd told him about the pregnancy when it happened. Why couldn't he know, anyway? Most relationships don't work out, so what's the difference? She would've found a way to support the baby. Her parents would've helped. She read once that regrets were part of growth. Without them, you don't have to think about the choices you've made. You don't have to learn from your mistakes. She wondered if she'd learned from hers.

There was always Jesse because he is my deepest regret.

There was that time she did see him from afar at the *Amma Healing and Meditation Conference.* Amma was the "Hugging Saint" and had been Alison's guru for a short while. And then there was the time Jesse surprised her by tapping her on the shoulder at the Juicy Kisses reunion at The Roxy. But she didn't want to think about that now. No, she wanted to think about the future...

When she got home, Alison sat in front of her computer and typed in Jesse Frankfort Photographer. She'd been following his work for years. He shot portraits for Rolling Stone and album covers for Led Zeppelin, Aerosmith, Jackson Browne, Stevie Wonder, and

Van Halen. He'd been Bon Jovi's personal photographer until the band decided to take a hiatus. So Jesse traveled the world, shooting the slums of Bangladesh, the mountains of Kyrgyzstan, the temples of Thailand. There was a current article saying Jesse had recently relocated to Todos Santos, near the southern tip of Baja, Mexico. He owned a photography gallery there called Inner Exposures. There was a picture. He still looked like himself—longish hair, smiling eyes. He wasn't wearing a wedding ring. That didn't mean he was single. She'd be respectful of his situation.

Alison took out a small pin from her purse and walked over to the living room window. She'd purchased the pin years ago at the *Amma Healing and Meditation Conference*. It was round and pink and had "Let Love Lead" printed on it in red, flowery letters. With it, she drummed a solid, simple beat against the windowpane. She was remembering the song, the one that played when she and Jesse first danced. Her body swayed with an inner pulse. She breathed onto the glass, creating a little cloud. She drew a heart with the words Ali and Jesse and decided to add him to her nightly prayers.

There was always Jesse because there was always Jesse.

A deep flush warmed her chest, neck, and face. This would definitely be her last year teaching. It was time to begin the rest of her wild and precious life.

~ 9 ~

WANDA

Thursday, March 21, 2019

Iт's ʙᴜʀɴɪɴ' ʜᴏᴛ ʜᴇʀᴇ ɪɴ Hollywood.

The sun's glarin' off these white buildings. Everythin's too harsh, and the palm trees don't offer any shade. I lean against the metal fence. It brands my back, leavin' a mark that hisses sinner.

I check my jeans lookin' for my keys, and I find the bus ticket that took me outta Mobile six days ago. I don't need it, but I still hold onto it. It's evidence that I really did it.

"Where to?" the ticket guy asked. I was out of breath so bad he must've known I was escapin'. He had skinny fingers, always pushin' his hair up from his square black glasses.

"Wherever the next bus outta here will take me," I said.

Then he saw my hand on my belly and decided to be a hero.

"Hollywood, California," he said, sliding a no-charge ticket under the bars of his window. "Leaves in fifteen minutes."

I never shoulda done it. I never shoulda come so far from

where I was born. But I had to do it. I had to save us both. My baby kicks me now, reminds me I still need to find my damn keys.

Thirsty. I drink from the plastic bottle I fill every mornin' from Ricardo's sink. I wish I could say it was holy water. It tastes like the kind you drink from fountains in bus stations and parks, prayin' to God no one let their dog slobber all over it. I heard dogs' mouths are cleaner than men's mouths. Way cleaner than yours, that's for sure.

Afternoons, I lie on the couch and nap. Dr. Vigman said it was natural to be so tired. I sit on the orange plush cushions with Ricardo's white cotton blanket on my double-beating body and sleep.

And dream. Sometimes nice ones where I'm walkin' with Grace.

That's her name. I decided. Grace.

We're in a field of lilies, and a puppy dog all golden and soft is smellin' the flowers and kissin' Grace's sweet, pure hand.

And then there's nightmares with your face near mine, and your mouth opens and out jumps flies and lizards. Bloody crosses, slow pour poison from a cracked jar. It's sticky and I can't breathe, and I can't see and I try to scream but can't 'cuz your vomit is swirlin' in my mouth. I wake up, chokin' to death.

And you laugh.

That's what happened this mornin'. That's why I went to emergency. I woke up and Grace wasn't kickin'. I thought the nightmare killed her. I waited 'til Ricardo left for work and went to the hospital. I was so scared, but the ER nurse said, "Shh! Listen." She put the stethoscope in my ears and the other part on my stomach, and I heard Grace, beatin' like a drummer in a marchin' band.

"But why wasn't she movin'?" I ask.

The nurse shrugs. "She's tired from dancing, I guess."

And she smiles at me from a real deep place. I know 'cuz it

hits me in my deep place, that place I only felt a few times in all my twenty years on this messed-up earth. I'm thinkin' of when you bought me that box of paints for my nineteenth birthday and said I should paint whatever I want on the walls of the trailer 'cuz my talent would make it our home. And I drew pictures of horses and mountains and we put 'em up and it was true, it became our home. So I smile back at the nurse and then I think of me burnin' it down and not knowin' if you're alive and the gates open and I can't stop cryin'.

"Here," she gives me some Kleenex. "I'll be right back. Promise me you'll stay."

I nod, wipin' my face dry. Where else am I gonna go? And what am I gonna do when I get there? And I don't think Grace is tired of dancin.' She's tired of runnin.'

She's pregnant too, the nurse. Her belly is bigger and lower than mine, like a watermelon on top of her thighs. She comes back with two cups of tea. She hands me one.

"Thanks," I say, feelin' kinda selfish, I hadn't asked about her. "How're you doin'?"

"Nobody told me I'd be so exhausted, and my emotions are all over the place. It's been quite a journey," she sighs. "I'm due in three weeks, April 12. The baby shower's in four days, on Sunday, March 24th."

"Isn't that cuttin' it a little close?" I ask. 'Cuz I know stuff 'bout baby showers.

"We didn't know whether to have a shower or not, and by the time we decided, that was the best date for everyone. You?"

"I'm due in four weeks on April 17!" I grin like we're two girlfriends.

"Baby shower?"

"No, decided not to have one."

She knows I'm lyin'. Everybody knows I'm lyin'. Then Grace moves, and my belly's flowin' hills.

"May I?" she asks, and I nod as she puts her hand on my stomach. "Oh, my name's Nurse Trisha O'Connor. If I'm going to touch you, I think you should know my name."

That makes us both laugh. She's feelin' my belly like an expert. That makes sense. Grace is lovin' it. She's jumpin' around like a cheerleader.

"She's a dancer alright," Nurse Trisha says. "She's doing an arabesque."

My eyes go wide like I'm talkin' to a Martian.

"A what?" I ask, puttin' my hand on my belly in case the nurse is gonna tell me somethin' weird, and I don't want Grace to hear it.

"When you extend your leg behind you and balance. It's ballet."

She steps to the middle of the floor, takes a big breath and starts shakin' a little 'cuz she's liftin' her leg out behind her, leanin' forward with the top of her body, slowly, slowly. One arm goes up, and I think she's gonna topple over, but she doesn't. She looks kinda graceful.

"Are you a ballerina?" I ask.

"Wanted to be," she pants. "A long time ago."

She's got a real nice smile. Her golden hair's tied back in a nurse's hairdo, but I bet it's pretty when it's all loose and curly. Her eyes are the color of almonds. I got a feelin' her baby's gonna be beautiful.

"You know what you're havin'?" I ask.

"A girl."

Maybe our daughters will be friends. Maybe we'll all be friends.

"Try it yourself." Nurse Trisha holds out her hand. "Here, I'll help you."

I take it, stand myself up and raise my leg, but I'm too big. She catches me as I tip forward and helps me find my balance. She does another whatever-you-call-it, and there we are, two watermelons doin' ballet.

"That was fun," she says and sips more tea. She glances at my left hand to see if there's a ring on it. "Is there anyone helping you?"

I haven't worn it in months, not since my fingers got so swollen. You had Travis loves Wanda engraved on the inside band. I remember you puttin' it on me at the weddin'. You were laughin' and cryin' at the same time. I couldn't believe I was gonna be your wife. I thought God had blessed me for sure.

I shake my head. The ring's probably lost now anyway. She nods like she shoulda known better than to ask.

"Is this your first?" I wanna stay bein' with her.

A look comes in her eye that's kinda sad and dark.

"Your husband must be pretty excited," I keep on talkin'.

"I don't have a husband."

"Your boyfriend, then."

"Don't have one of those either," she shrugs. "Got a girlfriend, well, had a girlfriend and we're going through a real rough patch. So..." And she just stands there, frozen.

"I'm sorry," I say, not wantin' to look like I don't know what she's talkin' about, but I don't, not really. "So who's the father if you don't mind me askin'? There's gotta be a father."

She wipes a whole lotta tears outta her eyes.

"Sorry, that's too personal a question," I say, and now it's me givin' her Kleenex. She blows her nose and throws the tissues in the trash bin. I see there are a whole lot of 'em already there.

"This is very unprofessional of me. I apologize," Nurse Trisha says and opens a drawer. "Here," offerin' me some cards. "I'm supposed to give you these, just in case."

I don't even look at 'em, but I have a hunch what they are. "Thanks," I drop 'em in my bag, the yellow one I grabbed before I lit the match.

"Alright then, Miss Smith...." She clears her throat and looks over my file.

I wanna tell her my real name. I do. I think she's gonna ask me to call her if I need someone to talk to. Or if she needs someone. Or buy baby clothes with. Or get an ice cream sometime. Or take the babies on a walk with. But I figure tellin' her the name Ricardo calls me is safe.

"Angel," I say. "Angel Smith."

"Right then, Angel." She closes my file. "Be well."

I don't blame her. It's probably against hospital rules. And why would she want to be my friend, anyway?

"Good luck," I say. "It's gonna work out. Whatever you're goin' through."

She heads out the room, but then changes her mind and writes somethin' on a pad and tears it off and gives it to me.

"Come to my baby shower. This Sunday afternoon. That's my address."

I'm kinda in shock. "Okay," I say. "You sure?"

She's smilin' again like before. "Yes," she says. "Absolutely."

She leaves and I'm on top of the world wantin' to jump for joy, but a sudden powerful sadness falls over me. I can't explain it.

It just does. And just as quick, the ground floats me up like the sun risin' at dawn, and I feel better thinkin' how Nurse Trisha's gonna be a good mother no matter what's goin' on in her life. A real good mother.

Me? I'm not so sure.

~ 10 ~

TRISHA

February 1, 2018

M<small>ARTIN</small> K<small>ANAKARIS</small> <small>ALWAYS SAID</small>, "I<small>F</small> you judge a character, you cannot play her." Trisha had been studying with him for four months, every Tuesday and Thursday night. He was a Scientologist and a womanizer, but he was also a brilliant acting teacher.

"Go beyond your bourgeois upbringing!" Martin would shout, firing up his students, his majestic shock of white hair glowing in the stage light. "Dare to cut yourself off from the mediocre, the mundane! To become a true artist, you have to be willing to become a monster!"

His class had lots of rules. You couldn't drink or take drugs twenty-four hours beforehand—so if you went two nights like Trisha did, you couldn't imbibe from Monday 'til after class on Thursday. That's when the students would go to the Hollywood Roosevelt and drink 'til closing. Most nights, a couple of the actors would leave together and wind up in each other's beds.

Trisha never felt comfortable with her sexuality or with her sense of self. Her dancing and singing were strong enough, but her belief in the character she was portraying wasn't. There was always that part of her that unconsciously signaled, "I'm not really like this part."

"You care too much what people think," Martin Kanakaris told her one Tuesday night. She was in the middle of the gentleman caller scene from *The Glass Menagerie* when he stopped it.

"Enough!" he shouted. "You're behaving like a contemporary girl in 2018. Laura is a virgin in the 1940s. She's never had a date in her life. You've blow-dried your hair and have too much makeup on. Your dress is too flattering. You're trying to show the audience your figure, how attractive you are. That's not acting. That's preening."

Trisha couldn't breathe. Everyone was staring at her. She'd never felt such shame before. She wanted to disappear off the stage and fly back to Canada.

"Look at Meryl Streep in *A Cry in the Dark*. Charlize Theron in *Monster*. You think they gave a shit about how they looked?"

Trisha couldn't speak.

"Say something, goddamn it!"

"No," Trisha answered, barely audible. The theatre was quiet. No one dared move in their seat. If they did, Martin would swing around and accuse them of being distracted and lacking empathy for their fellow artists.

"No!" he bellowed. "What Meryl and Charlize care about is creating a believable character. A real person. Not some weak imitation. Do you understand?"

"Yes," said Trisha. Her stomach tightened.

"What's the matter?" he asked.

"I don't feel well," she answered, her tongue wiping the sour taste from the inside of her mouth. Her teeth felt grimy— like she hadn't brushed them.

"It's fear that's making you queasy," he assured her. "Don't let it. Tell fear to fuck off. Shout it. Fuck off fear!"

"Fuck off fear!" shouted Trisha. Her body rocked as tears spilled out.

"Are your eyes leaking?" Martin asked. "Rise above your insecurities and do the work. Just do the work."

She had tried. She worked around her hospital schedule and rehearsed for hours with her scene partners. She visited the Samuel French bookstore on Sunset Boulevard, looking for parts that would stretch her capabilities. She just couldn't disappear into the character she was playing.

"I don't know how," she sniffed.

Martin stretched his long legs. He sighed and took a sip of Tispouro-laced espresso from his thermos, then swiveled around in his chair to face his adoring audience.

"If they were here," he addressed them, "what would Meryl or Charlize say to her?"

The students were silent. They were too scared to speak, too nervous he'd engage them in a philosophical battle they could never win.

"Go moment by moment?" Trisha asked, her voice strained.

He swung back. "Yes, Trisha O'Connor!" he beamed, his chest expanding with pride against his khaki jumpsuit, clean white tennis shoes shining. "Go moment by moment. Now pick up Laura's unicorn."

Trisha hesitated, then lifted it from the menagerie shelf.

"What does the glass feel like? Is it slippery? Is it rough?"

Martin asked. "Look at it closely. Can you see imperfections in it? Does it cast shadows on the wall?" He stood up. "How does it feel when you hold it to your ear? Does it make a sound like a seashell?" He approached the stage. "If you lick it, does it taste like salt? Like watermelon? Like whiskey? Be with the unicorn like you've never been with anything before. Fall in love with it." He took another step. "Do you understand?"

"I think so," Trisha answered.

"Try it," he coaxed. "Let the artist in you create."

Trisha raised up Laura's unicorn, allowing the stage lights to filter through. She twirled it in her palm and noticed the rainbow refractions stamped on the white wall behind her. There was a tune when she lifted it to her ear—a song she'd danced to in her father's bar. She pirouetted and leapt, zigzagging upstage and down, imitating the fiddle she heard in her head. She touched her face with the unicorn, then ran it down her arms and cradled it like a newborn. Finally, she sat cross-legged on the floor and grew statue-still. She tucked the unicorn in the left side of her bra, lay flat on her back, and fell asleep for an instant, totally at peace.

The students' applause shook her out of it. She stood up and bowed, like the curtain call at *Riverdance*. But this time, she wasn't way in back of forty dancers. This time, she was alone on center stage.

"Now that is going moment by moment," Martin said. "Good work, Trisha!"

It was thrilling. It was one of the happiest days of her life. Martin Kanakaris knew her name without glancing at the scene list. That day, she became a real actor.

Trisha knew she did the right thing by coming to Los Angeles. She felt closer to Erika than ever, more in love with her wit, her talent, her goodness. She loved spending time with her. It was so easy. Erika treated her well, like she was special. She hardly ever felt that before. Not as a child—not since her acting class, really. This was what falling in love was like, and that was a new experience too. When she imagined the future, Trisha could see herself with Erika. They'd make a perfect Hollywood couple – actor and writer. She was beginning to think about Erika's question, about having a family. She liked Erika's mother, grandmother, and brother. She liked kids. She hadn't said yes to getting pregnant, but she hadn't said no either. If she were going to have a child, it was starting to make sense that Erika might be a good partner to have one with.

Trisha had a good job at the hospital, a tough-love acting teacher, and something else she hadn't felt before—the possibility of success. She might actually work in the industry. She loved her new community. She never talked about things like "technique versus talent" before. And then there was the magic word: "charisma." If you wanted to be a movie star, her acting classmates agreed, charisma was essential. Trisha would say she didn't want to be a star, just a working actor who had guest parts on TV series and good roles in independent films. She was shy about her ambition, but secretly she wanted to make it. She wanted to be a star. She wanted to prove to everyone back home that they were wrong.

But Trisha hardly had any auditions. She was thirty years old with no American theatrical experience. She was lucky to get an agent—but that came through Erika, so Trisha never felt secure in the contract. The only acting job she booked in the eight months since she arrived in L.A. was the one-day hooker part on *Days of Our Lives*.

After a stressful week at the hospital, Trisha got a call for a two-line part on *Grey's Anatomy*. The role was for a patient in

Emergency. Perfect, she thought. I know how to play that.

Her lines were, "How long do I have to wait?" and "No, thanks." Sitting in the casting office at Prospect Studios were four other actors: a Black woman, an Asian woman, a Latina and a trans woman.

"Are you all here for the part of Patient #1?" Trisha asked.

They nodded.

In an instant, she fell headfirst through the familiar trap door of disappointment. Trisha recognized that at the level she was at in her fledgling career, she was interchangeable with other actors. She gave as good a reading as she could. She put everything she had into those two lines, but it didn't really matter. Trisha might not have been in the front row, but she was certain she could assemblé and jeté as well as or better than all the other dancers. She would practice her arabesques and pirouettes over and over 'til she had to sit down. She even fainted once. She played Monopoly with her cousins like it was a matter of life and death. It didn't matter that everything she did, she did one hundred percent. It didn't matter that she worked in a hospital and could bring verisimilitude to the role of the patient. It didn't matter that she went moment by moment. She didn't get the part of Patient #1. A cloudburst of negative emotions flooded her mind. She called in sick to work and stayed in bed all day.

"Can I come over with some chicken soup?" asked Erika.

"No," answered Trisha. "I just need to clear my head."

"What do you mean?"

She didn't want to discuss her history of rejections with Erika. Especially not with someone she was still trying to impress. She couldn't call her parents because they'd tell her to come home, and she hadn't made close friends in her acting class to commiserate with.

"This acting thing is tough," Trisha said. "It's starting to re-mind me of my dancing career. I'm tired of competing without win-ning. I need—I need to win."

"There are so many variables to getting cast," said Erika. "You've got to understand that or acting will kill you. I have several friends who couldn't handle it and left. I won't love you any less if you decide to give it up."

Trisha threw off the covers. "If you really loved me, you'd be more encouraging. I didn't work as hard as I did to come to Los An-geles to give up acting so easily."

"I'm sorry. I didn't mean anything by it."

It was dinner time. Trisha hadn't eaten all day. And she was thirsty.

"Well, maybe the timing is good for us," continued Erika. "Take a break from acting and we can seriously start to get preg-nant."

"What? Are you joking?" Trisha shot up from the bed. She hurried to the kitchen, opening the fridge. She tore off the seal from a bottle of strawberry kefir and gulped it down.

"No! It's perfect timing. When the baby's six months old, you can go back to it," offered Erika.

"You really don't know me, do you?"

"What's the big deal? It's not like you're giving up a series. You're still getting started here. Six months won't make a difference in your career."

"Six months is almost how long I've been trying to get work here! So, I give that all up and take off another six months and have a baby?" Trisha pulled her fingers through her hair. "And during all this, you get to just be you and do what you love?"

"Wait a minute!" Erika raised her voice. "You think writing is easy? It's taken years to work my way up from xeroxing scripts and getting coffee to being an assistant in the Writers Room. And I'm nowhere near where I want to be!"

"But the difference is you can always write." Trisha threw the container in the blue bin and went to the bathroom. "I need someone to say 'yes' to me for me to act."

She observed herself in the mirror for the first time that day. Her eyes were swollen. Her lion's mane was all over the place.

"So join a theatre company," Erika said. "Or do something on your own that brings out your other talents. Just don't lie around and sulk."

"Sulk?" Trisha stripped off her pajamas. "Thanks for your empathy. I've got to go."

"Where are you going?"

"You said not to talk about it. So I won't."

When Erika offered Trisha the freedom to even things out with the "catch-up arrangement," Trisha agreed even though she couldn't understand how someone would be fine knowing their partner was going to be unfaithful—giving them permission and encouraging the infidelity, in fact. Trisha had already gone to Akbar, a gay-friendly bar in Silverlake, and increased her repertoire by sleeping with two different women. The sex had been casual, playful, experimental. When she didn't get this acting job and didn't feel Erika was compassionate or supportive enough, Trisha decided to compete. She would compete in a game she would make up. She would compete and win.

Trisha shampooed her hair and shaved her legs. She put on a pair of tight jeans, a red silk blouse, and a black leather jacket. She got in her car and drove across town to Silverlake. She was in the mood for a cold beer.

Trisha would reveal a lot about her life to Erika. That was what partners did. But there was something she would never tell Erika. It would be her secret. That in their "catch-up arrangement," Trisha would surpass Erika's twenty-five lovers by one.

ALISON

April 8, 2018

Poetry had always intimidated Alison. In fact, she confessed to one of her tenth-grade classes that she wished it hadn't been added to the curriculum. Principal Tumaini Otieno called her to his office the next day.

"Poetry is exquisitely simple, Alison. It's the purist of the fine arts because each word is chosen with the utmost precision." Tumaini picked up a gold-framed photograph from his bookshelf and handed it to Alison. "Another word could never take its place. Like true love. It's only with that special person, and not another."

The picture was of a handsome man, maybe forty-five years old, with a bushy moustache like soldiers had in the First World War. His eyes were amber brown, and his teeth were stained from cigarettes. His smile was glorious. She had the sense that this man in the photo loved not only the person behind the lens, but the whole world behind that person as well.

"His name was Fernando Ramirez. He was a poet from Buenos Aires." Tumaini reached into his pocket, touching his turquoise-painted clay rosary beads. "We were lovers."

Alison remembered this man. Tumaini brought him to a Christmas party.

"He's very handsome," she said.

He pulled a small, navy leather book out of his desk drawer and gave it to her. The title was embossed with gold letters. *Promesas*. She opened the first page and read the inscription out loud: "These words are me and not me. In the end, there is only love."

"I miss him," said Tumaini.

Where did the sun go? Alison wondered. It must be close to dinnertime, and here she was with her friend, who was crying. He took the book back from her and held it to his heart. She placed her hand on his shoulder. He wiped his eyes with his fingertips, adjusted his tie, put the book back in the drawer, and became her boss once more.

"Your students have a right to know how poetry feels," the principal said. "Take a class. There's an excellent professor..."

That class turned out to be Professor Vincent Gaiman's UCLA extension course in American Poetry from Emily Dickinson to Charles Bukowski. She fell in love with it, all of it—free verse, sonnets, haikus, ballads, cinquains, sestinas. She imagined Emily Dickinson and Charles Bukowski at an outdoor café—she sipping Jasmine tea, he guzzling red burgundy—reciting, singing, spitting out songs of passion as they became besotted with each other. Alison also fell in love with the excellent professor.

"Go to Beyond Baroque," Professor Vincent Gaiman told her as he walked her to the elevator of his secret condo in Westwood. "You've got to read your poetry out loud."

"I'm too nervous," she said.

"Then you must do it!" He held her hands and kissed them. "Your nerves are telling you that you've got deep emotions to share. Just jump."

He never said he'd be there to catch her. Their affair lasted three years from 2012 to 2015. She was forty-four when it started and forty-seven when she ended it.

"Your crimson hair was the first thing I noticed about you when you walked into my class," Vincent had said. "It reminds me of Tennyson." His voice was deep and clear as he recited:

Now sleeps the crimson petal, now the white;
Nor waves the cypress in the palace walk;
Nor winks the gold fin in the porphyry font.
The firefly wakens; waken thou with me.

She believed him then. Now, three years after the breakup, she knew better. He probably sensed her deep loneliness. She had two unsuccessful marriages behind her. He was married and collected mistresses like butterflies. Their once-a-week touch, taste, talk— it gave her whatever it was she needed then. Alison had never been the kind of woman to have affairs, even when her marriages were struggling. Even when her husbands were unfaithful. She never blamed them. Her heart wasn't one hundred percent with them. There was always something missing. She felt terrible about sleeping with a married man. But her hunger for revitalization numbed her sense of right and wrong.

Alison joined a poetry workshop at Beyond Baroque. She remembered walking through the purple desert bushes and onto the coral porch for the first time. "Limping up the Aisle" was painted on the front arch of the white stucco building. There were three other women in the poetry group—a bartender, a therapist, and a nurse, along with three men—a math professor, a dentist, and a carpenter. They met at one another's places twice a month. They liked and supported one another's poetic sensibilities. It was, like Principal Tumaini Otieno said, "exquisitely simple."

Ever since adding Jesse to her nightly prayers, lines of poetry would come to Alison in the middle of the night. As soon as she drifted off, they would jab her awake like an impatient boxer.

NesQuik

He stirred her into life—
a heaping teaspoon
of Nestle Quik
in a glass of cold milk.

Sometimes she couldn't get back to sleep. In tonight's dream, Alison and Jesse were in a small town in Ireland, getting sugar cookies to take back to the concert. The bakery's name was "Harriet's Never Going to Leave You." It was painted in solid white letters on a dark green awning. She found the name of the store funny, and so did he. They laughed until she laughed herself awake at five in the morning.

Getting out of bed, she went to the kitchen for a glass of water. She wrote the name of the store, "Harriet's Never Going to Leave You," on her notepad by the phone. She taped the note on her bathroom mirror beside the Amma Post-it Note, near the lipstick-written "Best Used By," convinced it was a sign from the Divine—something important that she had to pay attention to.

A fragment of a memory began to taunt her. It was like an itch she couldn't reach. It was too far in, too deep, too lost to be found. She went to the bottom drawer of her night table and emptied it onto the bed. Old letters, diaries, crystals, and pictures splayed out across the sheets. She found a photograph dated September 15, 1988. She was twenty years old, leaning against a tree that was covered in chewing gum, looking stoned and drunk, probably because she was. She was wearing a brown suede coat with a fake fur collar and pink-and-green leather boots. Jesse took this picture when they were in Paris, at Père-Lachaise Cemetery.

The itch persisted. She searched deeper and found another photograph. It was dated a day later, September 16th, 1988. She and Jesse were on the Pont de la Tournelle with Notre Dame rising behind them. She remembered Jesse handing his Nikon to an old man on the bridge and asking him to take their picture. She was wearing the same outfit in this photo as the one the day before. He was in a dark blue corduroy jacket, jeans, and a denim cap. He held her in front of him, against his chest. They glowed in the light of the sun's early exhalations.

Anyone passing by would've bet Alison and Jesse's love would've lasted a lifetime. Who would've known that a month later, all that promise would be gone? Surely, not the Frenchman on the bridge who said, *"Les amoureux très heureux,"* when he lifted the camera to his eye and captured their image.

Alison's mind went for a spin. She wanted to dance like she did before—a go-go girl on fire, a source of true magic, a presence of the possible. She wanted her life back, like it was when everything was still in front of her. She wanted her dreams back—yes, even the crushed ones. She'd hold them in her arms and apologize for making them suffer, for not living up to their hopes, for abandoning them.

"Can't get no," Jagger whistled himself awake, "can't get no," and he flew out the open window. She never knew what made the parrot fly out and what made him fly in. It didn't matter, she decided, as long as he was flying.

But that itch—it was still lodged in her back between her shoulder blades, just behind her heart, the place on the body where feathers would sprout if people grew wings. She liked that thought. She could be an angel on earth. She could help someone else live the life that was meant for them, like she was going to do for herself now.

And like the sun's surprise on an overcast day, it all came back—the two of them locked inside the gates of Père-Lachaise Cemetery, hiding behind bushes near Sarah Bernhardt's grave and emerging with the stars. Jesse brought out fifteen flashlights from his backpack.

"We are capturing art," Jesse said as they beamed through the darkness, stroking her skin with translucent fingers.

She shivered—red hair floating in the indigo beside the gum tree near Jim Morrison's grave, body twirling to the beat of Jesse's clicks, naked except for the pink-and-green leather boots—a tipsy Venus de Milo. Her body was the vessel. The moon flowed in through the top of her head, flowered through her veins, and blossomed through her pores. She was luminous silver.

"Jim Morrison would approve," Jesse said.

He embraced her and helped her put her clothes back on, and they climbed out over the walls of the cemetery and taxied back to Hôtel Les Dames du Panthéon. They lay down on the small bed. He entered her with dawn's greeting. She received him with earth's blessings. They created their child that morning.

These photographs are the ones Jesse gave me that last morning we were together, she realized. That last morning together in her apartment in Hollywood so many years ago. She taped the one at Jim Morrison's grave to a page in her red notebook. She wrote:

Missing you
I made a nightshirt
of kisses, so when you sleep
my lips touch your body like
the lightness of rain

She mused about memories and dreams, how they were stories streaming from the subconscious universe, poems from the self, from ancestors, from lovers, from other dreamers.

She wondered if Jesse was dreaming the same dream. "Harriet's Never Going To Leave You." Maybe Harriet would've been their baby's name. A little girl.

The other photograph—the one on the bridge—she taped above the Post-it Note on the mirror in the bathroom. It wasn't a photograph of just her and Jesse anymore. It was a photograph of the three of them, because Harriet was there too.

The dream, the photographs, and the memory were all signs. They had to be.

~ 12 ~

WANDA

March 21, 2019

Iᴆ I ᴅᴏɴ'ᴛ ғɪɴᴅ ᴛʜᴏsᴇ keys, I'll have to break into the motel again. It's hard with all them bars on the windows. It's like I'm breakin' into jail. At least Ricardo never gets pissed at me like you would.

I leave ER and start walkin'. It's what I do all day, try to find work, but as soon as they see me, they know somethin's not right. I hide her with big shirts Ricardo lets me wear—those white Mexican ones with embroidery on the front panels, the kind of shirt that screams, "I'm hidin' a sinner and her baby." He washes 'em every night but I still smell the sweat on 'em.

I check my bag. No keys in there either. I'm in front of a blue buildin' on Santa Monica Boulevard, a couple of blocks from Motel El Centro. Looks like it was some kind of store before—hardware or car parts. There's baked, black oil stuck to the part where the wall hits the sidewalk. No amount of scrubbin's ever gonna get rid of that. Like your garage. You could pray for floods to clean that place away, but it'd never be like the first time we went in there and you said you was gonna rent it and make a goddamn fortune.

I told you not to swear and you grabbed my hair and pulled me real close and yelled, "I'll do whatever the fuck I want, whenever the fuck I want. Understand, Wanda?"

I wouldn't let you see me cry, but Momma saw. All she said was men are like that, and I should just get used to the fact. But Daddy never laid a hand on her or me and my sisters. So I don't know what she's talkin' about. He never laid a hand on Momma to stop her from hittin' us, neither. He'd wait 'til she left the room, and he'd say stuff like, "Your momma's havin' a bad day. Gotta cut her some slack." So we did, Betty Ann, Janine, and me. And for a while we were close 'cuz of that. When they moved outta the house, they took me with them to parties and bowlin'. But when I turned seventeen and started datin' you, they stopped. I guess they didn't like you.

Momma likes you. She told me you're a real looker, way better on the eye than I am, and what did you see in me anyway? She dresses up real pretty for church. All the women do. What for? Doesn't Jesus like 'em any ole way, and isn't Sunday a day off? But she flirts around all the men like a cat swishin' her tail, givin' everyone a quick sniff under, makin' sure they got a whiff of the perfume she got at Bel Air Mall. Not real obvious. Just kinda like when she gets up from the pew and tosses her hair and her hand moves real slow against her thigh and you can hear the silk of her slip rub up onto the nylon of her stockings.

Or when Pastor Higgins says somethin' funny in his sermon. She throws her head back and lets out a laugh that never sounds like any laugh that ever come out her mouth before. It sounds more like a bird gigglin.' And you glance at her, and I swear out of the corner of my eye I can see you get a little hard in your Sunday jeans I pressed that mornin.' And Momma gazes back your way and crosses one leg over the other and lets the hem of her shiny dress that seems kinda wet in the sunlight travel up to the tip of her white satin garters.

They're old, those garters with stretchy snaps that cling to the tops of her stockings like little pearl clams. She's had 'em ten years and washes 'em every Sunday night like they're righteous, in warm water and Palmolive dish soap and hangs 'em up on the shower rod in the bathroom, so everyone can see. Open for business, they say. All you have to do is part them and she's yours.

Daddy just stays quiet like he always does. But you tease her about 'em, don't ya?

"You musta been some hot chick in the day, Momma-Evelyn," you say.

She pours you another cup of Nescafe and says, "What d'ya mean musta been?" and gives you a wink.

Daddy turns red and stuffs a forkful of runny scrambled eggs into his mouth and shakes his head like you and Momma are actin' weird and speakin' Japanese or somethin'. But I understand what's goin' on.

I just remembered where my keys are. I left 'em under my pillow. I don't know why I hide 'em there. I've got five keys. The black one's for Ricardo's room, the red one's for Momma's house. I don't think I can ever go back there. The little gold one belongs to Daddy's shed, where he said he kept secret papers for me to find after he died. The silver one goes to the trailer, which I'd guess is a pile of steamin' ashes by now. Then there's the copper key, the one I found on the street in front of Dr. Vigman's office right after he told me I was pregnant.

I went to see him by myself 'cuz I didn't know what to expect. And I wanted to be sure before I told you. He said I'm eight weeks gone and needed to take it easy 'til the first three months is over. He said congratulations and that he's happy for me and that he'd be delighted to have me as his patient. He has kind eyes. The kind of eyes a grandfather has in children's books when they look at their grandchildren like they're precious. That's the way he looked at me. No one ever looked at me that way. Wait, that's not true. You did. You looked at me that way. And then you didn't.

Dr. Vigman's number was in the old phone book Daddy kept in the garage in case we ever needed a number we couldn't get on the computer. I looked up obstetricians and when I saw his name, it just felt right.

Momma asked why Dr. Mason wasn't good enough for me to go to. I said I just wanted someone new. A specialist. She looked at his name.

"Vigman? Sounds like a Jew," she sneered. "Well, at least he's not from India. All the doctors come from India these days, I tell you what."

I call the copper key the good luck key 'cuz it was lyin' in the mud near the sewer, and the sun hit it a funny way like it wanted me to see it and pick it up. It's the one I'm lookin' for when I can't find my keys. It's the one I'm hidin' when I put it someplace safe. It's my Grace good luck key.

My head hurts. I let my hair free. It comes down slow and heavy. It must be the pollution here makin' it feel bad every night before I take a shower to wash away my past.

I stare at the blue church on Santa Monica Boulevard—at least that's what I think it is. The sign says somethin' 'bout salvation. I could use some. I'll pray for you to be not dead. Right now, that's all

I want to be true.

I walk in. The congregants look at me like I'm a space alien, like a white person's never been in their church before. That's 'cuz we probably haven't. I sit down on a metal foldin' chair. It's ice on my thighs. It feels good to sit and take a load off. I search through my bag and find a dollar to put in the collection box. I walk up quick and drop it in.

I go back to my seat and wait for somethin' to happen. A short man comes to the front of the room lookin' like the busboy at the Denny's on Hollywood Boulevard. He's wearin' a white jacket and black pants like the kind Elvis wore in *Blue Hawaii*. That's your favorite movie, *Blue Hawaii*. You made me watch it five times. And when I didn't want to watch anymore, Momma'd make popcorn and sit beside you like she was on a date.

He says somethin' in Spanish and everyone nods. They all bow their heads and pray.

I guess church is the same no matter where you are and no matter what language. So I pray for your life. I pray for Grace to be safe and healthy. I know I should be prayin' for some kind of for-giveness, but from who to who? Me forgivin' you for hurtin' me as bad as you did or you forgivin' me for stabbin' you like I did?

Even now, inside a house of God, the coolness on my legs melts away and I rage like the fires here I've heard so much about. My bruised thighs blister through the chair, scorchin' it like I did our home. My tongue is bitter bile. I taste Satan's eyes glarin' down on me. They cry with tears of babies smashed down from high cliffs into black waves. They make me feel like hell is in me, and I'll never be saved.

I look at Jesus on the cross.

"Help me," I pray out loud.

He's brown and burnin' and bleedin' for real. The thorns pierce His head. I hear the loud poundin' of nails and see mud gush out His wounds. It's so dark, His blood. It drips heavy on the floor and soaks into the chairs where we sit.

The congregation sings real loud, praisin' Him. My head hurts like your knife missed my throat and stabbed directly into my brain. The people slip off their chairs and get down on their knees, raisin' their arms to heaven as His blood rises from the floor and laps at their ankles. They clutch their Bibles and their babies, liftin' 'em higher and higher. They don't wanna drown. They're starin' hard at the cross, waitin' for Him to answer.

So why am I thinkin' 'bout that time I painted the front of the garage with Camaros, and you were so happy you bought a bottle of champagne and we sat across the road and watched cars slow down to get a look, and you sang "Burning Love" and kissed me and looked at me like I was precious and told me I was a real artist through and through?

My feet scream. His blood boils the orange flip-flops I got on sale at Safeway for ninety-nine cents. I take the edge of Ricardo's shirt, reach down, and wipe them off. My hands are stained like I pulled out nails from my own palms.

Everyone sings, "Hallelujah." I look at Christ on the cross on the wall. He twists his head and stares back at me. He looks like Wilmer Valderrama from that '70s TV show. He winks. He wants to make love to me.

I join in singin' "Hallelujah," but I stare at the collection plate, wishin' I could take back my dollar. I know which one is mine from the purple nail polish I used this mornin'. It was still wet when I put the cash in my bag.

I rise up, run, turn back one last time before I leave the blueness. Wilmer Valderrama is a pourin' mess of misery. "Wanda!" He shouts at me in silence. "Wanda, why have you forsaken me?"

"Maybe 'cuz you're a liar," I yell back. "A goddamned liar!"

Elvis hollers somethin' fierce at me in Spanish. Everyone's lookin' at me like I'm crazy. I'm thinkin' they're not wrong. I put my hands up and cover my ears, but His screams leak through my fingers. I run out the church like a bat out of hell, keep on runnin' 'til I get to El Centro Avenue and climb in the back window to Ricardo's room.

Even under the covers, I still hear Him callin' my name. He's beggin' me to love him like I used to. I swear I woulda married Him when I was thirteen. I woulda been a nun for Him. Maybe I shoulda. But then I wouldn't be carryin' the only thing I've ever loved this much. I love Grace more than Christ Himself.

And Pastor Higgins is roarin' in my head, "Jesus saves, Wanda! He saves all sinners! Let Him save you!"

And I roar back, "But how's He supposed to save me if He couldn't even save Himself?"

~ 13 ~

TRISHA

March 18, 2018

Sнε κνεw нεr lover would leave if she said no. Trisha had asked for more time to consider Erika's ultimatum. She knew they were at a crossroads. Did she really want to have a baby? And what about her acting?

"Let's resume this conversation at dinner tonight," said Erika.

"I can't. I'm going to that poetry workshop in Venice. Remember?"

"No."

"I swear, you're so distracted." Trisha pulled her hair into a ponytail. "Martin said I needed to explore my inner thoughts, get them out, and expressed. He recommended poetry. He said it's good for understanding subtext in acting, so I went online and found a workshop and signed up."

"Since when do you write poetry?" asked Erika.

"Since I was a teenager," Trisha raised her voice.

"How come you never told me?"

"I don't know..." Trisha put on her Hokas. "There's lots of things I haven't told you," she said under her breath.

She grabbed her keys and headed out for an afternoon run. Half a block later, she looked down at the ground. She never looked down. Her father always said, "Look straight in front of you, Trish. That's how you'll get to your goals." But today, she didn't. She looked down, hoping to find a flattened stone, a four-leaf clover, something from the universe of signs and symbols to tell her what to do with her life. She was thirty. She was stuck.

That's when she saw the red bottle cap on the sidewalk. She didn't even realize they still made Coke in glass bottles, but the cap was the same as it always was, just a little crushed. She slowed down, peered at the name and date carved into the sidewalk under it.

Johnnie Baloney, 1992. What a funny name. She'd been running these sidewalks for a month, ever since Erika moved from West Hollywood to Silver Lake, and this was the first time she noticed something that had been there for twenty-six years. She stepped on the name so many times, but she never saw it before.

She picked up the bottle cap and put it in her pocket. She turned to the house in front of her, hiding behind a tall, glorious pine tree. A witness tree. When Trisha and Erika took a long weekend trip to visit Tom Wolfe's childhood home in Asheville, the tour guide called them "witness trees." It was one of those "if trees could talk" kinda things. Trisha wondered what the tree in her parents' front yard would say, back in Toronto. That her father never really understood his daughter? That her mother never fulfilled her own dreams? That their love was conditional?

The house was a Craftsman bungalow painted tan with a forest green roof and trimmings. A pinecone fell to the ground. The door swung open.

A little boy ran out, with a tall man chasing behind him. They had the same black hair that cascaded to the middle of their backs—they could've been two of the Three Musketeers.

"Well, hello there!" said Trisha.

The father smiled so wide that Trisha thought his face would lift off. There was a gap between his two front teeth. The boy smiled too, and he had the same gap.

"Hi!" the man said. "You live around here? I've seen you jogging."

"Sometimes," Trisha responded. "I stay over at my girlfriend's just down the street. She moved in a month ago. I'm going to be moving in with her, soon, I think—maybe."

"Are you going to the park?" the little boy asked.

"Sure! I was just on my way there," Trisha answered. "Hey, I was wondering. Do you know Johnnie Baloney?"

The little boy pointed up at his father. "Him," he said.

"Yep, that's me," laughed Johnnie Baloney. "Nice to meet you."

"I'm Little Johnnie," said his son. "You can call me L.J. because I'm almost five."

"Nice to meet you both. You can call me Trisha."

"I was seven when I wrote my name on the wet cement," Johnnie Baloney said, twisting his hair around his hand, pulling it through the back of a Dodgers baseball cap. "But my brother rubbed the 'O' out and added the 'EY.' So, I went from Johnnie O'Balon to Johnnie Baloney." He adjusted a smaller cap onto his son's head. "It became my nickname. I've been going by it ever since."

"You've lived in that house since you were a boy?" Trisha

asked.

"I moved away to go to UC Santa Cruz. When my dad got sick, I came back to care for him. Then we had L.J., and I never left."

L.J. counted to one hundred forwards and then backwards as they walked toward the playground. The sun was an hour away from taking its final bow. The park lights came on, making the playground resemble a set on a vast green stage.

"You married?" Trisha asked.

"Was," said Johnnie Baloney. "My ex-husband went back to his wife."

Trisha raised an eyebrow and picked up an abandoned tennis ball. She bounced it several times before she threw it closer to the courts.

"He was married. We met. We fell in love. He divorced her. We got married. We had L.J. He fell out of love. He went back to her. You know," his eyes twinkled, "your typical Silver Lake love story."

He lifted his son onto the swing. L.J. pushed his legs under, then straightened them out as he rode higher and higher. His hair flew around his face, tickling his cheeks, making him shriek with laughter.

"I'm thinking of having a baby," said Trisha. She wasn't sure why she blurted this out to a relative stranger. But there was something about Johnnie Baloney—maybe it was the silliness of his name and his friendliness—that cut through formalities.

"On your own?" asked Johnnie Baloney, looking at her as if for the first time.

"With my girlfriend," Trisha said. "But it'll be me carrying it. She can't."

L.J. slipped off the swing, and the three of them walked over to the sand box. Johnnie Baloney and Trisha sat a few feet away on a wooden bench.

"I hate the idea of going to a sperm clinic." She lowered her voice so L.J. couldn't hear. "So, I don't know. Maybe we'll adopt instead. But then you have no idea what the background is, or if the kid has genetic problems...." Trisha trailed off, realizing she didn't understand the first thing about talking to parents regarding these concerns. It could be very sensitive, these issues.

"It's a big commitment for sure," Johnnie Baloney nodded.

"Huge responsibility, being a parent," Trisha agreed. "That's my main concern, actually. Do I have it in me to be a good mother? And what does that mean, anyway?"

"Can I have my apple?" L.J. melted into his father's arms. Johnnie Baloney took a small Granny Smith from his jacket and gave it to his son. L.J. nuzzled his head up between his dad's neck and shoulder and closed his eyes, holding the apple with both hands.

"Good luck," Johnnie Baloney whispered to Trisha.

She watched him carry his sleepy son out of the playground. The apple dropped out of L.J.'s hands. Johnnie Baloney caught it mid-air and put it back in his pocket. Trisha got the impression this routine happened every day. And that it was perfect.

~ 14 ~

ALISON

April 25, 2018

Alison saw Harriet in all sorts of places—parks, coffee shops, supermarkets. She looked for women in their thirties who had an air of confidence and ease. Of course, Alison knew her child didn't really exist—but if she had lived, Harriet would be like these women Alison saw in the streets.

Sometimes Alison would spot a young woman with long auburn hair, a combination of her color and Jesse's. She'd walk a couple of feet behind, pretending to herself that they were on a mother-daughter afternoon together, shopping, eating, talking. At some point, Alison would speed up and walk in front of her "long-lost daughter," then turn back as if she forgot something, just to get a good look at the young woman's face. Was there anything in her eyes, her mouth, her forehead, that reminded Alison of Jesse or herself? Usually not, but that was fine. It made her feel like a mother, and the strangers didn't know they were players in her game.

Sometimes, Alison would go up to the woman and ask her a question about where a certain bus stop was, or could she recommend a nice coffee shop, or was there someplace special to visit because she was a stranger to the area. Each one—and there were eleven to date—was polite and friendly. "Just go down two blocks on Melrose," or "Sure, there's a Pain Quotidien on the next corner," or "The Farmers' Market is three blocks from the ocean," they said. Alison would smile and thank them and think about asking them to join her, but she never did.

When the young woman was gone, Alison would pull out her iPhone and take a picture of something that would remind her of their encounter. Once, she took a picture of the Olympic Boulevard sign because that's where she saw Harriet crossing the street. Then there was the time she took a photo of the Starbucks Harriet came out of—or the time she took a picture of the storefront Harriet had been looking into when Alison first noticed her. It was Moondance on Montana Avenue. The next day, Alison went back and bought a pair of gold hoops with a pearl in the center.

She knew exactly what she was doing. She wasn't Looney Tunes. She was an orphan, longing for a family. She always felt better afterwards. She'd go home, dance around her place with Jagger, make something to eat from a Trader Joe's pre-assembled package, and write a poem. She started writing a poetry collection called *Harriet's Never Going to Leave You*. She brought the first one to the workshop after dreaming about the green awning with the sign on it.

Never Knowing

We are a secret
we three—
scraped out
and tossed away.

I never told you
about that soul floating up
into a cloud
of never knowing.

So let's pretend
it's alright
when it's the reason
I'm not.

The poetry workshop discussed what the name Harriet meant. Trisha, the nurse, looked it up on one of those baby name websites. "The keeper of the home," she read off her cell. "Does that make any sense to you, Alison? Why you chose that name?"

This was the first time Trisha held the workshop at her new home. She'd finally moved in with her partner. Her boxes were balanced along the walls.

"It chose me," Alison answered. She liked the way she was perceiving things. It was new for her. Poetry was a path into her deepest thoughts—the ones she didn't know she was thinking until she wrote them down in her red notebook. Searching for the right word was like digging for buried treasure and finding a diamond. She was connecting to a mystical universe somewhere outside herself, and she was also part of it—a leaf seeing itself floating on a stream. She raised a glass of Frascati.

"To the mysteries of poetry," Alison said.

"To the mysteries of poetry," the poets echoed.

When it was Trisha's turn to read, she took everyone to the backyard. In soft, lantern light, she held up her poem.

"I had this image of life happening from the yellow roses Erika planted—about babies growing in our garden, like those Anne Geddes photographs," Trisha smiled. "It was really weird but also funny, so I tried to capture that."

Her hands shook so much the sheet of paper threatened to fly away. She cleared her throat, took a deep breath, and settled into herself. A power and a sensitivity filtered through her voice. It was more of a performance than a reading. The group had tears in their eyes after she read the last line, "precious one." They applauded.

"That was beautiful," said Charles. He was the dentist, over six feet tall with short, wavy blond hair, the perfect midway between regular and handsome. His teeth were gleaming white.

"I mean it," he continued as they reassembled in the living room, "you should write a book of poems for babies. I know someone who could do the illustrations if you want."

"Really? I've never thought about doing anything like that." Trisha reddened.

"You could do anything you want," Charles said. "You're very talented."

In the kitchen, the cup of tea Erika was drinking slid out of her grip and crashed into tiny pieces on the floor.

"Are you okay?" shouted Trisha over her shoulder.

"No problem," Erika answered. "Everything's fine."

Charles bit into a chocolate chip cookie.

"See it as a gift to mothers," Alison said, drawing a cushion to her lap. "'Poems for Babies' is a good title."

Alison regretted what she said as soon as she said it. She knew someone would ask if she had children—then would come the fumbling, embarrassed comments like "you're a teacher and helped more children than any mother ever has," and "I bet you're a wonderful aunt," and "consider yourself lucky." They'd cling in the air until she'd respond with "thanks for saying that," or "yes, I am blessed," or "it wasn't in the cards."

No one said anything. Erika came in with cookies for the road. People gathered their belongings and headed for the door. Amidst the goodbyes, Alison blurted to no one in particular, "I had an abortion when I was twenty!"

She didn't understand why she said it; it just came out for some reason. She hadn't told anyone but Suzy.

"Me too," said Marlee.

"Me three," Carolyne raised her hand.

Alison didn't know what to say. Unlike women younger than herself, she felt awkward and a little embarrassed. She said goodbye, walked out quickly, and got into her car.

Alison turned on the ignition and sat, thinking about what had just happened. She adjusted the rear-view mirror to look at herself, to see if her public admission had changed her in any way.

"Hey!" Trisha knocked on the car door.

Alison jumped, caught in her private moment. She rolled down the window.

"Can we go for a ride with the top down?" Trisha asked.

Alison reset the mirror. She always knew when one of her students wanted to talk to her. They'd show up in the doorway of her homeroom and just stand there, waiting for her to speak.

"Sure," she said. "Hop in."

They drove out to Sunset Boulevard and headed east. Alison pushed a button, and the top went down. There's no hiding in a convertible. They could see everyone, and everyone could see them.

Trisha unbuckled her seat belt and stood up. "I'm a Canadian girl in a convertible on Sunset Boulevard!" she whooped into the night. She raised her arms over her head, waving her hands. "Alison is my Fairy Godmother!"

"Sit down, for Heaven's sake!" Alison laughed. "What are you, sixteen?"

"Never," Trisha said as she buckled herself back in. "This is so much fun!"

The nocturnal air was brisk and damp. They giggled as they drove unsheltered, wind spiraling the hair around their heads, mist kissing their faces. Alison opened the glove compartment and took out two kerchiefs.

"Let's put these on. You'll look like Grace Kelly."

Suddenly, they were two mysterious women in a '60s movie, traveling in a green convertible to someplace unknown. Los Angeles did that to Alison from time to time—dropped her into a film. It was the architecture, the palm trees, the constant references to images engraved in the subconscious from all the television and movies she'd ever seen. Alison felt alive. She glanced over at Trisha, who was grinning ear to ear.

"Thelma and Louise," Alison declared. "That's who we are."

"Never saw it." Trisha reached into the glove compartment and found a pair of sunglasses. "Perfect," she said, putting them on.

"Well, it's a great movie," said Alison, "except for the ending."

It was 10 p.m. Another convertible honked three times as it passed them, a black Porsche with two older men. They belonged to an elite club, it seemed—the Convertible Club.

Trisha leaned in. "That must've been hard for you tonight," she said. "I'm so sorry."

"I surprised myself." Alison shrugged. "I mean, I'm not ashamed, or anything like that. I just never said it out loud to a group of people before." She pressed her foot a little heavier on the gas. "You ever have one?"

L.A.'s flatness created mirages. Dodger Stadium glowed like a huge alien ship they could almost touch, but it was miles away.

"Oh, sorry," Alison turned the steering wheel, "I guess if you're gay, abortion doesn't come up very often."

"Erika's my first woman, actually." Trisha's kerchief was slipping off. "But no, never had one. Never been pregnant, either."

They rolled to a stop at the intersection of Sunset and Echo Park. The traffic light cast a scarlet veil over their faces. An old dog walked along the boulevard. It knew its way home. The light turned green.

"Maybe you're lucky," Alison merged into the left lane. "You never had to make a choice."

Trisha removed the kerchief. She refolded the chiffon square into a neat triangle when the breeze lifted it from her hands. For a second, it floated between them like an angel, until Alison caught it mid-air and gave it back.

"Wow, that was a little magical," Trisha said, retying the kerchief. "Right?"

"Convertible magic," Alison laughed. "Happens all the time."

Trisha removed the sunglasses, looked up and watched the tops of palm trees race by. The moon was just on the other side of them— there it was, and then it wasn't.

"I don't know." Trisha shook her head and shoved her body deep into the back of the seat. "I really don't know what to do." She folded her legs into her chest and rested her forehead on her knees. "I'm so confused."

Alison put her hand on Trisha's shoulder. It was hard, making these life-changing decisions that women had to make. That was the real elite club–Womanhood.

Two young guys came out of Royale Liquor. One was carrying a six-pack of Tecate. The other was eating from a bag of Funyuns. They gawked at the women idling at a stoplight.

"Cool car!" one of them shouted. Alison looked back at them through her rearview mirror. They were running across the boulevard, howling at the moon.

"Erika wants to have a family." Trisha sat up straight. "She wants me to have the baby because she can't."

"And do you want to?" Alison made a U-turn.

Trisha started fumbling with the buttons of her jacket. "It's such a responsibility. I don't know. I'm in my early thirties. I'm not a kid anymore, but I certainly don't feel like an adult even though I'm supposed to be one. I'm a nurse now—it's my job to care for people in life and death situations. And I'm trying to be an actor too!" A button came off in her hand. "And fucking look at me! I'm a mess!"

Puffs of late-night moisture settled on the windshield. The sky was far, far away. Little stars twinkled like the lullaby.

"You need advice?" Alison asked. "Is that why you wanted to talk to me?"

"I guess," Trisha nodded. "I mean, what do you think?"

Alison turned on the wipers. The rubber was old, eaten away by bugs and time. They left streak marks across the window. She'd have to get them replaced before her trip.

"Honestly, I think if there's a baby out there meant for you, then it will come," said Alison. "I know that now. I didn't then." She thought about how different women were thirty years ago. She wished she'd been braver.

A stillness floated into the car. Alison made a right at Dillon Avenue. There were just a few lights on across the block. A spotted owl flew to the top of a pine tree.

"Do you ever regret having the abortion?" Trisha asked.

"Never." Alison pulled up in front of the white brick house. "And always," she added, pressing a button. The convertible top shifted back into place.

"I'm sorry," Trisha squirmed in her seat. "I shouldn't have asked you that—"

Alison turned off the ignition. She looked straight ahead, folding her hands in her lap.

"I don't know if having a baby was part of my life's plan or if not having her was part of my life's plan. What I do know is my daughter has always been a part of me. Ever since she was conceived—and even after the abortion, and even now, sitting here—I can feel her. Her absence. My life is lonely for her."

She turned to Trisha. "But I've taught thousands of kids over the past two decades, and I know I've made a difference in their lives. Would I have done that if I had taken the other path?" She shrugged her shoulders. "Probably not."

Alison rested her palm on Trisha's cheek—something she never got to do to Harriet. Tears welled up in both women.

"I had an abortion at twenty because at that time, there were no other options. None that I could see, anyway." Alison pulled out a packet of tissues from her purse and handed one to Trisha. She always had tissues at the ready for her students. "So do I regret it?" Alison took one for herself and wiped her eyes. "No. It was what I thought I had to do."

Trisha nodded, unbuckled her seatbelt, and put her hand on the door.

"A woman doesn't need to have a child to be complete," Alison said. "But I think you'll be a wonderful mother if you decide to try. You'll both be wonderful mothers—you and Erika. What a lucky baby!"

Alison scrunched the wet tissue in her hand and tossed it into her purse.

"But if you had to do it all over again?" Trisha probed.

First, they were two women in a poetry workshop—then two women in a '60s movie—now two women, at the crossroads of their lives.

"Personally, I would have the baby," Alison answered. "In a heartbeat."

Trisha let out a sigh like her body was emptying out every doubt she'd ever had, every fear she'd ever swallowed, every wish she'd ever suppressed. She let in a rush of sparkling night air. It looked like she wanted to stay and keep asking questions, but suddenly she seemed in a big hurry. She kissed Alison on the cheek and ran inside.

Returning from Silver Lake, Alison didn't want to step into an empty house. So she walked west along Ocean Park twenty blocks to the beach, took off her shoes and stepped onto the freezing sand, letting the wind wash over her for a good, long while. She thought about Harriet. She would be thirty years old now. The same age as

Trisha. That realization twisted something loose in Alison's chest. Maybe Harriet would be married with her own children...

Alison sat down at the water's edge, her toes searching deep into the crushed shells, roots looking for sustenance. So many years ago, and here it still was. The absence of her own child would always be present. Two unsuccessful marriages and no children. She never felt connected enough to her husbands to want a family. Or was it fear of loss that still haunted her? She was a feminist; she believed in a woman's right to choose, but she still dreamed about what could've been. There was the beginning of a life force—and then, there wasn't. It was the life of Harriet. And it was a real life. Alison gazed up at the scattering of stars. She'd been convinced her choice was the right one at the time. She didn't want to ruin Jesse's future by bringing an unplanned child into it. She felt scared and on her own. Her parents would've been so disappointed knowing her choice. But now, sitting on the sand, Alison would've liked to have an actual daughter sitting beside her.

She stood and took a few steps deeper. The undercurrent was strong. Her feet slid out beneath her into the swirling darkness— then just as suddenly, a wave carried her upright. She wouldn't drown on this ocean's watch.

Later, as she returned home—skirt wet, feet wet, face wet, bearing her clogs, dragging her purse, leaving a trail of salt water behind her—the people driving down the street took her for some solitary homeless person. But Alison knew she wasn't alone. She was searching for words, images, truths. A poem was forming.

Daughter

You are guiding
me back home

arms around
my shoulders

back into bed
and under the covers

back into the
peaceful healing sleep

of forgiveness

~ 15 ~

WANDA

March 22, 2019

"D<small>ADDY</small>?"

"Wanda? Where are you? Your momma's worried sick—"

"I'm fine. Just a little tired. I need you to tell me if —"

"Momma wants to talk to you—"

"No, Daddy!" I yell. "Don't put her on!"

I hear her grabbin' the phone away from him sayin', "Wanda! You're in big trouble." Her voice rattles through the payphone. "Travis is gonna cut the baby right outta you!"

So you ain't dead.

"That's what he said, swear to God! You shoulda seen him lyin' there in University Hospital in a room he's gotta share with a Mexican," she shouts. "And if that ain't enough, the doctor is some injun the government sent to medical school. Ain't no government sendin' Travis to medical school. But there he is, this fuckin' medicine man tellin' your husband he's gotta stop drinkin.' I'd say that's the pot callin' the kettle black if you ask me."

"Let me talk to Daddy—"

"Daddy went back to watchin' wrestlin', honey." I can hear her puff on a cigarette she rolled last night. That's what she does, rolls ten, and that's her limit for the next day. But she bums 'em wherever she can, ends up smokin' a pack.

"Momma, please—"

"Travis says he's gonna scratch the doctor's car up and screw with his tires soon as he gets out. Show him who's who."

"Please."

"What?" She stops for a minute.

Maybe she'll hear me. Daughter to mother. Flesh and blood to flesh and blood, askin' for help. "I'm scared," I say.

"You should be," she says, spittin' out flecks of tobacco got caught in her teeth. "You been sideswiped by the devil, Wanda. You think you're gonna get away with arson and attempted murder? That's a lifetime in prison, stupid. What kinda mother you gonna be in there?"

I shut my mind down 'cuz I don't wanna imagine nothin'.

"Travis is gonna track you down like a deer, so don't bother prayin'. Not even Jesus gonna care enough to save you now."

I can't help it. I see Momma and Jesus together. She's combin' his hair. He's lookin' up her skirt.

"I want my grandchild, and you're gonna give her to me." Her voice is a saw cutting through me. "Cuz I got news for you, Wanda. I'm a better mother than you'll ever be."

My hand's so weak it can hardly hold the phone.

"God speaks into darkness," she says, "and He's gonna punish you."

I hang up the phone. I can't slam it real loud, like I want to. I do it soft, so she'll keep talkin' 'til doomsday. I just let it drop. It hangs there in the booth, like the dead deer you want me to be, swings back and forth, back and forth. I see veins and guts spillin' out the mouthpiece and hear a baby deer bleatin' to the heavens on high. I wipe it with the sleeve of Ricardo's shirt.

I'm just 'bout to step outta the phone booth, and then I remember a time you were flushed and watery in our bed, tellin' me you got a fever, you can't go to work. I put my hand on your forehead, and yeah, it's burnin' up bad. So you hold my wrist and lead me down on top of you. I say I don't wanna get sick, but you don't stop and neither do I. Your fingers open me up, and I feel your electricity stab into me. It's always like that. You're rough, but then you get all movie-star romantic until the very end when you get all wild up in the deep inside middle of me. And I forget everythin' 'cuz you fill me to my edges and beyond. Your fever is in me now, but I don't care, 'cuz you chose me. Travis chose Wanda. Momma couldn't believe it. But I could. Our sweet was like tastin' a fresh strawberry just washed in the rain. I ride your body into paradise, and I swear it's the same paradise Jesus preaches when he preaches the rapture. I tighten all over to keep you inside me, and I pray, oh God, oh God, oh God, oh God...

My legs don't wanna hold me up. I put in more change, punch in the number to the hospital, and they put me through.

"Travis, it's me."

You don't say nothin' for a while, but I hear you breathin' like you got a bad cold. I see you lyin' with a bandage on your stomach, tubes goin' in and outta your head. You haven't shaved, and the thick blond hair climbin' out your face makes you look like a teddy bear. Your eyes are blue and clear like the glass marble I won off that girl in Mrs. Montgomery's class. I can't remember wantin' anything so bad—except maybe you, in Milton's bar, standin' by the pool table, singin' "Ring of Fire" 'cuz you just won fifty bucks. You winkin' at me was all the sky and sea in the world fast rolled up in your eyes. One blue breathes into another—blue like the perfume bottle you got me from the fancy store on Cottage Road, the one shaped like a cut diamond, so much heavier than I thought it would be—blue like the ring you won me at the county fair—a Navajo blue, like that paintin' of the water lilies we saw in Mrs. Abney's art book. It's a blue only God could make. So why did he give it to you? Why would he make your eyes that holy?

"Fucking bitch," you say.

I see you givin' me a box of chocolates for Valentine's. I kiss you thank you, and I drop the box by accident. I see them fallin' in slow motion, your boot smashin' 'em like fat brown bugs, my face mashed up with 'em. I see you ask forgiveness, with a bunch of daisies in your hand. You crawl up inside my arms. "I'm so sorry, Wanda," you say. "You mean the world to me. I'll never drink again." You touch my neck in that ticklish way and make me laugh even though I don't want to. You pull my head to yours and cry into me and say, "You're my woman 'til death do us part. I'm so sorry, baby. Please forgive me." And I forgive you, and we love each other all night 'til dawn but my jaw still hurts.

"You tried to kill me," I say.

"You tried to kill me!" you shout back.

Your voice slices me open a thousand different ways. The baby kicks. I wrap the phone's cord tight 'round my fingers.

"You tried to kill Grace!" I shout.

I hang up, real loud this time. I look out the phone booth, people walkin' by. I knock on the glass, but no one looks back at me.

I wanna tell 'em what happened. The truth and nothin' but. They turn their heads away from my eyes 'cuz they don't wanna be discovered. And soon with you on the hunt, neither do I.

~ 16 ~

TRISHA

April 26, 2018

"Wouldn't it be amazing if we could actually have a child together, just our DNA, just you and me?" Erika said, coming into the bedroom. "I wonder what she'd look like—'cause you know she'd be a girl."

"Let's see," Trisha mused. "I'd want her to have your height, my legs, your eyes, and our hair—curly and black. She'd be stunning if we say so ourselves." They both laughed, looking at each other, appreciating their moment of unity.

"Do you think I'd be a good mother?" Trisha whispered. This had been lying heavy on her heart. She hadn't learned about love from her parents. How could she give it if she hadn't received it?

"Yes," said Erika.

"You're not just saying that?"

"Nope."

"But my father was pretty crappy. My mother not much better. The unconditional love thing? I never got that."

Trisha walked over to the window. The North Star was behind a night cloud, struggling to be seen.

"Then you'll have the chance to correct all their wrongs. Be the mother she wasn't and the father he wasn't."

"Is that how it works?"

"I think so." Erika sat beside her on the bed. "Doesn't it make sense to you?"

"Yes, it does." Trisha turned to face her.

They moved into each other's arms and stayed that way for several minutes. They hadn't been this close in weeks. It was quiet, except for their minds dancing wildly.

"I love you," said Erika.

"I love you. Okay—I'll do it."

"OMG! For real? You want to?" Erika jumped up and down like a little girl getting a present directly from Santa. "But don't do it for me. It's got to be for you too."

"For real. And I'm doing it for us, for both of us." Trisha jumped with her. "Yes, it feels right. So—so let's do it!"

"Yes!" she said, kissing her again. "So, do we use an anonymous donor or someone we know?" Erika asked. "I don't want a man interfering in our possible future family."

"I think it's fine to have a third parent, if he's a good person." Trisha got into bed. "Maybe it's someone we don't know yet."

"What do you mean?" Erika climbed in.

"I'll go out there and hook up with a guy," Trisha answered.

Erika arranged the pillow behind her. "Are you saying you'll sleep with a man and never tell him if you get pregnant?"

If they were a heterosexual couple trying to have a baby, they'd be having sex right now—lots of it. But intimacy was so far from Erika's mind that Trisha began to long for that "catch-up arrangement" period of freedom.

"Why not?" Trisha said, gazing at her pile of clothes waiting for closet space. "At least that way we can both agree on his looks."

She'd given notice on her apartment in West Hollywood and moved into Erika's new place in Silver Lake. The neighborhood was diverse. Gay, straight, non-binary. The future was here, and she liked it.

"I get to go with you to some bar, and we both pick him out?"

"Yes, that's only fair," Trisha smirked.

"What about his medical history?" Erika asked. "He could come from a long line of sociopaths for all we know."

"Most people who get pregnant don't do extensive background checks," Trisha said. "It's only gay people who know all the gory details. And their children turn out just as screwed up as everyone else's."

It was 11:00 p.m. A helicopter rumbled in the distant sky.

"You'd be willing to have sex with a total stranger?" asked Erika.

Trisha put her hand on her lover's thigh. "I'd prefer you," she said.

"Sorry," Erika jumped back to set her alarm for 6:30. "I've got to get up early to finish reading this script."

Trisha turned away, cuddling her pillow to her chest. "Look, clinics don't show you pictures of sperm donors, right? And looks are important to us. So yeah, I'd at least think about it."

She'd been working in the ER. Seeing how people abused their lives—it took a toll on her. She wanted caresses from her partner, assurances. She questioned how important she was to Erika. She turned to ask, but Erika was twisted away from her, in a tight fetal position, already asleep.

Trisha turned out the light. Her career was starting to pick up now that being "other" was cool instead of the secret lurking in the corner. It felt like it happened overnight, but in reality, it took years. Now Hollywood was asking for—nay, demanding— diverse talent. Erika had just been promoted to story editor on *Orange is the New Black*. She liked being one of the sexy gay women on the lot. She'd grown out her hair. It was dark and wavy and hugged her back. She had plenty of covert sexual offers at the studio—conceited straight men, single women who never experimented in college, married women who had—but she wanted to be respected for the writer she was. She refused as sweetly as she could, saying she was a "married lady," even though she wasn't.

Trisha turned over and pulled up the comforter. And who would stay home to take care of the baby? Could they afford a nanny? Maybe her mother would come from Toronto and help in the beginning. Who was she kidding? Her mother wasn't comfortable with babies. She had said that her happiest time was before Trisha was born.

She needed to sleep. She traded with someone's morning shift because she had an audition in the late afternoon for a two-line part of a woman on an elevator for *The Good Fight*. She closed her eyes to try to imagine herself in an elevator, but instead her mind sent her back to when she was a young girl doing high jumps in a field of snow. She wanted to go back to Toronto to see the end of winter. She wanted... She wanted...

The alarm pierced the gray deafness of sleep. Trisha pushed away from the dream. It was a bad one. She was caught in a spider's web and couldn't get free. She sat up and sipped some water from the glass on her side table, then stared at the calming green color of the wall just to keep from getting dragged back in. A smile flickered across her mind.

"I know who!" Trisha sang out, jostling her partner awake.

"I don't want to get up," Erika groaned, covering her face with her hair.

"Remember that guy I told you about? The one who lives down the street on Dillon. With his little boy." Trisha took another sip of water.

"What?" Erika brushed her hair to the side, rubbing her eyes awake. "Who?"

"Johnnie Baloney." Trisha spritzed water on Erika's face.

"Stop! Stop that!" she laughed. "Who?"

"Handsome guy, black hair, tall—"

"Him?" Erika stretched her body. "You spent an hour at the park. That's not enough time to know anything."

"It's longer than with an anonymous donor," answered Trisha. "And remember, it'll be me with the syringe of semen pumped into my uterus! So maybe I should have the final say!"

It came out all wrong. Trisha knew it. Erika stepped into her slippers. Couldn't they just talk and not worry about how something sounded? Like they used to when they first met. On Sunday mornings, they'd make love and get brunch at The Kitchen. They'd hang around all day, talking about anything that came into their minds—a stream of consciousness language only they spoke. Nothing was too sacred or scary to discuss. That was another way Trisha realized she was falling in love—it was the only time in her life she felt seen and appreciated. There was such openness and freedom between them. Now, Erika wanted to change all that, and Trisha was afraid.

Trisha put on her red terry-cloth robe and went into the kitchen. They needed to talk about these things. Were they going to get married? Did it matter? Would they be good parents? What about religion? Erika was Italian and raised Catholic. Trisha was technically Protestant, but she hadn't been to church since her confirmation.

She peeled two oranges from their garden and sliced them into sixteen sections. What about schools? A child could make their relationship better. Or worse. What about divorce? Custody? There was just too much. Her brain was overcrowded. It was giving her headaches. She arranged the orange on a plate like a shining star.

"We're really going to have to start interviewing nannies." Erika came into the kitchen, a blue towel wrapped tightly around her body.

"I was just thinking about that. We need to talk about—"

"I hear it takes forever, and what if we have to import one from another country? There'll be tons of legal stuff, paperwork, etc. And do we want a strange person living in our house?"

"How are we going to afford all that?"

The bees were in the backyard, buzzing at the lavender bushes.

"Maybe I'll sell *Lemon Sky*."

"Your feature script about your romantic adventures in Italy?"

"I think it's pretty commercial."

Trisha dropped a pod into the espresso machine. "You'd quit your job at the show?"

"No, of course not." Erika took a couple of orange pieces and put them in her mouth. "Wow, so juicy!"

"So, what? I quit mine at the hospital?" She pressed the red button. "We wouldn't have enough money—"

"No, you keep that because we can count on it—"

"So, I put my acting on hold?" asked Trisha, clanging the knife into the sink. "Is that what you're saying?"

"I'm saying we need to start thinking about who's going to be at home with her."

"Agreed! Are you saying it's going to be me?"

"No, not exactly. Look, we'll get someone part-time at first, and yes, you'll take a maternity leave from the hospital, and I swear we'll work it out so we're both okay with the arrangement."

"You and your arrangements." Trisha washed the knife. "What if I get an audition?"

"We'll hire someone to babysit."

"And what if we can't find someone?"

"Then I will stay home with the baby until you get back from your audition."

It was early in the morning, yet Trisha felt exhausted, like she hadn't slept at all. She settled her body against the kitchen chair.

"Let's be realistic," Erika wiped the juice off her hands. "You'll be carrying the baby, so yes, I am expecting you to take care of her for the first several months. You'll be the birth mother, so you'll be the one to feed her and all that. If I could, I would." Erika moved to the doorway. "We'll figure something out, I promise, if you get an audition. And if you change your mind about all this, that's fine too. Just be honest with me."

"And then we'll break up, right? If I change my mind?" Trisha shrugged, walking back into the bedroom.

"Why don't I meet Johnny Baloney first?" said Erika, following her. "Let's have a dinner party. He'll never know the reason. It'll kind of be like an audition. We'll get to spend time with him and see if he deserves a callback."

"Funny," said Trisha, smiling.

Erika pulled her lover close and kissed her on the lips, lingering longer than the usual morning peck. "Sorry if I've been obsessed with all this. Let's plan a sexy date for this weekend. Champagne and everything."

"That would be nice."

Erika threw on black sweatpants and a white T-shirt. "Hey, don't you have to get ready for work?"

"I have time." Trisha waltzed back down the hall letting her pajamas fall off her body, hoping she'd be followed. She wasn't.

She stepped into the shower, soaped her body. She began to touch herself. She held her breasts, massaging them slowly, imagining Erika's hands there instead of hers. Then, blotting Erika from her mind, she was still angry with her, frustrated.

Trisha explored between her legs, rubbing herself with calm determination. And just before she was about to orgasm, Johnnie Baloney stepped in. This morning was the first time she thought about him or said his name in weeks. After their chance meeting, she found herself slowing down when she ran past his house. She hoped she'd see him and his charming smile, or L.J., or the grandfather. She hoped they'd invite her in for tea and cookies and *Sesame Street*. But there was never anyone there, so she kept on jogging straight into the park. She saw them at the playground twice. She waved and he waved back, but he never asked her to join them, so she let it go.

But this morning, under the rush of warm water, he was there. She closed her eyes, and he kissed the back of her neck. His body was muscular, his chest covered with tiny dark hairs. She leaned against the glassy wall of the shower. Her fingers moved faster, deeper, harder. Her hips rocked forward. She didn't want to burst too soon. It had been a while. Her body was ready but she wanted the sensations to last a little longer. She lifted the hand-held showerhead and decreased the pressure. She focused the spray onto her face, her breasts, her thighs. The temperature was perfect. She wanted to stay this way for a few more minutes, in her own private bubble. She would never tell Erika about her fantasy with Johnny Baloney. She liked secrets. That's how she survived her years as a lonely teenager in Toronto. She read erotic literature she bought at used bookstores on Yonge Street. She hid them under her mattress. First there was *Lady Chatterley's Lover*, then *Delta of Venus, The Unbearable Lightness of Being*, and *Emmanuelle*. Secrets were how Trisha balanced being in this new relationship with Erika— and her many one-night stands. But now, with the decision about motherhood, her acting career, and her partner's assumptions, what was she going to do? Her body was taking over. She longed for Erika to come in and catch her. Maybe then they'd play like they used to— but it was too late, she was still angry, and it was just too late. She couldn't stop herself—her muscles contracted into one another, and she came in a paroxysm of waves.

~ 17 ~

ALISON

June 23, 2018

JAGGER WAS FLYING BACK LESS and less. When he did, he'd gaze at Alison, fluff up his wings, and kiss her cheek with his curved beak.

"Can't get no. Can't get no," Alison sang to him.

"Can't get no," he'd cackle, circling his way back out the window into the canyons of Santa Monica.

She remembered seeing the Dalai Lama in Los Angeles with her parents in 1984.

"Just say 'yes' to the Divine," he said. "Try it. You might like it. Just say 'yes.'"

So she did. Did she want a free sample? Yes. Did she want dessert? Yes. Did she want to start a new account? Yes. She did, as a matter of fact. Yes. She wanted to set up a bank account where she could access her money from anywhere in the world, like Italy or India or especially Mexico. She wanted to go to Todos Santos, Mexico, to look up Jesse. And why not?

Saturday morning, when she was filling out the bank application online, a new email popped up. It wasn't from a student or subscription service. It was from Professor Vincent Gaiman.

Dear Alison,

I trust you are well. I'm getting in touch to let you know that Cindy passed after a two-year battle with breast cancer. She is now at peace.

I feel it's time to resolve and heal our past. Would you be so kind as to meet with me?

Best, Vincent.

She hesitated until she realized this was an opportunity for her. Yes, she responded. She'd meet him in the cafeteria at 4:00 p.m. that afternoon. Yes.

Alison chose a pink sweater and a pair of jeans from her spur-of-the-moment suitcase in the trunk of her car. She took a shower, washed her hair, blew it dry, and wore it fanned out across her shoulders. She stood in front of the mirror and unzipped her cosmetics bag. She applied foundation, concealer, eye shadow, liner, and lipstick. Her quiet beauty was revealed.

She drove east along Sunset, turned right at Hilgard Avenue, and parked near Kaplan Hall. UCLA's greenness oxygenated her. Students ambled past, hypnotized by their phones. She was hypnotized by their youth, and so was Vincent; she knew that. She hoped no one would sit too close. She didn't want him to compare.

Her past slapped her in the face when she walked in. This was where they'd met for coffee the first time. The second time was in his office. The third was in his secret condo in Westwood. Then, three years of Wednesday evenings there, except for holidays and semester breaks. Class first, lovemaking after. Then a Swiss turkey wrap from Trader Joe's, and a glass of port, and his anecdotes about the time he drank with Bukowski at the Brown Derby, or the time he saw Leonard Cohen at the Buddhist retreat, or the time he dined with Kate Braverman at The Source.

Her skin flushed, remembering it all.

A half-drunk cup of coffee sat in front of him. An Arnold Palmer rested across the table. It's what she ordered that first time. He assumed she'd want one now. He emptied two sugar packets into his drink and stirred in an infinite figure eight. He looked up when she entered. His face had always been a canvas of blurred lines. He said he loved her, but it never showed in his eyes. They were distant, protected, opaque—except for when he taught. Then they expanded into the world of each writer as he transformed himself into Delmore Schwartz, Grace Paley, and Jack Kerouac. Alison thought that's why she fell in love with him—not for him, but for the authors and poets he brought to life.

"Beautiful," escaped his lips.

He stood up. He looked older. He was just fifty-five, but his wife's sickness had aged him. His hair was black with gray threaded throughout, still long, but thinning on top. He was wearing a pair of tight jeans and a black leather jacket over the forest green cashmere sweater she gave him on his birthday a year before they broke up. He said he loved it, but he didn't know how he could explain it to Cindy.

"Thank you for coming," Vincent said.

She hugged him. She didn't know she was going to. He put his arms around her, and for an instant they were thrown back in time, the brilliant professor and the adoring, mature student.

"I'm very sorry about Cindy," Alison said.

"We tried everything," he said, taking the spoon out of the coffee. "It turned out she was chemoresistant." He placed it on the napkin.

"That must've been hard on you and the kids."

"It was," he nodded. "She was a trooper going from treatment to treatment. Braver than I could ever be." His eyes glanced away, as if searching for another outcome. Then they returned to Alison's face, hoping for a signal, a sign from her that everything was going to be all right. Someone's lap dog started barking. "At the end, we stood around her bed and told stories. Family memories, you know?" He picked up the napkin and placed it between the cup and the saucer. It absorbed the small amount of liquid sitting there. "And then she was gone."

"At least she's not suffering now," said Alison.

She wondered if their affair had anything to do with Cindy's illness. She heard that cancer could be caused by stress. She wished it hadn't happened. Another regret to add to her list. But who else could recite the works of such great writers with such passion, and talk about their lives and loves the way he did? I'll give you their genius, he teased, and you'll give me you.

And it was good, the sex, because she was making love with Theodore Roethke, Ernest Hemingway, and e. e. cummings. Vincent knew what he was doing. He seduced literary groupies throughout his entire academic career. The young, earnest, pretty women who dreamed of becoming the next Joan Didion, Dorianne Laux, or Toni Morrison. It made him feel powerful. It made them feel like muses. He was always hard. They were always wet.

"No." Vincent appraised her red hair against the pink of the sweater, her gray eyes highlighted by her makeup, her moist lips. "It's different when someone is sick for a long time," he said. He picked up a third sugar packet, poured it slowly into his coffee. "I got used to the fact that she was dying."

"I imagine it was difficult for her," she said.

"It was," he said.

"No, I mean with you and all your affairs."

She looked past him. A group of students, all young and beautiful, were mesmerized by one of their classmates who was standing at the head of her table, telling a story, imitating someone, speaking in a British accent. Theater students, Alison could tell. They came to Kaplan to study Shakespeare. They were louder than everyone else. They wanted to be seen. The young woman bowed, and her audience applauded. Vincent turned around in his chair to watch the commotion. Alison saw his shoulders stiffen.

"Someone you know?" she guessed.

"Just a student," he said. He took his jacket off and draped it over the back of the chair. "I really have missed you."

"Don't you think this conversation is inappropriate?" Alison sat forward. He was no longer her mentor. He was just a guy she'd had an affair with. He was just a guy.

"Cindy knew she wasn't going to make it. We accepted the inevitable. It's like I've been a widower for two years, really." His cell phone rang. He took it out and read the caller I.D. Then he shut it off. "She'd want me to be happy."

Alison raised an eyebrow. "That's very understanding of her."

Vincent looked hurt. He held out his right hand for Alison to take, like she had in the past. She placed her hands on her lap.

"My wife knew about my affairs. She understood I needed them. They didn't make her love me less."

Alison crossed her legs. "Your wife sounds like a saint."

Vincent stared into his cup of coffee. She hadn't touched her Arnold Palmer. There was still a sharp divide between the iced tea and the lemonade. She wanted to mix it all up with the straw. She wanted to disturb its perfection of color and dimension. She wanted to throw it in his face. They used to sit side-by-side when they met here before his classes. She'd talk about her homework, the poem she'd written, and the biography she was reading. He'd listen while his leg grazed hers, his hand finding its way under her dress.

She could sense him wanting her to want him.

"Why didn't you return my calls? Was I such a bastard?"

"No," said Alison. "You saved my life, actually. You brought me poetry."

Vincent bowed his head like a boy receiving communion. He needed to hear that they meant something to each other, something more than another professor-student affair.

"I'm glad."

"It changed my life. It may be my next passion. Poems help me express my unconscious. It's what I've been doing these past three years—writing poetry."

"Any about me?"

Alison took a beat before she shook her head. "We weren't that kind of love, Vincent. There was always Cindy."

"She and I stopped having sex after our last child was born—but you knew that. I told you the truth." His voice tripped in his throat. "I gave you everything."

"To a point," she said.

"Yes, to a point. And you knew that too." He ran his fingers through his hair. "You weren't some gullible twenty-one-year-old graduate student who was going to write the next Pulitzer Prize-winning novel. You were a mature woman who realized what she was getting into." He touched the indentation on his finger where his wedding band had lived. "I never told you I was going to divorce Cindy."

"I never wanted you to." Alison knew nothing would ever come from their relationship. That was why she was in it. After Jesse, she guarded a part of herself because she couldn't risk feeling that kind of pain again. A married man was safe.

The drama students were leaving. The young woman passed by their table and touched Vincent's shoulder. She was stunning and looked no older than twenty-one. Her long, golden hair curled down her back.

"Hey, Professor Gaiman!" Her fake eyelashes fluttered. She was wearing tight blue jeans with strappy red heels and a white tank top that barely covered her breasts. "How's life?"

"Hey, Melissa! It's great, how's life for you?" Alison watched the heat travel up his face.

"Awesome," Melissa leaned into the handsome, bearded young actor beside her. "Just awesome. See you in class!" Melissa giggled as she led the pack into the early evening sunset.

Vincent sipped the cold coffee. The cafeteria was emptying out. It was five o'clock on Saturday evening. People had dinners to eat, parties to attend, and secrets to reveal. Alison looked at her watch and leaned away from him. An ant scurried across the table. Even it had somewhere to go. She drew the Arnold Palmer to her lips. She hadn't realized how thirsty she was.

"So, you and Melissa...?" she inquired.

He reached for her hand again. "I always need a beautiful woman beside me." He ran his thumb along her fingers. He was good at this, she remembered.

"I have something special for you," he said, taking out a folded sheet of paper from his jacket pocket.

She recognized it immediately.

"Go on, read it out loud," he handed it to her.

"Here?" she shook her head. "I don't want to with all these college kids around."

"My office?" he suggested.

Alison wondered if she had left the window open for Jagger. If not, he'd wait for her on the ledge until she got home. They both rose from their seats.

Vincent's office had the same smell as before, leather and ink. She liked it then, and she liked it now. They sat down on the couch. She unfolded her poem and read it out loud.

Our naked bodies

A snake
came into
our room
through a
crack
we didn't know
was there.
It wasn't
big just
the right size
to go
unseen.
The room
grew cold, perfect

for eggs
to hatch.
And then
there were three,
so beautiful
so quick
so cunning
slinking
between our sheets
coiling
around our fingers
slithering
through our legs.
The snakes grew larger
eating each other 'til
only one remained.
The original.
The one
that entered through
the crack
we neglected
to fix,
wrapped itself around
our naked bodies.   *sometimes I wonder—why?*
I swear it smiled   *why didn't we just*
as it squeezed   *put putty in*
us
to   *the crack?*
death.

Alison felt a sudden escape of wetness. She'd been hoping for it, but it still surprised her when it happened.

"I'd like to keep this," she said, folding the page into her jeans' pocket.

Then she lifted her sweater over her head. She was wearing a new bra under a pink silk camisole. He stretched out his hand, and his fingers played along the curve of her breasts.

This was how he first touched her six years ago. They'd been sitting on the couch, this couch, discussing Delmore Schwartz's "In Dreams Begin Responsibility." She'd kicked off her sandals then and folded her legs to get more comfortable. He'd leaned towards her to arrange a cushion, she'd assumed. But instead, his hand had grazed the front of her blouse.

"Yes," she said again. "Yes."

Vincent moved in closer and kissed her neck. She didn't care for cologne on men, and he wasn't wearing any, just a faint trace of lavender soap. He remembered. She liked how he took care of himself. Manicured nails. Shined shoes. Close shave. Her fingers re-called the smooth skin of his face. It was easy kissing him—like she'd never stopped kissing him. He took off his sweater, then his T-shirt. She kissed his chest, her mouth moving down to the top of his belt. She stopped, slid out of her boots and jeans, letting him watch her body go from clothed to almost naked. She was happy with her new purchases from Victoria's Secret. Her panties matched her black, flowery lace bra. He stripped naked and stood there, letting her see how much he wanted her. That's what she was hoping for. There was something else she needed to know, but that answer wouldn't come 'til later. She slipped off her camisole and bra.

She teased him, moving aside her panties so he could watch her glisten. This was what they did when they made love before. It was part of their routine. It gave her a sense of control. He liked that. He got down on his knees and licked her until she couldn't hold on any longer—and then he stopped. Now he was in control, and she liked that. He let her calm down, then he lay her down on the couch and climbed on top of her, kissing her lips, letting his tongue cover her mouth with her taste on it. Then he got up and moved behind his desk. He came prepared. He brought out a framed mirror, the one they used to watch themselves with in the bedroom in his secret condo. He positioned the mirror against the desk so they could see their bare bodies reflected in the glass. He'd taught her to touch herself the way he liked. He loved to watch. She sat up and spread her legs as her fingers moved over her breasts and between her thighs. Then he entered her. He was still strong, "like a lion," she remembered him saying once. Their bodies moved in a connected rhythm, the heat between them building, memories of their love making reflected images on top of them now. She closed her eyes, and he gazed in the mirror as they came together. And then they were still.

She got up from the couch and went to the bathroom, carrying her clothes like a bundle of flowers.

"Are you okay?" he asked.

"Yes!" she shouted. "Yes, I am. Yes."

The light was changing into that deep gold Vincent said made the world look like a Turner painting.

"Care to stay for a glass of port?" he asked her. "For old time's sake. I just read a new biography of Anne Sexton that I—"

"Sorry," she answered. "I have plans."

"A date?"

She followed her reflection as she slipped back into her undergarments. Not bad, she thought. She decided not to add "for a fifty-year-old woman" to the end of her sentence. She wasn't going to qualify anything to anyone. No more comparisons. She was going to accept herself just as she was.

"None of your business, Vincent." She was just going home, but he didn't have to know that.

"Right," he answered. "Of course."

She let the cold water run in the sink.

"You know," he continued, "I'll be teaching a new class on the poetry of balladeers and songwriters like Bob Dylan, Neil Young and Leonard Cohen."

She cupped her hands, splashed her face and drank 'til his heat left her body.

"I think you'd like it," he tempted. "It starts in a month."

She pulled on her jeans and sweater and stepped out of the bathroom to find him putting on his clothes.

"Just one drink?" he asked, still barefoot.

"Hmmm," she murmured.

Vincent stood there, a little kid asking for something he really wanted, but knew he shouldn't have. She glanced at his pedicure and looked around the room. The degrees from Berkeley were still up on the cream-colored walls, the same pictures of Cindy with their three children on his desk. They'd be off to college by now, all of them. He was pretty much on his own.

He went over to his desk and reached into the bottom drawer for two glasses and the bottle of Sandeman. It was the same port they always drank together, though not the same bottle, of course. He'd probably gone through hundreds since her. She thought of him with these young women, these Melissas, and it didn't make her jealous. It wasn't like that when they were together. She'd made him swear on his children's lives that she was his only mistress. He'd said he would never cheat on her, not even with his wife. But he did. Alison had seen the extra bottles of port on his shelf. She ended their affair on her forty-seventh birthday with a note that said, "Thanks for the poetry."

His cell rang again. He had turned it back on while she was in the bathroom. He reached for it, checked the caller I.D., and answered it.

"I'll call you later," he said softly and hung up.

Alison had been the woman on the other end of Vincent's cell—a bit role in the movie of his life. She wasn't interested in playing that part with anyone anymore. It was her turn to shine.

The port was dark and unhurried as it emptied out of the bottle. He walked across the rough carpet and handed her a glass. He lifted his to meet hers.

"To you," he toasted.

Alison raised her glass and smiled, but she was no longer there. She'd already moved on.

~ 18 ~

WANDA

March 28, 2019

"Travis Williams checked out," the hospital lady in Mobile says.

Why am I back at the same phone booth on Hollywood Boulevard? It's the only one I can find. I don't know what else to do. I'm lookin' for a home, and since I've already been here, I think this is it.

I call my sister, Betty Ann, but she don't pick up. Neither does Janine. I'm kinda used to that 'cuz they got troubles of their own, but I figured they wouldn't know it was me 'cuz I'm callin' from a phone booth. I call Daddy. Momma picks up like she's waitin' by the phone. I stay on, 'cuz I'm pretendin' to myself real hard. I'm pretendin' she loves me so much she's become a different person.

"Travis been talkin' to Pastor Higgins," she says.

"Really?" I ask, and I'm seven years old again, and she's told me Santa Claus is in the living room with presents for me and my sisters.

"God as my witness. He's been talkin' a whole lot to Pastor Higgins, and he went to AA. Travis has seen the error of his ways, Wanda. He bent down on his knees and asked me to forgive him for being a bad son-in-law. He was cryin' all over the place. I told him to hush up and get up, but he wouldn't, not 'til I forgave him. So I did."

I stand there frozen, half-knowin' she's trickin' me into believin' so she can do somethin' real awful.

"You lyin' to me, Momma?" I wipe the sweat spreadin' underneath my bra. I've seen her like this before—sayin' somethin' sweet, then doin' somethin' nasty like goin' out drinkin' after she swore she was too sick to meet Daddy at the bowlin' alley. "Let me talk to Daddy."

"Swear on my grandchild's life, Wanda."

So I have to believe her. What grandmother would lie about that? Yeah, right.

"So he don't wanna track me down like a deer and cut her outta me?" I ask.

"Don't be crazy, Wanda. You know better than that. It was the hospital medicine doin' the talkin'."

My feet shift under me tryin' to find solid ground. Is there an earthquake happenin', or am I crazy?

"Where's Travis?" I ask.

"He's on his way to find you."

My throat tightens the same way it did when you held your knife against it.

"He knows where you are," she says.

How? How in God's name do you know I'm in Hollywood? There's a silence so strong I think I've gone deaf. So I'm guessin' you figured I'd have to leave by Greyhound 'cuz I don't have a lotta money. And you inquired who was on duty at the station that night and found the guy with the skinny fingers and black glasses, showed him my picture, and he didn't wanna tell you at first 'cuz he remembered I was runnin' from somethin', but then you gave him twenty bucks and he remembered a sweaty pregnant girl he gave a ticket to. Yeah, it wouldn't take a genius to figure out where I am. I don't hear nuthin'. Not Momma, not the cars, not my own heart clangin' against my ribs. But I sure feel everythin'. I'm a black hole with a million meteors whizzin' by, crashin' into my brain, makin' me think I'm gonna explode into a zillion more.

"I can just leave," I tell her.

"He's so sorry," Momma says, blowin' her nose showin' me she's cryin', "and you're carryin' his child. You know you love him even though you hate him sometimes. That's just how marriage is, Wanda."

My tongue is stone. It don't wanna answer.

"You gotta forgive him, Wanda, 'cuz Travis is just that kinda man."

"What kind is that?"

"The kind a woman like you makes better."

I'm feelin' a sweet sensation at the back of my neck, like a bird's wing brushed close by, and I see you and me at the beginnin' of us, all shiny and full of hope, at the bar dancin'. You holdin' me so tight I thought you'd never let me fall.

I shove myself upright. Gotta stand tall for this. Gotta be on guard.

"He did bad things, Momma. I'm afraid for the baby."

"He promises he'll never touch another drop of liquor again. And he'll never lay a hand on you, ever. He wants to be a good father

135

and husband. You gotta give him a second chance, Wanda. Do the right thing for once in your life. It's what Jesus would do."

Clouds are flyin' by. It might rain.

"Travis is givin' you a second chance," Momma keeps talkin'. "He didn't tell the police what you did."

I get tired real quick like a rollercoaster finishin' up the ride.

"Just ask Jesus what to do," she says.

"He's the one who told me to do what I did, Momma!" I hear myself laugh. "You think if I bow my head and pray some more, Jesus is gonna change his mind?"

"Yes, baby girl," Momma laughin' with me. "I think He will 'cuz He knows Travis is a good man down deep and He knows you're a good woman too."

I've no choice but to rest against the dirty glass of the phone booth, or I'll fall over. There's stickers from a massage parlor called Pretty Woman clingin' to the surface. They're half-scraped off, but a part of a girl's face is still there, lookin' at me.

"When did he leave Mobile?" I ask.

"Yesterday," she tells me.

The massage girl's face is pretty— the part that's still left. Her forehead's scratched away, and there's a beard drawn with a blue pen in crooked circles on what's left of her chin.

"How?" I ask.

The girl's big, round eyes fix on mine. She's sendin' me thoughts, tryin' to tell me somethin'.

"On that same bus you took outta here."

I hang up without tellin' her what I'm gonna do. I look into the girl's eyes like they're a mirror and we're the same person 'cuz I'm scratched away too.

Momma knows everythin'. She always does. Like after that first time lovin' you, she grabbed my shoulders and called me a whore. I was so quiet and careful comin' home, but she knew just like she knew I knew 'bout her sneakin' around on Daddy with Mr. Lewis, the high school math teacher. She just couldn't care less. She looked me straight in the eye and told me her life was for her to live and Jesus Christ to judge. I said the same thing back, and she slapped my face so hard she near twisted my head 'round my spine.

"I'm the queen of this life," she told me. "Don't you ever forget it!"

And I yelled back, "I love Travis Williams. Don't you ever forget that!"

I got some gum in my yellow bag. I take out a piece and chew it up so it's nice and soft. I stick it on the massage girl's eyes. She can't see me no more.

I walk fast to the motel and sleep 'til Ricardo comes home. He makes us fancy ham and cheese sandwiches on a skinny fryin' pan, and I swear it makes him so happy when I eat. He tells me what he's learnin' in chef school.

"Béchamel," he says.

It sounds like a spell, a magic word like that nurse's arabesque word, but it's a French sauce he's excited to try on me. I repeat it back to him, but it comes out all funny soundin', and he laughs and hugs me tight, smellin' of cinnamon and flour.

"Hollandaise," he says. "Velouté."

I can stay like this forever, I think. But I know as I'm changin' into Ricardo's Pachuca T-shirt, I'm gonna show up at the bus station tomorrow. I'll hide across the street, and you won't see me. I'll observe and decide if Pastor Higgins and AA has made a difference in you like Momma said. I wonder what you'll be wearin'. Maybe that sky blue shirt that matches your eyes I bought for Christmas at The Gap. The one you swore you'd never take off.

"Because I love you like a wild man loves his wild," you said.

I wonder if you shaved that beard off, if you're still in pain, if you'll talk to anyone on the bus? Knowin' you like I do, I know you'll talk to whoever's sittin' beside you, tell 'em all 'bout the baby. You'll tell 'em you opened a classic car garage on Airport Road, that you're your own boss, that you married your high school sweetheart who's real good in art. You'll tell 'em that bein' with me is heaven sent, that when you drive your '68 Camaro all sparklin' and black, we sit so close that when we take wide turns, we're a whip made of steel and glass, huggin' the edges, holdin' each other, kinda like dancin', kinda like skatin', kinda like makin' love 'cuz there's no space between us. Just rock-solid superglue.

I'll watch you get off the bus from across the street, watch you step onto the sidewalk in front of the Florentine Gardens Club with the white metal fence. You'll look all confused, but still proud, 'cuz that's who you are. You'll take out a cigarette you promised to stop smokin', and you'll see the white Hollywood sign on the mountains behind you. Then you'll spot the white cross comin' out the top of the church, and you'll think you're a crusader, 'cuz you're comin' to take me back to the Holy Land. And maybe I'll step out from where I'm hidin', but only if I see somethin's different 'bout you.

"Travis," I'll call. "Over here!"

You'll turn 'round and through the colored cars cruisin' by see me, all round and pure and real like a full moon risin'.

"Wanda!" You'll fall to your knees. "Babe, I'm so sorry I could die."

And I'll see that Momma was right. You are a changed man. I'll cross the street, and I'll tell you I'm fine on my own, but if you want to have some food, we can eat someplace. And then you'll go back to Mobile, and I'll stay here, and we'll be friends from a distance, and I won't touch your face, and you won't touch mine, and we won't kiss, and you won't rub my back, and I won't hug your chest, and it won't be like Jesus sent you to find me and hold me forever—'cuz why would He make me love you if we wasn't the sweetest creation this side of heaven?

~ 19 ~

TRISHA

May 12, 2018

Johnnie Baloney was at the swings with L.J. and the grandfather when Trisha invited them all to her sperm party. She didn't call it a sperm party, of course, not out loud, at least. She just called it a party. Anyway, Johnnie Baloney said they'd be delighted to attend for an hour or so, before L.J.'s bedtime. A ready-made family made sense to Trisha. It would be good for the baby. Erika would learn to appreciate it. And with L.J. coming, she could see how great a father Johnnie Baloney was.

Erika invited her brother, Steven. He was two years older and a hedge fund manager for tech start-ups. He graduated from the University of Miami with a master's in finance, worked for Charles Schwab and Morgan Stanley before he struck out on his own. They didn't talk politics, but Erika was pretty certain he was a Republican who may or may not have voted for Trump. He was divorced with three kids, and he looked like his sister. They were both tall with black hair and brown eyes. As far as DNA went, he was the closest thing to Erika herself. He'd be the uncle if they picked him, even though he'd be the father.

Steven brought a work buddy named David, who was practically the blond version of him, only a few inches shorter. He would be an obvious choice. David struck just the right balance between known and unknown. They wouldn't have to trawl a bar to find a donor, and he wasn't the type to stick around. He was good-looking, smart, and possibly perfect.

Trisha also invited a male nurse from the hospital named Clifton. He was Jamaican, athletic, and playful. Clifton was over six feet tall and moved like he was always dancing to a Bob Marley song. His eyes were magnetic—once you looked at them, it was hard to look at anything else. He sang in a reggae band that was destined to make it any day now; he was certain. He tied his dreads back with a gold scrunchie.

To make it seem like the party wasn't just for finding sperm, Trisha invited some women from the poetry workshop. Marlee was an African American actress who did commercials when she wasn't bartending. Carolyne was a therapist whose practice was focused on cancer survivors. Alison was a high school English teacher who was older. They were all straight women who wrote poems about love and loss.

The possible mothers-to-be served grilled Asian chicken and Erika's famous salad. She went to the farmers' market on Sunset early that Saturday morning and bought three kinds of lettuce—romaine, Boston, and mizuna—along with kale, watermelon radishes, arugula, spinach, cucumbers, cherry tomatoes, and mint. Erica steamed sweet potatoes, parsnips, carrots, let them cool down, and added a rice vinegar, soy sauce, honey, and peanut oil dressing that was her second claim to fame. They bought the grass-fed organic chickens at Whole Foods, marinated the pieces in lemon, ginger, teriyaki sauce, and honey, and grilled them on the barbecue that had come with the house. Dessert was blueberries, strawberries, cut-up peaches, and cherries soaked in rum and raw sugar with dollops of organic vanilla ice cream made from coconut and almond milk. They could laugh at themselves. They were very L.A., a perfect fit for the Silver Lake demographic—all that was missing was a dog, and yes, a child.

Trisha floated around, kissing everyone on the cheek. Maybe the candidates, Johnnie Baloney, Steven, David, and Clifton, would all be interested in making a sperm cocktail? They'd do their thing in the bathroom and present her with their contributions. She'd mix it all together, insert a turkey baster, and voilà, nine months later, a baby. No one would have to know who the real father was.

She giggled to herself. How was she ever going to get these four guys to masturbate into a cup? That seemed like more of a frat party thing. She went over to the bar and opened another bottle of Prosecco.

Men possess sperm. Was this why they possessed the world? But without an egg, sperm is worthless. Women and men need each other for what they lack themselves. That was fine with Erika. She could purchase whatever she was missing. No dating, no negotiating, no deceit—just money, a fertility clinic, lots of tests, plenty of paperwork—and a baby without any attachments.

Erika was adamant about reminding Trisha of a lesbian couple they had met, who got taken to court by the sperm donor. He was a gay friend who said he didn't want anything to do with the baby at first—only for him and his husband to appear on their doorstep two years later, demanding fifty-fifty custody. After four years of fighting and $150,000 in legal fees, the men got what they wanted.

Trisha examined the prospects from afar. Could she trust them? Would she want to co-parent with any of them? What if she and Erika broke up? Would he be there for her and the baby? She added ice cubes to her drink. The night was getting warm. She needed to stay sober.

Steven picked up the bottle of Prosecco and topped her glass.

"So, when are you and my sister getting married?" he asked.

Trisha took a sip. She wondered if she'd met him first, would she have fallen for him? He and Erika were so alike.

"We aren't even talking about it," she responded.

"You know what the leading cause of divorce is?" he asked, taking an hors d'oeuvre off the tray.

"What?"

"Marriage," he smirked, popping it into his mouth.

Erika was wearing a royal blue linen pantsuit with a white T-shirt and red tennis shoes. Her hair was down, her face make-up free. Her deep brown eyes roamed the room until she found their neighbor.

"I'm so happy to finally meet you," Erika said, bringing Johnnie Baloney a glass of bubbly water. Trisha stood a few feet away. She wanted them to get to know each other. "And this must be L.J."

Johnnie Baloney glanced down at his son and then kissed the top of his head. "Say hi to Erika, L.J."

"Hi," L.J. said, "Can I have a cookie?"

"If your dad says it's okay."

L.J. gazed up into his father's eyes with a look that said, if you love me, you'll say yes.

"Yes," said his father.

"Yes!" His son hugged him around the waist and marched off to the dessert table.

"But only one," Johnnie Baloney called after him.

"What a beautiful boy," smiled Erika.

Trisha inched a little closer. She liked how their conversation was going. So far, so good.

"I hear you're planning a pregnancy," Johnnie Baloney ventured.

"Yes, though it's kind of private at the moment," said Erika. Trisha took this opening to step in.

"Well, nothing is private anymore," Trisha interrupted. "Do you know who your egg donor was?"

"You mean was she a friend?" he asked.

"Yes. And was that important to you, knowing her?" replied Trisha, as nonchalant as possible.

"No. And no. She was a long number in a file," he said. "We're really grateful to her. Them. We had an egg donor, and another woman was the surrogate. Her, we met a couple of times throughout the nine months. She's from Long Beach. She needed the money to repay college loans."

L.J. came back and grabbed his father's hand and started to pull him towards the dessert table. "I want you to have a cookie too," he said.

"I'm talking, L.J. Please wait patiently."

L. J. shrugged and started eating only the chocolate chips in his cookie.

"So, you didn't really know them as people?" repeated Erika. "And you preferred it that way."

Trisha gave Erika a look that could be translated, "Leading the witness, your Honor."

"We were at the birth, and then we took L.J. home. We haven't spoken to either the surrogate or egg donor since. Cleaner that way. Less confusing."

"Do you want a second child?" Erika blurted out.

Trisha sat down with her drink. She couldn't believe Erika just put it out there like that. Johnnie Baloney looked from one to the other. Then he looked at his son, who had just finished eating the rest of the cookie. L.J. took this as a cue to start pulling his dad towards the dessert table again.

"Come on, Dad. You can have one too."

Trisha's face flushed. Johnnie Baloney had been asked this question before—it was so obvious now. He knew why he'd been invited, why his whole family had been invited. Trisha liked Johnnie Baloney. She appreciated his easy manner and wide-open attitude. Her imaginings in the shower didn't make her nervous. On the contrary—they made her feel safe. A sexual fantasy with a gay man was fine because there was no possibility of them ever getting together. Therefore, he was no threat to Erika.

Trisha couldn't take the suspense, waiting for Johnny Baloney's reply. She glanced over at Clifton, who was cornered by Carolyne and Marlee. Maybe they wanted babies too. It wasn't just lesbians anymore. It seemed like every woman of child-bearing age wanted designer sperm in her freezer.

Johnnie Baloney frowned and stood up, hoisting his son to his shoulders. "Nope. Sorry," he said, heading for the dessert table. "One's perfect for me."

Trisha finished her fourth glass of Prosecco. An hour ago, she thought it was too sweet. Now she cherished the pale, candied bubbles. Erika walked away feeling righteous, but Trisha sat there for a couple of minutes, wondering what her next step would be. She needed some air.

She snuck outside to stand in the center of the citrus trees. They gave her oxygen. She reached into her skirt pocket and pulled out a small notepad and pen. She jotted down a few words: confused, career, baby, motherhood.

"I do that too."

Trisha looked down, startled.

"Sorry," said Alison. "Didn't mean to scare you." She was sitting at the base of a tree, mindfully breathing in the fragrant evening breeze.

"Oh, hi! I didn't know anyone was back here."

"I do that too," Alison pointed to Trisha's notepad. "Write things down. Lines, ideas, phrases. Except my notebook is large and red. That's what you're doing, isn't it? Poetry?"

"Kind of. My acting teacher, Martin Kanakaris, said that these fleeting thoughts are the source of your creativity. He said to write them down, or you'll be applauding them in someone else's work one day. Not that I want to be a famous poet. Making it as an actor is hard enough." Trisha sat down opposite Alison. "You?"

"Be famous?" Alison shook her head. "No, not at all. I just want to know what I'm thinking on the inside. The deep inside."

"Yes, exactly! The deep inside."

Trisha could see that Alison had been a beautiful woman when she was younger. She was still great-looking with her red hair and positive energy.

"Right." Trisha rose and tugged at a lemon. "We decided we're going to try and have a baby."

"That's wonderful!"

"That's what this party is for."

"And you invited me because ..."

"I like you," handing her the fruit.

"Thank you," taking it.

"And we needed more women, so it wasn't that obvious."

"Oh, I see," Alison's eyes opened wide. "You're looking at the men as father prospects."

"Shh." Trisha put her finger to her own lips. "It's a secret. The guys will never know."

As if on cue, a burst of male laughter splashed out the back door. The two women outside giggled.

"Any luck so far?" Alison asked.

"The evening is young." Trisha straightened her skirt. "I'm going back in. Got to keep focused."

"I'll stay out here for a bit. The air is so different from Santa Monica. It's drier, more like the desert." Alison tossed the lemon up with her right hand and caught it with her left. "And so is the light. I bet sunsets are stunning here."

"You can see them forever. I love your poetry, by the way," added Trisha. "I think it's very soulful."

"That's very kind of you to say. I've been reading all these poets—Dorianne Laux, Charles Bukowski, Ocean Vuong. They're so inspiring."

"You should publish one day. I think you're really good."

"Thank you," Alison blushed. "I like yours too."

"Really?"

"Yes," she nodded. "I enjoy listening to you read your work."

"Thank you so much!" Trisha curtsied. "I think it's because I'm trying to be a person when I read, and not a "Poet." I feel connected to myself. Do you know what I mean?"

"Yes, I do. And good luck with the search," Alison winked.

"Hey, if it's meant to be ..."

Trisha went back in, took several long pulls from a newly opened bottle of an effervescent French rosé, and went up to Clifton.

"You are so great to work with." She hugged him. "Your dreads are so sexy."

"How're you doin?" He raised his eyebrow.

"You know," she spun around him, "if I met you before Erika, I'd still be straight."

Someone turned up the volume of k. d. lang's "Constant Craving," and Trisha felt the whole room tilt. She did a two-step and then kicked her leg up high. She thought the song would save her, but David came up from behind and pulled her out to the middle of the floor. He was one of those men who still believed he could change a woman's mind—all she needed was to spend a night in his bed. So when David touched her left breast, she pushed him towards the dessert table. Johnnie Baloney, his fingers moving through his own hair like someone playing a harp, was whispering something in Steven's ear. David looked back at Trisha and shrugged his shoulders as if to say, "Hey, your loss," then bit into a chocolate brownie and danced over to Marlee and Carolyne. Johnnie Baloney was still whispering into Steven's ear until they both howled with laughter.

Wait, was Johnnie Baloney coming on to Erika's brother? She thought Steven was straight, but you never knew with those right-wingers. Will there be another trip to the donor clinic, another egg hunt? Or would Erika become Auntie Mother? No, Erika had a hard time with regular menstruation. It would have to be me, Trisha realized. It always has to be me.

She swigged more rosé. While the pink fizz flitted on her tongue, she wondered if life would always be everybody wanting something from someone. I'll do this for you if you do that for me. Wouldn't it be amazing if, at that moment, the music stopped playing and each person stepped forward and came clean and told everyone at the party the truth about what they wanted? Why was it a secret, anyway? What's wrong with telling the truth? Erika would say she wants to be a mother. Steven would say he wants to make millions. Johnnie Baloney would say he wants to fall in love. Clifton would say he wants to be famous. David would say he wants to have sex. Marlee would say she wants to have romance. Carolyne would say she wants to have security. Alison would say she wants to have possibility. What would she say?

The Turkish carpet whirled beneath her feet. She looked up at the ceiling. The lights were bouncing like ping pong balls at a Bingo game, but no one was yelling "duck and roll." She took a couple more sips and convinced herself that everything was fine. Her body had other plans. It released the anxiety she'd been suppressing all day. A swarm of red hives erupted on her neck and chest.

Clifton lifted Trisha to the sofa. He gave her two Benadryl and made her drink a glass of water. What a beautiful man. She wondered which of the women he'd go home with. Or maybe he'd go home with both, impregnate both, and have two kids in nine months. Twins—but not quite.

"Babies." The alcohol and antihistamines sloshed around in her head. "We're all gonna make babies for each other."

She lay back on the sofa, clutching his arm as she dropped further and further into the abyss. The door to the cold room of sleep gaped open. A spindly leg peeked out. This would be the fourth recurrence of the spider dream this week, but this time, they were larger. They'd scuttle across the floor, their knotted webs waiting to snarl her up and carry her down, down, down... She knew that webs meant entrapment. But was she the spider or was she the prey? If she was the spider, then that meant she was the seductive one, the methodical one, the patient one who would somehow weave her dreams, whatever they were, into reality. But if she were the prey, that would mean she was waiting to be eaten, waiting for life to drain away, waiting for freedom to be sucked right out of her.

Maybe a baby is a bad idea. That was her last cohesive thought before the drugs took charge and banished her from herself. Later that night, she woke up sweating and alone. She called Clifton, and she was right. He did go home with both women, though not together. He drove Marlee home first, spent an hour in her bed, then called Carolyne and was eagerly invited into hers.

"You like one better than the other?" whispered Trisha.

"They're both nice. I like kissing Marlee, and Carolyne's hips got rhythm, so I like them the same."

The sofa was narrow. She was afraid of falling off.

"Did you use birth control?" she asked.

"They told me they're on the pill."

"I bet they did," she laughed and pushed her legs out from under the cover. Someone had taken her silver heels off and put them near the sofa. Beside them were her fuzzy burgundy slippers. She slid into them and stood up.

"Don't you men realize that it's the only thing we really need you for?"

She steadied herself against the sofa's arm. Clifton's laughter was a sparkle of jewels. He didn't sound tired. How could that be after bedding two women—in two different locations?

"You find anyone?" Clifton asked. "To help you and Erika

make a baby?"

A cup of mint tea on the coffee table caught her eye. She raised it to her lips. It was cold by now. She was still wearing the silver party skirt and silk blouse. The small notepad and pencil were still in the pocket. A crumpled napkin hid under the edge of the rug. She brushed her hair out of her eyes. That's when she realized she'd been crying in her sleep.

"Oh, no! Were we that obvious?" she probed.

"I never used to be so popular as I am now," he answered. "Been invited to lots of parties lately. I ask, "Can I bring anything?" and the hostess says, "No, just bring yourself, if you know what I mean."

Trisha nodded her head. She knew exactly what the hostess meant. "And how about you?" Trisha couldn't believe she was asking him just like that. "Interested?"

"I can't be no daddy now," Clifton responded in all seriousness. "Maybe when I be famous."

"But you won't have to be the father or anything like that. We just need your sperm, Clifton."

She thought he hung up; it was so quiet.

"Clifton? You there?"

"I can't be no daddy without being the daddy to my baby, Trisha."

Too bad, she thought as they hung up. Our baby would've been beautiful.

The TV in the bedroom was on. Erika was watching *Saturday Night Live*. Trisha could hear Alec Baldwin doing his Trump impression. Trisha wrapped the blanket around her body. She didn't want to go to their bed. She didn't want to argue. She didn't want to tell her that maybe it wasn't going to work, that maybe she wasn't cut out for motherhood—that maybe love just wasn't enough.

~ 20 ~

ALISON

June 23, 2018

Aʟɪsᴏɴ ғᴇʟᴛ ᴀ ʙᴜᴍᴘ ᴜɴᴅᴇʀ her tire on the way home from Vincent's. She started to panic, terrified she'd crushed some innocent creature. She pulled over and checked, but there was no blood, just two huge nails prodding out of a broken piece of wood, air whistling from the holes. The tire would be flat in no time. She took out her cell before she remembered she'd blocked Vincent's number three years ago. She clicked on her email, then shut it off. No, he would not be the knight-in-shining-armor. She wouldn't give him the privilege of coming to the rescue. She made her lopsided way to the fire station on Sunset just west of Barrington Avenue.

When she rang the bell, a tall fireman opened the door. She squinted at his nametag. LIEUTENANT SEAN PRESTON, it said.

"Can I help you?" he asked. He was chiseled-out-of-rock handsome, with the greenest eyes she'd ever seen. He could've been from Central Casting, and he'd probably saved hundreds of lives.

She smiled to herself as she stood there, still lightheaded from the recent lovemaking. "My tire is losing air. I was hoping someone could change it. Do firemen do that kind of thing?"

Her voice came out flirty. She wasn't interested in the fireman, not beyond fantasy anyway.

"Do you have a spare?" he asked.

"In my trunk. I've never used it before," she stepped towards her car. "I think there's a jack here too."

"Don't worry," he said, "I'll be right back."

Was it chilly, or was her body still communicating to her? Either way, she felt like dancing. Three years of celibacy was a long time. It's not that she couldn't have slept with a few of the men she knew, even a couple of women. She just wasn't interested. But now, with the resurgence of her new self and the completion with Vincent, she was enjoying the return of her playful side, her feminine side.

She noticed a yellow sign on the red brick wall. It was an illustration of a baby in a woman's arms. SAFE HAVEN was printed in black letters above them.

"Can you pop the trunk for me?" He hefted a jack and a wrench.

"Of course." She clicked her key and the trunk complied.

"Nice Mustang," he said. "2012?"

"Yes."

"Cool. One day I'll get a convertible," he said, moving the spur-of-the-moment suitcase to get to the spare. "Going on a trip?"

"Yes," she answered, stepping side to side, almost hopping. "Not sure exactly when or where, but I'll be ready when the time comes."

"I haven't traveled much," he said as he lifted it out without much trouble. "Just Mexico for a destination wedding. One of my buddies. He and his fiancée figured it would be a good time for everyone." He pried off the piece of wood with the two nails.

"Was it?" Her stomach growled. There was no turkey Swiss wrap from Trader Joe's waiting to be devoured after sex.

"You bet." He popped off the hubcap. "I met my wife there."

"Bride or groom?" she asked. She'd stop at Bob's Market and pick up a steak to broil and a potato to bake. And a salad.

"Pardon me?" He twisted off the lug nuts.

"Was she part of the bride's family or the groom's family?" Maybe she'd even have dessert.

"Neither. She worked at the front desk at the hotel. Love at first sight." He blushed as he took off the tire and lined up the spare. "Married six years now. Two little girls."

"Well, congratulations! It was meant to be." Alison took a couple of deep breaths and looked up at the sky. Her body felt lighter, calmer. The moon was almost full. Waning or waxing, she wondered. She could never tell.

Alison looked at the yellow sign again. "What does that mean?" She pointed.

He stopped his work to glance over. "It means we're a safe haven for newborns."

"And that means?"

"That means," he tightened the bolts, "that instead of abandoning a baby in a dumpster or a forest, the girl can leave it here. No questions asked."

"Really? What do you do with it?"

"We take it to Child Protective Services. And it'll go up for adoption."

When Alison was twenty, she never considered going full term and then giving the baby away. Why would she put herself through that?

"Has anyone ever left their baby?" she asked.

He double-checked to make sure everything was secure. He lowered the jack and lifted it out from under the car.

"Nope, not yet." He rolled the flat and placed it into the compartment in the back. "There you go." He wiped his hands on a towel. "You probably won't be able to save it. I'd get a new one soon, if I were you." He swung the suitcase back in place and slammed the trunk shut.

"Thank you!" Alison slipped back into the car. "I really appreciate your help."

"Happy to do it," he said and waved as she drove off.

She zigzagged her way back, finding new roads off the boulevard. After the steak and apple pie à la mode, her bones told her she needed to soak for a good long while. She was listening.

As she marinated in the coconut milk bath salts, a warm sensation emanated from her heart center. She let it envelop her body as she relaxed into a series of deep, slow breaths. She pictured the white lotus flowers from the long-ago Amma meditation and felt unafraid, vulnerable, and open. The first lines of a poem came to her. She said them out loud so she could recall them later, when she would write them in her red notebook.

*I stepped back
into my life today –*

An hour later, she fell into bed, wrapping the comforter around her body. It hugged her like her old guru, Amma, had. Bouncing between the conscious and the unconscious, her mother appeared before her, holding a newborn deer in her arms.

Alison's eyes shot open. She sat straight up. She threw back the covers.

Her parents never had the chance to live the second half of their lives. They were robbed of it. Her mother holding the newborn deer. This was a message. It had to be. Alison was starting the second half of her life. She would live it with a beautiful vengeance. Yes! And it would be so simple.

She went to the bathroom. She turned on the light. She ran the faucet 'til the water turned icy. So simple. Yes! Alison splashed her face, the back of her neck. So simple—a breeze lifting a leaf, a sunrise, a bird flying. Could it really be so simple? Yes! She'd have to wake up early. She'd have to be ready before dawn every morning. It could be a long wait. But it would be so simple and worth it. Yes! Yes!

She would open her heart again. She would love. She would save a baby.

~ 21 ~

WANDA

March 29, 2019

I RUB MY EYES TO make sure I'm here at Denny's and not watchin' a story on the back of my eyelids.

You eat four eggs over easy, six pieces crispy bacon, four pieces sourdough toast smothered in butter, roasted potatoes, and drink a whole two pots of black coffee.

"Thank you for comin' to meet me when I got off the bus," you tell me with the golden sun shining on your face, makes it impossible for me to turn away. "I prayed deep and long that you would."

"Travis," I say.

You excuse yourself and walk to the men's room to wash your face and brush your teeth. I hug myself to give me the strength to get up and go, but my skin feels like velvet when I'm near you. So I wait. You come back, take a deep breath and speak, starin' straight at me, no glancin' away, no sly smilin', no side twitchin'.

"Your momma said you'd come," you say.

I was right about the beard. It's gone.

"She couldn't know," feelin' my cheeks get red hot. "'Cuz I only talked to her yesterday, and you already left the day before."

"She knew. She loves you, Wanda. So do I. You know that, or you wouldn't be here now, so beautiful in front of me, waitin' to hear my regrets 'bout the mistakes I committed on you—"

"Travis," I try again. "It's too late."

I wish your name was Owen, or Warren, or Hugh. How'd God know that Travis is my favorite all-time boy's name?

"Just hear me out, and then I swear I'll do whatever you want," you tell me.

I sit back, pretendin' to be a tree trunk rooted to the ground. The plates are still on the table. A fly's cleanin' its wings on what's left of some egg yolk. You flick it to the ground.

"I came all this way, Wanda. Can you please do that for me?"

I nod 'cuz I don't know what to say. Your hair is longer, like how I always said it looked good on you. 'Cuz if you was gonna sing like Elvis or Johnnie Cash, you should kinda look like a rockabilly too. Your cheek has an eyelash on it. I want to brush it away, but I know I can't touch you. Even though I want to.

"I'm so sorry, babe."

I can see that you haven't slept much. The whites of your eyes are red from medicine and worry. You know I'm starin' at your fine-lookin' face. You let me a few seconds longer.

"What I did to you was wrong. I was drunk. I was crazy evil, and it was Satan who was cursin' through my body." You take a sip of your coffee. My skin feels itchy all of a sudden. "I swear to you, I'm so, so sorry, Wanda. I'm a God-fearin' man, and Pastor Higgins said it's when I'm under the influence of alcohol that I give over to the dark side."

The sun hits your eyes and makes them look like slick glass.

"I was deceived by the devil. But that's not me anymore 'cuz I haven't drunk since what happened, and I give you my word on our baby's life I ain't drinkin' no more, so help me God."

A big truck rumbles down Sunset Boulevard soundin' like thunder in the clouds. I hear a little boy cryin'. He wants dessert. My baby kicks.

"I know it's hard for you to believe me 'cuz I've been actin' this way since you met me. But you know I'm strong-willed, so if I say my drinkin's over, it's over—"

"That's not true, Travis."

I hear your heart pound like you're a bad dog caught tearin' up a pillow. I can hear mine too. It's racin' in my temples, then darts back down into my chest, then shoots up to behind my eyes, and I pray I don't start cryin'.

"Pastor Higgins said you'd doubt me," you frown. "He said you'd have every right in the world to do so."

If I could push farther back against the seat, I would, but my stomach's takin' up all the space between me and the table. I just don't want you to hit me.

"You promised me before," I tell you. My voice sounds stronger than I feel. "You believe you're gonna quit, and I believe you when you say you will." I look down so I can think some more what to say. The fly is twitchin' on the carpet. I squash it with my shoe, take it out of its misery. "But you didn't before, so why should I believe you now?"

You pour yourself another cup of coffee. You put in two sugars and top it with three of those plastic creamers. I taste my tea. It's cold. My toes scratch across the floor as I slip my feet outta my shoes. I wish I'd put purple nail polish on 'em.

"You want more hot water, babe?"

The sun's just startin' to think about where it's gonna spend the night. There are little lamps with gold shades on each of the tables. They're off for now, but they'll be on soon. I hear people talkin' 'round me, but my eyes are stuck on you. You're lookin' away.

"Hey, Miss, could we get some service here?" you ask a dark-haired girl. She's wearin' a cross that looks like it's made of tiny rubies. Probably just glass. DELPHINA, her nametag says. That's Ricardo's grandmother's name. I feel guilty, like I'm cheatin' on you with him though we ain't done nothin'. I remind myself you tried to carve your name on my neck with the sharp edge of a knife.

"Where're you from?" I ask. "Your name is so pretty."

"Mexico," she answers, a little afraid she might get caught.

"Tequila?" I ask.

"That's not a place, Wanda!" you laugh, spittin' out your coffee. "That's an alcohol."

Delphina glances over at you, then says to me, "No, I'm not from Tequila, but I been there." She picks up an empty plate. "It's a nice place. I'm from Santa Cruz. You been?"

"No, she hasn't," you answer for me.

She gets all stiff and pours more coffee and spills some on your pants.

"What the fuck!" You stand and shake your leg like a dog.

"I'm so sorry," she says, grabbin' napkins and givin' 'em to you 'cuz she doesn't wanna touch you there.

"Get her some hot water, and you better be careful!"

She pours slower than I've ever seen anybody pour. I smell her fear even when she walks away.

"Stupid Mexican," you say under your breath. You reach for

my hand. "Wanda, I'm talkin' to you from my soul. You gotta listen from your soul."

"That's what I'm doin, Travis."

You get up and come sit down beside me in the booth. I try to move away, but you hold my hand, so I stop.

"Then will you forgive me?" you ask, and I'm wondering if Grace will have your blue eyes.

"I'm not the only one you need to ask."

Your touch is gentle, different. You put your fingers on my stomach. I stand up, but you pull me down and say real quiet, lookin' directly at her through my skin.

"I promise to be the kind of father I know is in me to be, sweet daughter."

"Her name's Grace," I say.

You move my face so it's right in front of yours. You wait 'til I'm lookin' at you straight on. I'm holdin' my breath 'cuz I don't know if you're gonna headbutt me or not.

"Grace is a beautiful name," you say. "Real beautiful."

My body goes soft like love's meltin' my insides. I can see you washed your insides of all the poison you blame. Your eyes are like the Pacific Ocean. I went one day, you know. I got on a bus on Santa Monica Boulevard and rode all the way to the coast. I walked in a tunnel under the highway. When I got out, I'd never seen anythin' so alive before. With all the sand under my feet and the seagulls above my head, I thought I was in one of those paintings with Jesus and the saints. Illuminated by the Holy Spirit. Like I could walk on water just as He did. So I tried, and I think maybe I did. But maybe it was the Saints holdin' me up.

"Wanda, I love you. I've always loved you, and I'm never not gonna love you."

You kiss me like we're seventeen again, and I swear the music in the restaurant is "Ring of Fire," and I'm disappearin' into you. Delphina comes back and asks if there's anythin' else she can get us. You're real nice to her this time. You smile and say she's the best waitress you've ever had in Hollywood.

"I didn't charge you for the drinks," she says, puttin' down the check.

"You don't have to do that," I say.

She clears the table. I watch her run over to a busboy and give him the dirty plates. You put three twenty-dollar bills on the table and get up.

"Matthew 6:14-15: For if you forgive other people when they sin against you, your heavenly Father will also forgive you," you recite like you been practicin' every day. "But if you do not forgive others their sins, your Father will not forgive your sins."

You place a folded piece of paper on the table and head out the door. Delphina comes back to collect the bill.

"He your boyfriend?" she asks.

She's waitin' for me to say no 'cuz she wants to tell me 'bout someone who treated her bad, 'bout her mother and why they had to leave Mexico, 'bout all the secrets only girls like us share.

"Husband," I say, pickin' up the paper. Motel 6 is printed on it in thick, black letters like you're still in second grade. Then the numbers 134.

I run down the street 'til I catch up. You hold me so tight we both can't breathe. Then you take my hand, and we walk to your room.

Your tongue is like a serpent's. My troubles melt off me as you enter my body with a gentleness that's strange and new.

"You OK? Is the baby OK? Does this hurt? Does it feel good? Should I keep on doin' this?" you ask.

I moan "yes, yes, yes" because I'm back in your heaven. Hair falls across your eyes just like His. I'm thirteen again touchin' myself as I look at the body on the cross on the wall of my bedroom. My fingers pretend to be His fingers. My sheets tangle up as a sound I've never heard before cries outta me. My body isn't mine. It's His. I will marry Him one day, I think, as dancin' currents overtake me, and I hang above a stream in midair, a quiverin' feather held up by invisible breezes. I float 'til I drop into the water and sink, down, down into the undercurrent of blue.

Momma finds me in the mornin' and tells everyone at breakfast I'm a nasty slut with the Son of God. I leave the table and take a shower so hot I dissolve into nothin'. But I can't stop. I don't want to. Jesus is my lover. Until I meet you. And then I'm saved all over again. Sweat and spit and you drenchin' all over me, pushin' me under the surface of God's river. I'm born again. Baptized by you.

And now, in room 134, you love me up so much we both cry out our Lord's name.

"If Jesus could forgive his crucifiers, I guess I can forgive you," I whisper, tears fallin' down my face.

"Thattagirl, Wanda. You got your senses back," you say, pourin' me some coke from a can. "Here."

"No," I tell you. "It's bad for the baby."

"Yeah, right. Sorry," you say. The ceilin' fan goes round and round, remindin' me of somethin' I can't place. "Want some water?"

"That'll be nice."

You come out the bathroom with a couple of glasses. "Water here's murky, not like in Mobile."

"You let it run a bit?" I sip mine. "Tastes funny."

"Tastes fine to me," you say, gulpin' some of your own.

So I drink mine down.

"You mind, Wanda?" You light a cigarette and stand near the window. It's locked shut so you exhale smoke into the thick, gold curtains.

"The baby," I answer.

"I'll quit again, I swear. When we get back home."

This is the first time you mention the future with me in it. You're naked in the first light of this night. Michelangelo would draw you. Your body is fresh scars made by me, red and mad as hell. Swollen stitches in your stomach where the blade went in. Burn marks on your back eruptin' over winged crosses and Jesus forgivin'. I see the cuts, the kicks. I hear the screams, the flames. It's Momma and Pastor Higgins and all the softness I'm feelin' blasts outta me like bullets from a machine gun. I sit up and wrap myself in the wet sheet. You crush the cigarette out against the wall.

"Travis, maybe this wasn't a good idea."

"Got you a present," you say, comin' close to me, touchin' my arm.

"Those hoop earrings we seen at Springdale Mall?"

"No, somethin' better."

Like a bouquet of flowers from a magician's sleeve, a red velvet dress comes outta your bag. It's wrinkled, but it looks like it's supposed to be that way.

"It's beautiful."

"I wanna see you in it." You hold out your hand to me. "Come on. Let's get washed up."

You lead me to the bathroom. You step into the shower. I join you. Even with my belly, our bodies are an easy fit. Water rushes down. Steam rises up. It slithers into my nose and slips down my lungs. My head clouds up like it's gonna rain in my brain.

"Travis," I say. "I feel..."

I think I'm gonna pass out. You hold me tight like you're expectin' me to. I'm travelin' down somewhere into some murkiness I can't explain. The only thing I feel is Grace kickin'. But it's too late. I gaze into your blueness, but I don't see Jesus smilin'. I see Satan laughin', 'cuz the joke's on me.

∞

Blazin' face. Movin' fast. Lyin' down. Blanket over me. Looks familiar. Long green and yellow lines try to make a shape of curls, but don't do anythin' that looks like somethin' real. Smells like it's been washed a million times but is still filthy from all the people who've slept on it. Room 134.

I'm in the backseat of a car I don't know. The radio's playin' a song I don't recognize. I sit up real slow, and the heaviness behind my eyes gets worse. I look out. Brown hills. Dead grass. No clouds. Sun comin' up. The back of your head is handsome. You're king with one arm out the window and the other on the wheel. You're singin' with the radio. I wonder why you're so happy.

"Well, good mornin', babe," soundin' cool as a cucumber. "I thought you'd never wake up."

"Where are we?" I ask.

"Just past San Bernardino."

I look out the window, but the mornin' sun's so harsh bright it blinds my eyes.

"Where?"

"Near Palm Springs."

I heard of that place. That's that place in the desert, with the windmills.

"Why're we here?"

"We're goin' home."

I sit up straighter. My mouth is sticky. I wanna pee.

"You never asked."

"How could I? You've been out cold."

I move so I got my feet on the floor of the car. My head feels fat and wants to fall off my neck. I look at my watch. It says it's just past six in the mornin'.

"What happened to the night?" There's a gnawin' under my skull pullin' tentacles from the inside of my face. "You put somethin' in that water, Travis? Some kinda sleepin' pill?"

"Wanda, what kinda man you take me for?" You start laughin', like you think this is real funny, like you're watchin' wrestlin' with my daddy, and some guy gets thrown over the ropes and lands in the audience.

"If I didn't wake up, then why didn't you drive me to a hospital?"

"Cuz you're a wanted criminal, remember?"

I put my hand on my stomach. It's soft. She's sleepin'.

"What would I say when they ask for your ID? Oh, gee officer, she's my wife who burnt down our trailer and tried to kill me. Here are the wounds to prove it."

I look at my body, and I'm wearin' the wrinkled red velvet dress. It's the color of cut tomatoes.

"Weren't you afraid somethin' was wrong for the baby?"

"I called your momma, and she said to get you in a car real quick," you shrug, "so that's what I did."

My arms are tinglin'. I wanna throw up. You couldn't've put somethin' into the water I drank 'cuz then you'd be puttin' somethin' into Grace too. Only someone evil would do that.

"Why'd you call her?" I ask.

"She's your momma. She wants you to be safe from them crazies in Hollywood. Jeez, Wanda, I've never seen so many homeless in all my life. I couldn't let that happen to you. I'm takin' you back so we can look after you 'til the baby comes."

It's quiet 'cept for a small plane flyin' close overhead. It's a desert quiet that feels unnatural and wrong.

"And then what?" I ask.

"What do you mean, 'and then what?'"

"'til the baby comes," I repeat. "Then what?"

You glare at me from the rearview mirror, look at me like I'm somethin' you want to throw in the dump.

"What you did to me was bad," you say. "Criminal bad. You gotta ask for forgiveness."

Gone is your sweetness, your lovin' kindness from yesterday, your gentle touch. Your voice is changed. If it was a hammer, it would hit me on top of my head.

"And how will I do that?" I ask.

You turn off the radio and say, "Start prayin' for your life."

You pull off the highway into a parking lot of another Denny's.

"I'm hungry. You hungry, Wanda?"

My yellow bag is in the front. You've gone through it. The cards Nurse Trisha gave me are lyin' beside you. You unbuckle your seat belt and hold them up.

"What's these?" you ask like I'm on trial, and they're evidence that's gonna send me to the electric chair.

"A nurse gave 'em to me when I was worried that Grace stopped movin'." I answer. "It's what they do. Don't mean nothin'."

"Adoption agencies?" you shout and whip back 'round so fast you're like Quicksilver. You grab my hair and pull my face an inch away from yours.

"You're lucky I didn't kill you, Wanda." I can smell the beer you been drinkin'. "Your momma and me both agree on that, 'cuz I coulda and I shoulda. So if you ever give her away, I'll go to every place I can find and get her back. I swear on her life and every breath that's in me. She's my daughter, and no one's gonna have her but me. You understand?"

And then it's like I'm watchin' the movie of me, and I already know the endin' 'cuz now I realize what you did, Travis. What you and Momma did to trap me into givin' you Grace. You never talked to Pastor Higgins. Never went to AA. You're the devil, and Momma is your accomplice. She probably gave you the sleepin' pills to put in my water.

My hair rips off in your fingers.

"Stop it!" I scream. "You're hurtin' me!"

"Shut up, Wanda! You belong in an insane asylum with how you talk to Jesus and see things. You think I don't know, but I do. Everyone does. So you better act real calm and get out of the car like everythin's fine. Say yes or I'll break your neck right after I cut her outta you."

You move my head up and down like I'm a puppet.

"Yes," I say.

"That's a good girl. We'll get somethin' to eat and then go back to our lives. And if you behave and go to church things'll be okay. If not, all I gotta do is change my story about what happened and tell God's honest truth, and you'll be in prison for the rest of your life. See, I told the authorities I was drunk, that I fell on my knife and my cigarettes burnt the place down. I didn't tell 'em you gutted me and set fire to the trailer. So as long as you're with me, you're safe. But as soon as you're not, you're fucked. Understand? Fucked big time."

I wish there was still music playin' on the radio so I could hear only that and not the screamin' in my head 'bout how you're gonna slice me open and leave me by the side of the road while you got Grace wrapped up in the bloody Motel 6 blanket.

"So you're not gonna do anythin' stupid, are you?" you ask.

You move my head sideways.

"No," I answer.

"Good little bitch."

I get out of the car, and we go into the restaurant like a happy couple expectin' their first child. You let me go to the bathroom, but you wait outside the door. I have the shits, and I'm shakin' like Jello. I wash my face. I come back out, and we sit down at a table.

You order pancakes, and I eat scrambled eggs and sourdough toast. You talk 'bout how good the garage is doin', that I should paint the back wall with mustang horses 'cuz that would be cool, and we'd get more customers, that maybe you gotta hire Harvey Nash 'cuz he's outta work, and you could use another mechanic, and he was in the car club at school.

"You remember Harvey Nash?" you ask me like everythin's normal, and you didn't put sleepin' pills in my water last night and kidnap me this mornin'.

You get a coffee for the road and ask me if I want anythin'.

"I'm fine," I say. "Thank you."

You pay. We go outside to the parkin' lot. There are so many cars goin' both ways on the highway, they look like the same ants runnin' away from each other over and over again. I know like I've never known anythin' clearer in my life. If I don't do somethin' right now, I might as well just give up and die. So I do what you told me to do, Travis. I start prayin' for my life.

I look up into the empty sky and ask our Holy Father to take my hand, and He does, and We run as fast as I can and climb over the middle divider with the cars and trucks beepin' and swervin' like the Red Sea, and We're the Israelites escapin' over four lanes of traffic. You come after me, but a whole bunch of RVs in a row stop you, maybe ten of 'em. Your face is so red from the desert sun I think you might blow up.

But I'm already on the other side with my thumb out. A car slows down and stops. I climb right in. We move away from you, slow at first but then faster and faster 'til you're a burnin' dot, disappearin' into the punishin' sun.

"I'm gonna get you if it's the last thing I do!" Your screams find me. "Don't fuck with me, Wanda! Don't you fuck with me!"

I start laughin'.

"What's so funny?" the lady driver asks.

"Just somethin' I'm thinkin'," I answer.

I'm thinkin' me and Grace are safe. Then I stop laughin'. I must really be crazy to think that we'll ever be safe. From you.

~ 22 ~

TRISHA

Monday, May 14, 2018

Oɴ Mᴏɴᴅᴀʏ, ᴀꜰᴛᴇʀ ᴛʜᴇ ꜱᴘᴇʀᴍ party, Trisha hadn't gone to work. She left the house at the usual time, but she called in sick and parked her car a few blocks from the house instead. She walked to Mom's Donuts and Chinese Food To Go on Silver Lake Boulevard. She knew Erika would never eat there. She inhaled a sugar donut and drank a large coffee—no herbal tea today. She was going to walk and run and think and indulge and figure it out, or she wouldn't come back.

Trisha jogged east on Silver Lake Boulevard. It was an open street, flat and ugly, save for the palm trees that punctuated the cloudless sky. She remembered the first time she saw them. Her taxi from the airport was going north on Lincoln Boulevard, and there they were, surprises out of a magician's hat—so tall, so cool, so unmistakably Californian. Palm trees were transplants, like her. They were portable with short roots and required a simple diet of water and sunshine. And love. That's all she needed too. Would there be any left once the baby came? She felt ashamed, but the question was in her head, and it needed to get out.

She popped into a secondhand clothing store and bought a blue baseball cap with the Hollywood sign embroidered in sparkling rainbow threads. She would always be a tourist in this city. Spring in Los Angeles didn't really exist because winter wasn't cold, dark, or barren enough. The never-changing, unmarked passage of time set her body on a slow simmering restlessness. In Toronto, the middle of May was when buds sprang forward like green warriors slashing through the remnants of winter. It was her favorite month.

Here in this desert city, it was the opposite. The predictability of the blue sky was wearisome. There was no sense of variation, no sense of ending in order to begin again. She was tired of it, even though she'd only lived in L.A. for eleven months.

Trisha needed a bathroom. She stopped at Tierra Mia on Alvarado Street. She liked the simple chairs and tables, the framed photographs of coffee farmers. She liked the latte art, so she decided to buy a cappuccino with two foaming hearts on top. She bought a bottle of water. Fuck it, she thought. She bought a chocolate brownie.

When she left the café, she noticed an old building across the street. It had a pink door. *SEÑOR GABRIEL: RESPUESTAS*, said the sign above it. There was a painting of an open hand below the words, a purple crystal in its palm. And under that, ANSWERS.

She looked in her purse for her lucky bottle cap, but it wasn't there. The last time she saw it was Saturday afternoon, just before the sperm party, when she'd dropped it into her skirt pocket. She wanted to feel a connection to luck. Instead, she felt abandoned. She pulled her thoughts together. She knew what she wanted to ask.

Was love enough? She needed an answer.

Trisha crossed Alvarado and rang the bell. She was led into a small room by a woman who nodded and pointed to a closed blue door. Trisha opened it and walked into an even smaller room. An old man in a cracked leather chair gazed at Trisha over blue reading glasses. He wore a long blue robe, his hair white bristles, shaved like a monk's.

"English?" Señor Gabriel asked, lighting a purple candle. "Or Spanish?'

His fingernails were short and painted dark green. Beaded necklaces hung around his neck, laden with stone animal carvings. Two sets of silver hoop earrings dangled from each lobe. A cigar protruded from his hand like a sixth finger. He gave it a puff, let the embers fall into a marble ashtray on the card table, then put it out.

"English, *por favor*," she answered.

She thought she was being funny, but obviously he didn't. He didn't bat an eye.

"Ten dollars, please."

She pulled out two fives and placed them on the table. He swished small, pale shells in a straw tray, chanting something that sounded like Spanish, but not really. Reaching out his hand, Trisha placed hers in it, palm-up. His moustache reminded her of her father's. It curved around his top lip and ended in an upward thrust, like it was smiling even when his mouth wasn't.

Still holding her hand, Señor Gabriel stared down at the shells. It must've been at least two full minutes. He moved a few around, studying them like he was searching for the essential piece to some arcane puzzle. Then he looked into her eyes, drilling deeper, as if she held that special piece in the back of her skull.

And then, it all hit her at once—the pressure from Erika,

Charles, the Prosecco, the flirting with Clifton, the crazy fantasies with Johnnie Baloney, her parents' distant form of love, the spider dreams, the insanity of making acting a career, the fear of being like her parents...

"I'm—so—sorry, sir," she sobbed, "I'm kind of—lost."

Señor Gabriel tucked a bright purple shell from his pocket into Trisha's palm. "Belief is the most difficult thing you can ask of a person. That is why it is so important." He placed his hands on hers. "*De lo divino*," he said.

"I don't understand..."

"From the divine..." He pressed her hands together.

The purple shell felt warm and sparkly between her palms.

Señor Gabriel got up and moved across to Trisha's side of the table. His hand touched her between her breasts, not sexual, but a gesture of protection. Then he tilted his head, as if to catch the answer falling into his ear.

"A baby will come." His necklaces reflected light from the sun stealing in. "*Un regalo de Dios*. A special baby."

Trisha smiled. "*Gracias*."

"*Buena madre*," he took the money and headed for the door.

"But I have more questions."

"*Buena madre*," he turned back to her before he left. "Good mother. *Buena madre*."

When she got home, Trisha placed the purple shell in the little ivory box where she kept her lucky bottle cap, but it wasn't there either. She'd have to find it. She'd walk through every inch of the house until she did. But not tonight. Tonight, she was too exhausted, too exhilarated, too expectant. She took a bath and went to sleep.

~ 23 ~

ALISON

July 16, 2018

Bᴇꜰᴏʀᴇ ᴛʜᴇ ꜰʟᴀᴛ ᴛɪʀᴇ ᴀɴᴅ the fire station, Alison was idling at mid-life, waiting for a signal to guide her forward into her future. Since that Saturday evening, she set her clock for 4:00 a.m. every morning. With renewed vigor, she raised herself out of bed and onto the orange yoga mat, stretched, and did her sit-ups. She put on dark sweats and running shoes and made a thermos full of her favorite coffee, Blue Mountain. Then she'd drive to Sunset and Gretna Green Way. There was an empty lot to the right of the fire station. She parked her car there. She'd always loved the light green color of her car, but these mornings she wished it were black, so she could disappear into the darkness. Waiting there gave her an unobstructed view to the entrance of the fire station. She could see if anyone came or went.

At 4:30 a.m., nobody was in the front office. Even the firemen were asleep. Alison checked to see if there were cameras, but she couldn't be sure there weren't any hidden. Sometimes she'd get out and sneak around the perimeter of the station's grounds like a security guard checking for intruders. She'd be able to see when a girl came to the front door, ring the bell, and leave a baby.

Alison thought about it a lot. She presumed the girl would determine that the best time would be the hour just before dawn. It held the perfect blend of despair and possibility. She wouldn't arrive any earlier in case everyone was still asleep. Then no one would come to the front door. If she came later, there'd be too much light to go undetected. Alison assumed the mother didn't want to be seen. She remembered her own fears thirty years ago, leaving the Women's Free Clinic. Alison would pick up the baby as quickly as she could and hit the road. She didn't want to be seen either.

Alison's parents believed that each person had only so much happiness allotted to them. It was handed out at birth, then used up in small denominations at celebrations and holidays. Some people got more. Some people got less. You didn't waste your portion, because when it was gone, that was it, it was gone forever. Alison didn't want to believe this. She chose a spiritual path where you could create your own happiness. But when she abandoned Jesse and when her family died, she felt that perhaps her parents' doctrine was true.

She was unhappy in her two marriages. The men were interesting, handsome and artistic. Emanuel was a classical musician. Alison was thirty in 1998 and still mourning her parents when they met. She hoped their union would be a healing harmony of Ludwig van Beethoven and Mick Jagger. She was wrong. Emanuel hated The Rolling Stones.

Lior was an artist from Israel who had relocated to Los Angeles in 2008. He was working with the assemblage sculptor, Chris

Burden, on the Los Angeles County Museum's restored streetlamps installation. She was forty when they'd met at Cloverfield Park, running the circuit at the same time but in opposite directions. Whenever they got near the fence by Santa Monica Airport, they'd smile at each other. When their paths crossed again near the kids' playground, they laughed with each other. After the third cycle, they stopped, and without skipping a beat, walked across the street to Zabie's Café, drank coffee, chatted for an hour about favorite authors, and then jogged the six blocks back to her place. She made BLTs and chocolate ice cream crêpes, and they laughed a lot watching Tina Fey host *Saturday Night Live*. Lior stayed over. The lovemaking was good. On Sunday morning, he took her to brunch at The Rose Café in Venice.

Finally, thought Alison. Someone I can easily connect with and maybe even love.

A couple of months into their relationship, Alison wondered if it was time to get married again. She felt happy enough. And maybe that in itself was enough. So they married at Santa Monica City Hall with Suzy and Tumaini as her guests and a couple of visiting Israeli army buddies as his. A few years later, she ended the marriage because her feelings for him paled in comparison to the ones she still had for Jesse.

Alison understood that her fear of being vulnerable was the reason she rationed out her happiness, a nibble at a time. She only gave the minimum required, so if it didn't work out, the loss wouldn't be as devastating as when she was twenty. But now being fifty, she knew that if she held back in any way, it would be like dying alongside her parents. She didn't want their legacy to be death. She wanted their legacy to be life.

This next bite of happiness would be bigger. Much bigger. This was what all the signs were about—all the divine messages she was experiencing. Alison wanted to live the life she was meant to live.

She would swoop the infant into her arms, steal it away from its future foster homes. She would take it out of California and head south. She would create a wild and precious life for them both.

~ 24 ~

WANDA

March 30, 2019

Ricardo doesn't say anythin' when he sees me.

He wants to. I can tell. I was missin' for over twenty-four hours. But he doesn't. He just comes in and stares at me sittin' there on the sofa, watchin' *Judge Judy*. I get up slow as possible. I lift my hands to my face 'cuz I'm ready for anythin'. He walks over. I shrink back, unsure what he's gonna do.

"I was just—"

He hugs me so close I think he's gonna squish us.

"Sit down at the table, Angel, I got some soup for you," he says. "Chicken and rice. You'll like it, it's got vitamins. It'll be good for you and the baby."

So I do. I don't tell him about you, but he knows somethin's up when I come out the bathroom later with hair fire truck red. I gotta go into hidin' for real now, 'cuz I believe you when you say you'll take Grace and kill me. I hand Ricardo the scissors I stole from Rite

Aid, and like a condemned man, he cuts my hair.

"You look so different," he tells me.

"Shorter," I say. "Like Ziggy Stardust."

When I look in the mirror, Wanda's gone. He steps closer and whispers somethin' I don't understand, clasps a silver chain 'round my neck with a small red rock hangin' in the front. It's the color of sunset.

"The stone is from my city. If you want to be safe, you should go to Tequila. My family will protect you. Don't forget the Lopez Cafe."

"I never thought of goin' to Mexico," I say. "But thank you all the same."

I take it off and dangle the necklace over my stomach like I heard you're supposed to. It starts movin' side to side, unsure at first, then whooshes 'round like a record. It makes me think of the collection you had next to the TV. You could care less 'bout me, but you sure kept those old forty-fives clean. They're all melted now, like that clock you laughed at in my art book.

The baby kicks. She's rememberin' them too. She's inside me, after all. She can't see what I see, but I know she feels what I'm thinkin'. My appetite's gone, and she's lettin' me know I gotta eat, even if the memory of you cuts like razor blades.

Grace'll be here middle of April. I gotta start makin' plans. I gotta find a doctor. I gotta find a job. I gotta find a new place to stay. I gotta stop cryin' in the middle of the night when the whole world is asleep but me and you.

You used to wake me and want to watch TV. Remember?

"I'm sleepin'," I'd tell you.

"Then wake up," you'd say, "and make me somethin' to eat."

It wasn't 'til I watched one of 'em cop shows that I saw what to do. I crushed a couple Benadryl into your beer, and you slept like a baby. You never figured it out.

But you got it figured out now, don't you? You can sense I'm thinkin' 'bout the same things you're thinkin' 'bout, like we're still connected by that electric sex, electric hate. Yeah, you got it figured out. You drugged me and tried to take me back, and that didn't work so you're polishin' your knife, askin' around, so sure you're gonna find me. Gonna find her.

Grace jumps so wild in me I almost fall over.

"Ricardo," I call out. "I'm so sorry."

But he's gone to work the dinner shift, cookin' love into everythin' he makes. I wish I could take a picture of him or draw one from memory. I used to be pretty good. Even you said so. I tear out the last page in his bible and find a pencil near the phone. I close my eyes and see him. His short black hair kinda stands straight up. I like to rub my hand on it. It tickles my skin like a paintbrush. His eyes are so dark the iris blends into the pupil. His lips are full. His smile is kind. His face is the face of his people, like in cowboy movies. It takes me a half hour. I shade it like the Rembrandt light I saw on his face. I fold the paper and put it in my wallet beside the picture of Grace's ultrasound.

I sit down on the bed and do those deep breaths I read about. I let the air warm my throat and reach down to her. I hold it in, makin' sure she's surrounded, then I breathe out. I do it three times, like I'm supposed to, but I better do it four. I think Jesus let go of my hand somewhere, or maybe I let go of His. So I gotta do everythin' I can.

I look to the mirror. Our Lady of Guadalupe gazes back at me, wearin' her shawl in green and gold, like the picture on Ricardo's wall but with Ziggy Stardust's hair and his mark of lightnin' on her face.

"¡Proteja al bebé!" she says. I don't speak Spanish, but I know she's tellin' me to keep Grace safe. So I put the red rock necklace back on. I take one of Ricardo's hoodies and steal the cash from his hidin' spot inside those fancy cowboy boots. There's 800 dollars in his left and 400 in his right. I leave him 200 and a note.

> Dear Ricardo,
> You're the kindest man I ever met. I promise I will pay you back.
> Angel

I search through my bag for a place to put a steak knife, just in case—and that's when I know Ricardo knows. I find a thermos of orange juice tucked in the bottom, along with two near-ripe avocados and three burritos wrapped tight with Saran Wrap and aluminum foil. He covered them up with one of his white, embroidered shirts. Maybe he doesn't know everything, but he sure knows enough.

~ 25 ~

TRISHA

June 1, 2018

"CAPTAIN COMPASSION?" TRISHA READ OUT loud. "Who names these guys?" They sat side by side at Erika's desk in the second bedroom that pretended to be an office, scrolling through sperm donor profiles.

"Probably some lab assistant who interviewed them." Erika kissed her partner on the cheek. "I wonder how many children have been born to these lab assistants. If I worked there, I'd pick my favorite guy and impregnate myself—if I could get pregnant, that is."

Erika passed the popcorn to Trisha. It wasn't unlike watching a movie. Every night now for a week, they'd go combing the internet for sperm donors from all over the world and read up on prospective candidates.

"Hey, maybe you can get a job at a clinic," laughed Erika, bumping Trisha's shoulder with her own. "Anonymous—but not quite."

"Okay, Captain Compassion. Let's see what you're about." Trisha cleared her throat. "Donor A-1974-16 is hardworking. He went back to school to pursue his dream of becoming a doctor. He was a humanitarian aid worker," read Trisha. "He plays hockey, soccer, and chess. He likes to cook vegan, and his life's ambition is to one day have a large family. Height is five feet nine inches, and ethnic origin is Chinese." She turned to Erika. "We like? We don't?"

Erika shrugged and grabbed a handful of popcorn. "He's a little on the short side."

"I think five foot nine is fine," Trisha said.

"No way, he's gotta be at least five foot ten," Erika frowned, ready to move on. "Besides, Captain Compassion's probably lying. Men always lie about their height on these things. He's five foot six on a good day, guaranteed."

Trisha laughed in spite of herself, but she could feel her body tense up. "They can't lie on these sites, or they'll get sued." She stretched her legs, releasing the stiffness that was creeping in. "They take tons of tests and go through intense screenings. They literally measure them and weigh them. He's five foot nine for sure."

"But I want our kid to look like us. My whole family is tall."

"Is height really that important to you?" Trisha got up and paced around the room. "This donor is a vegan humanitarian with a medical degree, for God's sake."

"Let's put him in the maybe pile," Erika relented. "My favorite is still 'Green-Eyed Optimist.' Let's read his bio again."

"You have a crush on him," said Trisha.

Erika blushed. Her partner was right. She'd never had a crush on a guy 'til now, if it was possible to have a crush on a file number.

Trisha pulled out the stack of stapled papers from the top drawer. There was a picture of donor C-1974-18, Green-Eyed Optimist, when he was five years old. He had a space between his two front teeth, kind of like Johnnie Baloney. He had blond, wavy hair and freckles. He looked like the kind of kid who lived next door and always said hi.

"Want more?" Erika asked, as she detached herself from the computer.

"No, I'm popcorned-out," Trisha sighed.

Erika went to the kitchen to refill the bowl. Trisha stood still in the middle of the room. She closed her eyes. She forced her body to relax. It started to sway like she was on a high wire between two tall buildings.

"OK! We have Green-Eyed Optimist. Let's begin with the most important thing—he's six foot two. That's all you need to know," Trisha shouted. "Let's book his sperm!"

"Come on, read it all," Erika responded. "But wait! I'll be right back."

Trisha could hear her open a bottle of champagne—their Veuve Clicquot and pour two glasses.

"To our baby," Erika toasted, walking back in.

"To our baby," repeated Trisha.

They took generous sips between their giggles.

"OK, ready?" asked Trisha. "Here's your boyfriend. 'Ambitious, creative, and funny, Donor C-1974-18 excels at languages and science. Altruistic, this former scout got over his fear of bees by volunteering at a honey farm for a non-profit organization. This witty and articulate IT specialist is also a ham-radio buff, who loves cooking and sailing. He shares a list of his favorite movies and activities in the 'Get To Know Me Better' section. Positive and empathetic, he enjoys spending time skiing and reading.'" Trisha sat down and crossed her legs. "And he's $995 a vial. What a deal!"

"I don't want to think about what he does to that little cup," Erika grimaced. "Yuck!"

She stepped away from the desk to shut the window, then turned back, grabbed a piece of popcorn, and threw it at Trisha. Trisha caught it in midair and put it into her mouth. They both rushed to the bowl to flick popcorn at each other, eating the pieces that hadn't landed on the floor.

"Just wondering," Erika said, hiding the bowl behind her back, "did you enjoy having sex with men?"

"Hey!" said Trisha, putting Green-Eyed Optimist's information back on the pile. Trisha knew this topic would eventually come up. "Remember, we agreed never to talk about this. And why bring it up now?"

"So, that means you slept with at least one guy after we made that arrangement." Erika grinned.

Trisha rushed off to the kitchen to dump the remaining kernels into the garbage.

"Sorry," Erika leaned against the doorway. "I know we made a promise to each other. But we're together now, going to have a baby, and I'm just curious."

Trisha stood over the garbage, the butter and salt smearing her fingers.

"Do you miss men?"

"You're going to keep asking, aren't you?"

"Yep," Erika kissed the nape of Trisha's neck as she washed the bowl and placed it upside down on the dish rack. It was one of the first things they bought together when they decided to cohabitate—a yellow Fiesta Bowl designated solely for popcorn.

"You think a few good kisses are going to persuade me to tell you?" Trisha teased. "You'll have to work harder than that."

"Then come to bed," Erika pulled her in by her hips. "Let's have a threesome. You, me, and Green-Eyed Optimist. A *ménage à trois*! What do you say?"

Trisha wiped her hands dry and turned. There was salt on Erika's bottom lip. Trisha licked it off. Erika stepped in even closer, and they kissed, long and tender—how they kissed when they first met.

"I say you're a little crazy," Trisha said, "but I like you that way."

Trisha walked into the bathroom. Normally, Erika would come in, and they'd move around the cramped space like cat burglars, artfully inching by each other, reaching sideways for toothbrushes and cotton balls, for face cloths and creams. Tonight, Trisha locked the door. She looked in the mirror. Her reflection stared back—cold and certain. She was on thin ice, and she wanted to keep on skating. She didn't want to fall through a hole and freeze to death.

"I did sleep with a guy," Trisha confessed a few minutes later entering the bedroom. Erika looked up from reading. "Charles from poetry. The dentist. He goes back and forth to Kansas City to care for his parents so he's not here a lot," she said. "He has a dental practice there too, and a wife, so there's nothing to worry about."

Erika creased the corner of the page and closed the book. She sat straight up. "Do I look worried?"

"It was only twice, both times in his car," Trisha continued.

"Car sex?" Erika smiled. "That's pretty hot."

Trisha leaned on the dresser. "I felt like I was sixteen again even though I never did that when I was sixteen. It was fun because I knew I could do it without any repercussion."

"Women?" Erika asked, placing the book on her night table.

"Women?" Trisha echoed.

"Did you sleep with women too?" she asked, pulling the covers up over her legs. It was getting colder. She was wearing dark gray flannel pajamas. The house was chilly. Rain was in the forecast. "Or was it just one guy? Twice?"

"I'm not saying another word. Ever." Trisha got into bed. "We agreed never to talk about it, remember?"

"So that's a yes." Erika slid under the covers. "Good, you had me worried for a minute. And now you've gotten it all out of your system. See? The "catch-up arrangement" always works."

"'Always works'?" Trisha looked surprised. "Do you suggest it to all your girlfriends?"

"We agreed not to talk about it, remember?" Erika curled into herself.

Trisha's stomach felt queasy. She didn't like being tricked. She set her alarm for 6:00 a.m. She'd go for a run in the morning. Even if it were going to rain, she'd go. She liked being out at dawn. There was only one other runner at that time, a Black guy in a baby blue tracksuit, maybe fifty years old, who greeted her with a nod. She nodded back. It was a positive start to her day. She massaged moisturizer onto her hands. She'd need to stay in shape for the pregnancy. She was going to be a mother. And keep on acting. Erika chose her. She was winning. It felt good. She turned out the light.

"Does Charles' wife know?"

"Excuse me?"

The room was too dark to see, but Trisha knew Erika was looking at her, eyes wide open.

"Think I should tell her that Charles had an affair with you?"

The oxygen in the room vanished. Trisha opened her mouth

to breathe, but nothing filtered into her lungs. Her chest hurt. She prayed for words to come out like rehearsed lines in a play. She was an actress, after all.

"Well, should I?"

"No, why would you do that?" Trisha's voice caught in her throat. "Olivia doesn't need to know about it. It was our "catch-up arrangement." Charles fit into it. It has nothing to do with her."

"You know her name. Sounds like you did more than just have sex."

"What are you doing?" Trisha sat up and turned the light back on.

"We're taking a big step forward, starting a family. Just testing the waters."

"Well, don't."

"Why not?" Erika stretched her long legs. "It's over, isn't it? You and Charles? Or are you two still fucking in the back seat of his car?"

Trisha vaulted out of bed, took her pillow, and went into the living room. She crunched it a few times to get it just right, then set it on the sofa. She lay her head in the middle of it. Her feet slipped under the throw blanket. She closed her eyes. Did Erika know she was still seeing Charles, or was she guessing? Maybe it's what happened with her other girlfriends—they continued their affairs past the "catch-up arrangement's" cutoff date.

"I'm sorry, babe! I was just kidding." Erika walked to the sofa. "Please come back to bed."

"No, I'll sleep out here tonight."

"It's just that in the past, well, it's happened."

"What?"

"Some of my girlfriends kept on hooking up and lying about it."

"Oh." Trisha felt terrible. That's exactly what she was doing.

"Please come to bed," said Erika.

She let Erika put her arm around her and lead her back to the bedroom. She'd break up with him. It was the right thing to do.

"Is Charles a good poet?" Erika asked as she unbuttoned her pajama top.

Trisha couldn't help it. She thought about the backseat of his Ford Explorer, how she was his first bisexual, how he was her first dentist, how much they laughed, how passionate it was for both of them.

"Yeah," Trisha said as she unbuttoned hers. "He's good."

~ 26 ~

ALISON

September 23, 2018

Sᴏᴍᴇᴛɪᴍᴇꜱ ᴀꜰᴛᴇʀ ᴡᴀɪᴛɪɴɢ ᴀᴛ ᴛʜᴇ fire station, Alison would go to the beach. She always had a red notebook, a straw hat, and a towel in the car. Wordsworth said that poetry was "emotion recollected in tranquility." She'd find a quiet spot near the water and write.

But this Sunday morning, she had an impulse to go somewhere else—do something else. So, she drove north on the 405. When she got to Sherman Way East, her car moved of its own free will, a diviner leading her off the freeway backwards through time.

The two-bedroom bungalow on Vesper Avenue in Van Nuys was small and unremarkable. During her childhood, the front door had been painted turquoise and had a little window to spy through. In her mind's eye, she was seventeen again, turning left and walking into the kitchen, with its chrome-legged white-Formica table and chairs. Her mother's embroidered linen tablecloth with a bouquet of wildflowers in the center and a garland of purple bluebells scalloping the edges was spread on the tabletop. The walls and cabinets were buttery yellow. White opaque curtains with fruit appliqué borders graced the two windows above the sink. A calendar from San Fernando Valley Pharmacy, where her father worked, hung on the wall near the Westinghouse refrigerator. Her mother would circle church functions and special school events with a bright, red magic marker. Alison could sniff out the odor of future engagements as soon as she entered her home.

Now the front door was painted gray and smeared with graffiti that straggled across the front brick exterior. The red moniker of a San Fernando Valley gang called "Barrio Van Nuys x3" seeped through.

Alison got out of her car and walked up the path. The little window was concealed with cardboard. The house was boarded up, ready for demolition. She pried the two-by-four wooden slats crisscrossing the entrance and slid into her childhood home. Alison looked up to the ceiling, hoping to see the delicate petal-like green glass chandelier her mother bought at the Rose Bowl Flea Market. It was gone, of course.

Her bedroom had pink-and-yellow daisy wallpaper. There were pictures of Leif Garrett and Shaun Cassidy on the walls, silver stars glued to the ceiling in the shape of the Big Dipper, her clothes always crisply folded in the oak dresser.

Her parents' bedroom was at the end of the hall. The bed was a box spring under a queen-size mattress. White lace pillows and a matching duvet lay neatly on top. The thick wall-to-wall forest-green carpet covered all the floors of the house, except for the kitchen and the bathroom.

Alison sold the house in 1999, two years after their funerals. Now it smelt of piss and marijuana. The walls and floors were thick with time and dereliction. She had come to say her final goodbye. And to make a promise.

She went out to the backyard through a broken screen door. Alison had played on the swings and slide set when she was growing up. Her father pushed her higher and higher until her mother would run out shouting, "Frank! She's going to go flying off and get hurt!" But that never happened.

It was still there, the swing set. Vines swirled through the rusted chains, and moss covered the cracked wooden seats. A squirrel rested on top of the rungs. Alison broke off a piece of a granola bar from her purse.

"Here ya go, Rocky," tossing it to him.

He caught it and vaulted high into the birch tree. Alison looked for the carved heart her father had tattooed into the white bark. She found it, though it was smaller than she remembered. She ran her fingers over the scars, trying to recover his presence.

When she began teaching, the stories her students told her about their lives made hers sound like an episode of *The Waltons*. But when some of them shared that they had lost their fathers and mothers—shot, imprisoned, drowned—that, she could relate to.

Around 2:30 p.m. on a Sunday in March of 1997, Frank and Gloria Bishop were traveling down a side road in Simi Valley, taking their weekend drive. Gloria pointed to a woman lying on the ground beside the road. She had a camera around her neck. The Bishops parked and got out to help. The woman seemed comatose, but her body was quivering like there was still some life in it. Frank Bishop placed his hand on the woman's shoulder—and the same murderous current that struck her dead killed him instantly.

When Alison's parents got out of the car, they didn't realize what had happened any more than the woman did. The woman had pulled over to get a picture of a fallen eucalyptus tree, but as soon as she touched its branches, she got electrocuted. When Frank patted her shoulder, he got electrocuted. When Gloria tried to pull Frank back, she got electrocuted. That mighty eucalyptus brought down a telephone wire with it, surging more than 14,000 volts through all their bodies.

That's what the police told Alison.

"Three Electrocuted Bodies Found"—that's what the *Los Angeles Times* headline read.

How does a child process this kind of death? This inconceivable, horrific, senseless kind of death? The love Alison had for her parents had no bounds. Frank and Gloria Bishop had always been there for her. They were stellar human beings. They were compassionate, God-loving people. Yet being good Samaritans destroyed all their lives.

Alison fell into a deep, existential depression. She was twenty-nine years old. Her friends at teachers' college tried to help. Mrs. VanDusen and Suzy had her stay with them. They became her second family. She joined a grief group.

"Mourning has its own timeline," Dr. Gedal had said. "It binds you to its schedule until it's ready to let you go. And it never fully lets you go, ever."

Someone in the group sighed, someone else cried, and Alison's heart went cold.

"It devastates you with a whiff of your beloved's perfume or a phrase of his favorite song. It surrounds you with reminiscences of regret and longing and makes you do things that aren't necessarily good for you."

Alison met Emanuel, the concert pianist, one Saturday evening, four months into the mourning period. They married soon after and were divorced a year and a half later.

The squirrel jumped off a branch and skipped along the ground. Alison followed it and noticed something glittering in the broken-up earth. She bent down and pulled out a dirt-covered baggie. There was foil inside. Alison unwrapped a five-inch square beechwood box with a tulip engraved on the lid.

My mother's earring box!

It was perfect. No water damage. And it was empty. Nothing inside.

There wasn't a time when Alison couldn't remember it not sitting on her mother's night table—except when she was five and stole it.

"Where's my tulip box?" Her mother rushed into Alison's bedroom, perspiring like she swallowed a whole red pepper. "Do you have it?"

"I took it for my dolls." Alison was scared. She'd never seen her mother behave this way.

"Don't you ever touch it again!" Her mother shook her by the shoulders. "It's not yours. It's mine. Do you understand?"

"Yes," Alison started crying.

"Good," said her mother. "Now give it back!"

That was forty-five years ago. And now here she stood in their old backyard, holding it.

"Why did you bury the box, Mom?" she said out loud.

In 1999, when Alison sold the house and most of its contents, she wondered where this box had gone.

"Mom, Dad, I'm going away." The wooden box felt light in her hand. "I'm going to save a baby, then drive to Mexico and find Jesse. And we'll see what happens." Alison's thumb traced the curve of the tulip. "I'm going to live the life I never lived. I'm going to live it as fully as I can. Hopefully, I'll have twenty to thirty years ahead of me —the same ones you were cheated out of. I promise to appreciate every moment, for you and for me."

Alison watched the leaves of the tree shimmer.

"Why did you bury the box?" she asked again.

Surely there was no way her mother knew that she was going to die so young. And why bury an empty box? What was her mother trying to hide?

Alison slipped the box into her purse. It was meant for her to find. Her mother was watching over her. She would take it with her wherever she went. It was another sign that she was doing the right thing—the fire station, safe haven, a baby, Jesse.

She was doing the right thing.

~ 27 ~

WANDA

March 31, 2019

I WAKE UP TO AN upside-down face starin' at me.

It's an old man face, white beard for a hat, gray cap for a chin. His eyes water like an old dog's, or maybe he's cryin' for all the life that went wrong. Maybe he's cryin' for me, even though he doesn't know my story. Maybe he knows other girls who've slept in this same place.

Momma should be cryin' for me, but she'll never admit it. She says Jesus is her friend, that He'll forgive all her transgressions. She wants you to love her up and down like you did me. I wonder if she's fucked you yet, or maybe you just let her keep on thinkin' she might, so she'd help you bring me back to Mobile.

I sit up. You're just more proof that Jesus is a liar. Maybe it's God who started all the lyin', and his only son learned it from him. I'm runnin' and hidin' to save my baby, and you're out there in the light of day tryin' to kill me. What God would call that right?

"Are you hungry?" the old man asks. He wants to trick me into eatin' so he can call the cops and hand me over.

"I'm goin'," I say, gettin' up real slow. I don't want to wake Grace if she's still asleep.

He watches me movin' like a turtle, lookin' like a bear.

"You want a shower?" he asks.

Now I'm real scared. Is he some pervert who gets off on pregnant girls? I pick up my yellow bag I been usin' as a pillow and walk to the sidewalk. I been sleepin' in an alcove of a red brick buildin'. You don't see too many of those here. It's mostly white clay. This place looked strong, like the smart little pig built it. It reminded me of the big fire station where we used to go on field trips. When I was twelve, I ran away from home, and I went there. A fireman gave me juice and then called Momma. He said he had to. That hour before she came, I never felt so safe in all my life.

"Do you need some help?" the old man asks.

I look at him for the first time—upright, I mean. He looks like he comes from a different country, a different time. Sounds like it too. He's tall like me, which is short for a man. He looks like he's dressed for winter, with a thick jacket and a red plaid scarf wrapped around his neck a buncha times. His cap is like a golfer's 'cept the sides are pulled down over his ears. Is it supposed to be cold? Did it turn to winter overnight? I can tell it's early mornin' from the sun comin' over the buildings, makin' everythin' look flat. Nothin' seems like California on this street.

The old man takes a step towards me.

"I'm goin' mister," I say. "Don't call the police."

"I would never do that." He sits down on the stoop, pulls out an orange and a folded knife from his jacket pocket. He snaps it open and peels one long piece, a curl of sunshine, and rests it in my hands like I'm a little girl and it's a gift.

"Skin's got vitamins," he says. "Smells nice too. Go on, rub it on your hands."

His hands look like they've carried a lot of weight, bulgin' at the veins. His nails are ridged and square, like he trims them with the folded knife too. Thick glasses hang off his long nose, and the eyes behind 'em are dark green, like the Japanese forest in Mobile. Whiskers jut out his face, his eyebrows full and curly, white mixed in with brown. He could be ninety years old, maybe even a hundred.

"You remind me of my daughter Rose, many years ago now," he says, separatin' the orange into perfect pieces. "She loved oranges. Especially when she was pregnant." He eats one for himself and gives me the rest. I haven't eaten in a day, not since Ricardo's burritos, so it tastes like a present.

"Pickles too," he says. "You like pickles? I have a jar in the fridge. Stay here."

I don't know why, but I do. He comes back with pickles, bread, cheese and a cup of water on a plastic tray.

"My name is Solomon Schonblum. I work here in the mornings, but nobody comes anymore. I check for graffiti and bombs. So far nothing, *kein ahora*," he says. "They're going to tear it down and make a Trader Joe's. We're building a new *shul* on Olympic."

He smiles with a mouth full of false teeth, a whole set of pearly whites that are dim and yellow.

"Did you know you were sleeping in front of a synagogue?" he asks. I shake my head, not sure what he means.

"That's what I thought. Hard to tell it's a synagogue, besides the star in the brick." He gazes up, and I follow his eyes. A star with six points. Two triangles, one on top of the other, upside down. I seen this in paintings. Chagall.

I look at me through his eyes. I'm a creature from another planet with my big belly and spikey red hair.

"You like chocolate?" he asks. "I have some leftover *gelt* from Hannukah." He reaches into his other pocket and pulls out a handful of gold coins, like a pirate would find in a treasure chest.

"Here, take," he spreads them out on the step. "Just knock, if you want." He closes the door and locks it from inside. I pick up a piece and tear back the foil. I put it in my mouth. I swear it's the best I ever tasted.

I look at him again through the small window of the front door. He walks a little crooked, one foot bent in from the ankle. He touches the walls with his fingers like he's sayin' hello to 'em. I'm watchin' his back, but I know he's smilin'. He's home. He lifts his cap and fixes somethin' underneath it.

Maybe it's a good thing to look at someone again, like it's for the first time. If I'd done that with you, I might've seen who you really were before it was too late.

I walk down Vermont Avenue, thinkin' if I keep on goin' south, I'll get to Mexico someday. I'll make it to Tequila. To Lopez Café in the middle of the square. You'll never find me there. But I know I can't get that far with Grace comin' so soon. I need a place to sleep that's safe and warm. A soft rain starts tappin' on my shoulders.

I turn back, knock on the door and count the Jews I know. Only one, my baby doctor, and he's real nice. Dr. Vigman's not as old as this man, but they remind me of each other. Momma said it was okay to have a Jew doctor 'cuz they were smart, but not to trust 'em as far as you could throw 'em. I never understood why you both hate 'em so much. You used to tell me how they rule the world, and it's a conspiracy. I asked how you knew that, and you said you read it online and since a professor wrote it, it must be right. I said, "You believe everything you read?" and you slapped me around, tellin' me to never question your authority. And who made you the authority? I guess I did, without knowin' I was doin' it.

I hear the old man walkin' back. His face warms up when he sees me, like he's been expectin' a visitor, and here I am.

"Hurry," he says, *Good Morning America* just started."

This place smells familiar. I don't know what, but it reminds me of somethin'. I've been a bloodhound ever since I got pregnant. The first time this happened here was at Ricardo's motel. His shirts reminded me of the smell of fresh paper I colored on in second-grade art class. Mrs. Abney would hand each one of us a white sheet and tell us to let our imaginations run wild. She told us to put our heads on the paper and just listen to it, sniff it, look at it, talk to it and let it communicate to us like it was a part of us that wanted to come out. A happy or sad part, it didn't matter, she said. So I lay my head down and did that. I was scared and skinny and didn't know anythin' 'cept that my momma was mean to me but nicer to Betty Ann and Janine.

My first drawin' was of a mother with three baby daughters, two were painted pink, one was painted gray. Mrs. Abney asked me after class if I was the gray one. I said I didn't know. She asked me if I wanted to talk to a counselor. I said no thanks. After that, I colored everyone pink.

When Ricardo washed and dried his clothes, I put them on the bed and lay down on them. My nose remembered the white paper in art class. He came in once and caught me talkin' to his shirt. I thought he was gonna get mad. Instead, he laughed and lay down with me and started speakin' Spanish to his jeans. If I ever let myself love again, I would love him for that.

"My name's Solomon," the old man says again.

"Like the King," I say.

"Exactly!" his eyes twinklin' like stars. "Everybody calls me Sol."

My nose is tellin' me this place reminds me of raisins. I started eatin' them when I found out I was gonna have a baby. I got a list of nutritious foods from Dr. Vigman, and they were on it. I held them to my nose and sniffed. I thought maybe I'd smell grapes or wine. But they had their own fragrance. Like dried up wind in a bottle. The synagogue looks like them too. Wrinkled, like it's gonna die soon. The white paint on the walls is chipped down to the floor. The lights are just bare bulbs because I bet a lot of people came in and took everythin' when they found out they were gonna build a new one. I heard people do that when someone's near the end of life. Unless you save all the things a dyin' person has before they die, their stuff will be snatched up by vultures like it's roadkill. If I die, there's nothin' to take, 'cept for Grace. Maybe that's a good thing. Maybe she'll end up in a nicer place with people who can take care of her better than I can. I'd rather have that happen than her end up with you and Momma.

"Can I use the bathroom?" I ask.

He nods and leads me down to a room at the end of the hall. The sign says Rabbi Lefkowitz. I stop.

"Don't worry," he says openin' the door. "There's no one here except for me."

We go into the room. It's small with dark furniture. The shelves are empty. So are the walls. "There's a private bathroom with a shower. The couch is a pull-out bed." He walks over to the desk. "I'll be in the kitchen, making toast. I leave at noon. I come back at 7:00 every morning. Here's a key for the back door," he says takin' it from the drawer. It's big and bronze. Another key, I think.

He leaves the room, and I hear the TV click on down the hall. I go into the bathroom. The shower tiles are tiny, like glossy green pieces of seashell. I turn the handles and the pipes groan, wakin' up from a long sleep. I pull off my big sweater and sweatpants and look in the mirror before steppin' back in. I'm gettin' bigger, and so is Grace. And God, we're beautiful.

~ 28 ~

TRISHA

June 11, 2018

"W HAT ABOUT MY EGGS?" ERIKA asked.

"Your eggs?"

"Yeah." She seemed shy, even a little scared. "My eggs."

"What about them?"

Erika's fingers twisted the charm on her gold necklace. "Maybe they're okay," she said, her voice uncharacteristically soft. "I mean, I know my periods are all screwed up, but I've never had my eggs checked." She stood against the sink.

"You haven't?" Trisha stood motionless—marooned on a bridge—dizzy over churning waters.

"Not my eggs, specifically. Menstruation has always been so wacky that I never thought about my eggs." Erika hugged herself. She had confessed to Trisha that she didn't like feeling vulnerable; she needed to be the one in charge. "Maybe we should think about them."

They were eating linguine with pink vodka sauce from Trader Joe's. Erika pulled a quick dinner together before Trisha had to leave for the poetry workshop that night at Alison's in Santa Monica. Trisha watched her partner reach into the oven and pull out the focaccia. She tore the steaming bread in half and dipped it into the sauce.

"Here, babe," Erika offered.

"No thanks! Too many carbs."

Erika shrugged and bit into it. They were listening to Sirius' playlist of country music. The songs were beginning to all sound alike to Trisha. She wanted to listen to something new, something different, something alternative, like Haim, Vampire Weekend or R3HAB. At the last poetry workshop, Charles mentioned that was the kind of music he played for his patients in L.A. She joked and said maybe she'd be his patient. He blushed. She liked that his cheeks burned red on account of her. She was hoping he'd be there tonight at Alison's place.

"You talk to your mom lately?" Trisha bit into the bitter arugula and shaved Parmesan salad.

"She'll be back from Milan this week," answered Erika. "I'm worried she won't be around much for the baby with all her traveling and lecturing."

Trisha poured more sangiovese into her glass. It was her wine of choice tonight, the blood of Jupiter. That's what she needed to help her walk over the bridge. Her muse was sulking. She liked nursing, but she was anxious to greet her artist-self on the other side. The red wine sweetened her tongue. She twirled the perfect al dente pasta onto her fork and into her mouth, the vodka sauce squishing out the sides of her lips. She wiped her chin with the linen napkin, took another sip—another step across the bridge.

"What a family you come from," Trisha said. "Everyone's so accomplished."

"I know, it's crazy," laughed Erika. "My grandmother invested in Basquiat and Haring in the eighties—made a bundle. We even have a family burial plot at Hollywood Forever Cemetery. She wanted to make sure we'd always be together, no matter what."

"That's kinda sweet, actually," said Trisha.

"So, if we're still together when you croak," Erika said, tickling her partner, "you'll have made it in Hollywood!"

Trisha smiled. She loved Erika's dark humor.

"I've got to get ready." Trisha gathered the dishes and put them in the sink.

"Um, Okay."

Trisha went to the bedroom, closed the door, and took off her uniform, her underwear. It was starting to happen, naked, looking at herself in the full mirror, the blood of Jupiter, the sensations. She opened the drawer and found her red lace push-up bra and matching thong. She put them on. She reached in the closet for her black silk skirt that fell halfway down her thighs and laid it on the bed, paired it with a red silk blouse with silver threads. She felt that performer's high again as she fashioned the evening's outfit. She added sheer black tights and kitten heels. In a yoga class, she learned the second chakra—the sacral chakra—was associated with sexuality and creativity. When she felt creative, she felt sexy. When she felt sexy, she felt creative. Tonight, her second chakra was jumping all over the place.

She walked into the bathroom to put on makeup. Trisha brushed out her curls, blond hair flowing like a lion's mane. She applied shimmery pink shadow to her eyelids and black mascara to her pale lashes, dusting her face with a translucent powder, adding gentle puffs of rosy blush. She smoothed a clear red gloss on her lips with long, sure strokes. Just for fun, she feathered her eyebrows with Max Factor Midnight Black.

"You look hot," said Erika, peeking in. "Wild and sparkly like you're going to an opening night party. You sure there aren't any women you're interested in at poetry?"

"Oh, I'm positive," Trisha strutted past her to the hall closet.

"Charles still in Kansas City?"

"Stop it."

"You know I'm kidding. And I don't see you with a dentist, anyway. Too conservative."

"Those are the ones that surprise you!" Trisha grinned. She wrapped a silver silk scarf around her neck. It was something Charles bought her at the airport the last time he came in. She loved how cool it felt against her skin.

"So, what do you think about me getting my eggs checked?" Erika resumed the conversation.

"Why would you do that?" Trisha took a last glance at herself in the hall mirror and smiled at her reflection.

"To see if they're viable," Erika answered, looking relieved. She'd had the idea earlier that day in a brainstorming session. The show was doing a pregnancy story.

"But you can't carry to term."

"Right," Erika agreed. "But that doesn't mean my eggs aren't any good." She relaxed a little—kind of swaying, kind of not.

"And, if they're good?" Trisha turned to her.

Erika planted her feet like a boxer. "Then we should use mine instead of yours."

Trisha tied the silk scarf into a loose knot. "Really?" She zipped the jacket up to the collar, then changed her mind and unzipped it down to the middle of her chest.

"It's always been my dream, right?" Erika touched Trisha's hand. "I'm the one who's always wanted a child. Not you. Look how long it took you to decide. So, the baby should be my egg, a tall mystery man's sperm, and your uterus. How does that sound?"

"Very romantic." Trisha raised her eyebrows. "I feel so special."

"You know what I mean."

"It's just that—we've talked about it so much and... I was finally happy about being the mother—really excited about it, actually. All you've wanted from the beginning was for me to have a baby. And now that I'm ready to do it, you're taking that away from me?" Trisha unraveled the scarf and shoved it into her pocket. "That's not fair, Erika! You should've checked your eggs way before you met me." Trisha grabbed her purse. "I want the baby to be mine. I want to be the real mother!"

"Don't get so upset about it," Erika said.

Trisha looked at her watch. The workshop started in an hour. She'd have to drive across town to Santa Monica. It would take at least fifty minutes. She didn't want to be late.

"This way we'll both be real mothers," Erika continued.

"Yes, I know—but I thought—I was going to be the one—that it was going to be me. I really wanted that." Trisha ran her fingers through her hair. "Look, I've got to go. We'll discuss it tomorrow—don't wait up. Everyone's reading their pieces tonight," she said, shutting the front door.

Trisha didn't get home 'til way past midnight.

~ 29 ~

ALISON

November 10, 2018

Alison took a nap every afternoon when she got home from
school. She needed one after getting up before dawn to wait at the
fire station, then teaching all day. She'd put her earbuds in and
listen to Deepak and Oprah's meditations, incense burning, lights
dim, cushions under her head and feet. The ones on "Perfect Health"
were her flavor-of-the-month. She wanted to be ready when it happened.

Oprah would speak on something personal, then Deepak
would lead the meditation. "Even when you think you have your
life all mapped out," he hummed into her ear, "things happen that
shape your destiny in ways you might never have imagined."

She knew she had to take a chance at happiness, even though
it meant risking the comfort of her everyday life. She'd close her
eyes, inhale and exhale, long and deep. Soon, she was under the
spell of the duo. They made good partners—Oprah—Chopra—like

a human poem.

Then she'd fall asleep. Her internal alarm would wake her twenty minutes later, and she'd resume her day at the same exact point she'd left it—packing up her stuff, emptying out her place, creating the opportunity to leave at a moment's notice because once she found the baby, she couldn't come back here.

Her place looked deserted, like no one lived there anymore. Most of her clothes and books were at Goodwill or in boxes, except what she needed for school. She was organizing a garage sale. There was only one drawer left to empty—the one in the kitchen by the fridge, the one that held the detritus of her life. It was messy. It housed a combination lock, a yellow screwdriver, menus from Satdha Thai Vegan Cafe, a roll of 1-cent stamps, a box of 2-inch nails, an old bottle of La Vie Est Belle Eau de Parfum her students got her for Christmas, a wine cork, some loose vitamins, and rubber bands. She found a ticket stub to "Hamilton," red nail polish, candles, postcards from her cousins' trip to Italy, keys, pennies, an old watch, and small packs of Kleenex. Junk, pretty much. She could attach specific memories here and there, but not to everything. She still couldn't bring herself to sift through the drawer for the garage sale. That would be the final act of letting go, the no-reason-left-to-stay that would catapult her out the door. That, and of course, a baby.

She hired students who worked as crew in the school plays to move her furniture and belongings into the courtyard. A few of her neighbors took the occasion to sell their stuff as well. One by one, her old possessions would become other people's treasures, like her house on Vesper Avenue. She thought she'd never be able to sell her mother's things—the costume jewelry, the crocheted doilies, the dishes—but she was clearing out, leaving, maybe never returning. She was traveling light. Still, she wanted to hold onto the wooden box that had been buried in the old backyard. Alison liked the idea of keeping her mother's energy near her.

Her mother used to polish the pale-wood box every Tuesday because that was "cleaning day." Alison was going to treat it the same way. Her mother would be proud. She took it into the kitchen, wiped it with a paper towel, then placed it on the edge of the counter and bent down to find the lemon polish under the sink. The can of Pledge was way in the back, so she had to get on all fours to retrieve it. To help herself up, she reached above for the edge without thinking, smacking into the box by accident, sending it flying into the air. Her body froze. After all these years, her mother's buried treasure would end up broken, and it was all because of her.

"Don't you ever touch it again!" Her mother's harsh words rushed back. "It's not yours. It's mine." She watched the box collide with the stove, the tulip-engraved lid snapping in half. Alison could feel her mother rolling over in her grave. It had only been two thin pieces of beechwood glued together—but when she picked them up, she noticed something that had been wedged between the slats.

She carefully freed a 3"x 4" photograph from the debris. It was her mother, very young, looking just like Alison when she was twenty—the same open face, the same long red hair. She was holding a newborn baby, but the baby wasn't her, Alison was sure of that. She was born pretty much bald, and this baby had a full head of brown hair. Her mother's handwriting startled her as she turned the picture over—the left-handed ink smear over the letters, the circular vowels, the slanted crossing of the "t." She hadn't seen it in years, but there was an immediate, intimate recognition. No one else wrote like her mother. The letters were feminine and bold— they bore a graceful urgency.

"Hi, Mom," Alison whispered. It was as if she were meeting

her mother again after so much time.

She examined the writing on the aged photo paper: "Sebastian, 1965." It was an uncommon name. Alison couldn't remember ever hearing it in family conversations. Her mother never mentioned another baby. So, Sebastian must've been a secret.

Alison decided to make herself a cup of black tea. She was going to let her brain steep for a good five minutes. She went through the family history. Her mother and father met in San Francisco in 1969. This Sebastian was born in 1965, four years before her parents even knew each other. So who was he? Maybe he was a friend's kid, or a relative's. But then why would her mother hide the photograph? She kept it by her bed in a wooden earring box she wouldn't let Alison touch. She buried it in the backyard. Why? Alison sipped her drink. Her mother's expression in the photo was solemn, sad. Was Sebastian her secret child? Maybe he was put up for adoption after this picture was taken. Or maybe he passed away.

Alison stirred a teaspoon of almond milk into her tea, a dollop of honey. Sebastian could've been her half-brother. Was it possible he was still alive? Maybe she could find him, what with all the new DNA tests. Maybe he was dead. Maybe she should leave him buried—like he'd been for the past fifty-three years.

Alison imagined herself and Sebastian as children, playing in the backyard on the swings. What would her life have been like if she'd known him? She wouldn't have been alone after her parents' freak accident. She would have been happier.

Maybe her mother was sending her a message, or maybe it was Sebastian himself. Maybe he was trying to tell her that her plan would work, that a child would come, that she could open herself up to love, to not be afraid, to be vulnerable, and that she could now live a life without regrets.

Alison put the teacup in the sink. Maybe there was no mystical meaning to any of it, no hidden code—just the sobering, cold truth. Her mother most likely had a child out of wedlock that she gave up and never saw again.

Alison could hear the neighbors setting up their tables. Someone offered to make a Starbucks run. She placed the photo on the mantle. Had her mother been anxious that she only had one picture of Sebastian? If it disappeared, she'd have no proof he ever existed. Why did she bury it? Was it a final act of letting go? Or was it self-condemnation?

"Hey, Ms. Bishop!" The bell rang. "We're here!"

"Thanks, Julian!" Alison shouted through the door. "Give me five minutes, okay?" She looked over at the remaining drawer. "Wait, give me ten."

"Sure thing," her student answered.

She found two white votive candles in it. She lit them with the element on her stove, placed them on the mantle on either side of the photograph as though they were guardian angels. The last cardboard box of books was sitting on the coffee table. It was marked, "For Seekers," and held her spiritual books. She tore off the tape and opened the flaps. Deepak Chopra was on top. She turned to a dog-eared page and carried it to the fireplace.

"There are no extra pieces in the universe," she read to her half-brother as if she were telling him a story. "Everyone is here because he or she has a place to fill, and every piece must fit itself into a big jigsaw puzzle."

She pressed her finger along the ribbed edge of the photograph. Knowing she had a half-brother made her feel more whole, blessed, and part of something bigger. She would search for him in the future and tell him all about their mother. She would find him.

She wasn't sure how, but she would try.

"Sebastian, wherever you are, I hope you grew up happy and healthy. I hope you had a splendid life." She placed her hand on her heart. "And now that I know about you, you will always be in here."

She touched her mother's drawn face. "Mom, I'm so sorry you had to live with this secret. You did the best you could at the time. I guess we all did. I regret I never told you about my pregnancy. You would've understood..."

She imagined her whole family in the backyard on Vesper Avenue. They were sitting around the picnic table, eating hot dogs and drinking lemonade—father and mother, Sebastian and herself. A tender breeze surrounded the four of them. It blew through their hair. It was love, pure and simple.

~ 30 ~

WANDA

April 1, 2019

A KEY IN THE FRONT door.

I get dressed and meet Sol in the kitchen. The stove is old with lots of burners, crusty with drippings. There's a tall glass of orange juice on the table, water heatin' in a pot.

"Thank you," I say.

His corduroy jacket hangs over a chair. He's wearin' an old pinstripe suit like you see gangsters wear in movies. His shirt looks like it used to be white. He's got a black-and-yellow striped tie with a big knot at the Adam's apple. A couple of bobby pins hold a knit circle on his head, the color of red wine.

"Did someone make that for you?" I ask.

He puts his hand on it.

"Yes, one of my granddaughters, Ruthie. It's called a *yarmul-ke*. Men wear it to remember to honor the Almighty."

"And women?" I ask.

"They are naturally closer to God." He taps his heart. "They don't need to remember."

This makes me feel quiet inside like I knew it all along, but no one wanted to tell me the truth.

"How did you sleep?" he asks.

"Like a baby," I say, drinkin' the juice. It's so orange I want to taste it forever.

"How did your baby sleep?" He stirs a couple scoops of coffee grounds into the boiling water.

"Like an angel," I tell him.

He makes toast with rye bread, cuts an onion into thin slices and puts a handful on one piece. He smears a whole bunch of butter on the other, slams them together, then cuts straight down the middle.

"Want half?" he asks.

"No." I make a face.

"It's very healthy, an onion a day." He takes a bite, the onion crunchin' between his teeth. "I had typhus when the war was over. An American doctor told me I would do better if I left the camp instead of waiting there for help, so we started walking. This was the first time in four years we were free. Some of us died because we were too weak and sick." He stops to wipe his glasses. "A farmer's wife helped us. She cooked vegetables, and we ate, little by little. Slowly, my stomach got used to food again. She gave us day-old bread, sour milk, radishes, and onions. Now look at me—I'm ninety-four, and I'm never sick, because I still eat an onion every day of my life."

"That's because your breath is so bad nobody comes near you," I say, "so you can't catch any germs."

My hand jumps to my mouth. My tongue just let loose like I'm eleven years old.

"I'm sorry," I say, wantin' to hide. But instead of being mad, he laughs.

"You're right. That's why I do it. Who needs people around? Everybody should mind their own business and not get too close."

I look at him real funny. He didn't mind his own business with me.

"You were sleeping under God's roof," he says, like he knows what I'm thinkin'. "You are carrying a child. Who knows? It could be the Messiah." He touches the top of my head. "Cheerios?"

He pours cereal and milk into the glass bowl without waitin' for my answer. He pulls out a mug and puts a sieve on it. He empties the boiled coffee through it. He sits down and drinks it straight. It smells strong.

"What shall I call you?" he asks, lookin' straight into my eyes.

"Angel," comes outta my mouth too fast to stop it. That's what Ricardo called me, and I liked it.

"Eat, Angel. You both need to be strong." He passes over a plastic bottle. "Here, some vitamins I bought for you and the baby."

That's when I let out a sob from some part of me I don't recognize. I look down to see if there's any blood 'cuz it feels like a scar just split wide open.

"What's the matter?" Sol asks.

"Nothin'," I shake my head.

This old man's kindness is a foreign language. I don't know if I can take it. I shake a vitamin into my palm, a dark pink gummy bear. I chew it and remember bein' five years old, pickin' raspberries with Daddy. He promised I could eat one of every twenty that I found. Momma was out gettin' haircuts with Betty Ann and Janine.

She said I was too little to go along 'cuz my sisters were eleven and thirteen, and they were better behaved, but that wasn't really true. She just liked 'em better. Anyway, I didn't need her to take me. I cut mine short while they were gone, put scissors to it myself.

Momma whipped me when they got back from the beauty salon. She said I couldn't just do whatever I wanted, that she was in charge. She told me cuttin' my hair was a sin against Jesus, 'cuz mothers were his helpers, and goin' against your mother is goin' against Christ himself.

She woke me up in the middle of that night. Her eyes were swollen like they'd been cryin'. She smelled weird. I didn't know why 'cuz I didn't know what poison smelled like then.

"You're a bad girl, Wanda." Her hair was all messed up, and she was sippin' from a small bottle. "Know why?"

I shook my head, rubbin' my eyes open.

"'Cuz you were a mistake," she hissed. "A mistake makes mistakes. That's why."

I started to cry. "I'm sorry, Momma."

"We were fine. It was just me and Daddy, Betty Ann, and Janine. I shoulda been more careful. Daddy never knew. He's a weak man. You're a mistake, Wanda. You never shoulda been."

She left, and in the mornin', I thought it was a dream. But I know better now.

The air in the synagogue kitchen feels thick. My head hurts. Grace moves. Sol's waitin' for me to say somethin'.

"Do you have any tea?" I ask.

Sol nods, pushin' his chair back and standin' up. "I had stomach aches when I was a little boy. My mother, may she rest in peace, she didn't know what to do." He puts the kettle on. "One night, my grandmother, Miriam, came to her in a dream. She was carrying me in her arms and told my mother to make chamomile tea." Sol looks through the cupboards while he's talkin'. "My mother woke up, went to the fields, found some chamomile plants, and made a pot of tea. And you know what? My stomach got better."

He opens a tin box.

"Now, I don't know where there are chamomile fields in Los Angeles, but I think mint is pretty good," he said, holdin' up a teabag. "And look what I have—" He unwraps a blue handkerchief of Oreo cookies. Like I said, his pockets are magic. Maybe even miracles. We dunk the cookies in our drinks. I don't think I ever tasted somethin' so sweet and minty in my entire life.

He turns on the TV, and there's Robin, George and Lara. They're smilin' 'cuz they're real happy to see us. We watch *Good Morning America* like it's what we've been doin' every day of our lives since the beginnin' of time.

~ 31 ~

TRISHA

June 25, 2018

"**I** HAVE THE RESULTS," **DR.** Thayer said, strutting into her office.

She was head reproductive specialist at the Los Angeles Fertility Center, a handsome woman in her sixties, her chin-length white hair streaked with black. The women leaned forward as the office grew quiet. Their future would be determined by what the doctor said next. Erika held her breath. Trisha's stomach ached.

"Your ovaries are healthy," said the doctor.

"Seriously?" Erika jumped up. "That's awesome news! That's the best news ever." She turned to Trisha. "My ovaries are healthy!" She wiped her tears on the sleeve of her shirt. "Oh my god, I was so nervous. This is amazing!"

"But they need to make more eggs," Dr. Thayer continued. Her doctor's jacket hung on a hook on the inside of the door. She wore a dark-green pantsuit with a gold silk blouse. She was older, dispassionate and highly regarded—perfect casting, thought Trisha—and so were they.

"How do they do that?" Erika asked, sitting back down on the couch.

"With a combination of hormonal medications," explained Dr. Thayer. Her chair squeaked as she reclaimed it. "The development of new eggs will be monitored by ultrasound and measurements of hormones in your blood."

One of the lights on the ceiling was flickering. Dr. Thayer got up and turned it off. She swung open the curtains to let more sunshine in.

"When egg development is at the appropriate stage," the doctor resumed, waving her hand at a glass bowl half filled with Hershey's Kisses, "the ovulation process is triggered by an injection of medicine to allow the eggs to mature in time for retrieval." Erika took three. Trisha declined.

"Retrieval?" Erika asked. "How does that happen?"

She sat directly across from the doctor. Her posture was tall and straight, consciously projecting "strong mother" energy. Trisha sat beside her, crossing and uncrossing her legs.

"We collect them by using an ultrasonic probe," Dr. Thayer said. "We guide the needle through the vaginal wall into the ovary to gather the mature eggs."

"Through my vaginal wall?" Erika unwrapped a kiss. "Ouch! That's going to hurt, right?"

"We do our best to be concise and quick." The doctor pushed a file of paperwork towards them.

"So that's a yes," said Erika, throwing the wrapper into the trash can under the desk. "It's going to hurt."

The posters on the office walls represented the people sitting in the waiting room. The one with two women had a blue frame around it, a diverse couple, one Asian, one African American. They held their child, a beautiful little boy who resembled them both. They were at the beach. You could see other kids playing in the water. There was something so complete about the three of them. They were a family—mother, mother, and son. It was beautiful, really. Trisha stared at the little boy and wondered what it would be like to have a child of her own—with her DNA. And a sperm choice of her own, as well. Her stomach was still aching. She glanced over at Erika, then dipped her hand in the bowl for a kiss.

"That's nothing compared to gaining tons of weight, swollen feet and back pain," Trisha smirked, plucking out the paper plume and unraveling the silver cone. "Not to mention sleepless nights, hours and hours of labor, a vaginal birth that could leave me torn up or a C-section that could leave me scarred." She popped the chocolate in her mouth. Erika wanted to say something but didn't. Trisha twirled the slip of paper between her fingers.

"I'm assuming you both have discussed third-party insemination?" The doctor looked from one to the other.

"Yes, of course," said Erika.

"It's just that we were going to get pregnant the regular way with a sperm donor," interjected Trisha. "I was going to get pregnant. So I'm—I'm just processing for the first time that Erika's eggs are viable and—I won't be the mother."

"I understand." The doctor leaned across her desk. "A third-party insemination takes that title away from you. You become the surrogate for the gestation of the embryo. You have no DNA ties to the baby."

"I am aware of that." Trisha leaned back in her chair.

"I can't continue unless you're both committed," Dr. Thayer said. "It's a very big decision."

"Yes, we know. We are," Trisha assured the doctor. "Sorry. This is new information, and I'm adjusting to that, and it's getting real, is all."

"Oh, yes," agreed Dr. Thayer. "It's definitely real."

There were voices in the hallway— another couple with another specialist.

"So then what happens?" Erika continued. "After you collect the mature eggs?"

"The sperm is collected," answered Dr. Thayer, putting a pen back in the desk drawer.

"Are you sure this isn't a collection agency?" joked Trisha.

Erika looked over at Trisha and laughed. "Funny!" she said, reaching for her hand.

"In a manner of speaking, it is." Dr. Thayer got up and retrieved a bottle from the mini fridge in the corner of the room. "Water anyone?" she asked. The women shook their heads. She unscrewed the cap and took a long swig. "We need separate and specific materials for a third-party reproduction. So the sperm is collected and prepared, and then we take it to the embryology lab where the egg and sperm are combined to allow fertilization. Twelve to sixteen hours after the insemination, we hope to have an embryo or embryos."

"What if we have a lot of them?" Erika unwrapped the second kiss.

"You can freeze them for later use or donate them to other couples."

Trisha got up and crossed to the window. There was construction on Wilshire. There was always construction on Wilshire. She wanted to be home, binging *Nurse Jackie,* eating popcorn with Erika beside her on the sofa.

"We haven't talked about that," Trisha said. "What should we do?" She knew Erika didn't want another month of discussions. She wanted to move forward. Trisha focused on the doctor. "So what happens after the embryo stage?"

"They're cultured and three to five days later are ready for implantation into the wall of the uterus."

"That's me." Trisha raised her hand, grinning. "I'm the uterus."

"Then we take blood tests to determine if there's a pregnancy," said the doctor.

"How long do you do that for?" inquired Erika.

"We should know in nine to eleven days."

"And then?" Trisha asked.

"And then, if you're pregnant," replied Dr. Thayer, "then we see you for prenatal check-ups. Approximately forty weeks later, you'll have a baby."

"That's so exciting!" clapped Erika.

"And if not?" asked Trisha.

"Then you decide if you want to use one of your frozen embryos or start fresh with a new sperm donor and egg collection."

"We want a girl," Erica said.

"That's determined with PGS – Pre-Implantation Genetic Screening. We recommend that for women over thirty-five."

"I'm thirty-six," offered Erika, "so we'll do the screening—and that's where you determine the gender, right?"

The doctor nodded.

"Wow! Amazing! So all I have to do is—?"

"Take the medication to increase your egg count," Dr. Thayer said. "That's your job."

"And me?" Trisha asked. "What's my job?"

"You have two. First, you get ready to receive the embryo. Then, you carry for nine months." The doctor rose from her chair to shake hands. "Good luck!"

On the way home, Trisha and Erika parked in front of the Los Angeles County Museum of Art. It was a spontaneous visit. They walked through the Urban Lights—the 202 rows of streetlamps on the front courtyard. They took selfies. They flirted with each other. It was almost like a date. They forgot about the medications, the probes, and the inseminations. Erika's long black hair flew behind her as she ran through the installation. Her egg would make a beautiful baby.

Maybe third-party insemination was the best idea. But what about me, Trisha wondered? Was this another example of someone else shining in the front row, while she leapt as high as she could in the back?

She thought about Señor Gabriel. "*Buena madre,*" he'd said— good mother. Did that mean she'd be a good mother? Or did that mean being a mother would be good for her? Either way, it was time to move forward with her plan—a secret plan that would destroy their relationship if Erika ever found out.

ALISON

November 17, 2018

A<small>LISON WAS ON HER WAY</small> to the Cheesecake Factory in Beverly Hills to have lunch with Suzy and her mother, Mrs. VanDusen. No one could replace Alison's family, but Suzy and Mrs. V. came pretty close. When the three of them were together, Alison experienced the kind of acceptance she remembered from her childhood. It was the sweetest kind of love. She was going to read them one of her poems.

Bright banners advertising *Amma's Healing and Meditation Conference* Los Angeles visit ran along Wilshire Boulevard like enthusiastic spiritual coaches. The smiling images of the Hugging Saint gently tugged Alison back into the past.

∞

It had been Tuesday, November 14th, 2000. She had called

in sick to school and had driven down to the Hilton for the *Amma Healing and Meditation Conference*. The walk from the parking lot to the hotel was a pilgrimage to purification. Alison was thirty-two years old and newly divorced from her first husband, Emanuel. They had stormed through each other like colliding nimbus clouds. Tumaini was right. It was too soon after her parents' death to be in a meaningful relationship.

Alison sat in the audience with one hundred and fifty Amma devotees. A reverential hush preceded a white-bearded man in orange robes as he escorted the Guru to her cushioned chair. Amma touched both palms together and began to speak in a calming voice. The man stood beside her in front of his own microphone, translating every word.

"My friends," Amma spoke through him. "Surrounding yourself with positive energy is like walking out of a perfume factory, smelling beautiful without having sprayed any of the scent on you."

This was Alison's first encounter with the Indian spiritual leader. She had seen an ad in the *L.A. Weekly* for the Amma convention. It was three years after her parents' untimely death. She needed help.

"And negative energy is like being in a charcoal factory," Amma's translator continued. "No matter how careful you are not to touch anything, you will still walk out smudged."

A little boy was singing. A young girl was laughing.

"You must help someone in need," Amma told them. "If you are on the tenth floor of a building, and a fire breaks out on the first, you must help that person below for two reasons. The first is to help that person. The second is to help yourself. Because soon, the fire will reach your floor."

Alison stretched her legs out in front of her. She rotated her shoulders. She let go.

"Imagine white flowers of inner peace," Amma said.

The white flowers Alison visualized were crisp and beautiful. They fell from the heavens, the clouds, the trees, and filled the air with the fragrance of coconut jellybeans. Alison peeked up at the stage. Amma opened her eyes and sat, taking a long look at each person in the audience. The mother saint who embraced the world gazed directly at Alison with so much joy. No one had looked at her this way in such a long time, not since her mother, not since her father, not since Jesse.

The audience was arranged in a semi-circle so you could see the people around you. Most of them had their eyes closed. They seemed at peace. Alison was hoping to achieve that for herself. Just as she was about to shut her eyes, she turned her head—

And there he was, staring up front at Amma. Alison froze, squeezed her eyes shut, then peeked one open, just to make sure. She was sure. He was wearing a white cotton shirt and jeans. Same rich brown hair but shorter, same golden green eyes but wiser. And older, of course—they were together in 1988 when she was twenty and he was twenty-five. That was twelve years ago. She hadn't seen him since. Such a long time ago. And they weren't together very long. But here he was, thirty-seven years old, sitting not fifty feet away from her. Alison couldn't catch her breath. Something was happening. Her stomach hurt. She covered her mouth with her shawl.

It was Jesse. And there was a beautiful blond woman meditating beside him. His knee was leaning into her knee; their bodies seemed connected; their smiles were the same. Yes, there was no doubt they were a couple. Jesse turned left toward his partner and kissed her on the temple. And for one brief second—the longest second in recorded time—Alison thought he glanced at her, recognized her, loved her. Then everything in Alison's vision evaporated into a pitch-black tunnel.

The music sounded kind of like Indian rock 'n' roll. It held a faint memory of a touch she had experienced years ago, a whisper of eyelashes on the small of her back. It was Jesse kissing her body, his hair flowing over her naked hips and thighs, his lips tracing the gentle curve of her spine. She felt a cold shock through her blouse. She heard the tumbling of white flowers of inner peace. They were her heartbeats, rolling softly through her body into a stethoscope.

Alison opened her eyes wide. Soft beige curtains in front of heavy green ones. A thermostat on the bare wall. Another pair of eyes, a red dot between them.

"Are you awake, precious one?" It was a voice she recognized. "Doctor Anand says you are fine. Perhaps a little overwhelmed. Can you sit up?"

Alison felt a team of strong arms lift her up from the bed and onto a chair. She looked to the source of the voice and saw a large bundle of white pillows sitting on purple satin cushions.

"You fainted during meditation. It happens," said Amma. "We brought you here to rest. Now you are awake. Perhaps you still need something from us?"

"I'm not sure," Alison murmured. "I thought I saw someone—Jesse. I'm not sure..."

The late afternoon sun was pouring the last of itself into the hotel room. Piles of peanut butter and ginger cookies lay on white china plates on the room service cart, along with bottles of Perrier and juice boxes—orange, grapefruit, and apple. Amma's eyes were the deepest brown, holding sequin-sized glimmers of the brightest light imaginable. She wore round, gold earrings with red centers, the same color as the bindi on her forehead. Her long black hair was streaked with silver, plaited and pinned up. She was munching on a cookie, a few crumbs calmly resting on her chin. She wore several bracelets on both wrists, carved beads from stone and wood, green and brown.

"Come, let me hug you," said Amma, holding out her arms.

At first, Alison was a planet, and Amma was the universe. And then, there was no separation, no two bodies, no two breaths, no two hearts. They were one, suspended in space like that precious time when Alison was just out of the womb, lying on her mother's chest, still attached, only minutes born.

She could've stayed in Amma's arms forever. She wondered if maybe that was what heaven would be like. If there were a heaven. If she gets to go. She had made decisions when she was twenty that seemed correct, but now, in this moment of bliss, she wondered about her own empty arms. They never held a child. They probably never would. And she had just seen Jesse...

Amma chanted something in Malayalam deep into Alison's right ear. Then she said in English, "Be of service to others. There is no greater love."

The embrace lasted only a minute, maybe less. And then it was over. The team lifted Alison up and away and waited 'til she was standing secure on her own two feet. Then they swooped in under Amma and raised her with one collective inhalation. They held on to her as she took another peanut butter cookie and disappeared into the next room.

Alison heard the TV playing as the door to Amma's room closed. She was pretty certain she heard Lorelai on *The Gilmore Girls* say, "If you're going to throw your life away, he better have a motorcycle."

Alison ran all the way back to the parking lot. She didn't want to bump into Jesse and his girlfriend—wife most likely. She'd rehearsed running into him a million times, but it never came out right. What could she say, really? That she lied to him by omission and then did what she thought was best? It was her body after all, therefore her decision. She opened the car door and slid in.

She took Lincoln north, speeding through traffic lights until she swung into her garage, where she rested with the engine turned off and her head on the steering wheel. She had just been blessed by Amma. Their moment of oneness was a miracle. So why did she feel like her body was dissolving?

She rushed into her cottage and locked the door. This weird sensation must be a vestige of mourning for her parents, mourning for the way things might have been with Jesse. But she had moved on—to Arlen and other musicians she met touring. Her marriage to Emanuel was a mistake, but lots of first marriages are. She was happy teaching. Her students appreciated her.

Sobs escaped like tortured prisoners. She opened a bottle of Chablis and downed two glasses. She smoked what was left of a joint and, on a Post-it Note, wrote the words Amma whispered in her ear. "Be of service to others. There is no greater love." She stuck it on the bottom right-hand corner of the bathroom mirror.

Alison had seen Jesse. Maybe she should've approached him. She should've said hi, reminisced, and then apologized. She was so sorry for how she'd handled everything. But he seemed happy, and he was with that woman. She would focus her love on her teaching. She would be of service to her students—

∞

A honk startled her. "Light's green, lady!" An older man shouted out the window of the car behind her. "We don't have all day!"

Alison nodded to him in the rear-view mirror, then smiled back at the faces of Amma waving on the boulevard. The Post-it Note is still on my mirror after all these years, she thought as she made a left at Beverly Drive. It was faded and curled at the edges, with layers of Scotch Tape to reinforce it. But it was still there.

She continued down the street into a city parking structure. At the restaurant, she'd order some bubbly water to settle her stomach. Then she'd tell Suzy and Mrs. V. about her Amma recollections. And she'd talk about Jesse too.

"He's the one that got away," Mrs. V. would say. It's what she always said.

~ 33 ~

WANDA

April 5, 2019

"S<small>TOP!</small>" I <small>SHOUT.</small> "T<small>HIS IS</small> a holy place!"

You're peein' on the walls, jumpin' from corner to corner, pullin' out your thing.

"If you want it," you taunt, "you can have it."

You grow bigger and I can't breathe. Your body's shuttin' me off from livin'. I reach for the cross in my bag, the one that was on our wall, silver with black rosary beads. I hold it up, and you melt like the Wicked Witch of the West.

I wake screamin' from the nightmare, sweaty and scared. You're always in 'em. But this one's the worst. Grace is jumpin', warnin' me 'bout somethin', like she knows the future 'cuz she's already there.

I can't see the tops of my thighs anymore. I'm tired all the time. I'm sad too. I wish my sisters were here sittin' with me in the rabbi's room. I know that's stupid 'cuz they never helped before, but

I want them to hold my hands and say everything's gonna be fine. I'll always be wishin' for a new them to take the real ones' places. It's so hard to let go, but I know that's what I need to do if I'm gonna give Grace a chance at a good life. I get up and go take a shower.

Me and Sol walk after breakfast. That's what we do every mornin' at 10:30 since I started livin' at the *shul*. It's been six days now. Sol says I need to get out and exercise. We go over to Vons on Sunset and buy some water and fruit. He's a pretty good walker for a 94-year-old. Says it's from survivin' in the forest when he was a kid with the other boys who ran away. Then they all got caught and worked in camps. He was lucky. The Nazis kept him alive 'cuz he could speak a lot of languages. They used him to talk to other prisoners. Sol said he was ninety pounds when President Eisenhower rescued them. That's when he went home to his town near Prague. His parents had been killed so he came over here by boat with his brothers. They're all dead now too. He's the only person left from the old country. That's what he calls where he's from. The old country. I guess Mobile's my old country I ain't never goin' back to.

Sol's got a son and a daughter, three grandchildren, and five great-grandchildren. His wife Sarah died twelve years ago. He talks 'bout her a lot. She made pickles for him exactly the way he liked, with vinegar and spices. Those are the ones he brings to the synagogue. He uses the same recipe. I eat one every day. He says they're good for my digestion. He bought me some raisins too.

"What are your plans?" Sol takes the breakfast plates to the sink. I'm at the fridge, puttin' the milk and butter back.

"My plans?" I ask like I've no idea what he's talkin' 'bout even though it's in my thoughts every second of the day. "Maybe I can stay here. For a little while, at least."

"In the *shul*?" He turns on the hot water. "Remember, they're tearing it down. And the rabbi wouldn't like it."

"Can I talk to him?"

He looks at me like I made a joke, then he shakes his head. "I don't think that's a good idea," he says.

I nod. A man of God can't harbor a criminal. And that's what I am, plain and simple.

"I'll get my jacket," I say.

He dries the plates and shuts the cupboards. He likes to leave things in order, the opposite of me.

"Here." Sol helps me put it on.

I look like a dressed-up bear in a circus. He opens the front door, treatin' me like a lady. I wonder what he'd think if he knew what I did.

"It's clear you're running from a terrible situation," he says, readin' my mind again. We start walkin' and go right. "You know, I'll never turn you in."

I don't trust him. He'd have to. God's his conscience.

"It's gettin' warmer." I change the subject. "I don't know who said the weather was perfect in California. They must've come from Alaska."

Yesterday he woulda laughed at that. Not today.

"Sometimes it's too hot to breathe, and it's always so bright," I go on. "I have to wear sunglasses like Kim Kardashian."

"Do you plan on keeping the baby, Angel?" he asks. "Can you go back home for help?"

I wanna keep talkin' 'bout Kim and Khloe and her family, but Sol won't let me. He stops on the sidewalk and turns to face me.

"How do you expect to take care of Grace?" he said, his eyes diggin' into mine.

A whole bunch of birds land on the roof of a Taco Bell.

"I'm gonna go to Mexico," I tell him. "I know a place."

"I'm serious, Angel," he says.

"Me too," soundin' as sure as I can.

"What about adoption?" He won't stop. "Have you considered that?"

I shoulda known today's early mornin' nightmare of you was a premonition. It was tryin' to tell me Sol's God wasn't gonna save me. I shoulda known somethin' bad was gonna happen. 'Cuz right there in the mornin' sun, your sky-blue shirt catches my eye. It's you, for real, across the street. I blink a couple of times to make sure I'm not dreamin' you, but there you are, as real as I am, standin' maybe a hundred feet away. My body gets all paralyzed, but I start chokin' like it's middle of the night and someone's put a pillow over my face, and I'm fightin' for my life, and oh yeah, that someone is you. The same shirt you wore to steal me back, wrinkled and dirty now. You're right across Vermont Avenue, waitin' for a bus to take you someplace. I know you're tired the way your body slumps against the bus stop. It's funny how I still know everythin' 'bout you, and I wanna forget you, but how can I when I know you like the back of my hand? Even if I cut my hand off, I'll still know you. You look homeless. And maybe you are—sleepin' under freeways by night, huntin' me down by day. You watch people, but you must not really see 'em, or else you'd see me now, frozen-caught like a rabbit —an easy target ready for the kill. My lungs fill up with the heat of crows' wings flappin' 'round me, and I beg 'em to carry me up and away from you, forever and always, amen.

"What's the matter?" Sol asks, his palm touchin' my forehead. "You're so pale. Do you need to sit down?"

I tell myself you don't know it's me 'cuz all you see is a fat stupid girl in a green jacket with short red hair under a white hat, walkin' with an old Jewish man. Guess who's hidin' in plain sight now?

"Please take me home," I whisper. "It's Travis. He's across the street."

Sol stands in front of me, shieldin' me. "Which one?" he asks.

"In the blue shirt. Blond hair. He's leanin', waitin'. That's him."

"Come on, let's go. He's not looking over here." He holds my hand. "It's fine. Let's go."

When we get back to the shul, Sol makes me a cup of chamomile tea. Everythin' in my head tells me you'll never leave California 'til you find me. You'll tell the police 'bout what I did. Probably already have. Seein' you like that tells me I gotta figure out a plan.

I go to my room and sleep, and the nightmare comes back. This time you sit on the rabbi's bed and tie my hands and feet like a baby calf at a rodeo, rope burnin' my wrists and ankles. You take your knife and cut me down the middle, one straight gash, and you reach in and pull her out. She's tiny and slippery, but you dig your claws into her and hold her up like a trophy fish. Grace cries so loud it jerks me awake, her screams becomin' mine.

"What's the matter?" Sol runs into the room.

"Travis is here in the rabbi's room." I shiver like I'm gonna never stop.

"Tell him to go away," Sol says, his voice sure.

You sit on the bed starin' at me—flies jumpin' out your eyes.

"I don't know how," I say, sweat pumpin' from my skin.

"Scream at him," he tells me. "Do whatever you need to do, because he's hurting you, and he's hurting the baby."

"Leave me alone!" I'm prayin' the holiness still left in this room will make me invincible.

"More." Sol squeezes my hand like he'll never let go. Nobody did that before. Everybody let go.

"Leave me alone!" I shout louder.

"Be tough!" Sol looks at me, the way he might've looked at the other prisoners. "Stronger!" He tightens his mouth, his whiskers gray soldiers marchin' to war. "From your soul!"

"Leave me alone, Travis! I hate you!"

I stand and cry into the world, make fists with my soaked hands, punch the air and yell so loud I'm sure they'll take me away.

"Leave her alone, you evil man, you!" Sol shouts, uncurvin' his spine up tall, starin' where I'm starin'. You shimmer in waves and layers, like a boilin' day when the heat's playin' tricks.

"He's gonna kill me," every bone in my body tellin' me. "No matter what I do or where I go, he'll find me and take Grace. He's the devil."

Sol puts his hands on mine. They've lifted so many stones. They've opened so many doors. They've held so many children.

"I have seen the devil. He was in Czechoslovakia. He was in the camps." Sol stops. He gets out his handkerchief and wipes his eyes 'cuz tears are fallin' out. "He was in the faces of the Nazis and their collaborators." He's speakin' from what he's seen, and it hurts him. "One thing is always true of the devil. He hates and destroys because that's what he has to do in order to survive." He wipes my forehead. "So, you and me, we won't let him survive. We will stop him. I promise."

His arms wrap 'round my back and bring me into his chest. It smells like mothballs and onions. I inhale real deep. I look over his shoulder and see the room is finally empty of you. I'm so tired I could sleep on his shoulder for a thousand years.

"For now, my dearest, take a shower, eat something, then we'll go to the clinic. After that, I'll tell the taxi to stop at Canter's, and we'll pick up some chicken soup. When we get back, we'll have some, and we'll talk, Angel, and you'll tell me what happened."

I'm guessin' he knows, kinda like Ricardo knows. He knows even though he doesn't really. He knows 'cuz he has secrets too. The worst has happened to him, so it can happen to someone else.

"I have nightmares too," he says. "Even after all these years. I saw things, unspeakable things."

He moves against the wall.

"We were lined up, and the head Nazi pulled out a young boy, maybe twelve years old, not yet bar mitzvah. He asked who his father was. A man stepped forward and said, "I am." The Nazi shot the boy in front of the father. Then he shot the father."

I put my hand on my belly.

"When I think that the last thing the father saw was his son being killed." Sol shakes his head. "I can't comprehend how there is so much evil in man. And yet there it is. All around us to see."

He wipes his eyes.

"I did things to survive that I am ashamed of. Things I could go to prison for. Yet I lived and brought into the world good children who may help it become a better place for everyone in it. So yes, Angel, sometimes we must do things that are terrible, but in the long run, maybe are for good."

Sol stands in front of me like a small mountain.

"To be a survivor is no sin, Angel. It is a miracle." He reaches in his pocket and pulls out a red-and-white mint wrapped in cellophane. "So, you'll tell me the secrets that give you nightmares,

Angel. And we'll decide what to do." He kisses the top of my head and walks out of the room.

I tear the candy open and drop it on my tongue. It helps the bitter taste of you go away. How do I tell Sol I took a knife to your body? How do I tell him you bled all over your wetness pourin' outta me? How do I tell a man of God the biggest mistake of my life was lettin' you live?

~ 34 ~

TRISHA

October 12, 2018

Eᴿɪᴋᴀ ᴀɴᴅ "Gʀᴇᴇɴ-Eʏᴇᴅ Oᴘᴛɪᴍɪsᴛ's" embryo had been implanted into the lining of Trisha's uterus on July 12th, 2018. It had gone smoothly. This morning, three months later, the women heard from Dr. Thayer.

Last night, Trisha turned to face a huge black widow spider in her dream. She squashed it dead with her running shoe. When she woke up, she Googled the meaning of spider dreams for the tenth time. Jung wrote that spiders were connected to the shadow self— you were either the manipulator or the manipulated. Both resonated with Trisha. She read that the spider represented creativity and mystery, growth and hidden power. She always thought spiders were misunderstood, kind of like herself.

This morning, a tiny one still dangled in the corner of her mind. She brushed it away as the sun's golden liquid filled up the bedroom. Erika had already opened the curtains. Trisha felt like a pearl in a glass of lemonade.

After French toast and coffee, she wrote a poem about color. She conjured all things yellow: sun, daffodil, butter, banana, lemon, mustard, corn, canary, dandelion, rubber duck, school bus. She wrote them down, but she realized it wasn't a poem. It was a list.

Sometimes she felt that all Erika wanted was an offspring and would've settled for any woman who said yes to getting pregnant. Most of the time, when she wasn't nauseous or tired, she felt that Erika was her true companion.

Trisha knew that the first three months were the scariest. She kept quiet at work and in her classes. And she certainly didn't tell her agent. This morning, Dr. Thayer called to let them know the embryo had become a fetus because the internal organs were starting to form. Now, she'd be free to talk to the pregnant women, all of them, from doctors to patients, and ask about their stories, their experiences, their thoughts. It was safe to tell everyone the news.

"Well, guess what we are," Trisha said.

"What?" asked her father.

"Almost twelve weeks pregnant."

Her father's reflux had gotten worse over the years. He slept on a thick wedge that angled the top part of his body eight inches above the bottom half. Even over the phone, Trisha could sense the acid starting to rise.

"When did this happen?"

"Erika and I've been talking about it since we got together." She heard her father take a long sip of something. Probably apple cider vinegar.

"Brigid, get on the extension!" he yelled to his wife. "Trish's got some news."

Trisha heard the upstairs phone lift off the cradle. Her mother was panting a bit from running into their bedroom.

"Hello, Trish? Is everything okay?" her mother asked. "What's the matter?"

"She's going to have a baby!" her father answered. "Can you believe that?"

Trisha could hear The Chieftains in the background. Sometimes her father would pick up his fiddle and play along as if he were on stage with them. Maybe that was what his dream really was: to be a musician and not a bar owner in Toronto. Maybe then he would have understood his daughter.

"Who's the father?" her mother asked, clearing her throat. "Did you break up with Erika? Are you back with a man, I hope?"

Trisha grabbed a sponge and wet it. The water splashed onto her arm. She watched the droplets trickle down to her wrist.

"No, we're still together."

"Then, what happened?" her mother persisted. "How did you do it?"

"His name is Donor C-1974-18," Trisha said, "but we just call him 'Green-Eyed Optimist.'"

Her father nearly choked on his phlegm. "Well, that's ridiculous," he wheezed.

Trisha wiped the kitchen table, soaking up the crumbs from breakfast.

"So you're the mother, and donor-whatever is the father?" her mother asked.

"Actually," Trisha felt her neck stiffen, "it's Erika's egg. I'm the surrogate."

"What?" her mother shouted. "Well why on earth would you do that? That's just stupid."

Trisha folded the newspaper and threw it in the recycling bin out the back door. They loved reading "Ask Amy" in the *Los Angeles Times* Calendar section to each other in the mornings, discussing the letters like the senders were their closest friends.

Dear Amy, Trisha typed in her head. *I'm a thirty-one-year-old woman who's having a baby with her partner. I'm not sure who the father is or even who the mother is, but that's not why I'm writing. What I'm writing to ask you is this: how do I tell my parents to go to Hell? Sincerely, Smothered in Silver Lake.*

"Erika can't carry to term." Trisha flung the sponge into the trash can. "So I'm the oven."

"Why would you agree to that?" her father asked.

A fresh coldness wept through Trisha's body. "What do you mean?"

"I had so much morning sickness, I couldn't stand it," her mother said. "But you know that, and you still went ahead and did it. Why didn't you talk to me about it first?"

"I thought you said you loved being pregnant?" Trisha said.

"That was only compared to how hard it was after you were born," her mothered answered.

Trisha wanted to lie down on the strip of grass beside the house. She wanted to feel the silky blades under her bare legs. She wanted to take a nap. Instead, she ventured back into the kitchen to put the dishes away.

"I talked to Erika about it, mother. She is my partner."

"Well, she better be," her father cleared his throat. "Congratulations, I guess."

"Thanks," she said, pushing an errant curl behind her ear.

"Are we even grandparents if the baby's not really from our

bloodline? There's no O'Connor in her or him, right?" her father probed.

"Or is there some gene or something that gets into the baby from your womb?" her mother asked.

Trisha sat down on the edge of the table, tipping over a pile of Erika's scripts. She could pick them up later.

"No, there's no O'Connor DNA in the baby. And you can be whatever you want to be," she groaned, pulling off her running shoes and socks. "Grandma or Grandpa or just plain Brigid and Geoffrey, for all I care." Her feet were burning.

"You'll probably gain a ton of weight." She could sense her mother smirking. "I did."

The tension in Trisha's jaw tugged at the muscle around her temporal mandibular joint.

Dear Amy. How do you bury a body without getting caught? Sincerely, Parricidal Daughter.

"We're two peas in a pod, your father and I," her mother said. "We're a little shocked, to say the least. You could've warned us about all this. I mean, what shall we tell our friends?"

Trisha walked through the house to the living room. She stopped at the front window to watch Erika weeding the garden in her denim cut offs, a red bandana tied around her hair beneath a baseball cap. Pale smudges of sunscreen coated her arms as she cleared the rows for future seeds. Erika was Mother Nature, sure and strong.

"Now, if the baby was yours, well then that's a different story–"

"Mother!"

"What's the last name going to be? 'Green-eyed Optimist'?"

her father joked.

"No, probably O'Connor-Rossi."

"Why is Erika's name last if you're doing all the work? Is she going to pay you to do this?"

"Mother!"

"Yes?"

"Go to hell!" Trisha clicked off. She grabbed her sun hat and stormed outside.

"She's such a bitch!"

"That bad?" Erika came over and hugged her partner.

"Worse." Trisha melted into the embrace. She buried her face in Erika's chest, inhaling the musty smell of sweat and soil. "And my father just laughed. What'd your mother say?"

"She's with her new boyfriend, and they get back tonight. I'll tell her then."

It was Saturday, late morning. The neighbor's kids were screaming a game of Red Light, Green Light across the street. A thick layer of cloud sheltered them from the lurking sun. It was going to be a scorcher.

Johnnie Baloney rode by on his bike and waved. L.J. was sitting in the child seat attached to the front. Trisha had stopped fantasizing about him. She decided that if she were going to have an imaginary playmate, it should be someone she didn't know personally, certainly not a gay man who lived down the street. She'd leaf through *People* magazine at Ralphs and make herself choose a movie star of the week. Chris Hemsworth, Idris Elba and Chris Pine were her sometimes between-the-sheets companions. She never fantasized about another woman. That made it feel like she was cheating on Erika. But some movie star hunk, well, that was sexy and safe. She did like the secret of herself and Johnny Baloney in the shower though, especially when they ran into each other. You've been naked with me, she'd muse to herself, as they discussed politics and the climate. She wouldn't let herself think about what she was doing with Charles. Was that cheating on Erika? No, it wasn't about Erika at all. It was about something else altogether. And it was going to end soon anyway now that she was past three months pregnant.

"You think your mother will be happy about the news?" Trisha asked.

"What's not to be happy about?" Erika returned to her digging.

Trisha didn't answer.

Erika had to meet with two producers from her show that weekend. She was moving up, and they wanted to get her ready to write an episode on her own. That meant Trisha would have the afternoon to herself. She had another audition for *Grey's Anatomy* on Monday. The casting director liked her. This time it was for a co-star role as a nurse. She'd wear her blue uniform and tell them at the casting call that she was an actual RN. Maybe that would make a difference. She would spend two hours working on her dialogue, even though she only had five lines, but that was three more than usual. She'd memorize them and go over her part until she knew it backwards and forwards. She was going to continue acting class with Martin for as long as she could and then resume after the baby came. She was looking forward to being a working mom.

When Erika left, she made herself a cup of decaf Earl Grey, pulled out her phone, and typed his number.

"Hi there, L.A.," he picked up immediately. That's what he called her, L.A.

"Hey, Kansas." She felt silly. "How's it going there?"

"Good. It's cold, raining a little." Charles sounded happy. "It's nice, I like it. It's real here. How's the weather in sunny California?"

She could hear him opening a door. "Oh, you know. Sunny." She put his voice on speaker and closed her eyes.

"Writing any more brilliant poems?" he asked.

"No, just lists."

There was a pause. It wasn't weird or uncomfortable. They were both grinning a little, looking nowhere special, two particles suspended, connected.

∞

Their first time was after the poetry workshop at Alison's when she served a lusty red wine that made everyone's tongue trip over their verses. Charles was conservative by nature, but his poetry was bold and laced with rough, evocative language. His face contorted when he read his pieces. Watching him was like watching someone just before they woke up from a wild dream. For Trisha, it was both unsettling and seductive.

The poems were vibrant that night. The roaring ocean, a couple of miles to the west, was the perfect soundtrack. Trisha left with Charles. Both had parked on the same side street.

"I liked your poem about nature," Trisha said. "Can we talk a little about it?"

She wasn't totally conscious of what she was doing. She just knew she wanted to be close to him. He was tall and blond, just like the sperm-donors they were considering...

Trisha and Charles sat in his SUV until it became too uncomfortable not to touch each other. Her fingers brushed his lips. He was surprised, but only for a few seconds. He kissed them, and then the inside of her wrist, and then her mouth. They slipped into the back seat. They made out because it felt good to do something they weren't supposed to and because it felt good. Trisha kicked off her heels and slid out of her skirt. He pulled her panties off as he un-zipped and entered her so quickly, he almost slid out because she was so wet.

"I haven't been with a guy in a long time," she said. "You should feel flattered."

"I'm very flattered," he smiled.

"Yes," she murmured, putting her hand between his legs. "I can tell."

He lifted her cream silk blouse and unsnapped her bra. Her breasts were exposed in the soft moonlight that filtered in through the windshield. They curved up to meet his mouth. Her nipples were redolent with the taste of red wine. His eyes took in her sculpt-ed thighs. She was glistening, aroused, welcoming him into her. Her skin was burning as she moved him closer to her. He swirled his tongue, tasting her, loving her. Then he lay back, and she put him in her mouth. She had done this before but had never enjoyed it. She had always thought she was supposed to do it, that it was expected of her. But now, it was the only thing she wanted to do. Then she straddled him, moving in a deep undulation that created a rhythm that consumed them both until they came with a force greater than either of them expected. She tightened her muscles, keeping him in her for as long as she could. Then she lay on top of him, quiet in his arms.

∞

"Hey, L.A.," Charles' voice brought her back to the present. "Can I read you something?"

"Yes, please." She sipped her tea. He closed a door in the background.

"It's Rilke," he said. "One of my favorites."

"I know." She could imagine his long fingers lifting out the blue silk bookmark, the letters smudged red with wine.

"Perhaps all the dragons in our lives," he read, "are princesses who are only waiting to see us act, just once, with beauty and courage." His voice was soft, intimate, just for her.

"That's so beautiful." She wandered into the nursery. She'd been afraid to enter these past twelve weeks. Today, she was brave.

"There's something you should know," Trisha said.

She opened the window and watched the orange curtains pulsate.

"I'll be back in Los Angeles this Thursday," he said. "I have some things to do first. Before the workshop. Closing up my L.A. practice there, you know."

Dear Amy, I'm in a web of my own creation. How do I stop myself from making a choice I don't want to make? I'm in love with my girlfriend. But there's this man I have feelings for... and I'm pregnant. Do I tell the truth? Sincerely, Scared.

"I know," she said. "How're your parents?"

"Fine. I'm glad I'm here taking care of them."

"Work?"

"Busy"

"Wife?"

"We're trying..."

"Good." She rested her hand on her stomach.

She noticed a penny on the floor in the corner of the room. Maybe Erika left it there for good luck. Would the baby look like Charles, or "Green-Eyed Optimist"? They were both blond, so if she turned out to have yellow hair, no one would ever suspect.

"Will I see you at poetry?" Charles asked.

There was something she needed to tell him. Many things.

"Yes."

They hung up simultaneously, neither one saying goodbye. They didn't want to admit to each other and certainly not to themselves what their affair meant, or didn't mean, in the grand scheme of their lives.

~ 35 ~

ALISON

December 4, 2018

ALISON KNEW SHE COULDN'T TRAVEL with a newborn—not without raising suspicion, not at her age, and especially not at the Mexican border.

She Googled "birth certificates" and found out you needed something called a "certificate of live birth" first. It was a legal document that required proof of pregnancy, names of the parents, evidence of a live birth from a witness like a medical practitioner, and the name of the place where the live birth occurred. Then, and only then, could you apply for a birth certificate. Alison, of course, wouldn't have any of this information.

So she looked up "adoption papers." They could replace a birth certificate, but you needed a birth certificate to replace. No, she had to find another way. She could go online to apply for the baby's Social Security number, but she'd need to input a lot of information. She'd have to lie. Her application could be red-flagged.

She could get caught. And then what would happen? The FBI would track her down. She'd have to confess she took the baby from a fire station on Sunset Boulevard. Was it illegal if she was planning on giving it a good home? Was that so wrong? Everyone knew foster homes weren't always safe environments for children. Who would prosecute her? The fire station? Safe Haven? California Child Services? God?

No one would report the baby missing if she took it from the front door of the fire station quickly. The young mother would never know. She'd think the baby was in the hands of the firemen. The firemen would never suspect that a baby had been taken.

After some more Googling, Alison learned that 931 newborns had been safely surrendered to Safe Haven between January 2001 and December 2017, according to data by the California Department of Social Services. Within that same time frame, thirty-three of those infants were reclaimed. What if the mother wanted her baby back an hour later or two days later?

"The baby will have a good home," she promised the computer screen. "I will make sure of that!"

One government site said the baby wouldn't need a passport if traveling by car, but it would still need a birth certificate. Another site said the baby would need a passport when traveling by air. She looked up the forms for passports, DS-11—but she'd have to deliver the application in person to a government office. That would be a problem.

Was she really thinking of stealing a baby? But if the baby didn't have a home yet, was it really stealing? She pushed away from her desk. What she wanted was the possibility of a new life, a child to raise, and maybe another chance with Jesse. But this plan was more than a little crazy. She didn't even know if Jesse was single. And what if he still hated her? She didn't want her future to be Jesse-dependent.

She went into the kitchen and made herself a cup of chamomile tea. She inhaled its earthy fragrance and gazed up at the wall calendar. In a month, she'd be fifty-one years old. She'd be done teaching by then. She'd be ready.

And where did this need to bring a baby to Jesse come from? She could never change the past. He'd definitely think she was out of her mind, and he'd ask whose baby it was. And if she told him the truth, he'd probably contact the Policia Federal and have her arrested.

She knew it was irrational, but something about what she was doing felt right, felt destined. When she closed her eyes and went deep into herself, she saw the same image she'd seen the night she came up with the plan—the image of her mother holding a newborn deer. It gave Alison inner peace. She didn't want that bubble to burst.

~ 36 ~

WANDA

April 8, 2019

Sᴏʟ ᴡᴀɴᴛs ᴛᴏ ᴅᴏ sᴏᴍᴇᴛʜɪɴɢ different today.

"Angel, let's go to the beach."

We walk up Vermont Avenue past the big hospital and take the bus goin' west on Sunset. We're the only white people. Truth is, no one's lookin' at us.

"This is the longest street in Los Angeles," he says. "It will take you to the edge of California."

Lots of homeless people, like you, livin' on the streets. Could be me soon.

We cross over a freeway that says Hollywood North and South. Sol gives me a peach from his pocket. I take a bite, and it's so sweet I can feel Grace smilin'. The streets have Spanish names, and then they don't—restaurants, stores, mansions, emerald lawns, a pink Beverly Hills hotel, the tallest palm trees ever. The road's a river, curvin' left and right. We cross over another freeway, maybe ten thousand cars, I swear. In front of a dove-white buildin' is a statue of the Virgin Mary. I love the Virgin Mary. She's glorious, her arms open so wide I feel her huggin' me. We pass a fire station. It sure looks like that one from home. I feel safe all of a sudden. I know it's crazy. But I do. I give Sol the pit and he wraps it in his handkerchief and puts it back in his pocket. We pass a park, then a big hardware store. Then there's mountains, and there's the Pacific, wavy and wide as the whole horizon. We get off and go into a gas station to use the restroom. There's a police car parked there just waitin' for me to come by so they can snatch me up.

"Sol," I whisper, not feelin' safe anymore. "I'm scared."

"You're with me." He puts his arm through mine. "Don't worry." I wonder what people think when they see me and Sol. Maybe they think he's my grandfather. Maybe they're thinkin' somethin' else.

"What if Travis told the police?"

He shrugs. "Then they're not looking for you at the beach, that's for sure."

There are two benches. We sit on one and split an orange. He puts the peel in his pocket too. Then we walk to the water. No matter how hot it's outside, he wears the same gray cap and wool jacket. He must've lost the part of his body that keeps him warm. He wears all kinds of colored scarves that his Ruthie knits him. He changes up his *yarmulke* every day, and he wears one no matter what, 24/7. I've been with Sol for nine days, and he's never worn the same one twice. Every mornin', I look forward to what rainbow choice he'll come in wearin'.

"What did you do in Mobile?" he asks, takin' off his jacket for me to sit on.

Lots of seagulls stand there on the sand, not movin'. They look like fancy waiters with sharp eyes and pointy noses waitin' for an order. At the same second, they all turn their heads to the ocean, pull up their feet and rise over the water, squawkin' like balloons whistlin' air.

"I useta work at my cousin Autumn's hair salon and a bar near the airport so Travis could open his garage. Costs a lot to set up a business."

"You're right," he nods. "I was in the furniture business myself."

"Like in a store?" I ask.

The sun's itchin' to say hello, pokin' its head through the thick clouds.

"Yes, a great little store. Schonblum Brothers on Broadway in downtown Los Angeles. We were there for thirty-five years. Sofas, beds, dressers, dining room sets, cabinets, credenzas, cribs, highchairs." He looks real proud of helpin' people make a house into a home. I imagine Sol talkin' and wavin' his arms, a little guy lordin' over lotsa tall customers, showin' off the wares. I bet he was good at bein' a salesman. He cares about people, and his customers musta felt that.

The tide's toyin' with us, comin' in slow, then fast, then even slower than before. Lookin' down, a bird might think the ocean was drunk.

"Is that what you wanted to do when you were a kid?" I ask. "Was the furniture business your dream?"

"I never had the chance to ask myself that question." He takes off his cap and puts it on his lap. "I was captured by the Nazis when I was a teenager. Most of my family was murdered. After I came here, all I could do was think about surviving. I didn't even speak English." He removes the bobby pins and his *yarmulke*. He rubs his hair to let the ocean breeze cool down his head. Then he attaches it back on. His hair has indentation marks, so the pins know exactly where to slip in.

"How come you still believe in God after what happened?"

Maybe I shouldn't've asked him. Maybe it hurts too much. Maybe it's too private—but he glances my way, then takes holda my hand.

"God didn't kill the Jews." He squeezes my fingers so I'll remember forever. "People did. Evil, stupid, prejudiced people. Lots of them, from all over Europe." He picks up a stone. "God is what helped me after." He stands and throws it into the waves. "God is what keeps me living. And the *Lamed Vavniks.*"

"The— the—whatniks?"

He picks up another stone, hands it to me like he hands me his peaches and oranges. The seagulls fly close, thinkin' we got food for 'em. All we got is stones.

"The *Lamed Vavniks.* The Thirty-Six. You never heard of them?"

I shake my head.

"God and Abraham had an argument. God wanted to destroy mankind because there was so much terrible in the world. But Abraham said if there were good people, even a small amount, it was worth it to save the world. They discussed, and finally God agreed on the number Abraham suggested, thirty-six. So if the world is still here, it's because there are thirty-six humble, righteous people holding it up for the rest of us."

"Thirty-six? That's not a lot."

"No," said Sol. "But it's enough."

I stand, brushin' the sand off my long skirt. Sol must be one of 'em thirty-six, I'm thinkin'.

"What about you?" he asks.

"Me?"

"Your dream," he says.

I skip a stone out as far as I can throw. It hops three times. Three long, graceful hops. Then a wave crashes and gobbles it down to the bottom. "Grace is my dream now." She elbows me. She musta heard us talkin' 'bout her. "I need to go to the bathroom again soon."

"You and me, we're a good team," Sol laughs. "We both pee a lot."

I'm already takin' off my shoes. "Let's go in the water first," I say. "You think someone will steal our things?"

Sol turns around. He holds his hand over his eyes and squints at the people on the beach.

"Do these people look like thieves to you?" he asks.

I look behind me, and there's a family playin' Frisbee. A little way down is a lady sittin' on a towel, writin' in a notebook. A sharp breeze lifts her straw hat off her head, and a whole bunch of red hair tumbles down her shoulders. The hat rolls across the sand to us. I pick it up, and Sol takes it back to her. They talk for a bit. They both look over at me and wave. I feel kinda silly, kinda special too, like I'm a kid at school, and my parents have come to pick me up. I wave back.

"Nice lady," he says, walkin' back over to me. "Comes here to write poems."

"What about?" I'm curious. I know a little somethin' 'bout art. But poetry? Nothin'.

"About what everybody writes about." He's takin' off his shoes and socks. "Love. What else?"

"She tell you that?" Maybe everyone tells Sol their secrets.

"She didn't have to," rollin' up the hem of his pants. "At my age, you know these things."

The clouds are breakin' up, and more of the sun peeks through. Some rays are bold, shinin' a spotlight just on us.

"Why are you so kind to strangers, Sol?" I ask.

"You never know," he shrugs, like it's the most obvious thing on earth, "that poem lady could be one of the Thirty-Six."

We both look over at her. Her straw hat is back on, and she's writin' away like she just got an idea from God or somethin.'

"Come, let me help you, Angel." Sol reaches for me. "Take my hand."

I know he could slip out with the current if I don't hold onto him. I grab his hand and squeeze tight. We make each other stronger. Maybe that's what being kind really is. It's helpin'. You do somethin' for someone, but really, they're doin' somethin' for you too. Everybody helpin' everybody. What a nice world that would be.

Me and Sol step in. I gasp as I feel the freezin' ocean, holdin' my skirt up so the hem don't get wet—but I don't even have to. The only thing touchin' the tops of these waves are the soles of our feet.

~ 37 ~

TRISHA

December 20, 2018

Trisha looked in the mirror in the nurses' changing room at the Hollywood Presbyterian Hospital. She studied her growing body. It was still foreign to her. Her hips and butt were bigger, making her look like a pear from every angle. Trisha had gained twenty pounds so far. She'd probably gain another twenty-five, at least. Her breasts were huge, overflowing all her old bras. She went up two full cup sizes in four months.

She was more than halfway through her pregnancy, or "their" pregnancy, as her obstetrician always called it. The baby was the size of an avocado by now. They were always comparing it to one fruit or another. She hoped she could feel it move. That happened in the fifth month.

Trisha changed back into her regular clothes. She pulled up a stretchy pair of purple pregnancy leggings over her wide hips. It had extra fabric at the tummy. She put on a gray sweatshirt with the words, "Eating Tacos for Two," printed on the front—a present from Erika.

Pregnancy was an unsettling experience. Something—someone—was growing inside her, and she had no control over it. There was an alien in her body, and it was making her tired all the time. She felt hungry, heavy, burdened with the extra weight of fat and responsibility. Her senses were no longer her own. Trisha's emotions rushed from joy to fear in the span of a moment. She couldn't stand the smell of meat, yet she was craving boiled bacon and cabbage, which she hadn't eaten since she was a little girl in Canada. Erika's lavender-scented deodorant made her eyes water. The feel of cantaloupe rinds on her fingertips made her squirm. The house was too hot, the yellow roses too bright.

Trisha was upset with herself. She felt guilty. Why did I do it? If Erika ever found out, she thought—well, I'll deal with it then. She hadn't wanted to feel like a temporary container, but that's what she was supposed to be. She kept coming up with metaphors: "a piggy bank for their savings," "an oven for their bread," "an envelope for their letter." And what if she wasn't just the surrogate, the stand-in, the substitute for Erika's egg and "Green-eyed Optimist's" sperm? What if she was the actual mother and Charles was the father of the baby growing inside her? How would she ever know? She was a nurse, after all. She recognized that if some medical emergency arose someday, then the truth would have to come out. But for now, she would keep her affair with Charles the deepest of secrets. Like she kept the number of lovers she had during the "catch-up arrangement" a secret.

Trisha was growing her hair out. Nine months would be long enough to see if she liked her blond curls past her shoulders. Erika hadn't noticed. She was too busy at work. *The L Word* had given her an episode. She stayed late at the office, writing draft after draft. At least she was happy. Her dreams were coming true.

Trisha pulled on her fleece jacket and left. Driving home, all she could think about was the previous night. Erika had surprised her by coming home early to paint the nursery. Erika always fancied herself a handywoman. They'd chosen a soft green called Baby Tendrils.

"She's going to love it here," said Erika, pouring the paint into the pan. "Any new thoughts about a name?"

"Let's wait 'til she arrives." Trisha hoisted herself out of the rocking chair.

"You know," Erika glanced up, "I'd like to name her after my father, after all."

"Norman?" Trisha moved in front of Erika, then turned around. It was her signal. "That's cruel and unusual punishment," she smirked. "Don't you think?"

Erika stood up, wiped her hands on her jeans and pressed her strong fingers into Trisha's knotted muscles.

"Ouch!" groaned Trisha. "Take it easy, please."

"Sorry," Erika said, bending down to kiss the middle of her partner's back. "It's important to me."

"Of course, I understand completely. You really loved him. I wish I felt the same way about my parents. But I don't. So you've got no argument from me. Norman it is!"

Trisha tried to loosen up, but her shoulders ached, and her back was sore. She breathed deeply, exhaled slowly, letting her body slacken like a rag doll.

"You know I wanted you to pick the name, right?" Erika said.

"Yeah."

"I want you to feel connected to her. And I thought that would happen the more pregnant you got. But I'm not sure that's happening. Am I right?"

"What are you talking about?"

"You seem more detached from her every day. Like she's not really there."

"It's just weird." Trisha moved away. "You know, having something growing inside of you."

"Life, growing inside of you! A miracle! You don't know how lucky you are. I'd give anything to feel that. It's the one totally female experience nobody can take away from us." Erika stepped closer. "Come back. Let me finish."

Trisha sat on the edge of the sofa.

"An 'N' name will do." Erika resumed rubbing her back. "You choose."

"Me?" asked Trisha. "Like what?"

Erika pulled a note from the front pocket of her denim shirt. "Well, I just happen to have a list—"

"Don't stop," Trisha begged. "Do that thing you do, I love."

Erika's hands kneaded into her partner's back.

"Oh yes," she groaned, "that thing. You know, if you decide to quit writing, you could always be a masseuse…"

"Nicole, Natalie, Nina, Naomi, Natasha—"

"Nina? Like in *The Seagull*?" Trisha asked.

"I guess," Erika answered.

"That's a good name."

Erika moved up to the shoulders. "Nina O'Connor-Rossi. You like?"

"I like," Trisha relaxed. "A lot. You?"

They kept the floor of the nursery natural wood, with no shellac coating in case of pollutants. They'd paint the shelf orange. It would be the new home for children's books and plush toys. The crib would be Ikea white with zoo animal linens. A chest of white drawers would replace the desk. A dark green lamp with a white shade would sit on top, with a round braided rug resting green and orange on the floor.

"Absolutely! Yes!" Erika said as she pulled Trisha up and danced her across the floor. "Nina it is!"

Whole Foods was just ahead on the left. Trisha needed more prenatal vitamins and green juices, more lentils and peas and legumes and anything to help with the gas, constipation, and heartburn. She was the poster child for the second trimester. Christmas was five days away. She'd buy a small turkey and all the traditional vegetables to go with it. She needed to write something too. The poetry workshop was coming up on Thursday. She hoped Charles would be there even though he'd probably be spending the holidays with Olivia and his parents in Kansas City. She missed the person she was when she was with him.

Before she entered the market, a hollowness swooped into her body. She sat down at an outdoor table. The name was finally chosen, yet Trisha felt her throat constrict. Why was it always like this? A moment of joy, an hour of dread. She put her hands on her stomach and closed her eyes. She'd tried to imagine the fetus, but nothing ever appeared in her mind, no matter what she pictured it as—a peppercorn, a pomegranate seed, a kumquat, a plum. She didn't feel connected to it because of her secret. She wanted that to change because what was important now was the baby and Erika. Nina was a lovely name. It meant "little girl" in Spanish.

A crow plunged down to pick up an abandoned potato chip.

Why did I do it? She rubbed her stomach. Why did I do it? She bent her head as a tear dropped onto her gray sweatshirt. Why did I do it?

It was Trisha's longing to be seen, to be the star just once in her life. She wanted the baby to be hers. She wanted to be the actual mother. Even though no one else would know, she thought it would fill her emptiness, her feelings of unworthiness. She had been an unloved child, never cherished by her parents. It's why she became a dancer, then an actor. She tried to be the best at everything she did so somebody would notice her. "See me," she implored from the stage. "Love me."

She understood that now. But it was too late. Trisha did not know who the real parents of Nina were.

Last night as moonlight unfurled over their bed like a hazy blanket, Trisha wanted to blurt out the truth, bare her soul to Erika, and confess her intentionally unprotected affair with Charles, as well as her unequivocal desire for the baby to be hers. But she couldn't take the chance that Erika might never forgive her or never love the baby.

"I'll be a great mother to Nina," Trisha promised, instead of coming clean. She rolled over to spoon with her partner.

"I know you will," said Erika as she adjusted the covers over them. "You get to be the parent you wish you had."

Trisha touched her partner's shoulder. "Kind of a do-over?"

"Yeah, exactly that," Erika mumbled as she dozed off. "And remember I love you."

But can you really love me if I have secrets? thought Trisha. Can you really see me if part of me is hidden?

It began to drizzle a soft December rain. Oh, how she missed the sparkling white Christmases of Canada, the ice skating at Nathan Phillips Square, the hot toddies at her father's bar. Perhaps she'd visit them with the baby next winter.

"Nina," she whispered to her belly, "whoever's daughter you are, it doesn't matter. You are loved. Really. I love you."

She would tell Erika perhaps, one day, maybe. And if Erika couldn't forgive her, she would at least try to forgive herself.

Trisha felt a swish in her belly like a mermaid's tail—a push— a flutter—a wave—or maybe just gas. It was so fast—almost like it wasn't there—but it was. She was sure now. And there it was again. She felt something and closed her eyes. She saw something—a little girl swimming in an avocado-shaped pool—kicking, kicking, kicking.

~ 38 ~

ALISON

January 4, 2019

Suzy took Alison out for her fifty-first birthday to Lunetta on Pico Boulevard. They enjoyed the tasty cuisine and laid-back atmosphere of the neighborhood restaurant. Just for fun, Suzy wore her black leather miniskirt from the old Juicy Kisses days.

"So, what do you think?" Suzy twirled, showing off her trim figure. Her hair was still short, but it had turned into a silver mop of wild curls.

"You look pretty good!" said Alison.

"You mean for someone who's about to become a grand-mother?"

"Yes, that too!" Alison slipped out of her coat. "And tell me again how that happened?"

"All I wanna do is have some fun..." sang Suzy, and they gig-gled like they were back in high school.

"Yep," agreed Alison.

"The last time I wore this skirt was the Juicy Kisses reunion at The Roxy." Suzy sipped her Seven-Up. "Remember?"

"I do. That was eleven years ago! We were forty then," sighed Alison.

"We're still gorgeous." Suzy stood up. "Gotta pee. I'll be right back."

Alison watched her childhood friend walk away and found herself thinking back on that memorable night in 2008.

∞

It was the Juicy Kisses' fifteen-year reunion. She had driven into Hollywood with her second husband, Lior. The band members wore Juicy Kisses costumes—black leather miniskirts and fishnet tights with high black boots, and studded corsets over red sheer tops. The fans dressed up in their best 90s outfits so everyone looked like they were extras from the 1991 Oliver Stone movie, *The Doors*.

Juicy Kisses had just done a short set. Alison was on the floor signing an autograph when she felt a tap on her shoulder.

"Hey, Ali. You—you remember me?"

She turned around. He'd put on a few pounds and was wearing John Lennon gold-rimmed glasses, but it was definitely him.

"It's been, I don't know... maybe twenty years, I guess?" he said.

Everything around her seemed to blur, like she had imagined it would over the years. She wondered if he heard how loud her heart was pounding.

"I—I remember you, Jesse." She tugged at her miniskirt, but it wouldn't go past her mid-thighs. "What—what are you doing here?"

He shrugged, hefting his camera bag to the other shoulder. "Oh—you know, still shooting. I figured I'd do a historical perspective with photographs from tonight's reunion and ones from the 90s."

"What?" Her mouth was parched. "You have pictures of Juicy Kisses from fifteen years ago?"

He smiled, dimples and all. "A few."

That would mean Jesse had searched for her and found her back then. Or was it just a coincidence that he was on a job shooting her band? The Roxy felt crowded all of a sudden. People were bumping into her. Someone stepped on her toe. She had assumed he forgot about her, but maybe he hadn't—

"Why didn't you come backstage and say hi then?" Alison had that strange sensation again, an iron claw digging deep and holding on.

"It was editorial stuff for *Smash Hits*. I shot from the audience and left right after the show." He looked at the floor like he was searching for something. "And you made it pretty clear you weren't interested in me, so I never bothered you."

"What? What do you mean?"

"You disconnected your phone, Ali. You moved out of your place and never contacted me. You disappeared!"

It wasn't supposed to be like this. In Alison's fantasies, Jesse always swept her into his arms and told her how much he missed her. He never raised his voice, like he was doing now.

"What was I supposed to think?" he asked.

Alison touched his arm.

He pulled away. "Hey, no hard feelings. We were really young. We did a lot of crazy things back then." He tried to sound calm, but

Alison could detect a slight edge, a crack in polished glass. "Life goes on, right?"

There was so much she wanted to say to him. The music got louder. Someone had put on Juicy Kisses' cover of "Sometimes Love Just Ain't Enough." Her drumming was solid.

"Right," she answered.

Lior came up behind his wife and hugged her. "Alison, you were fantastic up there. So much fun to see your past!"

Jesse stared at them. Lior moved Alison's hair to the side and kissed the back of her neck. She was embarrassed by this intimacy in front of Jesse. She knew this was silly, but that's how she felt—as if she were betraying Jesse with Lior.

Jesse put out his hand like he had done the first time he met Alison in the Hollywood Hills Coffee Shop. "Hi, I'm Jesse."

"Nice to meet you." Lior's grip was military-trained. "I'm Lior, Alison's husband."

She watched the men sniff each other like two lions protecting their prey. Her husband was a commander in the Israeli army. There was no mistaking his authority, his position. Jesse held on to Lior's hand for an extra second before letting go—the final roar staking its historical claim.

"Anyway—I'm flying out to Stockholm tomorrow." Jesse's gaze rested on Alison. "Nice seeing you again, Ali. You look great."

"You're always leaving, aren't you?"

There was a surprised look on Jesse's face. No, not surprised, hurt. She wanted to take the question back. It revealed too much. Now she'd have to tell her husband about their past. Lior would instinctively know there had been something between them because she'd intentionally omitted his name from her stories of lovers and friends. And now Jesse knew that Alison was still carrying unresolved issues from their time together.

Alison turned to Lior, communicating with her eyes for him to let this go. When she looked back at Jesse, he was heading for the front door.

It was so obvious he hated her. The way he moved away when she touched him. How could he not hate her? She abandoned him. She moved with no forwarding address, didn't leave a note, or talk to him ever again. Until tonight. And it was only because he had the courage to come up to her. If she had seen him first, she would have snuck out the stage door or maybe even fainted like she did when she saw him at *Amma's Healing and Meditation Conference*. She was a coward.

Another song started playing, louder than the previous one. They'd been two feet apart. She'd touched his arm. And all she wanted to do now was follow him out to Sunset Boulevard and get in his van and fly away with him to Sweden. She wanted to pretend that they'd never been apart, that the twenty years since their time together had been just a dream, and that their three-month relationship was real life, authentic life, Alison-Jesse life. She wanted a second chance.

But she didn't follow him out. How could he ever forgive her if she couldn't forgive herself?

"Come on, my love," Lior said, leading her to the dance floor.

She would pour everything into her marriage instead. She'd help her husband with his business. She had good friends who cared about her. She had a fulfilling career. She'd traveled and been with interesting men. She'd learned so much about love and loss, grieving her parents. But her true love? Her soul mate? Not Arlen, not Emanuel and no, not Lior. She hurt inside like a post-surgery patient before the meds kicked in. Because it was Jesse. It was always Jesse.

∞

Alison jumped in her seat as a busboy at the restaurant poured two glasses of water for the table. She didn't like thinking about the last time she saw Jesse. She never tried to find him to explain. She'd been too embarrassed.

"I'm starving," Suzy said, returning from the restroom. "And I'm never taking this skirt off. I got hit on by the bartender!" She took a breadstick from the basket. "Okay, birthday girl, if you could have anything at all, we're talkin' anything, what would it be?"

"Anything?"

"Anything."

"I want—I want—" Alison leaned in. "Suzy, do you think it's too late for me?"

Her friend broke the breadstick in two and gave her half. "Like my mom always says, 'Honey, it's never too late.'"

Alison smiled. "I think I'll be traveling soon. Maybe this spring." She moved closer to her best friend. She wanted to confide in Suzy and tell her about Safe Haven and her plan. But Alison could hear Suzy calling her "crazy," so she sat back and picked up the menu instead.

She'd write Suzy from Mexico and invite her to visit. In the meantime, she'd prepare a letter for Mr. Bottler, the property manager, breaking her lease, and leaving it with two months' rent on the kitchen counter, so she could travel at a moment's notice.

~ 39 ~

WANDA

April 11, 2019

I GOTTA FIND NURSE TRISHA and tell her I need help, mother to mother.

"She's on maternity leave," says the lady at the front desk.

I shoulda figured. The baby shower was a couple of weeks ago. She was ahead of me. I think 'bout us doin' ballet like watermelons, and it makes me laugh. I grab onto a chair and steady myself with it.

"You look just about ready to pop. Everything okay?" The lady sounds worried, like she's wonderin' if I'm about to give birth right here in the waitin' room.

"Yes, ma'am," I work hard breathin'. With Grace growin' up in my ribs, my lungs don't have room to move. "I'm not due for another week."

"Want something to drink?"

She gets up and hands me a water bottle, and I wonder how hair can be that black, that pretty like polished marble flowin' past her shoulders.

"Thank you."

ESTHER CHEN, her nametag says. VOLUNTEER. She goes back to the computer, clickin' away as the air conditioning turns on real loud.

"You know when she'll be back?" I ask her. "That ER nurse?"

Sol told me he thought I should give myself up to the police.

"Do you want to keep running away your whole life from this crazy man? He's the one who should be locked up, not you," he said. "And what kind of life would that be for your daughter? She's an innocent person. Why would you want to bring her into that kind of danger? Think about this, Angel."

It's funny he calls me Angel. I've grown to like this person I'm pretendin' to be. She's a better version of me. Maybe I'll change my name to Angel when all this is over, and I can become her.

"You have any relatives who can take you in?" Sol asked.

"Only my sisters," I said, "but they have their own problems. And that's where Travis will look for me first, so I can't go to them."

I didn't tell him that Betty Ann's livin' on welfare with her married boyfriend, and Janine is in Bessemer doing rehab for the second time. Even though Momma treated 'em better than me, it wasn't enough. You gotta love pure, from the heart, and the only person Momma loved that way was herself. She sure fucked us up is what I think and then a kick from Grace tells me to stop thinkin' and start doin' what I need to do.

"Her name's Nurse Trisha," I say to Esther Chen. "I forget her last name."

"Sorry," she says. "I'm not sure when Nurse O'Connor gets back. Is this an emergency? You can see someone else."

I shake my head. I only want her. But I can't go to her house. That would be rude. She was nice invitin' me and all to the shower, and I dropped somethin' off for the baby, but I can't go there now and pretend we're friends. Time's runnin' out. I open the bottle and let the water ease down my throat. Maybe this is how Mary felt carryin' Jesus. At least she had Joseph leadin' the way. Maybe Sol's right. Maybe I should turn myself in. Everythin' I did, I did in self-defense. I did it to protect Grace. Maybe the courts will have mercy on me and let me go. Maybe I'm a fool, thinkin' all this crazy hope stuff when I know I got no way out.

"Where's the ladies' room?" I stand up.

"Take the hall behind you," Esther Chen points. "It's all the way down on the right," she says, hestitatin' like she wants to tell me somethin', ask me somethin'. She's got some story, Esther Chen's thinkin' about me. Hey, it's not a story. It's my life.

"What?" I ask.

"Oh, nothing," she says. She takes a sip from the Starbucks cup sittin' next to the phone beside a blueberry muffin. "Let me know if you want some more water."

"Will do."

I turn and go down the hall and hear the front glass doors behind me screech open like a train goin' off its tracks. Street noises come rushin' in, sirens blarin' like loudspeakers declarin' war. It gets hot real quick. I think it must just be me, and I keep on walkin', but I still feel the lick of wicked fire on my back with every step I take.

"I'm searchin' for my wife, Wanda Williams," you say.

I freeze.

"I got copies of her picture here. Any place I can put them up?"

I jam my body against the wall. I know it's you, but just to make sure I creep back to peek around the corner. Esther Chen's desk faces out toward the doors, so I know I'll see you from the back. It's you alright. You're lookin' cleaned up in your white cowboy shirt and your blue jeans, your hair in a ponytail. But I know the devil when I see him.

"She's carryin' my baby," you say, proud and desperate at the same time. "You seen her?"

I move a couple steps back down the hall so you can't spot me even if you turn around. I can still hear you. I know you so well. I know you're showin' Esther Chen that picture Daddy took of us not six months ago, holdin' it up like you cut off my head. We're in his backyard for his fiftieth birthday barbecue. I'm wearin' shorts and that pink T-shirt I got at Walgreens you said looked sexy 'cuz my boobs were bigger. You called me "hot momma," and we laughed, and that's when Daddy took the picture. I'm all blond and happy and startin' to grow the baby with my bellybutton poppin' out "like a pimple of love," you said. You're huggin' me from behind with your hand on it, makin' sure everyone knows it's yours, and aren't you a big man for gettin' me pregnant. When I told you the baby was a girl, you had to take a couple shots of whiskey before you could accept the fact that it wasn't my fault.

"There's no bulletin board for that," I hear Esther Chen say, "but if she's a missing person, you should go to the police."

No Esther Chen, I scream in my head. Don't tell him that!

"Oh, they know all about her," you say. "She's a criminal."

The pressure in my chest pounds so violent I think my ribs are gonna crack.

"My wife's sick in the head." You keep talkin'. "She tried to kill me. She's real dangerous. Her picture's up in all the police stations. I figure Wanda's still here in Hollywood, and she'd come to this hospital 'cuz where else she gonna go? My baby's gotta get baptized, y'understand? I can't have my daughter livin' like a sinner."

I picture you waitin' a couple seconds for Esther Chen to notice how blue your eyes are. You're smilin' now, I bet, gazin' at her like there's no one else in the world you'd rather be with.

"What's your name, sir?" Esther Chen asks.

I'm so scared a trail of hot pee trickles outta me. You're gonna sniff me out right here in the hallway.

"My name's Travis Williams." Your voice gets ready to sing. "Nice to meet you, Ms. Chen—"

You're goin' for the handshake, but I hear her shove her chair back, scrapin' it hard against the floor.

"I can't help you, Mr. Williams," I hear Esther Chen say. She says it real loud, like she wants me to hear, and that place in my heart reserved for love gets just a little bit fuller. My vision's blocked, but I swear I can see her gettin' up to face you eye-to-eye. Maybe she recognizes the girl in the photograph is me, but it doesn't matter. No woman's ever gonna give another woman up to a man like you, not if she sees who you really are. No woman but Momma. She'd throw me into the bay and let me drown a thousand times, then sail away with you standin' behind her, a smile on her face like a spikey piece of hell.

"If she shows up, call me," you say. "My phone number is on the bottom."

The glass doors shriek open, and you stride back into the hellish sun.

I puke in the toilet, drink more water from the half-empty bottle. My body wretches so bad I'm sure Grace's gonna come out my throat. I sit on the cement floor and rest against the stall. Someone comes in. Maybe it's you comin' back to kill me. I stop fightin', but

Grace doesn't. She's carryin' me. I close my eyes and see her with Nurse Trisha's little baby, dancin' the arabesque, holdin' hands like me and Sol at the beach, helpin' each other help each other. Grace is all that matters. She's all that's ever mattered. But as long as I'm with her, she'll never be safe—from you.

"Are you okay?" I hear Esther Chen ask. "I can show you a back exit. Come on."

I wipe myself clean and throw my panties away. She gives me another bottle of water and the rest of her muffin. She rushes me to a heavy door leadin' out the alley, pushes it open and walks me through, her hand on my shoulder.

"Do you want me to call the police?" Esther Chen asks.

I do, I'm thinkin'. I want them to come and arrest you, but they'd handcuff me and shove me in a car, and my life would be over.

I shake my head.

"I have a list of women's shelters. You'll be safe there."

Sure, I'm thinkin', 'til I leave, and you'll be waitin' for me like a hunter waits for his prey.

"You stay here," she says, "It's at my desk. I'll go get it."

I nod my head.

"Good, I'll be right back."

Grace is jumpin' like a butterfly caught in a spider's web. I slam the door shut behind me. And I'm movin' as quick as I can, fadin' into shadows all the way back to the *shul*. I slip through the back door and hope Sol's not there. I got some serious thinkin' to do.

I guess that's about as much of my story as Esther Chen's ever gonna know.

~ 40 ~

TRISHA

March 17, 2019

"T HE BABY CAN OPEN AND close her eyes now," Trisha said as she chewed the lox-and-onion scrambled eggs at Wexler's Deli. "Can you believe that?"

"What does she see?" Erika took a bite of her pumpernickel bagel. She joked with Trisha about ordering the "Big Poppa Breakfast" with pastrami and cheddar cheese.

"That's me," she laughed, hooking her thumbs beneath imaginary suspenders. "I'm 'Big Poppa.'"

"And I'm just big!" Trisha joined in, brushing crumbs off the ledge of her belly. "The baby sees total darkness, I guess. Or variations of light. Anyway, I'm stuffed," she rested her hands on the baby bump. "But that's not gonna stop me from eating this black-and-white cookie!"

"Shouldn't you be careful?" Erika leaned forward.

"With what?"

"You know," she mumbled. "Your caloric intake? A black-and-white cookie, I mean...?"

Trisha had been right to worry about her pregnancy. She could hardly fit into the front seat of her car. She was as big as a house, walking into walls and brushing against strangers. She had terrible heartburn. She burped every ten minutes. She peed when she laughed; she peed when she coughed; she peed when she sneezed. She did Kegel exercises twice a day, but she still had to change her panties thrice a day. It was near the end of the last trimester. There was no turning back.

"So I'll be a little extra pregnant for the commercial shoot this week," Trisha shrugged. "Isn't it perfect that it's for Maxwell House? One of my favorite commercials from my childhood, and I get to be the calm, expectant mom, drinking decaf. I've come full circle," said Trisha. "I'm really excited, my first commercial!"

"You're going to be great," Erika smiled. "I love the way you drink decaf."

"Thanks!" Then Trisha squirmed in her seat. "The baby shower is in a week! We shouldn't have left it so late. I'm feeling anxious about the shoot and getting stuff ready for the party."

"I know," Erika poked at her pastrami. "Sorry."

Trisha pushed her dirty napkin to the edge of the table. "The baby's beginning to use her senses. She tastes what I taste. So a black-and-white cookie will taste really goddamn delicious to her because that's the way it tastes to me!"

Trisha's emotions were all over the place. She wanted to dart away, but her bigness blocked her in. A neighboring family looked up from their phones and stared as she knocked against the table.

"I said I was sorry. I'm anxious too." Erika sighed, reaching for Trisha's hands. "I know Nina listens to my voice."

Trisha held back tears. She'd already sobbed in the shower that morning, her sensations somersaulting beneath the pelt of warm water.

"You do?"

"Yeah." Erika helped ease Trisha back into her seat. "I know she hears me."

Trisha glanced over at the family. They'd all gone back to their screens. A mother, a father, and two teenage boys. How does a family drift into non-communication like that?

"What do you say?" Trisha reached for the discarded napkin and blew her nose.

"Once upon a time there was a little girl, a magic princess, a beautiful fairy..."

"That's so sweet," Trisha smiled.

"I'm going to write a story book for new parents to read to their unborn child. *A Fetus Fairytale*. What do you think?" asked Erika.

It reminded her of the idea she'd had with Charles, the poetry book for babies. She hadn't mentioned it to Erika since she was the writer of the family, and Trisha was only an amateur—except when she read her poetry out loud in the workshop. That was when her body could barely handle the emotions coursing through it. Her face would flush. Her hands would sweat. It was like the high she got when she acted. She would always be the little girl from Toronto who needed to be seen, and Charles had seen her.

They still called each other. They didn't have much to say to one another, but she'd be buzzed for the rest of the day. He was coming to the baby shower.

Wexler's Deli was busy that morning. Hungry diners were lining up. Erika was ready to leave. Trisha pulled out her prenatal vitamins and stacked them on the plate. She sipped some water and popped them into her mouth, one at a time.

"I'm gonna take dance classes once the baby comes. I'll look like me again," she grinned. "Just thought you'd like to know. And my agent said there are more and more parts for mothers, so I'm hopeful."

Trisha split the black-and-white cookie down the middle. She was vanilla. Erika was chocolate. When she stuck one piece on top of the other, they made a perfect half-moon shape. She dipped the double-edged treat into her tea. Tiny pieces soaked off and floated near the rim of the mug. She bit into the moist cookie and chewed it 'til a rich, sweet paste rested on her tongue.

"Ready?" Erika got up to leave.

"Sure." Trisha followed. She was the tortoise. Erika was the hare.

They drove from Grand Central Market along Alvarado, past Señor Gabriel's fortune-telling parlor with the pink door. The sign was still there: *SEÑOR GABRIEL: RESPUESTAS.*

A line of ten people stretched out on the sidewalk. She wondered if he'd remember her. Trisha pressed her forehead on the car window. It had been a little over a year since she'd stood in that doorway looking for answers. *Buena madre*, Señor Gabriel had said. She never told Erika about that, either.

When they got home, a familiar heaviness hijacked Trisha's body. She threw her purse on the sofa and trudged to the bedroom. Her need for immediate naps, just like in the first trimester, was back.

While she was sleeping, her cell phone rang. Erika picked it up—maybe it was a friend RSVPing to the shower. The name on the screen read "Kansas." She didn't recognize the caller and let it go to voicemail. But she slipped the phone in her pocket before she went outside. In the backyard under one of the orange trees, Erika played the message from Kansas.

"Hey there, L.A. It's me. Been thinking about you. Missing you. Wrote another poem. Can't help it. You're under my skin."

Erika counted the other calls from Kansas. There were over forty-five, dating back a year. That meant almost a phone call a week from Kansas—Charles, obviously.

Erika strode into the house and down the hall. She opened the door to her sleeping lover.

"Hey there, L.A! It's me," Erika said, her voice low and even, but brimming with intensity. "Been thinking about you. Missing you." A nerve twitched in her left eyelid. Heat climbed up her chest to her cheeks. Her palms were slippery. Her legs were shaking.

Trisha opened her eyes and saw her cell phone in her partner's grip. There was a sudden rush of cold in the room.

"Wrote another poem," Erika echoed Charles' message. "Can't help it. You're under my skin."

Trisha swung her legs over the edge of the bed and tried to stand, but the weight of it all wouldn't let her. "I'm sorry..." she said. "It's—it's not what you think."

"You have no idea what I think!"

"It's been over for a long time, I swear! He—he thinks he's in love with me," Trisha twisted the hem of her blouse straight, "but he's not really. It's just—some fantasy he has that keeps him writing poetry."

Erika took a step closer, looking at her partner as if for the first time. "And you?" crossing her arms. "Are you in love with him?"

"No." Trisha struggled up. "I love you!"

"Then why do you and Charles talk? I thought he moved permanently to Kansas City."

Trisha knew right away that Erika had checked her history of calls with Charles. A wave of nausea rushed up from her stomach to her throat. Was this really happening? Was it all going to come out now—a week before the baby shower, a month before the baby was due? She took a sip from the glass of water still on her night table.

"Are you going through my phone?" Trisha faced her partner. "That's so wrong. That's an invasion of privacy."

"Oh, really?" Erika laughed and flung the phone on the bed. "I think infidelity is way more 'wrong' than an 'invasion of privacy'!"

"Charles and I are done." Trisha wiped the sweat above her lip. "It was only twice, like I said."

"His phone calls go all the way back to April 2018. That's close to a year!"

"So we talk about our poems, the workshop."

"Right." Erika leaned against the chest of drawers. It seemed like she needed its support to keep her standing. "Is that why you always came home late?"

"You were asleep. You have no idea when I got home."

"You were always tired the next morning. Tired but happy," said Erika, swinging around and leaving. "That, I remember!"

Through the open door, Trisha could see Erika pull down a carry-on from the hall closet. "So what if it went on longer?" Trisha shouted. "You started all this with your 'catch-up arrangement.' I never would've had sex with other people. It was like you wanted me to."

Erika came back in, opened a drawer, and pitched underwear into the suitcase. "How many times were you with him?"

"It's in the past. I swear. We haven't met up for months."

"How many?"

"I'm sorry. Please forgive me," pleaded Trisha. "I made a terrible mistake. Please don't leave."

"How many?" Erika moved into the bathroom to get her toiletries.

"Not since October."

"So that's what—? Five? Five months?"

Trisha hesitated. "...Yes..."

It was quiet for a moment, then Erika bolted back in. "As soon—as soon as you knew you were—pregnant?"

Trisha exhaled. Finally, the truth. But there was no air left in the room, no oxygen for the women to inhale. Their ribs ached from trying.

Erika clutched her sides as if she had just run a marathon. "And did you use protection?"

Trisha hoped that the truth would set her free. But she felt the opposite, imprisoned by it instead, and with a life sentence. "We did not."

"So," Erika's voice a shattered piece of glass, "the baby—could be—his?"

"It's possible."

"His and—yours?"

Trisha shrugged. She could feel herself giving up.

"And—and not—mine?" Erika asked.

"It's—it's possible," Trisha murmured.

Erika nodded, zipped her bag, and rushed down the hall.

"Wait!" Trisha moved after her. "You're acting crazy. We have the shower coming up."

"The shower? Fuck the shower!" Erika stopped at the front door. "Why didn't you tell me?"

"Because—I thought you would leave me and the baby—like you're doing now," Trisha answered. "I—I can't do this alone."

"But you did, didn't you?" Erika's eyes were burning. "You were more than happy to fuck this man, get possibly pregnant with him, have his child, and keep it a secret!"

Trisha reached out to touch her partner. "I'll have a DNA test done when Nina is born, so we'll know for sure."

Erika shifted away. "How? How could you do this?"

Trisha moved closer. She could sense the fighter in her return. "How? How could you give me the promise of motherhood and then take it away? How could you use me as a substitute for you like I'm an understudy, going on only when you can't?" Trisha's whole body heaved as if the baby were sobbing too. "What about me, Erika? Didn't you love me enough to love my child? Or did it always have to be yours?"

Erika mumbled something but shook her head instead. Her throat tightened. The sound of the children playing across the street lay heavy between them.

"I'm going." Erika twisted the knob.

Trisha blocked the door. "And this 'catch-up arrangement' bullshit. You did it with all your girlfriends, didn't you? That's—that's why you never had a long-term relationship! They never believed you really loved them—I mean, how could they?"

Erika glared at Trisha. Her face was pale, her hands sweaty.

"Your girlfriends fooled around—with your permission—and always left you for one of their affairs," Trisha kept on. "Didn't they?"

Erika wiped her eyes, but she couldn't stop them from crying. "All I ever wanted was a child—"

"All you ever wanted was a replica of you," Trisha lashed back. "A little Erika. Well, maybe you got one—and maybe you didn't. You use people—"

"—And you don't?" Erika arched an eyebrow. "Does Charles even know that he might be the father?"

Trisha's phone rang. Perhaps it was Kansas again, trying to reach her. Or perhaps it was her father saying they wouldn't be coming to the shower. She waited for the ringing to stop.

"We never talk about it," Trisha admitted. "But I have a feeling that's why he's coming next Sunday."

"Well, I won't be here." Erika pushed open the door. "So as far as I'm concerned, you and he can go take a flying fuck!"

"But what if Nina is yours?" Trisha placed her hands on her stomach.

Both women looked down at her huge belly. A baby girl was in there, floating...

"Then she's not yours at all!" Erika's voice grew louder. She picked up her suitcase and stepped into the blinding sun. "You'll move out, and that'll be that! You have no rights. You're just the uterus." She got into her car and drove off.

Trisha stood there, paralyzed. Her greatest fear had come true.

~ 41 ~

ALISON

March 20, 2019

Dᴇᴀʀ Jᴇssᴇ,

We've already had three encounters in our lives, and that's pretty miraculous if you think about it. The first was our beautiful romance in 1988. The second time was when I saw you at Amma's Healing and Meditation Conference in 2000—maybe you saw me? The third time was at the Juicy Kisses reunion at The Roxy in 2008. I was twenty, thirty-two, and forty.

Now I'm fifty-one. It's time for me to tell you what happened and why. I'm neither proud nor ashamed of my actions. What I did was the best I could do at the time. I understand that now.

So here goes. In 1988, when I got home from Europe, I discovered I was pregnant with your child. I was young, and we hardly knew each other, but I was beyond happy. Don't ask me why. Probably because I was so in love with you, and I thought you felt the same about me. I wanted to tell you when you got back from the tour, but I couldn't. You were high on your professional future, and I was afraid an unplanned pregnancy would ruin your dreams, ruin our relationship. I see now that you deserved to know then.

I had an abortion. I decided that I would never tell you. And what was our love worth with this huge secret between us? Nothing. So I moved away and out of your life forever. Or so I thought.

I'm so sorry I didn't share the news with you. We could've figured out what to do together. Maybe the outcome would've been the same. Maybe not. We'll never know.

That's it, really. It's just three lines in this letter, but that decision changed my life. Perhaps we'll have the chance to talk about it one day.

I'm a teacher and a poet. I wrote this for you:

Todos Santos, Mexico

I imagine myself
in Todos Santos
in a white lace dress embroidered
with red flowers. I'd toss my hair
into a ponytail, tie it up
with a blue ribbon.

I'd swing your photo gallery
door wide open, and see you
sitting at your desk, your brown hair flecked
with gray, in a ponytail too.

You'd look at me, your eyes

curious at first, the same beautiful soul
shining through those eyes
and then you'd rise
and step closer

"Ali," you'd say,
and you'd invite me in
to scan the walls
with all their photographs
of the rock bands, the prostitutes
the street art—and right in the middle
a photograph of me—
the one from thirty years ago
on our last morning in Paris.

I'd just taken a shower
and you decided to stand me
by the window.
I was shivering, but
it didn't matter to you
or to me.

"Let me photograph you wet,"
you told me back then
when we still loved each other.
Droplets like sprays
of deep-sea pearls. The hotel's scarlet
curtains drawn back, exposing
the pale blue sun.

"Just you. Just me.
Think of a secret.
A deep one.
Don't tell me.
But think it."

You pointed your camera
and I looked at you
through the lens—

When we see each other again
in Todos Santos,
you'll move closer, your new wrinkles
crinkling up your face.

"It's you," you'll say
with all the saints,
"It's really you."

"I imagined you
around every corner," I'll whisper.
"Wherever I went,
I was looking for you."

~

All my love,
Alison

Alison folded the letter into a white envelope and sealed it. On the front she wrote a line from one of Rabindranath Tagore's poems:

You can't cross the sea merely by standing and staring at the water.

She dropped it into her purse. She'd give it to him in person in Todos Santos, Mexico. It would be right to finally tell Jesse the truth.

~ 42 ~

WANDA

April 12, 2019

I T'S RAININ' TODAY.

That's good news for me and Grace, 'cuz I figure you won't be out searchin' for us. You'll be in a bar shootin' off your mouth. I been thinkin' 'bout what Sol said and decided to check out an adoption agency from one of the cards Nurse Trisha gave me.

I hope maybe I'll see Ricardo on the bus, but I don't. That makes me sad. I promise myself I'm gonna pay him back his money, no matter what. I touch his necklace every night before I go to sleep. It's under my pillow with Grace's key. It's my only key now. I threw the rest away, even the small gold one from Daddy 'cuz I'm never goin' back there again. If people have children, they gotta do the best they can for 'em. That's what I decided. Even if things are tough, it doesn't matter. They gotta love 'em in that forever way 'cuz their children will know it. No matter what happens, they'll know it. Momma was abusive, and Daddy didn't protect us, and that's job number one for a parent. That's what I'm gonna do for sure. Protect Grace. I try not to cry 'cuz I don't want Grace to be sad. Today I stop myself. Other times I can't.

I still love Betty Ann and Janine. It wasn't their fault what happened. Betty Ann was Daddy's favorite, and Janine looked like Momma. And me? Here I am, twenty years old, and I still feel like a mistake. Who knows, maybe my sisters will visit me one day, and we'll talk about how we grew up. I kinda doubt it, but like Sol says, if you're gonna believe in somethin', why not believe in miracles?

The Care Adoption Agency's a small gray buildin' with a dry cleaner on one side and a check cashing service on the other. It's got a big glass door that surprises me. Shouldn't it be private, givin' your baby away?

"Please come in!" the man at the desk says.

I didn't expect a man. I don't know why, I just didn't. He's not as old as Sol, but he's got false teeth too. He's wearin' a toupee to cover his bald spot, but it's still visible, plain as day. I want to laugh, then I remember nothin's funny these days. I edge closer to his desk.

"May I help you?" he asks, soundin' like he went to college and got his degree in politeness.

As soon as he hears me talk, he's gonna think he knows everythin' about me like I'm just another stupid girl got knocked up by the wrong guy, and now I want out. But he don't know me at all.

"I have some questions," I say, real deliberate, like I'm smart, like I'm doin' a project for social studies.

"Certainly." He's got a smirk on his face, thinkin' he just caught a big fish. He slides his chair along the desk and picks up some papers. "Please fill out these forms, and I'll tell Mrs. Richmond you're here."

Ten minutes later he brings me back to a room painted pink with tall windows and pictures of happy families.

"I'm Mrs. Richmond," the lady says as she gets up. "Thank you for coming in."

I sit across from her. She reminds me of Mrs. Brown, the principal at Chickasaw High. This woman is black and maybe twenty years older than me, with shiny hoop earrings like Mrs. Brown used to wear. Her hair is slicked back with perfumed oil. Her fingernails are extra long and painted blue, curlin' down at the ends. There are pictures of her and three kids on the walls. Her husband is white. The kids are mixed, one even looks Chinese or somethin'. Probably adopted. Makes sense.

She looks at my application, then up at me. I feel like my stomach's gonna plunge through the floor and take Grace with it. Mrs. Richmond knows I made everythin' up.

"How does it happen?" I ask, before she can kick me out.

"Would you mind answering a few more questions first?" she says.

She picks up a red pen and gets ready to check the boxes. I wonder how many I have to get right? I'm not waitin' to find out.

"I want to know what happens if I give up my baby."

She puts down the pen and sighs. She's done this so many times, she must be ready to quit. She leans back and crosses her legs.

"We have several families waiting for a child to love and include into their lives. You can look at their online pictures and histories. You can talk to them or even meet them for an open adoption. If you prefer to just choose and never meet, that's fine too."

I pick up a framed picture on her desk. It's of the three children, two girls, maybe eight and ten years old, and a boy who looks like he's six. They're all wearin' the same school uniform.

"They yours?" I ask.

"Yes, all adopted," she beams. "Three different women helped my husband and myself make our family."

Maybe she's for real. Maybe I can trust her.

"When are you due?" she asks.

"In a week," I say. "Maybe sooner. It's a girl. I want her name to be Grace."

Tellin' someone to name my baby for me—I stand, too rattled to stay seated. She just nods.

"Any health issues?" she goes on, soundin' like a doctor on *Grey's Anatomy*.

"No."

"Drugs?"

"No."

Mrs. Richmond cocks her head like she's tryin' to get some water outta her ear. She scratches her nose with one of her nails and leaves a red mark. She's bothered by somethin'. Me, I'm guessin'.

"You need to be honest with me," she says. Now she's just like Momma when she accused me of stealin' her perfume and it wasn't me. I didn't tell her who it was, so she strapped me anyway. Momma caught Betty Ann sprayin' it on her Barbie 'bout a week later, and she just beat me again for not tellin' her sooner.

"I said no, didn't I?" My voice stands up for me.

Mrs. Richmond takes off her glasses to rub her eyes. She looks tired. Maybe she had a bad night. Maybe her kids are havin' nightmares. Maybe her husband's cheatin' on her.

"You did," she agrees. "I'm so sorry." Her weddin' ring's dull. I could shine it up for her. A little toothpaste and a rag would do the trick.

"Are you hungry?" she asks. "I can get you a healthy snack from the common room. Would you like some Trail Mix?"

Is this what she feeds her children?

"No," I shake my head.

"An apple?

Just 'cuz a woman can't have a baby doesn't mean she's gonna be a good mother. All them women should be standin' in front of me now, provin' how much they'll love Grace. Instead of the way it is with Mrs. Richmond makin' me feel like I'm a drug addict loser.

"I had a big breakfast."

"Okay," she nods and smiles a little. "How's the baby?"

"Good," I answer. "I went to a clinic for a checkup a week ago."

"Which one?"

I don't tell her. I cross my arms, shieldin' Grace.

"I want to help you," Mrs. Richmond says starin' at me and then down at my application like it's a menu at a bar and she's dyin' for a drink. "It says here you're not married."

"That's right."

"We still need the father's consent." She might be tired, but she's turned into a block of cement.

"I said I wasn't married." I smooth my sweatshirt over my belly.

"Is he willing to give up his child?"

That's when you show up behind her. You're smilin' so wide your teeth are gonna crack apart and fall onto her glossy hair.

"Does he know you're here?" she asks as I watch you take out that same rope you used on me from my nightmare. You twist its rawness 'round your hand, showin' me how you'd like to twist it 'round my neck.

"You see, Angel," Mrs. Richmond keeps on talkin', "in the state of California, we need both parents' consent. We can help you find a lawyer to prove that the father is abusive or negligent, if that's the problem. But it takes time and money."

I wish I could push this lady through the wall. That just makes you sneer even more 'cuz you're readin' my thoughts, aren't ya? No, Travis, you are my thoughts, my hatin' thoughts.

"So, what you're sayin' is I can't give my baby to a good family 'less I get the father's consent?" I stand.

"That's right," she nods.

"Why's it up to him? I'm the one carryin' her. She's way more mine than his."

"I understand." Her voice frays. "But he has the legal right to show up with the police and remove his child."

I take in air to steady myself. I won't let Mrs. Richmond see that she's my enemy.

"I got drunk at a party," I lie, "and when I woke up, the guy was gone." I can't believe the words comin' outta my mouth. You make me into a deceiver. Mrs. Richmond doesn't even bat an eye. She's heard it all before. "I didn't even know his name."

"Was it consensual?" she leans forward.

I'm sweatin' hard. I didn't like Principal Brown either. She told Momma I was smart but lazy, and that made Momma swing even harder.

"Or was it rape?"

What if Mrs. Richmond gets me to say you raped me, even though you didn't? Not when we made Grace, at least. That night was magic with the rainstorm and all. You and me makin' her precious life. I loved you once. Does that mean I still do even though I hate you with all my heart?

"No, it wasn't rape," I say.

I bet she has a security camera on, and she'll send the tape to the cops. And they'll come lookin' for me and take me to prison, and I'll give birth to Grace there, and you'll come with a lawyer and take her away, and I'll never see her again.

"You didn't write your phone number down, Angel," Mrs. Richmond says, back to the application. "What is it, so we can contact you?"

A blue ray of sunshine stumbles in, makin' everythin' glow sapphire, even Mrs. Richmond. Even you.

"I don't have a phone."

"What's your address?" she says, her pen itchin' to move across the page.

"I'm stayin' with friends."

"Do you need to talk with a counselor?" she asks. "I can arrange that. But we can't go forward without the father's consent."

You're starin' at me, with a look of victory on your face. Now you're twirlin' the rope 'round Mrs. Richmond's neck.

"No!" I yell. You're pullin' it tighter. "Stop!"

She must think I'm yellin' at her. "Angel, please. In my experience, most fathers don't want to take care of the child—"

"That's not true." I'm burnin' up as I watch you eye my belly. I know you want Grace.

"Just try to find the father, and—"

I start to sway and grip her desk for balance.

"I think I've upset you, Angel," says Mrs. Richmond. "I'm— I'm very sorry. I didn't sleep well. My son had a toothache, and he was up all night." She offers me a Kleenex. "You're perspiring, dear. Would you like some water?"

I shake my head no.

"Please sit down."

I do. I hear a fly buzzin'. It's hittin' itself against the window tryin' to escape. Doesn't it get all bruised up doin' that? It just keeps on at it, cripplin' its wings bit by bit. Mrs. Richmond looks where I'm lookin'. She gets up and opens the window, freein' the fly into the outdoors. Then she shuts it tight and looks at me, waitin' in the quiet for some confession to happen.

I point to the little boy in the picture. "Where'd you get him?"

"A young woman," she says, "not unlike you. She was a runaway, didn't have any money." She sets down her pen to really look at me. "She did the right thing, you know. Henry has a better life with us than he ever could've had with her."

I'm tremblin' now. My feet are jumpy.

"But what did she do with all her love?" I can't stop myself from shakin'. "Her love for her child. What did she do with that?"

I get up again, back away from Mrs. Richmond, back away from you. "Did it just quit when she gave her baby over to you? Or did it fester like a bloody wound and poison her, little by little, every day for the rest of her goddamned life?"

Mrs. Richmond doesn't say anythin' for a couple of seconds. Her mouth is dry. I can tell by the white chalk collectin' at the corners.

"We haven't kept in touch," she says.

I snatch up the application and run out past the polite old man. He says somethin' but I can't understand him. I slam the glass door behind me. I hope it shatters.

It's rainin' harder now. I rip up my dishonesties and watch them swirl down the gutter. I walk with my face tiltin' straight up to the clouds. I open my mouth, and the heavens drip into me, coolin' me down in bits and pieces, washin' what just happened away. I see a cat sittin' inside a window, lookin' down at me, starin' like they do with those see-through eyes not blinkin'. You remember the one lived next door to my parents? 'Course you do. The orange female named Sassy Pants. She had the longest whiskers you'd ever seen, you said. They were licorice red and almost touched the ground when she ran. Remember the day you got drunk on grapefruit juice and vodka? You said her mustache needed trimmin'. I begged you not to, but you wouldn't stop 'til they were just bristles under either side of her nose. And then the neighbor said Sassy Pants started walkin' into doors and walls and fallin' off ledges. She couldn't keep her balance. She was dizzy and cryin' all the time and stopped eatin' so they had to put her down. They buried her under the sunflower patch in their backyard. I knew then, didn't I Travis? Everythin' I needed to know 'bout you I knew then.

The cat in the window turns its back on me and disappears into the room. I'm soakin' wet as I get back on the bus. I'm so tired I could cry. A girl my age stands and gives me her seat. I wish to God I never pulled you outta that blazin' trailer. I wish to God I never. I hate you—my husband. The man who tasted my skin and made it weep.

~ 43 ~

TRISHA

March 24, 2019

IT RAINED THE AFTERNOON OF the shower. Trisha thought about calling it off. In the end, she decided to go through with it. She made up a story about Erika not being there because of a family emergency, and it wasn't really a fabrication. Their breakup was a family emergency.

The week since Erika's departure had been brutal. Trisha worked two double ER shifts. She broke down in front of her patients several times—especially if they were pregnant. She had to get up at 4:30 a.m. to be on set for the Maxwell House commercial by 6:00 a.m. That was the only good part of the week, being in front of the camera. She called upon her acting teacher's words and transformed into a calm, expectant mother, even though her insides were warped with anxiety. She texted Erika three times a day but never heard back.

Trisha prepared Erika's famous vegan noodle dish, drenched

in heirloom tomato sauce, and topped with roasted eggplant, yellow zucchini, and cashew Pecorino cheese. She even baked black-and-white cookies for dessert. She hoped the aroma of all this food would somehow find its way to Erika and entice her back wherever she was, like a fairy tale or a cartoon, where the beloved would sniff the delicious smells and float back on a breeze of sense memory, back to her lover, back to the possibility of happily ever after. That's what Trisha hoped.

Friends from every world came—Trisha's hospital world, poetry world, acting class world, Erika's TV world, the world of family, and the world of neighbors.

"So," Johnnie Baloney chuckled, "you obviously found someone."

He stood there, charming as ever. L.J. was almost a year older than the first time they met, running on Dillon Avenue. He had a black-and-white cookie in each hand.

The doorbell rang, even though Trisha put up a sign informing guests the door was open and to please come right in. She excused herself from Johnny Baloney and opened the door—and there was the pregnant girl from the ER, standing there in the rain, holding an umbrella and a Rite Aid plastic bag.

"Oh! Hi!" Trisha said. "You came!"

The girl blushed and nodded.

"Angel, right?"

"Yeah." She shuffled from one foot to the other. "Angel Smith. But I can't stay."

"Well at least come out of the rain—"

"No, that's okay," said Angel. "I wanna thank you for bein' so nice to me when I was at the hospital and—and give you this for your daughter," she said, handing Trisha the bag.

Trisha looked inside.

"I made a mobile for her to hang above her crib. It's wild horses and bright stars." The girl's eyes shone. "I think it'll help her dream of beautiful places."

Trisha pulled out the mobile with great care. The top frame was made of long twigs glued together in an octagon shape. The cut-outs of the horses and stars were hand-painted in bright gemstone colors. It was so natural and so special, kind of like the girl herself.

"You made this?" Trisha hugged her. "Thank you!"

"Yeah," The girl was both surprised and delighted, as if she hadn't been in another's embrace in a long time. "I'm gonna be an artist!"

"Seems to me you already are one. I'll tell my daughter about you and how we danced a ballet!" They giggled as their bellies bounced up against each other like two basketballs in a basket. "You sure you don't want to come in?"

The girl positioned the umbrella over her other shoulder. There wasn't enough room for two pregnant women to stay dry under it. "Can't. Gotta go." She clutched the railing. "I hope everything works out with your girlfriend."

"Me too."

The girl started walking down the front steps, then turned at the bottom. "Good luck!"

"You too!" Trisha reflected on this girl's life. How difficult to be so alone. And then she realized she was alone too. There had been no communication from Erika. That was wrong. She was just three weeks away from giving birth.

"You're gonna be a good mother!" The girl shouted behind her as she lumbered down the path and made a left onto Dillon.

"Madonna in the Rain," Trisha thought as she waved goodbye. That would be a great title for a poem. She reached into her pocket and ran her fingers over Señor Gabriel's purple shell. She carried it every day, either in her purse or on her body, like she had with the crushed Coke cap. It brought her a sense of calm. She thought she lost it once, but Charles texted her the next day to say he'd found it in the back seat of his car.

Trisha walked out to the street, hoping she'd see Erika driving up. Instead, she saw Alison in her green Mustang. She waited for her to park.

"Well, don't you look like a ripe peach!" Alison said, taking an umbrella out to protect them both. "You're gorgeous! How do you feel?"

"Not gorgeous." Trisha hadn't told anyone what had happened. But there was a poetic kinship between these two women since that late-night drive along Sunset. "Erika left me."

"What?" Alison slipped her arm through her friend's. "Are you serious? That's just awful! What happened?"

"I don't blame her. I did something..." Trisha stopped on the path to the house. She stared at Erika's yellow roses against the white-painted brick. The garden was just beginning to open up again. The rain made everything more colorful, more vibrant, like glistening oils on a silver canvas. This was one of Erika's passions, along with family, writing, and food. Trisha didn't know if there was still room for her in Erika's world. "I can't tell you what it is—what I did, but—she left me," tears mingling with raindrops. "I just hope she'll forgive me someday."

"We've all done things we're ashamed of," Alison said. "Have some compassion for yourself. You're carrying her baby. She'll forgive you."

"I hope so." Trisha felt a kick. "Ow! Nina's really strong! I need a drink!"

"Nina's a beautiful name! Come on," Alison enticed. "I'll make you some lemonade. I hear this place has amazing lemons."

Trisha and Alison walked into Clifton singing his own composition for the baby shower, sounding like the love child of Bob Marley and Adele. His voice was amber honey lifted straight from the hive. His moves radiated from his hips—a little Elvis, a lot of Bruno Mars. The two women from Trisha's poetry group, Marlee and Carolyne, who were also at the sperm party, were there too. But neither one had gotten pregnant. From the look on their faces as they ogled Clifton, they'd be willing to try again... and again.

"Something to drink." Alison handed Trisha a freshly made glass of lemonade.

"Thanks!" Trisha gulped it down. "I needed that! And how're you? What's been going on in the workshop?"

Alison sat down beside Trisha. She was wearing a long denim skirt with flower patches running down the side and a gold gypsy blouse. She was a woman you couldn't ignore.

"Not much," Alison answered. "We're on a hiatus."

"But you're still writing, yes?"

"Yes. All the time." She smiled. "I'm thinking of submitting my work to poetry magazines and online journals."

"Definitely, you should."

"I want to get published. There! I said it out loud!" Alison spread her arms wide. "I want to be a poet!"

"I think that's awesome." Trisha hugged her. "Go for it! And your first collection will be *Harriet's Never Going to Leave You*, and I'll be first in line to buy a copy."

"Thank you," Alison said. "That's so lovely of you to say."

The doorbell rang again. Could it be Angel, the pregnant girl, deciding she wanted to come in after all? Trisha lifted herself off the sofa and waddled to the front door.

Charles stood there in a royal blue rain jacket, holding a small gift bag. She was always surprised to see how tall he was—over six feet—and how handsome. His green eyes told her how happy he was to see her.

"Can we be alone for a minute?" he said as the rain hushed behind him.

Trisha put on a sweater and led him to the backyard where the air was an intoxicating mélange of wet grass and citrus.

"You look beautiful," Charles said, backlit by the emerging sun. A red glow emanated through his ears like he was an alien species. Trisha giggled.

"What's so funny?"

"Guess!"

"Yeah, I know," he tugged self-consciously at his left lobe. "Olivia says they're big. Cute, but big," he said, handing her the gift bag lined with pink tissue paper. "Here, for the baby."

Trisha peeked inside. "A bunny training toothbrush kit for infants. Perfect! Thank you!" She headed for the lemon trees. "So, you and Olivia are back together?"

"For now." He followed. "I have a question. You don't have to answer it and— it's okay, really it is, if you don't—"

"Ow! Ow!!" Trisha grabbed his arm.

"What's wrong?"

"Braxton Hicks, I think." She leaned back against a tree. "My womb is having contractions. They taper off. Just gimme a second to catch my breath."

She rubbed her belly. He stood with her, his clear eyes steady on her face. She inhaled deeply, then slowly exhaled.

"I feel better now," she said, looking up at him.

"You sure?"

"Yes. They're completely normal. Okay, so what's the question?"

Charles brushed her cheek with his hand. "Do you ever write poems about me?"

It wasn't the question she was expecting.

When he didn't get an answer, he continued. "Does Erika know about us?"

Trisha sighed. "Yes—yes, she does."

Charles seemed tired, like he hadn't been sleeping well. He slumped a little, losing his stature. He moved back several feet.

"Should I—should I leave?"

Now that Erika knew about Charles, the power of their secret affair and its consequences had evaporated. Trisha ran her fingers over a lemon blossom, releasing the sweet fragrance of new life. The choice was clear because there never really was a question. She loved Erika.

"No, she's not here."

"My wife doesn't know anything about us," Charles offered. The yellow-and-green trees stood behind him like soldiers, ready to defend if necessary. "And never will."

She remembered reading her poems out loud in the workshop and always looking at him afterwards for signs. Always looking to the outside for applause when it should have come from within.

"I sense you," he said. "I can't help it. Whenever I taste something sweet, I think of you."

The leaves released a halo of raindrops above them. He turned his head, looking up at the wrung-out clouds in the darkening sky.

"The baby?" His voice was soft, almost inaudible. "I've—I've been wondering about it. A lot." He shifted the weight in his legs as if he were balancing on a raft. "You said not to worry about birth control—and then you said you and Erika were going to have a baby..."

Trisha heard cars on the street. More people were arriving. They'd be wondering where she was, where Erika was. She wanted to lie down in the wet grass. She wanted absolution. She wanted Erika to come home.

He touched her cheek again. "Is it mine?"

That was the question she'd been expecting. There'd be no way of knowing for certain 'til after the baby was born. "I don't know," she answered, her curls luminous in the golden rays of sunset. "I don't think so, but I can't be sure. I'm so sorry."

The week without Erika had left her plenty of time to rumi-nate. No matter what the outcome, Trisha decided she wanted to teach the baby about unconditional love. That was something she'd never experienced. It was something she wanted to give herself too. She would try to have compassion for herself, even though she lied to Erika and Charles—a terrible lie born from a profound parental wound. Erika was a strong woman. She'd been raised with endless amounts of hugs and kisses. They would both be strong mothers, no matter whose child it was.

"I could love you," said Charles. "You know that, right?"

Trisha stretched her sweater across her belly. "I think you love your wife, Charles."

"Olivia doesn't see me the way you do."

Trisha hugged him as best she could. He was a young boy at that moment, a young boy needing to be loved.

"You and I see the wounded parts of ourselves in each other—the hidden parts we're afraid to expose." It was suddenly clear to her—an epiphany. "So, you write poetry. And I act." She stood on her toes and brushed a wet strand of hair off his forehead. "If Olivia loves you, and I think she does, she will understand the poet in you— the wild, romantic artist in you. Give her a chance. Let her see the real you," she entreated. "It's not fair to her if you don't."

Charles moved away like he was going to leave, then stopped and stood very still. "How do I do that?"

"Let her read your poems." She reached for his hand. "Better yet, you read them aloud to her."

He turned to her, his eyes shining into hers. "But I wrote them for you."

"It's easy to write a poem to someone you don't know. It takes real courage to write to someone you do."

A crow was cawing its warning to other birds. It was getting late. Time to fly home.

"I'm just a needy actress," Trisha continued with a glint in her eye. "You'll get over me as soon as you hear me ranting about my career and auditions, and the unfairness of Hollywood. I swear you will."

Charles nodded. He slipped his hand out of hers.

"You wrote your poems for Olivia. You just didn't know it at the time."

They walked in silence back down the path. She kissed him on the cheek and went into the house alone.

The music had stopped. Trisha moved into the living room

and put on a k.d. lang and Tony Bennett duet, "Because of You." k. d. lang was how she and Erika met almost two years ago at that party in West Hollywood. Anything k. d. sang was "their song," Erika had said. If the food didn't bring her back, maybe the music would—

"May I have this dance?"

There was Erika, standing in the middle of the floor, her arms open wide. Maybe it was the quiet that followed, or the stillness of the guests, but it seemed like the room stopped for a brief moment— like in *West Side Story* when Tony and Maria first see each other. Erika and Trisha looked in each other's eyes and saw forgiveness.

Steven took pictures of them on his iPhone. Erika was tall and thin. Trisha was short and round. They looked like the number eighteen.

Later that night, Trisha studied herself in the dresser mirror, her green nightgown covering her huge body. She never really felt desired as a young woman, but now, she knew that a man wanted her, and a woman wanted her. She felt special. She felt cherished.

"It's a good time to talk," said Erika. She had taken a long bath. She was wearing her flannel pajamas.

Trisha nodded, "I felt totally abandoned."

"Me too." Erika stood very still.

"What I did was wrong," Trisha confessed.

"Yes, it was. And I'm sorry for leaving like that and being out of communication."

"What if something happened to the baby?"

"I listened to all your messages," Erika said. "I just didn't answer them."

Trisha sat on the edge of the bed, nodding her head. "Where did you go?"

"My mother's."

"So, she knows?" Trisha suspected Erika might go there seeking comfort and advice. Trisha would never contact her parents for either.

"My mother told me to put myself in your shoes. So I did." Erika faced her partner. "You were right. I offered you something, and then I selfishly took it away. I deeply apologize. I can understand why you did what you did. It was still pretty terrible—what you did and... and I'm not condoning it, and never will—but I'm not condemning it either. All I'm saying is—I understand why. I understand why you did it."

Hoots and coos from the neighborhood owl seeped in through the bedroom windows—soft at first, then louder, then somewhere in between. The women had gone out at midnight when they first moved in, just to observe the owl's night home. It was the top of Johnny Baloney's pine tree. The witness tree.

"Will you ever forgive me?" Trisha asked.

"I'm here, aren't I?"

Like the letting down of a heavy curtain, Trisha began to cry. Erika joined her. Their sobs were a lament of love and regret. "We can do a DNA test so there's no question..."

"No, I'll love Nina no matter who her parents are. She is our daughter. That's what's important." Erika wiped her eyes with a tissue. "You want to hear something crazy?"

"Always," Trisha grinned.

"I felt like I was at our wedding earlier, y'know? That k.d. lang and Tony Bennett song was our special dance... Crazy, right?" Erika plopped down on the bed and sat cross-legged. "So—so what do you think?"

"Sorry," Trisha said, going to the bathroom to wash her face.

"What do I think about what?"

Erika followed and stood behind her, talking to their reflection. "About a real wedding—about getting married." She bent her head and kissed Trisha on the cheek—the same spot where Charles had touched her earlier. "Do you—do you want to?"

Trisha recalled Erika asking the same question just three months into their relationship. "Do you want to?" It was about getting pregnant. And now here she was, just a few weeks to go, asking her about getting married.

"Yes." Tears moistened Trisha's eyes again.

"I'll adore any child that's ours," said Erika. "I promise."

"I promise too." Trisha put one hand on her stomach and the other on her lover's cheek. "Do you really want to marry me? After what I did?"

"I love you," answered Erika.

"I love you," Trisha echoed her partner. "Yippee! When?" She carefully pirouetted down the hall. "Before or after the baby comes?"

Erika swiveled her hips, just like Clifton. "Before."

"So, like next week?" Trisha didn't know whose heart was beating faster—hers or Nina's.

"Sure. We'll go downtown to City Hall. Then we'll go to Langer's for the hot pastrami and corned beef. And we'll order Cokes!" She reached out her hand for Trisha, and they danced their way into the bedroom.

Later, they lay in bed with both pairs of hands on Trisha's growing belly. The baby moved, then moved again. Trisha rolled onto her right side. She encircled her stomach with her arms. Erika spooned a little closer, their bodies fitting together like a Russian matryoshka doll, one inside the other, inside the other.

~ 44 ~

ALISON

April 14, 2019

Aʟɪsᴏɴ ᴅɪᴅɴ'ᴛ ᴋɴᴏᴡ ᴡʜᴀᴛ ᴛᴏ wear to Trisha's baby's funeral.

"What? Wait–" The phone burned against her ear as she stared into the darkness of her closet. "What happened?"

"No one knows," Carolyne answered. She had a soothing voice. Alison sensed she was a good therapist. Her poetry was always sensitive and deep.

"Was it the umbilical cord?"

"No." Carolyne sighed. "They did an emergency C-section, but the baby was already dead."

Black was what you wore to funerals. It's what she wore to her parents'. Black was for old ladies and presidents. The baby was so young, not even born. Maybe white, to honor her innocence. Amma always wore white, for purity and holiness. Alison sat down on the bed, her body a boulder. No, she would wear black, of course.

"How's Trisha doing?" she asked, wiping her tears with the

sleeve of her silk blouse.

"Devastated," Carolyne replied. "They don't understand how it could happen when nothing was wrong the whole pregnancy."

Alison grabbed one of the burgundy velvet cushions and cradled it to her chest. She slowed down her breathing ... in for three ... out for three.

"The baby shower was the last time..." Carolyne sighed.

Alison could still see Trisha and Erika dancing in the middle of the living room.

"Me too," said Alison.

Carolyne was silent on the other end while Alison struggled to remember the poems Trisha wrote about her pregnancy. She tried to glimpse a phrase in her mind's eye, but her thoughts were scrambling over one another, trying to find purchase. She rose from the sofa and pulled Trisha's poems from the workshop folder in her file cabinet. If not for the move, her house would be in chaos, but her files were always in order. It was a teacher's habit. She was always losing her phone, but she knew where to find anything that one of her students or poetry workshop participants had ever written. Before she left Santa Monica for good, she'd have a ceremony on the beach. She'd smoke a joint, raise a glass of wine to her creative friends, and burn everything from her files in a fire pit on the sand. It would be a ceremony of liberation, the poems embraced in smoke, wafting up to the stars.

"Anyone else coming from our poetry workshop?" Alison inquired.

"I don't know," Carolyne said. "Hopefully, Charles will fly in. He was pretty devastated when I told him."

Alison couldn't imagine a harder call to make.

"Anyway," Carolyne exhaled, "see you at Hollywood Forever."

Alison placed Trisha's poems on the nightstand. She'd read them later. She went into the bathroom to wash her face. She wrapped her hair back and held it up with a tortoise shell clip. An empty wine glass from the night before balanced precariously on the edge of the tub. It was the last of the new rosé. She went to rinse it in the sink, but it slid from her grip. When she caught it, the thin glass broke in her hand, and a sleek piece sliced across her thumb. That broke the dam. Alison shattered into herself, doubling over, her bloodied hands holding onto the sink. It was that feeling again, a wide emptiness. It hadn't happened in so long, she'd almost forgotten it, but now it pounded in her stomach like a jackhammer grinding a wall of ice. She could've folded in two, slipped into a crack in the wall. She eased herself down instead and rolled into the child's pose, bending her knees, and touching her forehead to the turquoise hexagon tiles.

A surge of depression was rolling in. She could sense it. Her personal sorrows were tangled up in its dense waves. Alison remembered from the grief group that she was experiencing a form of post-traumatic stress disorder. A sense of meaninglessness settled into her being like dredged-up sludge. Baby Nina's death reminded her of her parents' deaths. It was like the subconscious rug was pulled out from under her. The unfathomable cruelty of these mortalities left her bereft and desolate. Alison wanted to collapse into the cracks between the tiles and live there forever. She tried to meditate instead and remembered Amma saying, "Meditation is listening to God." Yeah, right. She was done listening.

"Dear God." She looked up. "What the fuck?"

The god Alison grew up with was protestant. The only path to Him had been through the Bible. She searched every page, but she still couldn't find her way there. She stopped singing in the choir.

She refused to go to church on Sundays. She became an agnostic. That's when she encountered New Age thought. This new universe was karmic—the pop concept of "do good and good will come to you." After her parents' death, she learned to embrace spiritualism and its meaning of karma—where your journey was the sum of all lives, not just this one, and suffering was a part of that. The kindness of Amma's prayers helped her put the rough patches into perspective. But no one deserved to suffer like Trisha was suffering. What was there to learn from this kind of despair?

Alison walked into her bedroom. Maybe the tragedy that Trisha and Erika were experiencing had absolutely nothing to do with anything else. Maybe their baby's death had no spiritual justification, none at all, just like her parents' senseless freak accident. Maybe life was unfair, and terrible things happened to good people, because that's just the way it is—and always will be. But did that mean you had to stop yourself from living because terrible things could happen?

Alison lay down and pulled the covers over her head. A gnawing snaked in her belly. It wasn't the regret of what she did. It was the regret of what she didn't do.

~ 45 ~

WANDA

April 14, 2019

Grace is almost here.

I bet you're checkin' all the hospitals in Los Angeles now, callin' them to ask if your wife's in their maternity ward. I'm not Mrs. Travis Williams anymore. No one knows me here, no one but Ricardo and Sol, and they'd kill before they'd give me up to you. No one knows my real name. No one knows Wanda Williams. Ricardo calls me Angel. Sol calls me Angel. No one can track me. I cut up my driver's license and threw the pieces into garbage cans all down Western Avenue, so no one could put me together.

Sol still gives me those dark pink pre-natal vitamins and makes me drink lots of water, but I know I'm empty inside. Grace takes all I can give.

Everybody talks to a pregnant girl. "When are you due?" "Is it a boy or girl?" "Is it your first?" Always the same questions. Everybody comes up and tries to put their hands on me, like I'm a public figure 'cuz I got a baby inside. I can't hide that anymore. Ladies see me as a member of the club. That part's nice, at least.

Everybody always says I'm "expecting." I didn't know what they meant before, but now I do. I'm expectin' a whole new person to show up. And what happens when she does? I can't call Momma, or she'll send police dogs to track me down. I can't call Daddy, 'cuz he's too weak to help anyone but himself survive. I can't call Betty Ann and Janine 'cuz it looks like they gave up on me the day I married you. Ricardo and Sol, they're the only people I trust. But I stole Ricardo's money, and I ran. And Sol, he wants me to meet his son-in-law, the doctor, and go to the hospital. And I can't do that either 'cuz you'd find me there, and then nothin' could stop you from doin' whatever you want 'cuz like the adoption lady said, you got rights 'cuz you're the father.

Sol walks 'round like there's a cloud on him. He's expectin' too. He's expectin' the worst. The *shul's* demolition starts in a week. The trucks'll show up like mushrooms after a storm. You don't know if they're poison, but you better stay far away, just in case.

"What do you want to do, Angel?" he asks again, walkin' the kitchen floor.

"We'll live with you," I say again. The first time was a joke, but now it ain't.

"In a few days, this *shul* won't exist anymore."

"At your house. With you," I pretend like it's so obvious, but I'm combin' my mind for answers. I feel like I'm in an elevator stuck between two floors.

"I live in a seniors-only complex. The board would throw us out in a day. The first baby is usually late." He leans against the stove.

I feel Grace kick. My whole body ripples. She's a pebble, and

I'm the pond. She's got strong legs, ready to step into life.

"That was true for our Alex. He was two weeks past his due date."

"You remember that?" I ask.

"Sure," he nods. "What else is important enough to remember?"

"I don't think my father would have any idea 'bout that. He barely remembers my birthday."

Sol goes quiet as he pulls out the fryin' pan.

"Here, let me do that," I say, decidin' to cook grilled cheese the fancy way, like Ricardo cooked it. I smear mayonnaise on one side of each piece of bread, fry it in butter, add the cheese, let it crisp up, then join the pieces together and watch 'em melt into one. I cut it in half, and we eat it with a bowl of Campbell's tomato soup, like Andy Warhol.

"Making art out of soup," Mrs. Abney used to say. "Now that was genius." I'm still tryin' to get my head 'round it myself. Maybe one day I'll study art again. Frida Kahlo, Jackson Pollack. I'd like that.

Me and Sol are doin' what we been doin' these past two weeks together. We eat breakfast and lunch in the kitchen. Sometimes Sol reads the newspaper, and I read the used book about what to expect when you're havin' a baby, I bought at the flea market on Vermont. Sometimes I try to do the crossword puzzle. I'm pretty bad at it, but he's even worse, so we just kid each other, tryin' to come up with funny words. He'll throw in some Yiddish like *oy* or *plotz* or *meshuga*. Me, I just put down any letter that comes to mind, and we laugh 'til we both have to pee again.

Today, he's quiet. He nibbles at his grilled cheese. He takes a spoonful of soup, then stands up and puts on his cap.

"You have to decide," he says. "I won't be able to help you anymore." He leaves without finishin' his lunch. It feels like he's mad at me for the first time since I've known him. I wander 'round the shul like I'm already in prison.

At night, I watch *Friends*. I've been watchin' reruns since I started stayin' here. It reminds me of when we all lived at home. That's 'bout the only time I can think of us laughin' together— Momma and her daughters. Daddy too, drinkin' beer while we ate popcorn. Tonight's episode is 'bout when Monica has to leave Richard 'cuz she wants a baby, and he's too old. She's so sad she can't sleep 'til her father comes over and tells her that Richard is very sad too. That helps her feel better. But you're not sad while I'm hidin' and you're searchin'. I know Monica ends up with Chandler, someone she'll be happy to have a baby with, so it all works out for her. But me? When Grace comes, we could be on the streets or in a shelter or sittin' on a Greyhound crisscrossin' the country forever.

The next mornin', Sol comes in at 7 a.m. like always.

"How did you sleep?" he asks like nothin's different, but we know everythin's changed.

"Okay."

"I can't stay," he says. "I have to prepare coffee and pastries at the rabbi's house for a meeting. We are discussing the budget for carpets and curtains for the new *shul* building."

"What's all that?" I point to a big wicker basket he's carryin'.

"Passover's coming. I'm getting rid of all the *chometz*. It's from the communal kitchen where I live. Look, bagels, flour, bread, cookies. All for you."

"Can't you go later to the rabbi's?" I ask. I don't want him to be mad at me. I don't want him to leave. "Did you bring the newspaper? We could do the crossword—"

323

"No, I have to change over the plates and cutlery for Passover."

"I know the story," I say, tryin' to impress him. "That's when Jochebed gives birth to Moses. The Israelites are afraid the pharaoh will kill him so Miriam puts him in a basket and floats him on the Nile for the sister of the pharaoh who doesn't have children. Like in the painting by Raphael when they find him in the water."

"I know that painting." Sol takes off his cap.

He's stayin'. I wanna cry, I'm so happy.

"It's one of my favorites," I say.

"Angel, will you make me some coffee?"

"Yes, Sol," I say as I get up and fill the pot with water.

"How do you know that painting?" He sits at the table.

"It's called *Moses Saved from the Water*. My art teacher, Mrs. Abney—she was my art teacher at Denton Elementary and then moved to Chickasaw High so I guess she was my teacher for a lot of my education. I was lucky."

"I think she was the lucky one," Sol says.

"I don't know 'bout that," I shrug, "but she was kind to me. Gave me confidence. Mrs. Abney was always showin' us pictures in books, takin' us to museums and galleries. She told me to copy any paintin' I wanted, and I tried that one. I liked how Raphael painted the women's bodies kinda movin', and the way the sun was on their dresses and the river. My copy was pretty good."

I feel the flush of pride warm my cheeks. I take two cookies from the basket and put them on a plate. They're Sol's favorite, the cinnamon-raisin *rugalach* from Diamond Bakery on Fairfax.

"What happened to your copy of the Moses painting?"

I offer him a *rugalach*. "Travis liked it too. He taped it on the kitchen wall. I guess it got burnt in the fire," I shrug. I get the other one, and he says a prayer over them. We eat.

"You think you might like to do art?"

"Like a job?" I ask.

"Sure, why not? You seem to know a lot about it. Maybe you could go back to school and study it and be a teacher like Mrs. Abney or a painter or something like that."

I'm feelin' red hot as a beet. How'd he know my secret wish?

"Something to think about, Angel."

I don't want Sol to see the tears startin' to climb outta my eyes, so I get up and take another *rugalach*.

"Is Mrs. Abney still teaching?" he asks.

"I think she retired and moved to Gadsden. Why?"

"Call her sometime, Angel. Maybe she could help you find a place to study art. Help you with a scholarship. You never know."

"I'm not goin' back home!" I yell.

"Who said anything about going home?" His eyebrows shoot up. "There are lots of places in the world to study art. Like Italy or France."

I search through the box of tea like I'm huntin' down a special one, but they're all the same chamomile Sol bought. "Okay." I lift one out. I never thought about a future like that. It makes my insides kinda sparkle. "Maybe I will. You never know. Maybe in Mexico."

"Good," he says. "Mexico is good."

He dunks his *rugalach* into his coffee and sweeps it into his mouth. He's experienced at dunkin', it's pretty obvious.

"So, what else happens to Moses?"

"That's easy," I pour hot water into a cup. "Moses brings the Ten Commandments and takes his people out of slavery and into freedom. It's my favorite bible story."

"Mine too," Sol smiles. "I like all endings that have freedom in them. Maybe it doesn't always look like freedom, but if you strive for it at least, somehow it will all come to some form of good."

He looks out the back window and sees somethin' that turns his eyes dim. There's nothin' out there but sky and telephone wires so I know he's lookin' within.

"That's what I pray for," he says.

I'm wonderin' how come there's so much hate in the world and how could anyone hate Sol? How come you hate me so much you'd destroy any chance of happiness I got?

Sol stands. "There's something I must do," he says.

I get nervous all of a sudden. "What?"

"Bless you and your baby."

"The kitchen's a funny place for that." I'm thankful he's not mad at me anymore. I sip my tea. "I thought only priests can give blessings."

"Only holy people," Sol answers, "and since we are made in God's image, we are all holy."

I'm havin' doubts 'bout that. I bet he is, as well. Too many of his kin were murdered. What kind of holy is that?

"Even me?" I ask.

He's lookin' at me knowin' I almost killed you. How can he let me stay here, in this sacred place? If God's watchin', maybe He's thinkin' I need to be punished. But if Jesus is watchin', He'll forgive me. At least that's what He's supposed to do. Maybe it's Grace They love, and not me.

"Especially you," he says and kisses me on the top part of my forehead.

He puts one hand on my head. He's a little man, so his arms are stretched out like Superman flyin'. He closes his eyes and starts to chant.

"May God bless you, Angel..."

Then he stops, frowns, looks at me. "Wait," he says, his eyes intent on mine. "Tell me your real name."

I shake my head. "God don't care if my name's real or not."

"But I do," he says. "I want to make sure the blessing gets to you."

Sol looks like someone I know. I been tryin' to figure it out. I almost see it now—the way his head bends, the way his eyes shine from the depths of his soul.

"Wanda," I whisper.

He puts his hand on top of my head and shuts his eyes.

"May God bless you, Wanda," he whispers back to me, "and guard you."

His voice is sweet, like he's makin' a wish to a five-year-old child. My body tingles stars.

"May the light of God shine upon you, Wanda. May God be gracious unto you and give you peace."

My eyes get all moist again. So do his. His face reminds me of somethin'. I don't know what. He pulls a handkerchief from his magic pocket, white with blue squares at the corners. He gives it to me. It smells like lemons. He pulls one out for himself, dark gray and already wilted. He wipes his eyes, but they keep cryin', like it's their job.

"Tears are like raindrops," he says. "You can't stop them when they come."

I nod 'cuz it's hard for me to speak. I wanna tell him how I like the rain, how I feel washed from the inside when I stand in it, how Grace was created in it.

"Rain is also a blessing," he says like he's readin' my mind again. "It enables life. It makes things grow." He folds his handkerchief. "Even if it's a big thunderstorm, each raindrop is light, holy like a baby's tear." He places it back in his pocket.

I'm blowin' my nose.

"You must have stood in it when you were a little girl because you're so tall now," he smiles. "Rain brings out the angels, Wanda. Did you know that?"

I shake my head.

"They dance in it."

I hear a man singin' a hymn from the big room even though I know we're alone. It's a radiant voice chantin' a tune I've never heard before, like opera but not, like a ballad but not that either. Then a choir of men's voices joins in. They're singin' to God like he's actually listenin'.

"Do you hear that, Sol?" I ask, sure he's gonna think I'm crazy like Momma and you do.

Behind my eyelids the singers are circlin' us, wearin' white and black satin shawls with long tassels hung over their heads, sweepin' the air with devotion. They're prayin' so deep love climbs up from the center of the earth like roots sproutin' trees.

"Yes," says Sol. "Always."

It's my turn to kiss him on the forehead.

"Grace does too," I say. "Feel."

She's dancin' a ballet, again. He lays his hand on my stomach.

"Grace, may you grow up to be like Sarah, Rebecca, Rachel, and Leah. May the Eternal One bless you."

He pulls out a red ribbon from the first pocket and ties it 'round my wrist.

"What's this?" I ask.

"A *kein ahora*," he says, "to protect you from the Evil Eye, from men like Travis, from those that would do you harm. Wear it until it falls off on its own."

Then he hugs me. I sense Grace settlin' down like she's 'bout to take a big breath, the kind you take before you jump off a cliff into a rushin' river.

"Can you take care of her for me?" I'm beggin', but I won't let him hear it in my voice. "You're my only hope."

His beard scratches my cheek. He steps away from me and goes to the sink. The water takes a long time to turn hot. He washes the dish, puts it in the rack.

"I've spent my last years helping here at the *shul*," he says, "and, God willing, I'll help at the new location." He wipes his hands on the towel, then places them on the counter and stares out the window.

I sit real still.

"It has been my greatest honor to help the rabbi and his congregants." He's shaking just a little but enough for me to see. "I lost God many times in my life. The last time—it wasn't so long ago."

He turns to look at me. "And then there you were," he says, his voice hoarse, "sleeping under the Star of David, a child within a child."

He is so beautiful, this man. And now I know what I been tryin' to remember. His face looks like the paintin' of *King David* by Chagall. His eyes have the same intelligence and kindness. Same narrow beard. Sol's is gray, King David's is black. And even though Sol isn't wearing a crown, it seems to me like he is.

"I am sorry, Wanda," he says. "I cannot look after Grace. I don't know how much more life there is left in me."

The hem of his pants touch the ground. He's gettin' smaller every day. I think on what Pastor Higgins used to say at funerals: "For dust thou art, and unto dust shalt thou return."

He reaches into his pocket. He takes out another red ribbon, only this one's a lot shorter. "Here," he hands it to me. "Tie this on Grace's wrist when she is born."

"She gets a *kein ahora* too?"

"Yes," he answers. "May she always be protected."

"She's protectin' me," I say. It's somethin' I been believin' for a while now but didn't wanna tell nobody. I didn't wanna jinx it. But standin' in the kitchen, tellin' the truth to each other—it seemed like the perfect time.

"Isn't that right, Sol?" I'm almost holdin' my breath wantin' it to be so. "Grace is protectin' me."

Sol smiles. "She's protecting us both." And he nods, just like King David.

~ 46 ~

TRISHA

April 13, 2019

Bᴀʙʏ Nɪɴᴀ ᴡᴇᴀʀꜱ ᴀ ᴘɪɴᴋ ribbon around her head. She is in a white cotton blanket in Trisha's arms. Trisha wears a soiled hospital gown that she refuses to take off. Her hospital ID bracelet is on her right wrist. She is sitting up with two pillows supporting her back. Erika stands behind the bed. She is wearing blue sweats. A Black nurse takes a picture on Erika's phone. No one speaks.

Nina has wavy blond hair. Her eyes are closed. They never opened. Her tiny fingernails are perfect. Everything about her is perfect. Except she isn't breathing. Never has. Not even for a second.

Nina stays in the CuddleCot. It keeps her body cold. They can take it home for three days if they want. To make memories. Everyone holds her. Erika sobs. Trisha weeps. What's the difference between sobbing and weeping? Nothing.

They bathe her. Diaper her. Dress her in a white onesie, then a christening gown. They cut a lock of her hair and put it in the hospital envelope to take home. They sing to her. They tell her how they will always love her. Someone comes with nontoxic gray ink to make imprints of her hands and feet on ivory stationery. Nontoxic? What does it matter now?

Stillbirth. She had given birth to death. Trisha feels ashamed. Everything aches. Is it something they did? Is it because of what she did? This sorrow has no words. It has no light to give, only greater reason for hating God.

Two days after Trisha gets home, she walks to Hollywood Boulevard. Her breasts are full and hard as diamonds. The stitches pierce her skin. She doubles over with each step, but still she walks. She has passed this place so many times but never entered.

Today, she goes in at noon. She made an appointment. The artist is an older Japanese woman with a nose piercing and two silver teeth. Trisha asks her to put it on her right shoulder. Three inches. No. Bigger, please. Five inches.

An hour later, it's done. Emiko gives Trisha instructions. Clean it three to four times a day. Put moisturizing lotion on it. Avoid direct sunlight. Don't scratch it. It's bloody and swollen now, but it will heal.

Trisha stares at the tattoo in the mirror, still red and raw from the needle. Baby's breath, the thin stem, the soft peach petals, and underneath, her name:

Nina.

~ 47 ~

ALISON

April 15, 2019

Tʜᴇ ᴅᴀʏ ᴡᴀꜱ ᴍᴇʀᴄɪʟᴇꜱꜱ ʙᴇᴄᴀᴜꜱᴇ it couldn't have been more beautiful. It had rained two days ago, but today the sky was a translucent azure blue. There was a poster-sized picture of the baby in Trisha's arms balanced on an easel at the doorway to the chapel. Two celadon vases filled with white bouquets of chrysanthemums, tulips, and roses stood on either side of the portrait. The baby was wearing a little pink bow. Trisha was wearing her hospital gown, touching Nina's tiny fingers, staring into her closed eyes. Erika stood behind them, one hand on Trisha's shoulder, the other on the baby's head.

The chapel was small and white. Packs of tissues were waiting on the second chair of every row. Alison put one in her purse. Only three of the poetry workshop members showed up.

"I've never been to a funeral for someone so tiny before," said Carolyne, hugging her jacket close to her chest. She didn't look cold. She looked like she was unraveling, trying to hold herself together.

Charles sat on the other side of Carolyne. He was focusing on the program, but it was clear he wasn't really reading. His eyes were glassy, staring at the pages like a flashlight in the dark. Alison took a look herself. A Unitarian minister would lead the ceremony. First, there would be music, then friends speaking, then family, and then the procession to the graveside. She had to put the program down.

"My heart is breaking," Alison murmured.

Carolyne stared up at the ceiling beams. Charles sat frozen. Alison looked behind her at the same crowd from the baby shower. Just three weeks ago, they were laughing, hugging, and eating.

"Charles, how's your wife?" asked Carolyne.

His head jolted up from the program. "Olivia is pregnant," he responded.

The women glanced at each other.

"I'm sorry," said Charles, the program slipping from his fingers. "That's so thoughtless of me. It's just—my wife told me, and then I got the call about Trisha and..." His eyes clouded up. He covered them with his hands.

"It's okay, Charles." Carolyne picked up his program, and Alison handed him the pack of tissues. "It's hard to know the right thing to say at a time like this."

The room grew quiet as the flautist walked on stage and played Bach's "Air Suite #3 in D Major." Erika and Trisha entered from the side door and sat in the front row. They were both wearing white.

"But congratulations to you and Olivia," whispered Carolyne.

Charles stood up. "Excuse me," he said, and moved to the back of the chapel. He stood in the corner and bowed his head.

The minister stepped onto the pulpit. "Let us pray," he said.

Harriet was never real. The fantasy daughters that Alison encountered on the street were never real. But Trisha actually held her baby in her arms. Nina was real. Dr. Gedal from the grief group told Alison it was healing to accept sorrow's presence, as long as you continued to move forward. But moving forward meant taking a chance. She'd been too afraid to risk it. She was too afraid to tell Jesse about the child that would've been Harriet. So she closed herself off and rejected him, before he could reject her, and their baby, and their future together. Instead, she chose to find joy in her students, even though their connection wasn't as deep or sustaining. Along the way, she subconsciously selected men she couldn't commit to, not with all her heart, not like Jesse. And after her parents died—well, she stopped trusting love altogether. Alison hoped that Trisha and Erika wouldn't be like her. She hoped they wouldn't close themselves off like she had.

"Even those who never fully blossom bring beauty into the world," the minister said as mourners dropped white roses onto the little coffin. The faint sound of petals hitting wood was a requiem. It was all too much. Trisha sank to the grass and wailed. Erika stood behind her, gazing up at a single velvet cloud, passing ever so slowly overhead. Everyone followed her lead without thinking. They all looked up, desperate to find some kind of answer from the universe.

Alison stayed with the cloud. The universe was saying something—maybe her parents—maybe her half-brother too. "Be of service to others. There is no greater love."

Alison was listening.

~ 48 ~

WANDA

April 17, 2019

BABY MOSES FLOATS ON THE Nile.

It's the Raphael paintin', movin' like a dream, happenin' live in front of me. The river curves tender pink into the reeds. Seven beautiful women gaze down at him in robes of orange, white and green. He's golden, and they all wanna touch him, be touched by him. Two bend down to pick him up as they murmur to each other in a language I can't understand. It's like I'm there, and they're here, and I'm hidin' in the bushes so they can't see me, and I sit up, wake up, drenched between my thighs. My mind's racin' along my limbs. Thunder beatin' through my veins. Either I'm bleedin' dear God no, or my water broke, and she's ready dear God yes. I pray to Jesus for help and reach my fingers down. They move back up to me, clear and damp. She's comin'.

I hear the *shul* men singin' again, louder than usual. I walk into the big room, proppin' myself up against the walls, grabbin' whatever I can hold onto. They're in there, in their dark suits, bowin' their heads, shiftin' back and forth with the top parts of their bodies like mothers rockin' their babies to sleep. Their faces look down into the prayer books. They're old. They're young. They're shinin'.

And then I hear you.

"My baby!" you howl. "I want my baby!"

I see you, Travis, hangin' from the ceilin' with rat claws for feet. You got three wolves' heads comin' outta your ropey neck, but all the faces are yours. Your long serpent tongues lick the walls. Your teeth are cracked fangs, oozin' green bile. I been waitin' for God to give me a sign, to tell me what He wants me to do for Grace. I see it now. He's been givin' me signs all along, hasn't He? The sign He's been givin' me is you, isn't that right, Travis? I gotta get Grace as far away from you as possible. Me bein' with her, she'd be easy to track. But without me—

I gasp for air as the holy water washes outta me. I gotta let her go.

"I banish you from my daughter!" I shout.

The air's loud with the flappin' of angels, all feathers and eyes and fire.

"I'll kill you if you ever come near us," I yell. "I'll die saving her if I have to."

I sway back and forth with the men. We stomp the ground like we're plantin' the earth back in order. The singin's so loud there's no room for any other sound, 'cept for the wings clappin' and my daughter's heart beatin'.

"I swear on every breath that's in me, for all eternity, Grace will never be yours!" I call up to the Heavens. "And so it shall be, forever and ever!"

You roar, your mouths frothin', your eyes rollin', lookin' like you wanna murder me. You punch at that window like you punched my face, but the glass don't break. You pull at the curtain like you pulled my soul, but it don't tear out.

I lift up, up, up to the dome ceilin', floatin' in God's sky.

"Amen," the *shul* men chant.

"Amen!" I answer back.

I look down and see myself standin' in *shul*, arms stretched out holdin' tender green shoots with buds glistenin' on their stems, and there's birds flyin' in and out of the prayer of dancin' men, their sacred shawls floatin' free and red ribbons twirlin', swirlin', whirlin' round the holiest part of me.

I don't remember findin' my way back down to the rabbi's room, but I guess I did 'cuz Sol stands over me when I wake up. He's got one of his worried expressions on his face.

"You've been sleeping a couple hours," he says. "The bed's wet. I called my son-in-law."

"No," I sit up. "I'm not goin'—"

"No hospital unless there's a problem." Sol takes hold of my hand. "I promise." Then he lets go and opens the door. "This is my daughter Rose's husband," Sol says like the man standin' there's a superhero comin' to save mankind.

"Hello, Angel," his son-in-law says.

He sounds calm, but I can tell he doesn't wanna be here. He's got a leather bag like those black-and-white movies where doctors are old and kind. But this man isn't that old. He looks my father's age. He's got brown hair and a short beard. He wears a gray backpack over his shoulder.

"I'm Doctor Leaf," he says coming in. "I'm going to help you through this."

I shake my head and press up against the wall.

"No one knows I'm here except Sol and you," Dr. Leaf says. His eyes look into mine like he knows me. "If there are complications, I'll have to call an ambulance. It's the law. If not," he takes a step towards me, "I'll be your guide, that's all."

I look up to see if any bits of you are still bubblin' under the surface of the ceilin'. I think maybe I see part of your forked tongue, but it's just a twisted piece of electric wire stuck in the paint from a long time ago.

"Do you understand?" Dr. Leaf asks.

I nod. I let out a breath I didn't know I was holdin'.

"Here, put this on." Dr. Leaf takes out a hospital gown from the backpack. "And we'll walk around and get that baby out."

"Want some tea, Angel?" Sol asks.

Grace moves. The eruption of her body wrenches the middle of me. It brings me to my knees.

"Oh, God!" I cry out, clutchin' my stomach like there's a hook grabin' at my insides, rippin' 'em out.

Dr. Leaf gives me his arm and I hold on. Sounds come outta me like when Pastor Higgin's cat had babies—only wilder and deeper. Then it stops as quick as it started. Must be those contractions I heard so much about. I guess I'm in labor.

"Yes, Sol," I nod, "chamomile with honey, please."

Dr. Leaf pulls out some Kleenex and wipes the sweat off my face. Maybe it's a Jewish thing, always havin' somethin' in your pocket to wipe the wet away.

"Can you take me on a tour of the synagogue?" Dr. Leaf asks.

"Sure," I say.

I'm not afraid now. Passover's comin', and so's my daughter.

She's gonna join the world, and her story will be a story of freedom.

~ 49 ~

ALISON

April 17, 2019

Aｌｉｓｏｎ ｗａｌｋｅｄ ｔｅｎ ｂｌｏｃｋｓ ｔｏ the Kathmandu Boutique on Lincoln Avenue. She entered past the jewel-toned harem pants and embroidered skirts. She went directly to the glass counter. She wanted to lose herself in the silver necklaces and brass earrings from Nepal. She needed something to mark the occasion of moving on. And she enjoyed the woman who worked there. They had had many complex conversations about simple things. Her name was Devna. Alison couldn't help but ask what it meant the first time they met.

"Divine," said Devna.

"That," ventured Alison, "is a lot to live up to."

"Tell me about it!" she laughed.

Alison found a sterling silver band with Blood Red Jasper stones in the shape of a flower. It fit on her ring finger. She would wear it on the drive to Todos Santos. It would bring her luck.

"I'll take this one," she said.

Devna wrapped it in blue tissue and attached a stick of clove incense tied with a ribbon of ivory lace.

"My friend's baby died." It just slipped out. Alison hadn't planned on saying anything. She lowered her head.

Devna's fingers stopped. An ambulance shrieked past the store. A stocky man with a short black beard sat cross-legged in the corner on the meditation cushion, eyes closed, fingers gripping *Awakening the Buddha Within*, a ladybug resting on his Indian shirt. A wisp of hair tickled Alison's ear. She touched her earring, the small gold hoops with the pearl in the center—the ones she bought after she had a Harriet sighting.

"My heart breaks for the mother," Devna said.

A second ambulance raced by, harmonizing with the first.

"Mothers," Alison added.

Devna shut the front door. She handed Alison a tea biscuit, her wrist tinkling with copper bracelets. She was one of those beautiful older women you see at art openings—long silver hair, strong bone structure, fine-lined skin, as if the artist himself had etched her into perfection. The fat man snored. The ladybug flew off his shirt, which looked exactly like the shirts the Beatles wore with the Maharishi, and landed on a statue of the Buddha.

"What can I do?" Alison asked.

"An understanding, an awareness, a decision will come to you," Devna said, reading Alison's mind. "Perhaps it already has..."

"Yes," Alison nodded and took a bite of the biscuit. It tasted like Sunday afternoons with her mother.

On her way home, she followed a Harriet into Bob's Market on Ocean Park. Alison sensed that this young woman would be her forever and always last Harriet. Twenty minutes later, when they both checked out, Alison had the exact same food in her cart as the young woman.

Alison placed everything she purchased on her kitchen table—two grapefruits, a medley of cut-up melon, a cucumber, a box of cherry tomatoes, a pack of sliced Swiss cheese, four containers of strawberry yogurt, a jar of almond butter, and a bag of double-roasted ground African coffee.

Like she always did when she had an encounter like this, she took a picture of everything she bought. She'd print, date, and tape the photo into her notebook along with the others.

Alison prepared a small bowl of the cut-up fruit mixed into strawberry yogurt, along with a toasted almond butter sandwich. She brewed the coffee.

A phrase materialized in Alison's mind like a photograph emerging in developer— *the washed heavens*. A second phrase appeared— *are wringing out my insides*.

Alison imagined herself back at baby Nina's graveside. Harriet and Nina were out there somewhere unseen. Maybe angels, maybe even friends.

She hoped more images would shape themselves into phrases. The velvet cloud floated back to her, the third line:

ready to be hung anew

Jagger flew in the window and brought in the rest of the poem.

The washed heavens

No more asking
for directions to places
I already live in—

*the washed heavens
are wringing out my insides
ready to be hung anew.*

*Daughter, you are
my brightest, my darkest—
talk to me
about adventures
only we can share.*

*Maybe one day
we'll get a chance
to meet like oceans
sing like sparrows
laugh like bubbles
sparkle like water
dance like pearls
touch like wings
fly like raindrops
to the upward-
facing sky.*

*Until then
I let you go.
Until then.
Until then.*

~ 50 ~

WANDA

April 17, 2019

"PUSH," THEY SAY. MY BABY'S comin'. "Push," they say. I breathe into Sol's hands. "Push! Push!"

My insides tear apart. Doctor wipes my brow. "Push," they say. She's jammin' into me. "Push," they say. I'm crackin' wide open. "Push," they say. "Push!" No! No! She's gotta stay in me where she'll be safe. "Push," they say.

Sol's weepin'. "Push! Push," they say. Me too. "Push! Attagirl! Push harder," they say. Ice on my parched lips. "Push!"

I hear Mother Mary singin'. "Keep going," they say. I hear Abraham rejoicin'. "She's crowning," they say. I see Jesus jumpin'. "Here she comes," they say.

The shul men are praying, they're chantin', they're stompin'. "Keep pushing," they say. "Push! Angel! Push!"

'Cuz she's almost here.

~ 51 ~

GRACE

April 17, 2019

hello here I am love what is this place where am I who are you where have I come from I was on a bus and then I was in the blackest of bright lights love appears and then drops rain off into nothingness and as I remember these things I've already forgotten them love the seam of impossible memory blessing and lightness and longing belonging and nothingness and then an explosion like the last time and the time before hello love forgetting and before into the backwards of infinity going the wrong way hello but who's to say really we are love not remembering all points in the now and the now keeps on moving and removing the past and the future dissolving evolving constantly from the here we go again connected by membranes now forgetting now a cord of blood the doctor cuts in two vanished into yesterday Moses in the basket waits and the road is longing for a river a bus ride to the ocean of the forgotten beginning of the edge of love that is hello

~ 52 ~

TRISHA

April 17, 2019

Forever Hollywood Cemetery's hours are 8:30 a.m. to 5:00 p.m.

Trisha drove through the gates as soon as they opened. The security man on a bicycle waved her in. He knew her. It was the third morning in a row. He had long purple dreads tucked into a red-and-blue Clippers cap. He wore a sweet musky fragrance that lingered with her as she parked. It blended with the scent of newly cut grass, throwing Trisha into the sense memory of mowing her parents' lawn in Toronto. She had to lean against her car for a moment.

She let herself wander the grounds without heading straight over. It didn't matter where she started. She'd end up at the same little mound of earth with a numbered code on a white flag marker.

"It's too soon to even think about a headstone," said Erika. "It's impossible to write something for someone you never met."

Trisha memorized the inscriptions anyway, hoping one would resonate.

HE SHALL GATHER THE LAMBS IN HIS ARMS
SHE HAS SOARED AWAY TO A BETTER PLACE
WE LOVE YOU

She stopped in front of Mel Blanc's grave. He'd been the voice of Bugs Bunny, Daffy Duck, Tweetie Bird and dozens more. She watched those cartoons when she was growing up. "THAT'S ALL, FOLKS," his epitaph read. Mel Blanc lived to be eighty years old. Nina didn't live a minute. Trisha sat down on the grass as an earthworm inched its way across the gravel.

"You walk just like a worm," her mother had said when Trisha was in her mid-twenties, "because you're always catching up to yourself!"

Trisha knew what her mother meant. Her heart hadn't found the key to itself then. But since coming to Los Angeles, Trisha had rekindled her passion for acting, and that was definitely a key. And in the past month, she realized being a mother would be another key. She had a lot of love to give. Motherhood would lead her to that part of herself that was truly her. She would finally be in sync with her authentic self. But now, what?

A homeless woman sashayed by, maybe 70 years old, in a belted beige trench coat with bobbed white hair and a red felt hat. She materialized each time Trisha visited, like a heroine waking up from a deep sleep in a 1940s movie. She pulled a beat-up pink suitcase on wheels and carried a Ralphs plastic bag. This morning, wilted carnations peeked out the top. Trisha assumed she camped overnight on the grounds, behind some huge monument, away from security cameras.

"Who are you visiting?" the woman's voice rasped through her toothless grin.

"My daughter," Trisha answered.

"Me too!" She exhaled invisible smoke from a cigarette holder. "Wanna see?"

The homeless woman took the path west. Trisha followed, the headstones surrounding them like crooked rows of sentinels. When they got to the Abbey of the Palms, they stood in front of the shrine to Judy Garland.

"She was your daughter?" asked Trisha.

"Yes," the woman answered, taking out a small tape recorder from the Ralphs bag. "She was the greatest singer of all time. Listen." She pressed a button, and Judy Garland's voice came out: "Soooomewheeere ooover the raaainbooooow..."

As the homeless woman lost herself in reverie, Trisha slipped away. That kind of thing was easy for her after Nina's passing. Since then, Trisha's life was vaporous. It was mist. It was always raining —a pointillist painting where you couldn't make out the shape of anything if you looked too close. It took her half an hour to cross the street—her shoes sticking to the cement, tugged down by some kind of imperceptible mourning mud. The spiders scurried back into her nights. She hated sleep. She hated waking up.

But the cemetery was a different world. She'd start at the entrance on Santa Monica Boulevard, buy a white rose from the pretty Russian lady, then go wherever she wanted. There were funerals every day. She'd sit in the back of the chapel with a pack of tissues in her hand. Her grief was so genuine, no one wondered who she was.

At home, neighbors asked about the baby. They expected to see her with a stroller or a baby wrap or a baby. When they approached her, she turned away. How many times could she fall to pieces in front of them? Their reactions made it all worse. She'd have to give them oxygen when she was the one who was drowning. She was safer here with the departed. They didn't ask questions.

There was only one grave she could find with such a short life. RUSSELL FULLER 1927 – 1927. No month, no date. He could've lived a year, or he could've lived a minute.

SEE YOU NEXT TIME AROUND
WITH YOUR TRUE FATHER
DEAREST KINDEST HEART

There were no real answers. Stillborn deaths just happened sometimes. Dr. Thayer told them they could try again once she'd healed. There were other sperm donors they could use.

She walked south to the oldest part of the cemetery where the first burial took place in 1901. These dead were long gone, and so were their mourners. There were no flowers on these graves, only dried leaves, and dust.

DEAREST DAUGHTER
REST IN PEACE
BLESSED FOREVER

Trisha sat down on the grass, her hand smoothing the folds of her skirt that rested on top of the furious scar. She angled her face to the sun. She lay down between two graves. She shut her eyes. A shadow of a butterfly passed over her. Its fragile wings beat together like a tiny heart.

TREASURED CHILD
SOULMATE
HEAVEN WILL BE HAPPIER NOW

She didn't feel anything lingering around her at the cemetery, like ghosts or spirits. Maybe at midnight it would be different—scary or haunted—and she didn't want to be here then. But on this fresh morning, there was a calm she hadn't felt before. She placed her palms on the headstones on either side of her body. A warm exhalation poured out of them, through her arms and into her chest. It was a force that became a letting go that created a transformation— from deep sadness to deep love. It was alchemy. Her teacher, Martin Kanakaris, talked about it in acting class—changing lead into gold, crushing coal into diamonds, conjuring words into characters. She never understood it before. But now, she did.

I have a daughter, thought Trisha, but she's not here. She taught me that I do want children. Erika was right. Family is important. Nina will never be forgotten. She will always be our first child.

They would never know if Nina was Erika and "Green-Eyed Optimist's" baby or her and Charles' baby.

"It doesn't matter anymore, does it?" she whispered to Charles at the funeral.

"I'm so sorry." He held her close. They embraced for a long time, for the last time.

She lifted herself from the headstones and took the path east, then veering off it onto the grass. A film crew was setting up for a movie. The trailers were lined up on the road. A 2nd Assistant Director ran up to her.

"Hey! What are you doing here?" he asked, clipboard in hand.

"Extras are supposed to report to that trailer down there," he pointed. "You're not allowed to wander."

She looked at him like he was an Australian sheepdog nipping at her heels.

"Well?" he said. "We don't have all day."

She stared at the white flag marker up the hill.

"And where's your wardrobe?" he demanded.

She tried to take a step, but her feet were caught in quicksand.

"Get going!" he shouted.

"I'm not an extra," she murmured under her breath.

"What's your name?" He studied the call sheet. "I'm going to report you—"

"I'm—I'm not—an extra," she repeated, louder, as heat rose in her throat like mercury in a thermometer.

"Oh," he said. "I thought you were—"

"Extras are people too, you know!" she yelled. "Who do you think you are, talking to a person like that? Talking to me like that—like I'm nothing—like I'm less than you!"

He took a step back as people started staring.

"How dare you! You don't even know me. You have no idea who I am!"

"I'm—I'm just doing my job—" the AD stammered.

"Yeah, all you care about is what you have to do. You never see the person for who they are. I'm an actress! I'm a nurse, I'm a dancer! I'm a wife. I'm a mother, goddamn it! I'm a mother!"

She turned, every part of her shaking, and faced the white flag marker. "My daughter's right over there!"

Trisha bent over in pain, her empty womb aching. Crew members clustered around to see what was happening.

"Oh! I'm sorry—I'm sorry for your loss..." the AD reached for her shoulder, but she tore it away.

"Please don't touch me!" she said. Pity only made it worse. She wouldn't let anyone console her, except for the security man with the purple dreads. He rode over on his bike when he heard her screaming.

"Let me take you to your spot, Ms. O'Connor," he said.

She shook her head. She didn't want to go. She nodded. She wanted to go.

"It's real peaceful there. You can sit all day if you like. Nobody's gonna bother you." He stood between her and the small crowd. "Come on, ma'am, let me take you there."

"Thank you," Trisha said.

He put one arm around her shoulder and the other under her elbow.

"I'm so sorry," the AD tried again.

"You gotta leave," the security man said.

"But—"

"Just move away, man. Have some respect."

The security man escorted Trisha to the mound. "You need anything, all you gotta do is ask. You got that?"

Trisha squeezed his hand as he helped her to the ground. "You're very kind," she said. "I have so many questions."

"Maybe you just gotta listen," the security man offered. "Lots of people come here to talk with their dearly departed. You'd be surprised how many get answers!"

She watched him walk away and waited for her insides to settle. Nina never breathed, never laughed, never cried, but she'd been present in their world since they started talking about having a child a year and a half ago. She'd been alive for Trisha and Erika that whole time. Trisha reached for the black Sharpie in her purse. A year and a half is a life. She wrote on the white flag:

NINA O'CONNOR-ROSSI

NOVEMBER 18, 2017 – APRIL 13, 2019

Trisha moved her fingers through the earth like a mother brushing hair out of her child's eyes. She grazed the purple shell in her pocket. She took it out and held it up to the sky, its lavender curves capturing the powdered light.

She held her stomach as the anguish of emptiness shot through her.

"But Señor Garcia told me '*buena madre*,'" she implored the world around her. "He said, '*Buena madre.*'"

She was listening. She would've taken any response—the chirp of a bird, the screech of a tire, the echo of Judy Garland in her ear—anything. She would've interpreted it into something she could grasp—some significance to it all.

She thought she heard a child singing.

Trisha peered at the eroding names on the surrounding gravestones. Their deathly silence couldn't stop her. Her fingers clawed at the ground. She buried the purple shell as deep as her hands could dig.

Then she wrote on the white flag:

IN LOVING MEMORY OF OUR PRECIOUS CHILD,
BORN ASLEEP

ALISON

April 19, 2019

Our holiest of days

crumpled tissues
hold prayers, circled
by smoke rings, puffed
into the air

where do they go
these longings?

did you know
there is another world
above this one
where all our moments
are still happening?

even the pretend ones

I take a golden rope
and lasso them down –
drape them like wet garments
beneath the curious sun

in the shimmering explosions
of our holiest of days
my pockets are full

it is time
to say
it is time

it is time

~ 54 ~

WANDA

April 17, 2019

Sʜᴇ sʟɪᴅᴇs ᴏᴜᴛᴛᴀ ᴍᴇ ʟɪᴋᴇ a mermaid into the stream of life.

The most beautiful baby lies on my chest, tiny hands and feet, warm and wrapped in a blanket like a burrito. Ten fingers, ten toes, two eyes dark blue, two lips the wings of butterflies, a nose a tiny button, whiffs of golden hair, and a soul as pure as the beginning of the beginning.

"Dear God, keep her safe in your embrace. Protect and bless her and let her be everything she is meant to be. Amen."

I try to sleep, but I can't. I have to keep guard. I hear them talk, the men. They're in the hall, tired from helpin'.

"Angel's got to go to the hospital," Dr. Leaf says. "She's weak. She can't take care of the baby."

I know he's sayin' what he's supposed to, but he don't know me. Grace gives me strength. My milk's comin' in.

"I'll stay with her," Sol says. "I'll make her eat."

"This is crazy, coming here," Dr. Leaf says. "What was I thinking?"

She moves on me like a gentle stream, suckin' on my nipples.

"I'll make sure she eats. When she's awake, we'll talk again—"

"Sol, isn't it time you stop helping people and take care of yourself?" The doctor's shoutin' from a distance now. I imagine him shakin' his head, getting' red in the face. "You're ninety-four years old for Chrissakes!"

I hear his footsteps as he paces the hall.

"You have to call child services," the doctor says. "Call the police."

"No," I yell as loud as I can. They don't hear me 'cuz my voice is tired too. I touch my red ribbon, my protection against evil.

"No," says Sol, my bodyguard. "Helping people," he says, "that's why I come here. Everyday. Because God may have work for me to do."

The doctor's not sayin' anythin'. He's stopped in place.

"Isn't that why I'm still alive?" Sol asks. "I don't want to die knowing I could've helped someone and didn't."

I look around the rabbi's room. It'll be torn down soon, I know. I wonder if the new *shul* will be the same. Maybe with Sol, it will be.

"You're a good person," Doctor Leaf says. "You make me feel ashamed of myself." I hear him step closer. Their shirts are rustlin'. I bet they're huggin'. "The baby is beautiful. So is the mother. I'll see you at *seder*."

The back door closes. Sol walks into my room. It's just the three of us now. He sits on the edge of the bed.

I turn my head to him, "What do you think the rabbi would say if he knew a baby was born in his bed?"

Sol's face ripples into a smile. "He would say it's a miracle."

It's so quiet. Just the sound of our lives breathin' in and out of our bodies. Grace is just beginnin' while Sol's nearin' the end. And then there's me, somewhere in between, suspended over holy ground.

"Try to sleep," he says.

"Not yet," I say, shakin' my head. "The red ribbon," I say, pointin'.

He gets it from my yellow bag. He ties it on her perfect wrist. Protection.

Just before my eyes close, the *shul* men start chantin'. The tune is a joyous one. I see them swirlin' around us. So does Sol—their faces turned up to the sky, holdin' onto each other's shoulders, skippin' round and round, prayer shawls flappin', feet dancin'. They're thankin' the Almighty for the miracle of my daughter.

Now we can sleep.

∞

I pump manna into the bottles Dr. Leaf brought in the backpack. I put them in the fridge, a choir of white nuns.

I take Grace on a walk through the *shul*. This is the first place she knows. It was sacred before, but now it's Jerusalem because she was born here. Even with its empty walls, its broken lights, its ripped-up carpets, it's beautiful—because she's here.

She's two-and-a-half days old now, and I feel I've known her my whole life. I wrap her in a baby blanket and watch her breathe. My hand holds hers. She opens her eyes. Her tiny fingers grab my red ribbon and won't let go. We're two against the evil eye.

She gets thirsty in the middle of the night, and I feed her 'til she's love drunk with my milk. I put white towels in the wicker basket Sol brought and lay her down on top with the nuns beside her. I cover 'em with a blanket Sol's daughter Rose knit for her own child twenty-five years ago, light purple with white stripes. I fill the backpack with some clothes and Ricardo's money.

Meanwhile, I'm waitin' for my hair to change color again. I cut it even shorter this time, dyed it black as coal. I look like some big kid. No one would recognize me as Wanda, that's for sure. And Ricardo and Sol wouldn't see me as Angel. I don't know who I am. I'm just not them. I place a letter by the coffee pot.

Dear Sol,

You saved our lives. I'll send you blessings for the rest of my life.

Thank you forever,
Wanda and Grace

He'll read it at sunrise. It'll be all over by then. I drew a picture of him and me in pencil on the *shul's* stationery. We're walkin' on the ocean. I fold it in my wallet next to the picture of Ricardo and Grace's ultrasound.

They knew all along I'd leave. That's why Ricardo made me burritos. That's why Sol slept here these last two nights—even tonight, the first night of Passover, he came over after the *seder*. He's deep in a dream now, back in the chamomile fields with his grandmother.

I leave the *shul's* bronze key next to the letter.

"*Shalom,*" I whisper.

We walk to the bus stop on Sunset and Vermont and wait for God's chariot to take us out of Egypt.

The road is a river. We get on the bus.

A band of fifty motorcycles rev up beside us, Hell's Angels, like knights on armored stallions. Their silver-studded jackets bounce back the moonshine that spills onto the boulevard. It's so bright, I think it's almost tomorrow. They ride with us, escortin' us past the Denny's, past the Starbucks, past the churches and the mansions.

When we pass over the second freeway, a man comes on the bus and sits across from us. I get goose bumps all over. I haven't seen Him since that day in Hollywood when He was bleedin' off the cross in the blue Mexican church. I watch Him like the beginnin' of a tornado. He still looks like Wilmer Valderrama. His eyes are the color of wet sand, tears crusted down his cheeks. He's bundled up in an old green army jacket, his head bent to rest against the window. His beard is stringy, his long dirty hair tied up in a knot. His fingernails are chipped and broken. Black mud is stuck in all the cracks.

Maybe I been too hard on Him. I can't expect Him to do all the savin'. Too much savin' to do in this broken world. We gotta do some ourselves. I reach into my bag and hold out some of Sol's Hannukah *gelt*.

"Here," I tell Him.

He turns, lookin' surprised that someone's talkin' to Him. When His gaze lands on us, I feel the sun on my face even though it's the middle of the night. He takes the chocolate coins, and I see swollen scars on His wrists. He nods thanks, then goes rummagin' through His greasy shoppin' bag. He pulls out an orange and leaves it on the seat.

"Vitamin C," He says over his shoulder.

He gets off the bus, and the bus keeps movin'. When the statue of Mother Mary appears, I know it's comin' soon. I remember seein' her on the way to the beach with Sol. Her silky arms were open wide, like they are now. Let me guide you, she's sayin', like I guided you through the desert. She glows so bright it's almost blindin'. Grace will be safe, she tells me, and I believe her. She's my only momma now.

I haven't seen you since she was born, since I decided what to do. Now you're gone, and He came on the bus to wish me good luck. I might've stopped lovin' Him forever if He hadn't. I still don't love Him how I used to. I'm not that Wanda anymore. Ever since I took the knife to your gut, I became a different me. I became the mother who'll protect her child from evil, no matter what.

That's why I get off the bus. That's why I walk like I'm full of what I'm doin' though inside I'm a paper bag waitin' to be blown away. That's why I cry.

"Stay sleepin', baby girl," I say into the blanket.

The fire station's red brick with a closed green door. One bright light shines down the driveway from the open garage where the trucks go in and out.

I rest the basket two feet in front of the door, so she won't get shoved aside when someone opens it. I been thinkin' about this a lot, pictured it in my mind, cursin' you every second.

And then I see the sign, yellow and black—SAFE HAVEN—a drawin' of a baby in someone's hands. The earth stops movin'. I'm grateful. I bow my head and ask for forgiveness. I stand there for a hundred years. I want to wait and tell whoever takes her all about me and you, and why I have to give her up, but I know I can't. I don't want anyone to see me, not the cameras, not the fireman, not anyone. If I stay, I'll change my mind, and me and Grace will be runnin' for cover our whole lives. If I coulda killed you, Travis, I woulda.

That'll always be my biggest regret, the one I'll take to my grave.

I touch Grace's face for the last time. Her innocence takes my breath away. There's an invisible hand behind me, pushin' my finger up into the buzzer, ringin' so hollow in my bones. A light turns on at the end of the hall, shinin' through the window. Someone's comin' to get her. They'll never know where she came from. They'll never know 'bout me or you, Travis. Grace will be saved.

Now I can go.

I gotta get on another bus.

I gotta get to the ocean.

I gotta run, keep movin', can't look back.

This is the only and forever way my daughter will be free.

~ 55 ~

ALISON

April 20, 2019

THE SOUND OF THE BUS brakes shocked Alison out of her notebook. Most buses didn't stop at the fire station so early in the morning. They just kept on going. These months of early mornings had become private pilgrimages into herself. She'd been filling up notebooks with poems and scribbles, wondering if it would ever really happen. Didn't Lieutenant Sean Prescott tell her that no one had ever left a baby?

The girl walked off the bus, quick and quiet, in black sweatpants and an oversized black hoodie pulled down to bury her face. She put a basket on the ground, right under the sign. She paused for a split second, and Alison could feel the world ending for her. This young mother traced the baby's face with her fingertips, locking the memory of that touch into her own body. Her hand went up to the buzzer, lingered for a moment. She pushed hard, stepped back, and dropped her hand into her pocket like she was hiding evidence at a murder scene. Then she ran back to the street and disappeared.

Alison moved quick and quiet, just like the girl. She didn't want any of the firemen to come to the front door first. She plucked the basket from the steps and rushed to her car.

The baby was wearing a pink cap—a little girl, Alison supposed. She was sleeping, a bottle of breast milk tucked close to her face. The baby's heartbeats echoed through her translucent-blue eyelids. Her face was flawless in a way that defied human constructs altogether. She was what Harriet would've looked like. All babies are that kind of perfection. They've just arrived, still fresh from the imprint of whatever place they've come from. The baby was the closest thing to God she'd felt in a long time.

The baby would be sitting beside her tonight—Alison knew she should keep her in the back, but she needed to make sure she'd be there for her if the baby started to cry. Alison didn't want the baby to wake up and feel alone. She was already lost to her real mother. That was hard enough.

Alison was about to turn the ignition when she heard the front door of the station open. A fireman, half-dressed in his pants and undershirt, came out to look around. He must've heard the buzzer the girl pushed. It was the same fireman who had fixed her flat tire. He didn't think to look at the car parked on the driveway next door. With a shrug, Lieutenant Sean Preston pulled out a pack of cigarettes.

Alison never realized firemen smoked. It seemed counterintuitive. That's okay, she thought. From now on, there'd be lots of surprises in the world. She was counting on them to guide her. She was ready. In the trunk of her car was her packed suitcase and Mother's carved wooden box. Alison placed her photographs in there—Jesse on the bridge, and her half-brother Sebastian. The baby was sleeping beside her.

For the last several months, Alison left a note on the kitchen counter along with two months' rent, just in case she found a baby. She couldn't risk coming back to her place with it. She knew that once a baby was in her possession, she would start her journey.

The note said:

Dear Mr. Bottler,

Thank you for the past two decades of my life. I am moving, with no forwarding address. Please inform whoever takes my place that they might be visited by an African grey parrot. His name is Jagger, and he likes to get on people's shoulders and dance.

All the best,

Alison Bishop

Lieutenant Sean Preston pulled out his phone and made a call. It was a short one. She chose to believe he was leaving an early good morning to someone he loved—his wife and two daughters, Alison decided. He took a couple of drags, then crushed the cigarette with his boot, spreading ashes and tobacco into the gray stones on the pavement. He looked up to the brightening sky like he thought it might rain. He went back inside and locked the door.

The baby was hers. She touched the blanket, like she remembered people touching the hem of Amma's robe. Alison lifted the newborn out of the basket. She held her as close to her heart as humanly possible—so tenderly, so gently—the mother-child embrace Alison longed for was finally hers. There was no separation, no two bodies, no two breaths, no two hearts. They were one.

"My sweet, sweet baby girl," she whispered. "At last."

Tears flowed out of her eyes and onto the infant's forehead. Catharsis. Alison inhaled the pure fragrance of new life—the baby's and hers—and wondered what the child would grow up to look like, be like. She knew she shouldn't think about that, but she couldn't help it. Love happens so fast.

They sat for a moment rocking from side to side, balancing on the brim of tomorrow and whatever came next.

~ 56 ~

WANDA

April 20, 2019

I TELL THE BUS DRIVER I'm gettin' off at the edge of California.

He says it'll be sunrise by then, so I won't have a problem see-in' it. But my eyes are already full up so I guess I'm not gonna be able to see for a long time. A cleanin' lady asks me if I wanna Kleen-ex. *No gracias*, I say, and get out Sol's handkerchief, the white one with the blue squares. It still smells of lemons.

When we get to Pacific Coast Highway, I'm thick molasses pourin' out onto the flat and gray road. I go to the gas station. No police car this time.

I clean my face. I look in the cracked mirror and don't know the black-haired girl who gawks back at me. I stuff what I'm wearin' in the garbage can in case the fire station took videos.

Before I put on the green sweatshirt and white wool cap, I wet a paper towel and reach under my bra to wipe my weepin' nipples.

Not too many cars this early in the mornin'. I sit on the same bench from Sol and my beach trip, but I get up real fast. That's my past now, and it's over.

I walk to the water. It glares back. Maybe it's mad at me for what I did.

I drink the chamomile tea I put in Ricardo's thermos. I peel Jesus' orange and eat it. It tastes like every glass of juice Sol poured for me.

I look at my wrist, and I see the red ribbon's disappeared. My breathin's hard and shallow. It ain't in Dr. Leaf's backpack. All I find on the beach is rocks and shells. Sol said it would fall off by itself, but I still need it. I still need it. My fingers hunt below the surface, with nothin' but sand fallin' through. Nothin'. I start to walk back to the gas station to see if it's there, but there's a cop pullin' up. I wanna fall to the ground and get washed out to sea. I wanna lose me. I wanna never wake up. But if I do that, I know you'll have won, Travis. So I swear on her life that I'll never let that happen. I gotta act like I'm someone else now. Because I am.

I look back at the ocean, and there it is—the red ribbon. A wind's got it wrapped up high, floatin' by itself, like an angel doin' an arabesque. It's wavin' to me. So long, see ya, been real nice knowin' ya ...

~ 57 ~

TRISHA

April 20, 2019

THEY TOOK TURNS. ERIKA WAS the caterpillar; Trisha was the cocoon. Then they changed positions. They slept as one, moving and breathing in unison.

Erika's grandmother told them that tragedies like this either broke you up or bonded you for life. Erika was willing to try again in the future if Trisha was up to it. Or they could adopt. Trisha said, "Yes." Motherhood felt like a place she wanted to live in, like a neighborhood she finally felt comfortable in. She wanted to keep on acting too. The space in her heart reserved for passion had somehow grown larger.

Erika kissed Nina's tattoo on Trisha's shoulder and fell back asleep.

Trisha dreamed about the Hollywood Forever headstones, Bugs Bunny, the weightlessness of loss, Erika, ruby-red slippers, and the metamorphosis of grief into love. That was alchemy too.

She felt a breath of freedom in the acceptance of transformation. She heard their neighborhood owl cooing. She read somewhere that owls were the messengers of angels...

She woke up with a start and glanced at the clock on her nightstand. Already four in the morning. She kissed her wife's arms. It would be dawn soon.

~ 58 ~

ALISON

April 20, 2019

Sᴜɴꜱᴇᴛ Bᴏᴜʟᴇᴠᴀʀᴅ ᴄᴜʀᴠᴇᴅ ᴀʀᴏᴜɴᴅ ɪᴛꜱᴇʟꜰ, a cat settling down in front of the fire. Alison was driving backwards in time towards the oldest parts of the city, and she was starving. The baby, probably hungry too. Alison guided the bottle back to her tiny mouth.

She left a goodbye message on Principal Tumaini Otieno's office phone, telling him he'd been a good friend, and they'd meet up again, hopefully in Mexico. She'd call Suzy from the road, and they'd sing '90s hits and talk about it all.

Alison passed Mom's Donuts and Chinese Restaurant. It opened at 5:30 a.m. Perfect timing. She'd go there before her journey really began.

She made a right on Dillon Avenue, pulled up, and parked several houses down from the little white brick house. She got out of the car, unclicked the baby's seatbelt, and lifted the basket into her arms. She hugged it with as much of her body as she could without letting her sadness seep into the baby. There were no words.

When Alison reached the porch, she placed the basket a few feet in front of the door, just like the girl at the fire station. She paused for an instant, just like the girl. And just like the girl, Alison knew this was the right decision.

"Be of service," the divine women said. "There is no greater love."

Her mother holding a newborn deer in her arms.

She kissed the baby on the forehead. Her lips rested on the delicate brow. The infant nodded her head, as if she understood what was happening. She was a traveler, this soul, going from one mother to another to another.

Alison rang the bell, then hurried back to her car to observe. A moment later, Trisha came to the door. She was barefoot in a pale green cotton nightgown. It was wrinkled and stained. The lace on the hem was torn. She almost didn't look down—but the baby began to cry. It surprised both Alison and Trisha. She backed away as if thrown by an explosion.

"Erika!" Trisha yelled behind her. "Erika!"

Trisha ran onto the lawn and looked in all directions. She saw no one. She turned and stared back at the wicker basket. Pink hibiscus flowers were swaying in the breeze. Yellow roses were trumpeting the new day. Green grass was cradling her feet. She took a last glance around her, then walked back to the baby. With all the trepidation of a new mother, Trisha knelt down.

A light rain began to fall.

∞

MapQuest said it would take twenty-three hours and for-ty-nine minutes to get to Todos Santos, Mexico. Alison pulled the printed map from her glove compartment. She liked having the di-rections on the seat beside her—a navigator on her travels. She'd marked the roads with a thick pink highlighter, the one she used to grade papers with. The smell always took her back to her mother's calendar in the kitchen on Vesper Avenue.

Alison hoped her mother was smiling down on her now. Her father too. Trisha and Erika would make perfect parents for the baby girl. They would notify the authorities and apply to be her adoptive family. It would happen. This was meant to be.

Alison drove west on the 10 Freeway, reciting the route in her head. She'd take the I-5 South to the I–8 East to the Carretera Fed-eral-5 all the way down into Todos Santos. She bit into a buttermilk donut—and then, that sensation in her gut again.

"Oh, God! No, no! Please not now," she prayed. "Not now."

Was she finally dying, this morning of all mornings? She pulled over at the Cloverfield Boulevard exit and drove in behind the gas station. She unbuckled the seatbelt, unzipped her jacket and stretched her spine. She unbuttoned the waist of her pants but couldn't find enough air to satisfy her lungs. Alison escaped the car and ran into a cluster of sycamore trees. A murder of crows rushed out of their homes. The dry ground crackled beneath her.

She stretched her arms above her head. She made decisions when she was twenty. She didn't want to be haunted by them any longer. She would be vulnerable and say "yes" to life. But first, she had to say "no."

"It is time." She spoke to the sky. "Good-bye, Harriet. I will always love you."

She stood motionless in her declaration, waiting for something terrible to happen. Nothing happened at all. The cars on the freeway didn't stop. The crows didn't fly back to their branches. The gas station attendant didn't come out to check on her. Yet Alison felt different. There was a stillness. She could detect a flicker of peace she'd been searching for so long.

Alison had always heard people talk about the soul like it was an organ, a fragment, a small, separate thing glowing in the middle of the body. But what if people had it backwards? Maybe the soul wasn't in the middle of the body. Maybe the body was in the middle of the soul.

The full blast of morning beckoned her back to her car.

And what if the soul wasn't finite? Instead, maybe it was infinite, and maybe it kept on living forever and ever and ever. That would mean Alison was part of Harriet's journey and now part of the baby's journey, as well. This thought made her feel connected to something greater than herself. Alison bowed her head and wept.

Then she took out her notebook and started to write. She had a box full of them now. When she got to wherever she was going, she'd edit them and put together a chap book. *Harriet's Never Going to Leave You*. She'd mail copies to everyone in the poetry workshop, and to Tumaini and to Suzy and Mrs. V. And she'd try to find a publisher. She was a poet. It was her calling.

She put the top down on the Mustang for the first time since she and Trisha drove on Sunset Boulevard the night after the poetry workshop. Alison reached into her glove compartment for a tissue and for her Very Berry Berry lipstick. She smoothed it on, ran her tongue over her lips. She let her hair loose, falling majestically over her shoulders. She wanted to feel on the outside what she was beginning to feel on the inside—liberated.

It had already been thirty years, not counting the Jesse sighting at Amma's and that other meeting at the Juicy Kisses reunion. Their timing hadn't been right then. What difference would a few extra days make now? She wanted to see Santa Monica Beach, visit the zoo in San Diego, drink mezcal in Mexicali, stand on pink cliffs, eat tortilla soup, swim in the Sea of Cortez, kayak in Loreto, put on her new clothes—maybe even pull out those pink-and-green leather boots she packed way in the back of her trunk.

Whatever happened with Jesse in Todos Santos, Alison decided she'd be fine. She would give him the letter and poem she wrote for him, and they'd talk about everything—their young love, the pregnancy, the abortion, the running away from him, her parents, her life, his life. If there was a second chance for them, there couldn't be any secrets. If it wasn't meant to be, she could always get back in her car and keep on going. She was open now, open to connecting to people and possibilities. She would lead with love instead of fear. And she'd try to find her brother, Sebastian. There could still be a family in her future. She was only fifty-one.

She swung left out of the McClure Tunnel, gliding onto the Pacific Coast Highway. The car felt too quiet. She wanted company. She turned on the radio. The Beatles were singing "A Long and Winding Road" just for her. Alison missed her mother. She missed her father. She missed Jagger. But she didn't miss herself anymore.

"You left me standing here, a long, long time ago..." Alison let herself absorb the sound of Paul's voice. "Don't leave me waiting here, lead me to your door..."

A hitchhiker in a green sweatshirt appeared on the side of the highway just as a handful of raindrops sprinkled the windshield. Alison would have to put the top up soon. A wet breeze whispered through her hair. She knew a sign when she heard one. She turned on her signal, pulled over, and slowed to a stop.

WANDA

April 20, 2019

Seagulls are wakin' up and divin' into the water for their breakfast.

They fly powerful over the waves in the same direction I'm takin'. I guess that's a good sign, so I put my thumb out as I walk and wait for someone to pick me up. I figure goin' south will keep me warm on nights I got no place to sleep. I figure there'll be plenty of 'em.

I touch the necklace that Ricardo gave me. It drapes everlastin' 'round my neck, the same place my bad husband wanted to carve his name. I'm not talkin' to him no more. 'Cuz Grace is free. My fingers brush the red rock. I'm gonna keep my promise and pay Ricardo back. I'll paint some pictures for his family's café. 'Cuz I'm an artist.

My lips kiss Grace's key, and everythin' changes. A soft cloud opens up and pours out tender blessings. And the sky is below and the ocean above, and I'm floatin' in the haze in-between. Tears are runnin' up my cheeks or maybe it's the rain that's caressin' my face. I can't tell the difference. The birds spiral out below in a circle, flyin' round, round, round like that record of Elvis. "Love me tender love me sweet never let me go," the shul men sing. They swoop me up with their prayer shawls for wings and fly me high into their midst. And the women in the Moses paintin' touch my feet, and Sol and his grandmother make me grilled cheese sandwiches, and the cleanin' lady on the bus gives me a peach, and a Hell's Angel kisses my forehead, and Nurse Trisha dances rock 'n roll, and Ricardo washes my hair, and for one shinin' moment, I am in my daughter's embrace.

A green car's slowin' down. I'm hopin' it's for me.

~ 60 ~

TRISHA

April 20, 2019

Trisha lifted the newborn from the basket, a red ribbon tied around her tiny wrist.

Erika bent down and found a piece of white paper tucked deep between the towels. There was something written on it —

"My name is Grace Ricardo Solomon," Erika read aloud.

The baby girl began to cry.

Trisha's milk began to flow.

~ 61 ~

GRACE

April 20, 2019

Home

ACKNOWLEDGEMENTS

A FEW YEARS AGO, I was having trouble putting a child seat in my car. I'd heard that if you went to a fire station, someone would do it for you. So I drove to my neighborhood station. I noticed a *SAFE HAVEN* sign on the brick wall. I asked what it was. The answer birthed, *The Lightness of Rain.*

That and some work I'd done in Jack Grapes' writing class. I'd developed two characters who were so different that there'd be no chance of them ever meeting—except by the maneuverings of a writer at her computer.

I told my husband my idea, and he said, "That's a book."

"A book? Me, write a book?"

"Yes," he answered. "You write a book."

So, with the help of the brilliant editor, Joshua Grapes, my wonderful friends who read my work, and the muse who pushed me back in front of my computer when all I wanted to do was eat dark chocolate and read Dorianne Laux's poetry, I wrote *The Lightness of Rain.*

I believe in both Fate and Destiny. I admit I like Destiny better because you have a hand in creating it.

My eternal gratitude to Peter Lefcourt who knew I could do it.

Thank you to Cheryl Edwards, Joan Ryan, Marlee Novak and Steven Hirshfeld who read my work and gave me invaluable notes, Mark Hanauer for the beautiful cover photograph, Nancy Nimoy for the evocative design, and my family, colleagues, and classmates who listened and responded with love and consideration.

Thank you to Murray Weiss for his belief in my book and Stephanie Kelly for her insights. Thank you to Jack Grapes for his wonderful classes and Joshua Grapes for his inimitable editing. Thank you to Gary Goldstein for his loving support and Danielle Matlin for her creative planning. Thank you to Milton for his teachings.

Thank you to Three Tomatoes Publishing and Cheryl Benton for her guidance and grace.

What I'd like to say most of all is thank you to the reader. Without you, all the 't's would be left uncrossed and the 'i's undotted. You complete the circle.

Always love,
Terri Hanauer
2025

ABOUT TERRI HANAUER

TERRI HANAUER IS A MULTIPLE AWARD-WINNING Los Angeles theatre director, most recently winning the Broadway World Los Angeles Best Director Award. Her first feature film, *Sweet Talk* is
streaming on Gravitas Films. She directed a season of HBO Cin-
emax's *Zane's Sex Chronicles*, and Amazon's *Smothered*. She is a
graduate of AFI's Directing Workshop for Women. She worked ex-
tensively as an actress and photographer in the States and Canada,
appearing on countless TV shows—*Seinfeld, Beggars and Choosers,
Six Feet Under, Without A Trace* (to name a few)—and the Mark

Taper Forum and the Arena Stage Theatre. She's a graduate of Toronto's York University with a Bachelor of Fine Arts degree.

Stevie Wonder blessed her baby when she was nine months pregnant, magician Doug Henning hypnotized and sawed her in half when she was his assistant, and the hugging saint, Amma, hugged her. She enjoys family, fashion, and float tanks.

Her first book, *The Party - How To Have Fun While Finding True Love*, a helpful and hopeful guidebook, was published in 2024 and is available on Amazon. Her second novel, *Love Crimes*, and a compilation of poems and short stories written with Brynn Thayer, *We Were Just Thinking…,* will be available next year.

Terri Hanauer photo by Mark Hanauer

www.TerriHanauer.com

THE LIGHTNESS OF RAIN
BOOK CLUB QUESTIONS

1. What was the author trying to say? What are the themes in the book?

2. Did you sense the presence of The Thirty-Six throughout the book? If so, where did you find it? Who is the thirty-sixth? Is it possible that there are more than one thirty-six?

3. There are many novels, plays, and films where the main characters are three women. Why do you think the number three makes for good storytelling?

4. Do you think Alison was right in hiding her secret from Jesse? What could she have done differently, and what would have been the likely outcome?

5. Would Wanda have made a good mother? Do you think she did the right thing? How do you feel about a character who regrets not having killed someone?

6. What is Trisha's driving force? Do you feel it propelled her into a happy life?

7. Did Trisha's double betrayal of Erika and Charles cause you to have negative feelings towards her? Can the reader find compassion for a troubled and ethically challenged female character?

8. What are your thoughts about the Sol/Wanda relationship? What did it teach you?

9. How do you think each character conducts their lives after the book's ending?

10. Did you have a favorite character? If so, who and why?

11. What does the title, *The Lightness of Rain*, mean to you?

12. Did Wanda's visions worry you? Why do you think she had them?

13. Is there a regret you have that, if you could go back and change, you would? How would your life be affected?

14. These three women were the unwitting guides to Grace's finding her rightful home. Do you believe in destiny or fate? If so, give an example.

15. Which secondary characters were most instrumental in affecting the three main women?

16. What do you think Grace's life will be like?

www.ingramcontent.com/pod-product-compliance
Lightning Source LLC
Chambersburg PA
CBHW020016120726
47903CB00004B/1306

9 789899 266182